# THE LIFE WE LEAD
## Ascending

By
# George M. Nagle

**The Life We Lead: Ascending by George M. Nagle**
Copyright © 2014-2017 by **George M. Nagle**

**George M. Nagle Publishing, LLC**
**http://thelifewelead.net**

Publishers Note: Though this work is inspired by
real life events, this is a work of fiction.
Names, characters, places, time lines and incidents have been altered and enhanced by the
author. Locales and publish names are sometimes
used for atmospheric purposes only. Any resem-
blance to actual people, living or dead, or to
businesses, companies, events, institutions, or
locales is completely coincidental.

Cover Design by Kelly Pernell of PBJ Creative
Studios
The Life We Lead: Ascending by George M. Nagle
1st ed.
13-ISBN 978-0-9862472-1-7
10-ISBN 0-9862472-1-9

Dedicated to
Marie Pauli Nagle

# CONTENTS

# •Chapter One•

"Ready to go, man?" asked Daen. He frowned slightly as he looked at his companion. "You look like you have a headache."

"Life is a headache, but yeah, let's go." James answered in a deliberately playful tone. He was now conscious of showing that something was wrong. He'd have to try harder to hide it.

The pair walked out of the hotel room and James locked the door.

Something was coming, and James knew it. He had a slightly fogging feeling, like missing sleep or jet lag, and a building tension in his stomach. This feeling was usually a warning, and judging by the degree of pressure he felt; this was going to be something big.

He hated the feeling.

A few moments later, a hard, cold burst of snowy wind hit them as they stepped out onto the street.

"Damn, man, this Russian weather is harsh. Glad this place is close. Ain't made for this weather, man. I just ain't. Feels like the air is freezing in my mouth. People shouldn't live like this." Daen's voice was muffled beneath the collar of his winter coat.

James silently agreed as they walked the block and a half to the bar the hotel clerk, Natalia, had recommended as having good food. They had barely taken their seats at the bar when two shot glasses filled with vodka appeared.

His eyebrows high, and with a huge smile on his face, Daen said, "Now that's service!"

They picked up the shots and downed them. James didn't usually drink at all, but he also believed that "When in Rome, do as the Romans do."

The old man behind the bar smiled, and said in Russian slang, "Americans." He apparently spoke English.

"You are Americans, da?" A rather drunken, red-faced man in his late forties with bright blue eyes, and short sandy blond hair, all but shouted to Daen and James, in an intoxicated slur. "I know many Americans!" the drunken man told them. "I... I... I have been to your country. I must buy you drink!" The man turned to the barman and called for another round.

"Thank you. That is very friendly," said James. In his head, he registered the stammer and the overly generous act. He shook his head and dismissed the suspicious thought.

"And welcome too, man. I need to warm up," said Daen, and everyone chuckled.

As the barman brought the drinks, James excused himself.

"But, a moment, friend, your drink is here," protested the drunken man.

"Need to let some out before I take more in," said James, smiling as he walked away.

As James made his way along the dusky bar, he noticed how uneven the floor was. He saw that only half the light sockets had bulbs in them. The tables were mismatched, and the walls had odd bumps that, in the poor lighting, made the wallpaper look like it was moving.

A young lady of about twenty was tending to the back area where twelve patrons were scattered. She wore a simple dress with an apron, and flat shoes. Her dark brown shoulder-length hair suited her rather plain face.

As James passed her, he noticed a thin gold chain hanging around her neck with a small golden emblem. It was partially covered, but it looked like a cross or maybe an 'X' shape.

"Could you tell me where the bathroom is?" he asked.

The lady gave him a dazzling polite smile, and looked toward the man tending the bar, as if seeking assistance. She apparently didn't speak English.

"Ah, where is the toilet?" said James in poor Russian.

The girl replied and smiled, then nodded to her right, as her hands were full of dishes.

James hadn't understood what she had said, but got the hint from her body language. As James started to walk toward the bathroom, he heard the front door open and close, followed by a burst of cold air that sent a shiver throughout the bar.

He casually made his way to the bathroom as his eyes automatically scanned the area for fire equipment, cameras, and exits. All he could see was the entrance to the kitchen, and a door he assumed led to a storeroom. Going to the bathroom was just an excuse to finish getting a feel for the bar, as he still had that slightly nagging, distracted feeling in his stomach.

The bathroom was small with timeworn, but clean, fixtures. The mirror that hung over the sink had a small crack in the lower corner. The window was just big enough to slip through, though the building next door would make it a tight squeeze in an emergency.

Exiting the bathroom, James noticed a small family had come in to have what was probably a rare night out. They looked happy to be enjoying each other's company, and smiled at James as he passed by. He smiled back and even winked at the two little girls, who started to giggle.

Reaching his seat, he noticed his glass was empty.

He looked over at Daen, who leaned in and whispered, "Man, the guy next to you must use the five-second rule on drinks. If it's there any longer, he snatches it up like it's open season. I don't know how he's sittin' there. He's already had three shots since we came in, and I don't think those were the first of the night."

"What do you want to eat?" Daen asked in a louder voice, pulling away from James and handing over a menu.

James simply said, "Whatever you're having is fine."

Daen, who spoke Russian, placed the orders with the young lady serving food from the back area. Just as he was about to say something else to James, the door opened again. He closed his mouth as if it would help stop the cold rush of air that was coming. "Damn, man, I'm not used to cold like this." He shivered as the door shut, and a new customer took a seat at the bar.

"This? This is not cold," said the drunken man next to James. "I have been in cold, and this is not cold. Moscow does not get so very cold like Siberia. The cold there is so bad that when you take shit, it starts to freeze before it hits ground. This is cold. Or when, can't go outside for few days because your eyes might freeze if slightly touched with wind. I, Petior, I have been in this cold. It is nice here," said the drink-snatching man, who had bought them a round of vodka.

"Damn, man, seriously?" said Daen with astonishment.

"Of course, seriously. I have been all over and never experience cold like this anywhere else," Petior said. "It is where hell would go to be frozen over."

James and Daen introduced themselves, using their customary false names.

"Stephen Lewis," said James, shaking Petior's hand.

Daen said, "Bryan Douglas," also shaking hands.

James and Daen rarely used their real names when they were together. Mainly because if they were together, odds had it they were on a mission for the group. This spring break trip to Russia was no different. Though, both Daen and James wished they were experiencing the much warmer weather like their college classmates.

While they waited for the food, James, Daen, and Petior were laughing, and enjoying getting to know each other. It was one of those rare moments that you instantly become friends with someone you just met.

James leaned over the counter to order another round of drinks, discretely communicating with the bartender to switch his out for water. The bartender found this odd, given the face he made at James, but he played along. The bartender was very skilled at covering up the fact that James wasn't drinking vodka like Petior and Daen.

During the meal, Petior gave them a highlight of his best adventures in what seemed almost an autobiography.

"Very early in Russia, you must be strong or weak. Not strong like Americans think. Their strong is like our weak. I remember when I was boy, just start at school. An older boy was beating on each of my classmates. New one each day. When he got to me, he got much more than he could deal. I remember, he pushed me, and I was small, and I hit very hard on my nose on ground. See?"

He pointed to one of the many bumps on his crooked nose. "That is first time it broke. I was bleeding, and my friends were calling out, and I lay there, and he walked over me, his feet on sides of my body. He turn me over to face him, and I kick very hard."

Petior started laughing in a deep, booming way, spilling half of his drink on his sleeve. "Ugh, bad to waste drink," he said as he began to suck on his sleeve.

"Well, what happened then?" asked Daen impatiently.

"Oh yes, I kick him very hard in balls," the man finished.

Instinctively, James and Daen cringed, subconsciously grabbing their groins, but laughing.

"He collapse on top of me, on his knees," Petior said. "So as he fell, I turned quickly and hit him in nose with my elbow. Blood all over. He is lying there on floor bleeding. Very still for moment. Everyone cheers for me. Then schoolmaster come. He have to take other boy to infirmary, but takes me to office. He ask what happened and I tell. He says I did what I had to, but he still have to beat me for fight. He gave me five lashes. I have mark from one still." Petior stood up and grabbed for his belt as if he was going to show the mark.

"Hey, hey man, no man. We believe you. We don't need the visual," said Daen quickly.

James shook his head and laughed.

The evening carried on this way for another two hours, the three men joking, and laughing, and thoroughly enjoying themselves. Daen was getting very drunk, while Petior didn't seem to be any worse than when they'd come in, though he did keep slipping in and out of Russian.

They learned that Petior had been a fantastic hockey player in his youth before joining the military. Also, that he had been recruited into the KGB before leaving to operate an import business for appliances.

James decided it was time to go. He paid the bill, and covered Petior's tab too, for which the Russian was very grateful. James steadied Daen as they said goodnight, and Petior was extremely insistent that they have dinner again tomorrow, meeting up at the bar first at 6 p.m.

Though James liked Petior, he was conscious of the fact he and Daen had a mission. Spending another evening with someone they'd randomly met didn't sound like the best use of their limited time, but Daen agreed before James could say anything, so he went along with it. He knew Daen would be in rough shape the next day, so they wouldn't be out too late, and James would have a chance to do some work if needed.

The cold walk back to the hotel didn't seem to bother Daen much, but James's back was happy to drop Daen on his bed ten minutes later. Walking a drunken man who is taller than you home on ice isn't an easy task, especially when walking into the wind.

James turned towards the bathroom. He'd taken a few steps when he heard the unmistakable sound of vomiting, followed by a splattering sound on the floor. He paused a moment, his eyes closed as if praying for patience. Then came a thud.

Daen had fallen off the bed and was trying to get up. James helped him up and steered him into the bathroom.

"Uhha, I think I'm going to be sick again, man," he groaned. "Why you puttin' me in the tub?"

"It's a lot easier to wash down a tub than a floor, and toilet, and everything else if you miss," said James.

"Okay, man," said Daen weakly before passing out in the tub.

James turned Daen's head to the side so he wouldn't choke if he threw up in his sleep, before cleaning up the vomit near the bed. He thought he might be sick himself from the smell of alcohol and that night's dinner mixed with stomach acid. He reminded himself that Daen rarely drank around him out of respect for their friendship and decided that, in the big scheme of things, it didn't matter.

What did matter was figuring out the channeling of heroin between Russia and the Italians. It still didn't make sense. The Russians hated the Italians, however, somehow they were connected, and aiding each other. Or at least, that was according to the initial file they'd gotten from Tom at the group.

James and Daen were members of the group. The group was a secret society that operated with the emphasis on being secret. They deliberately referred to themselves as 'the group' because it was an ambiguous term. They even went as far as to burn the records of the members once they were officially part of the team.

The group was essentially a spy agency except that it wasn't a government sponsored organization. Multi-millionaire Bernie Baruch founded it at the start of the Cold War in 1947. He was an advisor to several Presidents, but felt he needed a mechanism to gather information without worrying about the constraints of the law.

Within a few years of Baruch's death, several branches were able to open. The group became comprised of independently operated offices that shared information without a central controlling location. It became an organization that actively found ways to help people that had been taken advantage of by criminal syndicates, while providing the evidence needed for law enforcement to get eventual convictions.

The way the group functioned really came down to some key fundamentals of the members. First, the active field members were all volunteers. As volunteers, they were free to leave at any point with no strings attached. It was common practice to finish something once started, but that was more of a personality characteristic that they all shared compared to a hard fast rule. Second, the members were in their late teens and early twenties. There is a natural bias that people assume young adults do not have the wisdom, experience, patience or capabilities to be effective or efficient spies. This bias is particularly true when the members went to great lengths to have strong academic and respectable lives. Capitalizing on these assumptions were just some of the principles the group members utilized to operate silently, and without too much suspicion. Third, each of the members had exceptional skills in at least a few areas. These talents and the desire to increase their abilities, was a major motivator for many of the members. Also, learning from each other to develop new skill sets often drove individuals to remain in the group for at least five years. Finally, there was a financial reward for being a member. Part of the funds for taking down a criminal organization would go to the group, while the remainder stayed with the member. Even on the off chance that the criminals knew who had taken their money, they couldn't exactly complain about the missing funds to the police.

However, like all things in life, they had to give up certain things that many of their peers enjoyed. Being able to hold consistent relationships, or even fully disclose their lives to family and friends wasn't allowed. It was also dangerous if they did tell people about the group, as it diluted the ability of the group to stay in the unknown shadows, and that was a fundamental attribute for the organization to function.

Daen and James found themselves in Russia because they were at the beginning stages of investigating a major drug cartel operation. This particular investigation was the largest the group had ever undertaken.

James was one of the most skilled members the group had ever had. He seemed to be able to master things quickly through a combination of natural intelligence, diligent effort, and logical thinking. His ability to read people in the blink of an eye was uncanny, and had saved him on several occasions. He rarely made mistakes, and even when he did, he was skilled enough to recover as if he hadn't.

In turn, James had selected Daen for this reconnaissance trip because they always worked well together, and because Daen spoke fluent Russian. His selection hadn't gone over so smoothly, mainly because, Daen, who was black, would stand out like a sore thumb in Russia. James felt this was an advantage because it would allow them to hide in plain sight. No one would suspect a black man of being a spy in Russia. Besides that, Daen possessed incredible skills at winning people over. He could be extraordinarily empathetic, and his genuine selflessness, and integrity radiated from him. To top it all off, he was incredibly resourceful, almost like a real life MacGyver.

Tomorrow would be a low-key day James decided, as Daen wouldn't be worth much in the morning. It would be a good day to walk around, and just observe, and James knew where to start. He'd start where he always did, at the bottom, and that meant the subway system with the people living on the streets. Those areas tended to have a lot of foot traffic, and that attracted drug dealers.

Just as James was climbing into bed, the sounds of fluids hitting porcelain rang out as his friend emptied what little remained in his stomach. James shook his head, rolled over and tried to get some sleep.

# •Chapter Two•

The next day, after leaving Daen a note, and enough rubles for some food, James went down to the subway station with his translation device in his pocket. To look more like a tourist, he wore his camera around his neck. The camera also had a great zoom lens if it was needed. This morning was more about getting a feel for the environment. Perhaps he'd get lucky and make some connections.

The vast subway system was very busy. It had clearly been beautiful at one point, but now the detailed tile work was missing sections, was dirty, and gave an ancient feel to the platform. The stained glass windows would fit perfectly in a Catholic church in Rome, except they showcased various landscapes that highlighted Russia's natural beauty, not heavenly images. The station did have modern vending and ticket machines, though cart vendors pushed their goods at everyone who passed by.

The cart vendors weren't the only ones commuters had to avoid. A few children were trying to sell candies and such, or were just flat-out begging. James watched them for a while and noticed a pattern. The kids never seemed to get too close to the cart vendors, who had taken space on the walls. They seemed to have their own zones of operation. They also had the best zones near the bottlenecks of the station.

A girl about six and a boy about the same age had positions toward the entrance. The girl seemed to target the men, while the boy targeted the women. Then came two girls. One looked to be eight, and the other a little older. They crossed into the younger kids' area, and caught those people the little ones hadn't spoken to yet. Finally, a teenage boy with small objects and trinkets for sale approached people the other four hadn't. He too seemed to have an area. It was like they were working as a team with zone coverage. More impressively, it appeared to be working.

A young teenage girl suddenly came through the crowd. She grabbed the older looking of the two girls selling candy and screamed at her. James hadn't see what the girl had done to offend the teenager, but the older girl suddenly began hitting the younger one. The crowd gave them room, and no one made any motion to stop it.

James moved toward them, but before he'd taken two steps, it was over. The older girl vanished while the younger one lay crying on the floor. As James reached her, she stood up, wiped her tears, and resumed her work. Looking down, James suddenly understood.

A candy wrapper lay on the ground. The girl had eaten a piece of candy, and the teenager was the boss punishing her for stealing. It was simple and swift justice. The older girl had done what she'd felt she had to do, but hadn't gone overboard. The younger girl had accepted her punishment and returned to work. Perhaps this wasn't what would happen back home, but it was a system of justice that allowed the kids to survive.

Walking away, James noticed a vendor watching him. He had a variety of objects on his table, but wasn't pushing them like the other vendors. James walked over, curious as to why this man had locked eyes with him. He pretended to look at the watches, pens, and handmade objects on the table, and even asked for a price a few times. The vendor answered curtly, but had lost interest in James, and was now watching the crowd, his eyes sweeping back and forth. Finally, James selected a small pin and paid the man, who spoke to him in English.

"Thank you for your purchase, but you should know not to get involved in our business. It is lucky that you didn't stop what you see with the girls."

"Why is that?" asked James, waiting for his change.

"Because our ways are not your way, and you would have to pay much more than she did," he said, his eyes coming to rest on James.

James realized that this man was the real boss. He controlled what happened here, and the teenage girl was just an enforcer. Despite his youth, he had a hard look about him.

"I see. Thank you for the advice," James replied in a measured voice. "Please, keep the change as a sign of gratitude for your help." He turned to walk away, but the vendor grabbed his wrist.

"You should show more respect, American."

James quickly twisted out of the grab, and locked the vendor's wrist and elbow, exposing the under part of his forearm, which had extensive tattoos. They stared at each other for a moment before James released him.

Smiling, James said, "Thanks again," and walked away to watch the crowd a bit more.

The morning commuters eventually thinned out, and the children vanished. James watched for a few more hours, but he didn't see any drug activity whatsoever. He decided it was time to try other spots. As he climbed the steps, he realized he was being followed. The vendor James had somehow offended had sent a boy after him.

*This guy is a bit unhinged,* he thought to himself.

James let the boy follow him for a while and he was surprised at the skill he had. The kid certainly was more talented than some CIA agents James had been followed by once. After a few hours of pretending to be a tourist, James decided enough was enough. The boy was obviously to report on him, and James thought going back to the hotel might free the child of his task. Plus, James had some work to do now to his and Daen's room.

He led the boy back to the shabby hotel. The boy followed him in, and James made a split-second decision. He decided to go to the room directly below his. Since his room was on the second floor, he simply walked across the lobby and down the hall. Stopping at what he hoped was the right door, James took a long time pretending to search for the key, giving the child plenty of time to see which room he was attempting to enter. This way the boy succeeded in reporting where James had gone, while James retained control of the situation.

Noticing the boy disappear out the revolving door, James walked to the front desk. "Hello, Natalia, how are you today?"

The receptionist was an older woman who loved to converse in English whenever she could.

"Mr. Lewis, I am good. You are good, too?" she asked.

"I am very good, yes, thank you. Can you tell me if room nine is open to rent?"

With a frown on her face, the woman answered, "Your room is bad? Everything wrong? I fix?"

"No, no. The room is fine. I just want an extra room. Bryan snores very loudly," James assured her.

"What is snorts?" she asked, her head slightly to the side.

James figured it was easier to demonstrate, which made Natalia laugh.

"Very funny," she said. "Yes, that room open. You would like, da?"

"Da," answered James. He handed her enough money to cover the room fees for the next few days, and collected the keys.

"Daen, how you feeling, buddy?" James asked in a semi-soft voice, as he entered their room a minute later.

A low "ugggggghhh," was all the reply he got.

"We're supposed to meet Petior in about ninety minutes. Since you were so gung-ho on going out tonight, you'd better shape up so we can go."

James sat down on his bed as Daen stirred in the other one. "I have some things to prep," he told his groggy friend, "but won't be long, so if you could..."

"How are you even functionin', man? You had almost as many shots as me, and you ain't anything!" Daen spoke in the loudest voice his head could take.

"I don't know what to tell ya, but how about you be in and out of the shower before I get back?" James grabbed his clothes and a suitcase.

"Where you goin'?" Daen poked his head out from under the covers, looking a lot worse than James had expected.

"Long story short, I was followed today, and we may have a visitor. I booked the room below this one, and need to make it look like I'm staying in it. I'm also hooking up some sensors in there, so need to run a cable. In fact, if you jump in the shower now, I'll drill while you're showering, so the sound doesn't kill you."

"Gimme two minutes, and that's very considerate, man." Daen shuffled out of bed and toward the bathroom, without showing any surprise at what his colleague had just said.

James finished packing. When he heard the shower running, he picked a spot about an inch from the interior wall behind a dresser set. He was betting each of the rooms in the hotel was set up in the same fashion, though after he started drilling it occurred to him that he should have verified that first. Even when his assumptions were logical, he liked to confirm what he could.

He finished the hole and ran the length of cable down into it. He hooked the other end of the cable to the monitor that would remain in the room he and Daen shared.

He grabbed his stuff and made his way downstairs. He approached room nine and then stopped. *Check first, genius*, he thought to himself.

Walking up to Natalia, he asked, "Excuse me, Natalia, has anyone else come in or out of the hotel since I left you?"

"No, you are looking for someone?" she asked.

"Bryan and I are meeting a friend for dinner. I was just making sure he hadn't arrived. Thank you," said James, giving her a smile as he walked away.

Entering room nine, James found he'd been correct to think the rooms were all set up the same. Only the furniture differed slightly. In this case, the dresser was long and flat, though in the same spot as the one above. A thin layer of dust now partially covered the furniture from the drilling.

James put his clothes and toiletries in the proper places. He then installed the two-way split mini-camera that would allow him to see inside this room using the monitor upstairs. He could see the bathroom door, as well as the large window on the opposite wall of the room's main door. His blind spot was the room entrance, but a hallway remote camera would let him see the room door, hallway, and lobby.

He taped some remote flash capsules inside the bathroom door, as well as near the window. This way, if he needed a quick entrance or exit, he could blind his visitors for a few moments.

Next came planting the guns. First, James had to plant a tranquilizer gun that he could get to with his hands potentially bound. He decided to plant it under the chair next to the window. The 9mm pistol was a tougher plant. It was his preferred weapon, but he'd only have eight shots if the thing didn't jam, and he didn't know how many visitors to expect. He decided to keep it on him. Finally, he taped an extra clip of bullets, and an extra cartridge of darts to the underside of the flat dresser.

He stepped into the hall and walked to the fake plant that sat one door down. He picked it up, and moved it to the other side of the corridor to get a better view, then attached a remote camera.

He made his way upstairs after setting a tripper on the door to room nine that would appear innocent enough, but would tell him if someone entered the room while he was gone.

*That should do it for now, until we see who and what come,* he thought.

Experience over the last year had taught James to bring more equipment than he should need. In the world of intelligence gathering, it was extremely rare to have shootouts and grand escapes like shown in movies. The golden rule was to be quiet and unseen, but prepared for anything to happen.

Forty minutes later, when he and a somewhat better looking Daen set off to meet Petior, James noticed that he had a tail again. It was a different boy. He wasn't as talented at following people unnoticed as the other kid was. He apparently had been waiting outside the hotel for a while judging by the way his bottom lip was trembling.

*Poor kid, having to wait in the cold all that time,* James thought.

James had a soft spot for kids who weren't in the best economic situations and had to struggle.

"Bryan, we have a tail," he said loud enough for Daen to hear over the gust of wind. "Boy about ten, shabby coat, one glove, mismatched shoes, and about seventy-five feet behind us. This is part of what I was talking about earlier. Right now, no play," he said as they walked.

"Follow," Daen replied, to let James know that they were on the same page. They went on about their business as if the kid wasn't there.

After a few more steps, Daen spoke, "And that one at ten o'clock?"

James looked up. "No change." He answered with a fake laugh, as if Daen had said something funny.

They walked the remaining block to the bar, where they found Petior waiting.

"My American friends, ha, ha, ha, come drink!" he said, even before the door closed.

James quickly gave the bartender a look, with a slight tilt of his head, as if to say, "Same arrangement as last night." The bartender nodded.

"Man, I can't have it, not after last night," said Daen, looking decidedly green.

"Drink with your friends," said Petior. "What are you, how you say, walking punsy?" to which he gave a tremendous roar of laughter.

"What did he just call me?" Daen whispered to James.

"Either a pansy or a pussy, but either way, it was funny." James crossed to the bar, picked up the drink the bartender pushed at him, clanged glasses with Petior, and slugged down his water.

"Whatever, man," was all Daen could muster. He drank with his eyes closed, and gave a slight shiver, but managed to keep it down.

It was apparent that Petior was about to order another round, but James cut him off by placing cash on the counter to cover the bill twice over. "Petior, we are very hungry and looking forward to tasting some excellent food tonight, and don't want to spoil it with too much vodka first. Shall we go?"

"Da, da, good point making, da, let us go now," said Petior, but James was slightly distracted.

Something was coming. His stomach was swinging as if James were on a roller coaster. The sensation was stronger tonight, and again felt like something about the bar.

His eyes scanned the room and did a fast head count. *Seven customers, his party, the barman, and the plain waitress.* The layout hadn't changed; nothing was out of place. This wasn't it, not yet, but he was on full alert.

James bet it had something to do with the kids tailing him. He'd felt this feeling last night, but later had dismissed it as just being jet lag.

He hadn't yet mastered these little warnings, and wasn't particularly keen for them to continue, especially when some were false alarms. Tonight, he was conscious enough not to let anything appear to be bothering him. Walking toward the door, he smiled and clasped Petior with his left hand, and Daen with his right, as they set off.

Upon exiting, the first thing James looked for was a kid. He saw a girl, and realized the kids were using an elaborate relay system. The girl was about eight or nine, and appeared to be wearing boys' clothes. Her hair was rather short and sticking out everywhere from underneath her hat. As they followed Petior to the restaurant, it was evident she was new to tracking people. She tried to mask it by begging along the way, which made her have to run to catch up every time she asked for money.

They walked only a few blocks, but it seemed much longer. They kept making odd turns here and there. When they stopped, and Petior knocked on an old wooden door, James wondered where they were. Nothing marked this place as a restaurant.

"What are we doing here?" Daen's voice was muf-fled again behind his coat collar.

"This is place. We go in back. Only special VIP use this entrance." Petior answered, with his chest puffed out.

A voice came from inside, speaking in Russian. Petior answered, and the door opened.

James was clueless. "You catch that?" he whispered to Daen, as Petior walked inside.

"No," answered Daen, walking over the threshold.

James looked back as he pulled the door closed, and saw the girl who had followed them turning the corner, no doubt heading back to report their location. At least she wasn't standing in the cold waiting for them.

They walked through a storeroom filled with pota-toes that looked like it served as an office. This room connected to a short dingy hallway that opened to the kitchen area. The kitchen looked like an odd assort-ment of modern equipment meets the eighteenth century. A large kettle was set over an open fire, near a large stainless steel counter. The refrigerator was also new, however, it was being powered with a large ex-tension cord.

"You see here? These plates and new machines?" asked Petior. "I get these for them, and they do me fa-vor in return. Food is very good too!" He said this louder than was needed, and the two women in the kitchen smiled, with the older giving Petior a wink.

The man who had let them in, led them to a hall with two additional doors and a staircase. They went up the stairs, and entered the second door on the right into a private parlor.

The room consisted of a large fireplace that took up almost a whole wall, a ragged sofa with beautiful hand woven coverings, and a table with four chairs. Candle brackets lit the room, even though light sockets and outlets were clearly visible. Two small windows on each side of the sofa let in extra light from the street.

The man produced a tablecloth from a cabinet in the hall, and gestured for them to have a seat.

"I will get best food, da?" asked Petior.

"Sure man, that would be great," said Daen.

Petior stepped with the man into the hallway, and began to order dinner.

"No vodka!" Daen cried out.

"Baaaa," came Petior's reply.

Daen looked at James for support, but James was already chiming in. "Petior, please, just water for tonight." There was some more grumbling, followed by laughter from the hallway. "What did he say?" asked James.

"Missed it, but probably saying how we 'Americans' can't hang with them drinking. After yesterday, he's right," Daen said with a frown, embarrassed to admit it.

Walking toward the windows, James noticed that the floor creaked with each step. It reminded him of the old Buddhist temples that used creaky floors as an alarm system against intruders. Peering into the street, he noticed the windows in the adjacent building made a mirror effect. His eyes fell on the outside windowsill of his window.

There was a marking of two downward slanted parallel lines. They looked like scratches, except the lines were burned into the wood. The top line had a small hook toward the highest end. The bottom line had a large, misshapen circle at the lowest point. Crossing the two lines in the center was a single vertical line.

James thought he recognized it, but was having trouble placing it. Then he remembered. It was one of the tattoo's the vendor had on his arm from the subway. James turned to call Daen over, but Petior was back, and beckoning him to join them at the table.

"Friends, tonight you have good Russian food from good Russian people. They bring best for you at no charge." Petior was clearly pleased with this arrangement.

"We certainly appreciate that, but we can pay. We're grateful to you for just bringing us here," said James, but Petior wouldn't allow it.

"You have paid enough. You bought all drinks last night and then today. It is my turn to return favor with my friends," said Petior in a passive voice.

James knew it would be offensive to refuse, so he said, "Thank you, my friend."

Daen said the same in Russian, which made Petior laugh.

"How does black man speak motherland tongue so good?" he inquired.

"What? A black man can't speak Russian?" Daen pretended to be insulted. In fact, he felt racism was funny. It was the same as judging someone based on the color of their eyes.

"It isn't too interesting of a story, I'm afraid to say, man. When I was in high school, my momma had a friend who was a professor. She said I should take Russian in high school, because I needed a second language for college anyhow. If I took Russian, I would qualify for more scholarships without much competition, since most people don't take Russian, but especially since I'm a minority. So momma made me take four years of it."

Daen laughed. "They were right too," he affirmed. "I got an excellent scholarship, and now I'm minoring in Russian. My professor laughs, and says, I'd blend right in if only I matched the snow."

They all laughed and clinked glasses. Daen and James had water, and as usual, Petior drank vodka. As the meal courses began, dinner was full of laughter, discussion, and excellently prepared food. Daen was starting to feel better, and had begun exchanging jokes with Petior in Russian.

"That is much more funny hearing way you tell it, Bryan," said Petior, a huge grin on his face. "I will need to remember to tell your version with pig, instead of fat waitress, is much better."

"I think you translated something wrong, Bryan," said James, grinning at his friend.

Petior attempted to point out where Daen went wrong in the joke. Apparently, pig just means pig, and the slang use in English didn't translate. This discussion led to more laughter.

"Hello, Petior," came a man's voice in Russian from the hallway that sounded slightly out of breath. A short, round man with a head full of white hair entered the room, walking slightly forward on his right side, as if he'd had his shoulder dislocated several times. His face had deep aging lines across it, though he was probably only in his fifties.

"This is my friend Roman. He is owner, and our host," Petior explained as everyone shook hands.

"Dinner was very good..." James began, but stopped because it looked like Roman didn't speak English.

Daen immediately jumped in, and expressed their gratitude. Roman stared at Daen as though he'd never met someone like him in his entire life, then leaned in, and whispered something to Petior.

"Excuse for moment please, friends," Petior said, as he followed Roman into the hallway. As they walked away, Roman removed a folded piece of paper from his back pocket. Petior took it and closed the door behind them.

"I wonder if that's the bill. I thought Petior said this meal was covered. Should we offer some money?" asked James, trusting Daen to know more about the Russian customs.

"Nah, man, he'd take it as an insult. Besides, that was a normal sized sheet of paper. When was the last time your bill for food was that big? Nah, just be cool, it'll be all good."

Petior opened the door and walked back in. "We are done now, here?" he asked. "May go for drink?"

"Dinner was great, man, but I don't think I'm up for a night of drinkin'," Daen immediately responded.

"Thank you, Petior. Tonight was very nice, but I'm with Bryan," said James.

"You are sure?" Petior said with a slight frown. "It is good, tonight. I hope before you leave we can do again."

# •Chapter Three•

A few minutes later, the three men were back in the cold, snowy streets of Moscow. They parted ways after tentatively planning to see each other at the bar one more time.

As James and Daen turned a snowy corner, heading back toward their hotel, Daen muttered, "Seems we have a short stack behind us again."

"The girl, yeah. A boy took off the moment we stepped outside. He was watching from the alley across the way." James began to explain the day's events. Everything from the kids selling candy, to how he'd set up room nine. "We may have some activity," he concluded, "but I'm not sure to what level. I wouldn't put it past them to have kids doing a lot of the work, or even be waiting for us back at the room."

While Daen digested this, James added, "You go in and up to our room. Check the monitors, and signal me in the hallway fifty seconds after we shake hands. One jump is all clear to enter room nine. Two jumps means to come up to our room."

"Okay," replied Daen.

The hotel looked unwatched as they approached and entered. They said good night to each other, shook hands, and James turned to the front desk to check for any messages. In reality, this was just an excuse to waste the fifty seconds before entering the hallway.

"Hi, any messages for Stephen Lewis?" he asked the clerk.

The man flipped a piece of paper and peered down.

Even though he wore a long sleeved shirt, a tattoo was partially visible on his wrist. James noticed another tattoo just below his collarbone, because the clerk had the top few buttons undone.

"No," the man replied curtly.

James felt a surge come over him. It was almost time for whatever was coming. He focused on the man, and gave him a quick visual scan, making mental notes.

*Checked with his left hand, right hand not visible. Probably right handed, and has a weapon. Made eye contact, so he is confident in himself. Limits tattoos to areas that can be hidden, so he's someone potentially in the public eye. Looks like he can handle himself well. No visible scars. Right eye slightly larger than left, weight shifted to right foot, so extremely right dominant; will probably be thrown off by left handed fighter. Lean and top heavy, so free-floating rib best point of immediate attack.*

"Thank you," said James, as he turned and walked toward room nine. The clerk picked up the phone, and spoke in Russian in a hushed voice.

*Thud. Thud.*

Daen had jumped twice.

James stopped in front of room nine. He made a show of putting the key in the door, but then stopped, pretending he'd forgotten something. He placed the key back in his pocket and turned. He thought he heard a small creak from inside the room as he headed for the stairs, and he noticed the tripper he had set earlier had been disrupted.

A few seconds later, he was in the room he shared with Daen. "The clerk is helping whoever's behind this little arrangement. Any conditions we need to remove?"

"No, man, I don't see any kids around, just two guys sitting in the room," said Daen pointing at the monitor. "Seems like these folks are serious about teaching you that respect. You sure all you did was challenge the fool in the subway?"

"Yes sir, but go figure that logic out. You want the room or the clerk?" James checked his gun, as he walked over to the balcony, already knowing Daen's answer.

"Dumb question, the clerk. What do you think, catch him in the hallway, or at the desk before you start?"

"The desk would be best. He knows how to fight and is very right dominant. Chances are he's packing, too. Let's try to keep this quiet," said James with a smile. "Say thirty seconds?"

"Works for me," said Daen, sliding his pistol into his jacket.

James checked his triggers for the mini-flashes. He then looked at the monitors, and saw both men facing the door that leads to the hallway from room nine.

He climbed over the rail and hung down. Just as he let go, he heard Daen exclaim, "Damn!" in a hushed voice.

Landing, James peered up, wondering what was wrong.

Daen's head appeared. "Petior just walked into the lobby." He dropped James a microphone pack, and went back into the room.

James hooked up his earpiece and said, "What do you see?"

"He's still at the desk, probably trying to get our room number. What do you want to... Damn! One of the guys left the room, and is walking toward the desk. They're shouting. I can hear them through the floor," said Daen.

"I am breaching the room, taking out the remaining guy with the flash, and will join you in the lobby. Go now," said James. Turning his back to the building, he shut his eyes and detonated the flashes. *Bang.* The sound was like someone dropping a heavy boot on a wooden floor.

James pushed open the window he'd unlocked earlier and climbed into room nine. He could hear noise in the lobby, but he had to neutralize the man in the room first. James quickly crossed over to the man, who was holding his eyes. James considered a sleeper hold, but didn't have time.

*Crack, crack.* James hit the man in the jaw twice, hard enough to dislocate it, and the guy dropped to the floor. James took out his gun. He barely had a foot in the hallway when he saw Daen running out the front door. James followed, but before he reached the door, Daen was speaking into the earpiece.

"The clerk and the guy that came out of room nine grabbed Petior. Saw them take him out the side door in the front of the hotel. They shoved him in a black sedan and took off. I have the plate. You okay?"

James knew Daen was smart enough not to give chase. The idea of trying to track a vehicle in an area you don't know isn't an action a member of the group would consider. It was pointless if you didn't have the ability to stop the vehicle.

"I'm fine. The guy in room... Hey!" James ex-claimed, as he rounded the corner and reentered room nine. The man was attempting to escape out the win-dow.

"Bryan, alley!" James shouted, as he sprinted across the room and out the window himself.

The man staggered to his feet in a weak attempt to flee as James tackled him, dropping his knee into the middle of the man's back. He twisted the man's wrists into the middle of his shoulder blades, making it ex-tremely difficult for him to move.

And there it was. What James earlier had sensed was coming had arrived. Now that he was in the mo-ment, James could trace it like all the others to a dream he'd had. It was more than déjà vu.

When Daen arrived, he used a zip tie to secure the man's hands. James stuffed a bit of fabric from the man's shirt into his mouth. Daen climbed through the window so he could help pull the other man in while James pushed. They let him fall on his head.

"Go see if there is a real front desk clerk tied up, and then come back. We need to minimize potential witnesses," said James, grabbing his gun from the ground, and tucking it away quickly before climbing through the window himself.

Daen left without another word, shutting the door behind him.

James propped the bound man in a chair, closed the window, and turned to study him. Now that James con-sidered him, the guy wasn't that old. In fact, he had to be two or maybe three years younger than himself. He looked familiar, especially something around the cheeks, but the left side of his face was rather swollen, and James couldn't place him.

James pulled out his gun again, and made sure the safety was on, and pointed it at him. The man looked around nervously. Enough of the young man's senses had come back to know he was in trouble.

"Do you speak English?" James asked.

The man looked around even more frantically.

"Do you speak English?" James repeated with more force.

The man nodded, continuing to look around the room.

"If you make any noise or yell, I'll shoot you in the head. I'm going to remove the gag, do you understand?" James looked the young man in the eyes.

The man stared at James for a moment before giving a single nod.

James approached him with his gun in a back stance, and got just close enough to remove the cloth with a tug before taking two steps back. The man wasn't secured to the chair, and James was going to go cautiously until Daen was back.

"Are you seriously hurt?" James asked.

The young man shook his head.

"What is your name?" No reply.

"I said, what is your name? What are you called?"

"Nikolias," the man answered.

"Where did they take our friend?" James asked.

"What friend? Is two of you," came the raspy voice of Nikolias.

"A man, a friend of ours, they took him from the lobby. Where would they take him?" James asked.

"Why should I tell you?" sneered Nikolias.

"Well, besides me having a gun pointing at you, imagine me pointing it at your sister," James said in a flat tone.

"I have no sister," Nikolias said with a defiant, but truthful manner.

"Your cousin then. The girl in the subway station who works to keep the other children in line," James said coolly, finally having placed Nikolias's face.

"What? You are lying," the man said, but this time his body language betrayed him.

"Oh, and I just happened to mention the subway and her job?" James asked, in a sarcastic tone.

"She is not my family. Do what you think. It is nothing to me," Nikolias lied.

"She is your family. I can see it in your face and cheekbones. And if your life, and hers means nothing to you..." James chambered the gun.

"You will not hurt her. You will not!" Nikolias started to shout.

"Quiet down." James waved his hands up and down to make sure Nikolias understood. "If you tell me where to find my friend, we'll let you go. We'll also help you find a way to get out of this area, with your family, if you want. We can help protect you," he said, as Daen entered the room.

"There was a clerk back there. It looks like they knocked him out, but he'll be alright. I saw the schedule. Natalia was supposed to work tonight man. Not whoever's back there," said Daen. He walked over and secured Nikolias to the chair. "What'dja get from him?"

"Nikolias here was about to tell us where we can find Petior, in exchange for his life, and his cousin's, along with my promise to help protect them if they want it," commented James.

"You made some progress then, about time you do something tonight." Daen grinned, grabbing the other chair. He faced it toward Nikolias and sat down.

Both Daen and James peered at Nikolias with anticipation, but he said nothing. He seemed to be concentrating very hard.

Daen started to speak to Nikolias in Russian, and Nikolias's eyes narrowed.

"We can help you," Daen said, "but you need to help us. All we want to know is how to get our friend back. Consider your situation. We are trying to be fair to you, and give you help in return for helping us."

"What makes you think I need your help?" Nikolias answered in Russian.

"You are our prisoner, but you are a captive of whatever group you..." Daen began, but Nikolias cut him off.

"What makes you think I want to leave?" growled Nikolias.

"When you help us, your bosses will not be too happy with you. You and your cousin will need to leave to survive," replied Daen.

"So he says," Nikolias said curtly, with a head gesture towards James.

"What did he say? Why did he just do that?" asked James.

"Sounds like he doesn't feel the need for our help. It seems he doesn't want to, or have a reason to leave," Daen replied, a puzzled look on his face.

"I am no traitor, and I will die to help our fraternity and country. I am loyal and believe in things, unlike you American dogs," Nikolias stated in English.

James bowed his head, closed his eyes, and rubbed his left temple for a moment with his left hand. He dragged it down his face before speaking again.

"Okay, tell us what the fraternity's cause is. What's so special about it that you're willing to risk your life, your cousin's life, because someone felt I disrespected them near a train?" asked James.

Nikolias laughed. "We know you're looking for drugs. You feel drugs are not disrespectful and destroying. You think we do not know that is why you are here? We see you peoples, and how you treat us. You all deserve death for your exploits on us, and our children."

It all clicked into place for James. "Bryan, please translate what I'm about to say. I want to make sure our friend here understands completely."

Daen nodded.

"You're right," James affirmed. "We are seeking those who deal in drugs. But, we seek it for the same reason you do. We do not," he gave extra emphasis to the word not, "wish to purchase drugs or sell them. We want to stop those who are doing it." He paused to let that sink in. "We've been able to make connections that somehow link several factions from different mafias together. We're trying to understand how it works, find those responsible, and bring them to justice. We're on the same side."

As Daen finished translating, James walked over and released Nikolias. The room was silent as Nikolias sat rubbing his hands, and looked at James and Daen. Daen hid his surprise at James's actions. His companion always seemed to keep things under control, and Daen was placing his faith in James's judgment. After a few long moments, Nikolias stood. As he did, James spotted a tattoo on his wrist.

"If we are on same side," the man spoke slowly, "you must show good faith. My weapon back, please." He stammered the last three words, doubting his own daring in making such a request.

"You can have your gun back." James removed the ammunition from Nikolias's gun and held it out.

"And the bullets?" asked Nikolias.

"Those you may not have back, at least not yet. However," James unchambered his gun and took out all the rounds, "we will remove our ammunition as well. Is that more fair?"

Nikolias considered him, and nodded.

"Stephen..." began Daen in an uncertain voice.

James cut him off with a look. He had this, and Daen needed to cooperate. Slowly, Daen removed his rounds from his gun.

"Nikolias, that symbol on your hand, is that the symbol of your fraternity?" James asked.

Nikolias raised his hand to show the tattoo, taking a step closer to them. "Da."

James asked, "Is that the same symbol I saw on the vendor at the train station, on the neck of the man pretending to be the clerk, and several other places, like the window ledge of Roman's restaurant?"

Nikolias gave a start of recognition at Roman's name, but didn't have time to answer James's question.

"Roman is a good friend of Petior's too," stated James trying to capitalize on Nikolias's knowing Roman.

Daen missed the subtle gesture by Nikolias, as he had focused on the tattoo. "What does it mean?"

Nikolias addressed Daen without addressing James's quick comment. "It is hammer and sickle stretched out and laying parallel as if making equal sign. The lies of the old country, but with sword of truth running through it to show it is not equal, and we will break it and rise from rebellion," said Nikolias. He ran his finger over each part as he described the tattoo and then continued.

"They use drugs to keep us down, hurt our family, our children, and make everyone dependent on them, for everything, so they have all power. They take our children. They only respect violence. We protect ourselves, and take out as many as we can in fight to get power back to people of Russia. To have strong, fierce, respected nation again."

James got it; the train station, the organization and control of the kids. It wasn't about the money. It was about keeping the drugs away. It was about teaching the kids life lessons they needed if the revolution were to happen. They were trying to do good using the tools and methods they had available to them.

"Why did your friend at the subway assume I was looking for drugs?" James asked.

"He said you make move to make friends with children. That you are strong, and healthy, and know how to fight. You watch before doing. This is what smart drug dealers are like," said Nikolias.

"I see," said James.

"How do you know Roman? He does not normally talk to outsiders," asked Nikolias, whose attitude seemed to be changing as his tone became more even.

"He hosted a dinner for us tonight because Petior is his friend. We got to meet him at the end of the dinner.

I'm sure the children you had watching us can verify our location," said James.

James knew he was winning Nikolias over. He added, "Perhaps we can go talk to Roman, and you can see for yourself that we had met him, and he can tell you about Petior."

"No, no that is not needed. I take you to Petior. We must hurry," said Nikolias.

# •Chapter Four•

A minute later, they were walking up the street. The three men went about a block before climbing into Nikolias's car. They drove in silence for about fifteen minutes, as each man was deep in thought.

The housing complex they arrived at was made up of five twelve-story buildings that formed a 'U' shape, and had a thin forest behind it. The sidewalks leading to the buildings were heavily damaged and missing large sections.

The buildings were very old judging by their condition. Several bricks were missing here and there from each of the buildings. Some of the missing bricks seemed to be deliberate, as if those spots had once held surveillance cameras.

The courtyard area had a fountain in the middle that was remarkably well maintained when compared to the buildings. Four concrete benches created a rectangle around the circular water display. This area was clearly a source of inspiration and pride for the inhabitants. A plaque on the fountain read *"HOPE ETERNAL"* in Russian.

They entered the second building on the left, which surprised James and Daen. They had expected the middle building to be a more suitable headquarters from a strategic point of view.

Upon entering the building, Daen looked like he was going to be sick. James knew why. The odor was terrible. The place smelled like a mix of burnt cabbage and old gym clothes.

They climbed five flights of stairs, entered the main hallway, and went to the second door on the right. Here, they found two more doors. Nikolias secured the door behind them, and revealed a hidden keypad to the door immediately in front of them. He entered a code, and the door to the left opened.

"If you enter wrong code, this door open," he said, indicating the door in front of them. "Four seconds after you close it, toxic gas is released. This is why it is sealed door. You can open this door," he pointed to the one on his left, "without a code, but then you cannot find hidden stairs."

Entering, they found a studio apartment. The old couple that lived there looked up, recognized Nikolias, and went back to what they were doing. As the door closed, a little panel opened on the floor. Nikolias placed his palm on the palm reader, and a trap door opened in the floor.

"Damn, man. Rather high tech for a building like this," whispered Daen to James.

"They gave up space in their home so we could set this up in exchange for free rent and vodka. They are old and do not need a lot of space," said Nikolias in Russian, clearly making sure the couple understood what was being explained. Daen translated for James as they went down the steps.

Nikolias unlocked the last door, and they walked through to find Petior gagged, beaten, and tied to a chair. Three other men were present; two had guns on Petior, while the third worked him over. Suddenly, there was a lot of confused shouting in English and Russian.

"Stop!"

"Put the guns down!"

"We will shoot him!"

"Stop. Don't shoot!"

"Hear them out!"

"I will not even count to one. You will release him and put down the guns!"

"Enough!" said a woman in the corner. While raising her hands, she moved between the two groups, capturing the room's attention. As her face came into full view, she appeared to be in her mid-fifties, but with the beauty of a much younger woman.

"They are not holding guns to Nikolias. He is standing with them, and defending them. We can hear them, and then decide our next step," she said.

She scanned Daen's face, and then James's before lowering her hands to her side.

The eye contact was enough. James's instinct on reading people, which had never failed him, told him it was wise to heed her instructions.

James lowered his weapon, as did the Russian men on the other side of the room.

"Man, are you sure about this?" Daen's weak whisper rang with fear and surprise. "You always tell me to trust my instincts more, and this goes against them."

In an audible voice, James said, "Lower your gun."

"What if this is a setup and they shoot us?" implored Daen.

"Then we will be dead, but this woman is a woman of her word, lower the gun," James said, his eyes locked onto the woman's eyes.

Lowering his gun, Daen said under his breath, "Damn, man, this goes against training," his head slightly shaking back and forth.

Without looking at Daen, James calmly said, "It does."

"They are friends of Roman's, his guests for dinner tonight," said Nikolias, after a tense moment of silence.

The men exchanged a glance but said nothing. The woman walked toward them.

She hugged Nikolias and then leaned back, lightly grabbing his face in her hands before kissing his cheeks. She said something to him in Russian, and he nodded, and smiled, as his fingers found her wrists near his face. A moment later, she released him, and stepped back a few paces.

"I am Ola," she said, addressing Daen and James. "This is Anton, Igor, and Valdnik." She indicated the men from left to right. They didn't acknowledge the introduction. "How is it that you know Roman?" she asked.

At this, Petior started to create some noise, and received a hard hit to the ribs for his efforts.

"Petior, please, my friend, relax," said Daen in Russian.

Ola looked slightly surprised. "You call this man your friend?" she asked.

"We do," answered James.

"Do you know your friend has stabbed one of our members? He may die. He has two small children who have no mother already. How will they survive without their father?" she asked, in a voice like an attorney addressing a hostile witness.

Petior began to fuss again and tried to talk through his gag. He was somehow making the chair jump beneath him. The visible parts of his face that weren't swollen, or covered in blood had turned a bright red. He was clearly trying to answer for his actions. Instead, he received another shot to the ribs.

"Do you intend to kill him?" James asked.

"Yes. If our man dies, so does he. Life for life," she said in a flat tone.

"He is how we know Roman. They are friends. I don't believe Roman would appreciate his friend being killed." James slowly turned toward Ola; his body language careful and deliberate to show he wanted a meeting of the minds, and did not pose a threat.

"Roman will have to understand, and he will accept it with a minimum of words." Ola spoke as though she knew a key piece of information that would sway Roman.

James quickly made eye contact with Daen. A tool was gone.

"If this man, the injured man lives, then so does Petior?" asked James.

"His," she indicated Petior, "and your chances of survival increase greatly. But if he dies, then so does your friend, in a most painful way. He will feel pain, as will our comrade's children for the loss." Her eyes narrowed, and her voice held a steel edge.

"Is he with a doctor, this man? What is his name?" James asked.

"He is Alexander, and no, we do not have a doctor we can freely summon. Alexander is in the infirmary. Why? You are not doctor. You can't help him." Ola spoke with a skeptical voice that hid a tiny hint of hope. Evidently, she cared about Alexander living.

"I might be able to help. I will need to see him, but perhaps I can help." James played on the hope she had tried to conceal, convinced her tone was a cover.

She immediately countered. "Are you willing to bet your life on this?"

"If I think I can help Alexander after seeing him, and if the tools I need are there, then yes, I am. If I fail and Alexander dies, then I die and not Petior," James said.

Petior began to make noise again. This time he got a blow to the left knee from Anton for his troubles.

"No, you both die," Ola stated.

He knew this wasn't negotiable, but James had an out. If he didn't think Alexander would make it, he'd simply have to find a different way to save Petior.

"Stephen, man..." Daen began.

James knew Daen's argument without hearing it. Petior was basically a stranger to them. However, as James saw it, that wasn't the point. He felt he had an obligation to try to help anyone he saw in a dangerous situation when he could. It was one of the main reasons why he was in the group.

He also had a feeling that Petior was in this situation because of Daen and himself. Plus, they had become friends over the last two nights. James decided to take action since he had a way out.

The human body fascinated James. Even as a young boy, he had always had an interest in the medical field. As soon as he was allowed, he started volunteering in the hospitals on 3rd shifts just to be able to gain some first-hand experience. While in college, he was studying biology, focusing on physiology and chemistry, with aspirations of becoming a doctor.

"Agreed," James answered sharply, silencing Daen. "If I begin to help Alexander and he doesn't make it, then we both die. If I don't try to help, then no harm from Alexander's death will come to me. If I do help and Alexander lives, then we all live. Oh, and no more injury to my friend. In return, Petior will sit quietly."

James made eye contact with Petior. Petior sat motionless for a moment before nodding. James turned toward Ola, who considered the request.

"That will all come to be. Come this way." She led James and Daen out of the room. Nikolias and Igor came too, leaving Anton and Valdnik to watch over Petior.

A few minutes later, after going through several doors and hallways that seemed to snake throughout the building, they reached the infirmary. It was like a small emergency room from before World War II, though, with some modern devices.

Alexander was in one of three beds, with a young woman at his side wiping his forehead with a cloth. He seemed to be having trouble breathing, but was hooked up to an oxygen mask, a saline drip, and a heart monitor.

He was the man who had posed as the hotel clerk.

"Anna has done all that is possible to make him comfortable," Ola explained.

Anna appeared to be in her late twenties, with exceptionally bright green eyes, and a kind face. She wore a bonnet, and had a clean, light-brown dress on with white shoes.

"Hello, Anna, I'm Stephen. I'm going to try to help Alexander, and I could use your help, please. Could you tell me what medicine you have given him?"

James smiled softly, but Anna frowned and looked at Ola.

Using sign language, Ola told Anna what James had said. Springing up, Anna went to get the medicine she had given Alexander.

"Anna has had no hearing for many years now," explained Ola. "When she was young, she was forced to work in an official's home. One day, he returned home early to find Anna had not done as he instructed in cleaning. He said that since she did not listen properly, she did not need her ears. He proceeded to burn her ears, so they closed forever. She wears the bonnet to cover her scars."

James processed the story but gave no outward reaction, as Anna returned and presented him with a bottle. Turning it over in his hands, James read the label.

"Demerol," he stated to the room in general. "Well, I suppose it's what they have." He turned back toward Alexander, whose eyes were now open.

Upon seeing James's face, the man immediately tried to get up. Igor and Nikolias rushed over and gently held him down.

"You!" Alexander exclaimed.

Ola came to the foot of the bed and spoke in rapid Russian.

"Alexander," James began, quieting the others. The man's eyes were full of anger, and the monitor was showing signs of increased heart rate, but his blood pressure was still extremely low. "I know that Petior stabbed you, and I think you have heavy internal bleeding. I'm going to look at your wound and see what I can do to help you."

As James lifted the bed sheets, Ola spoke to Alexander in a reassuring tone. Gauze covered the man's chest, with the darkest red spot indicating the location of the injury. It was the middle of the left side of the chest, which led James to believe Alexander had a punctured lung. If that was the case, his chest was slowly filling with blood.

"Do you feel like there's a very heavy weight on your chest, making it hard to breathe?" James asked Alexander.

He nodded.

James asked Daen to bring over the portable X-ray machine he had spotted, and began raising Alexander's bed. "I'm going to be as fast as I can," he said. "I know this position won't be comfortable, and I apologize for it. I think you have a punctured lung."

James stopped short of putting Alexander in the full position. It would essentially cut off his breathing if James had him there too long, and it would take a minute to get him fully set up.

"Do you know how to use this?" Daen whispered.

"Yes, I was a volunteer in radiology two summers ago," James replied.

He had never actually used the equipment, but had watched enough to understand the basics. Two minutes later, they were ready to go, aside from putting on the traditional lead radiation bib. The X-ray was a one shot deal, so it wasn't worth taking the time to for it.

"Alexander, stay with me. Nikolias and Igor, I'll need your help to lift him so I can place this plate for the film behind him. At the same time, Ola, if you and Bryan can manually bring his bed up to support him as I get the film in place, that would be best. Anna will need to hit the radiation. Once she's done that, Nikolias and Igor, we'll need to then lift him back up so I can get the film. Ola and Bryan, you'll reset the bed manually to how he was when we came in. Everyone clear?"

Ola signed James's instructions to Anna, who had evidently run the machine before, while Daen translated for everyone else.

"On three." James verbally counted up, and held up a finger for each number counted. He had the film in his left hand ready to be placed. When he got to three everyone worked seamlessly together. He pointed to Anna to signal for the radiation.

"Now," he said to kick off the second half of the maneuvering. Moments later, he retrieved the film and handed it to Anna for processing.

James used the time while the X-ray developed to grab those tools he thought he need to address the lung. He was working on the assumption he was right. He also grabbed a defibrillator and had it ready to go. Alexander's blood pressure and heart rate had been continuously dropping.

Anna came back with the X-ray. The lung was damaged, but the puncture had missed the heart. James noted that Alexander's lungs were rather small for an adult, which added an unneeded level of complexity to the situation.

The man was starting to fade. James moved quickly and removed all the bandages. As soon as they were off, James reached for iodine. At that moment, the monitor flat-lined. Simultaneously, there was the unmistakable sound of a gun being chambered behind James's head.

James moved so fast no one expected it. He turned and disarmed Igor before the man could respond. He removed the bullets, and tossed the gun, and said, "I'm trying to save his life. Leave me alone."

"Leave it," commanded Ola to Igor, who had gone to retrieve the gun.

James did a quick wipe over the ribs with the iodine. He made the incision, placed the draining tube, and secured it. It was a bit sloppy but fast.

"Turn him toward me," he instructed. Nikolias and Daen gently lifted Alexander. "Stop, that's good enough," said James, when they had him at the correct angle. Anna had already started supporting Alexander in that position with pillows, and the blood was beginning to drain.

James placed a manual respirator on Alexander and had Nikolias operate it. Now the tricky part was shocking Alexander's heart back. *If it doesn't take the first time*, James thought, but he didn't have time to worry about that. He gelled up the paddles, and told everyone to move away. Anna was ready for the signal.

"Clear," James said and nodded to Anna.

Two tense seconds had passed before they heard a bleep on the monitor. They had a heartbeat. Alexander then took a breath on his own that seemed to be the signal that others could breathe again too.

"We still have work to do. Ola, can you please ask Anna to get... never mind." James had started to ask for blood, but Anna had already gotten it. James gave her a big smile, and she smiled back, as she hooked up the bag. James returned to Alexander's side to tidy up the draining tube.

"He live now?" Igor asked.

"I've done the best I can. I'm sure the doctor will be able to mend him better, but yes, I think he'll recover," said James, with pride in his voice. James reflected on how good he felt as he walked over to the sink with the others.

After washing and drying his hands, James returned and punched Igor squarely on the right cheek, knocking him to the floor.

"Don't ever put a gun on me again," he said in a clear, but unemotional voice. The room was stunned.

Ola broke the silence. "Igor is sorry, I am sure."

She plainly understood. James would do what he needed to do, but he wasn't going to be pushed around. He had patience, and that made him a formidable enemy, but it could also make him a strong ally.

James turned to Ola. "Can we please bring Petior here, to address some of his wounds?"

She nodded and motioned for Igor to bring him. While they waited, Nikolias told Ola everything that had transpired. James and Daen filled in where needed, but didn't say too much. They knew it was far better for this to come from Nikolias. About halfway through, Petior arrived, and James set to work to dress the wounds of his Russian friend.

# •Chapter Five•

The next day, James received a call from Ola saying the doctor had agreed Alexander would make a full recovery and that he, Daen, and Petior were free to go. She apologized that she wasn't able to personally tell them, but said Nikolias would arrive in a moment to escort them out.

The three men had been placed in a room made of solid brick. The door was made of solid steel and could only be opened from the outside. A guard had been stationed outside the door with the real purpose of executing the captives if Alexander died.

Nikolias bounded into the room just as James told Petior and Daen they were free to go. "I will take you back to hotel," he said smiling, as he showed them out of the room and to the car.

Daen took the front seat, while James sat in the back with Petior. As they drove, Nikolias and Daen spoke in Russian, hitting it off now that the crisis had passed. Daen easily demonstrated his admirable trait of making friends quickly.

"My American friend, how can I repay you for this debt of my life that I owe you?" Petior asked, in a sheepish voice.

"We returned the favor. You came to try to help Bryan and me," James replied in a soft voice, looking over at Petior. "We saw you enter the hotel and get into a fight, but how'd you know we might be in danger?"

"No, it is different. I notice children following you, so I follow to see why. Very different than you saving my life. You bet your life to save mine. Not same. I will not forget this my friend. My life, it is yours," said Petior, with such conviction, that he almost shouted it.

James didn't know what to say, so he merely nodded.

"I do have question," Petior continued. "Who are you, Stephen? You and Bryan, you are not normal Americans. I know many people, and I know how to see people. I see more than you think. You know how to do things. Things like spy, but you are not spy like I ever know," he whispered to James. "You are not CIA or FBI. I am former KGB, for reasons we do not discuss, but I know this. So, who are you, Stephen?"

James paused, considering Petior. He made a choice to trust him. "We are part of a group that is trying to understand how different mafias are working to continue the drug trades," he said quietly.

"You are talking of Russian dealings with Italians into America and how they get it from Slants," grumbled Petior. "This is a fast and dirty thing you ask. You want none of it. Trust me, I know, it will break you into million pieces."

"Slants, what or who are the Slants?" James asked.

"Is that not what you call them, Asian people?" Petior inquired.

"Oh, I see. Tell me, Petior, why will this break me into a million pieces, and how are the Asians connected?" James asked.

"You are good man. Strong, smart, and fierce, but this goes too deep and too ugly. You do not want to follow. I know some, and it is too ugly. Save your youth for a happier life," Petior said, looking down.

"Petior, what can you tell me? I appreciate the warning, but if I can rid the world of this evil, I will." James stared at Petior, who finally looked up.

With a slight lurch, the car stopped in front of the hotel.

James knew it was now or never. Petior's body language signaled he was shutting down, no doubt to protect James from himself.

"Nikolias, drive around the block once more please," said Daen, who knew with a quick glance in the rearview mirror that James needed more time.

"I do not understand. We are here," said Nikolias, but Daen insisted. As they drove, Daen began telling Nikolias the pig joke from the night before.

James grabbed Petior's shoulders and gently pushed him back into the seat. He needed Petior's body to be in an open position. This would make it easier for Petior to tell James what he needed to know.

"I take responsibility for what I ask," James told his new friend. "I truly believe it is a horrible thing I'm seeking, and that ignorance is often bliss. But for men like me, like us, that is never an acceptable reality. If you value what I have done for you, please at least point me in the right direction. You have the power to help me, and I certainly need it." James made sure he didn't blink as he said this. His tone was measured, half pleading and half demanding.

"Da, I know of what you speak. I will put you in contact with man in UK that can give you information. Calum will send you to Asians. They know of the Italians' ways and will help you. They hate them." Petior took a pen and piece of paper from the seat pocket in front of them, and wrote down a phone number. He gave James the paper just as they pulled back up to the hotel again.

"But I ask you, please, do not call him," Petior said slowly. "I know, wasted words, but I ask it anyhow, my friend."

The men exchanged goodbyes as well as contact information. A moment later, Nikolias and Petior speed away as James and Daen walked into the hotel. They were looking forward to a hot shower and a soft bed.

Natalia was at the front desk reading as they approached the lobby. When she saw them, she quickly picked up the desk phone, whispered something, and began to talk in a normal voice.

"You know, it's interesting man," said Daen, "I wonder why she missed her shift last night."

James gave an acknowledging grunt, and they continued through the lobby. He too suspected it wasn't by chance.

Entering the room they shared, they found a man wearing a coat with a turned up collar and bowler hat peering out the window. "I hear you have been busy these last hours disrupting the peace, capturing my men, saving lives, and earning the respect of the people. Oh, and not to mention enjoying my hospitality. Thank you for what you have done. I trust you won't wear out your welcome or earned status with us."

The man turned, and it was Roman. He had no trace of an accent. Clearly, James had been wrong about his ability to speak English. He went on in his out-of-breath voice. "I have covered your costs for the trip here. I have booked you on a plane leaving tonight, in first class. You will find you have enough time to shower and pack before your flight if you don't delay.

Simply take what you need for your flight, and walk out to the black Mercedes in front of the hotel, and the driver will take you directly to the airport. The remainder of your things will be shipped as you like."

He said nothing else but placed their tickets on the bed and walked out.

James and Daen weren't sure what to make of this, but James suspected the call Natalia had made was to Roman.

Daen checked the tickets. "These are first class. Hey, all our equipment is packed. Look they have shipping labels ready to go. All we need to do is fill in the address back to the hot spot. What the..."

"I don't know, but this is one of those 'Go with the flow' moments," James said.

"Really man, why?" Daen questioned. "A man we don't know just did all that for us? What about not being in someone's debt and all that jazz you talk about?"

"We aren't in his debt. He's in ours. Or he feels he is. This is his way to try to level the field," James answered.

"Are you nuts? How'd you work that out? Okay, yeah, maybe the others, but him?" Daen was clearly skeptical of James's reasoning.

"Well, Roman is related to Alexander. I suspect his friendship with Petior is business related, given that exchange in the hall with the paper last night. More than likely illegal business, actually. Roman is obviously in a position of influence with Ola and the others. Natalia does some spying directly for him, but not for the freedom group, as she didn't bother to tell them about us splitting rooms."

James said all this in a matter-of-fact tone as he gathered fresh clothes for a shower. He was exhausted and was getting grossed out by his body odor.

"Man, I know you're right. I don't know how you know that, but you're never wrong." Daen shook his head and began filling in the shipping labels with the proper identification codes. The hot spot would reject the shipment without these special codes.

James continued talking, almost as if Daen hadn't said anything. "Alexander has small lungs, a trait that's genetically inherited and one that Roman shares, assuming I've interpreted his breathing properly. They also have identical height, hair color, and ear lobes. My guess is they're father and son, but that Alexander is a bastard child." James's voice cracked slightly. He was getting tired, but continued, "Ola spoke of his family and its importance. However, that group believes in dying for the cause. So why be so worried about one member's life, unless he's super valuable to someone high up?"

James stopped speaking to pick up the shirt he accidently dropped. He then went on. "The fact that Ola spoke about Roman understanding means she knows Alexander is Roman's son. That must be why she felt Roman would be okay with Petior dying if Alexander did. What's perplexing is that Ola and Petior, didn't know each other. That concerns me."

James continued thinking out loud as he moved slowly toward the bathroom. "The fact that Roman stayed away from us during dinner, even though he had to know about us by then, given the symbol burned into the windowsill where we ate, tells me he has to be in debt to Petior. Plus Natalia, who apparently knows Roman, just happened to be absent last night? It

sounds like Roman got her to switch shifts with someone. I think Roman's comments sum up the remainder
nicely, don't you?" James said, as if remembering that
Daen was there. He turned on the shower and un-
dressed.

"Translate that for me in English, not crazy James
thinkin'," Daen said.

"I think Roman is like a commander in that freedom
group. Or at least the one that pays the bills. I think
Ola is the one who runs everything full time, though.
We already discussed Roman and Petior's rather lucid
relationship, but Petior doesn't seem to be involved
with the freedom movement. Roman is the key, like he
sees two sides of a coin."

Daen nodded and opened his mouth to speak, but
seemed to answer his own question. Then, as if trying
to find something to nitpick, he turned towards James
and said, "Identical hair? His hair is whiter than you,
man."

"Eyebrows," James said simply, closing the door
completely, and getting in a much-needed shower.

"Damn, man, how the..." he paused. "Whatever it is
that allows you to do that, well, it's impressive every
time you do it. But you are a nerd man, no doubt. Like
seriously, who notices all of the detail like that?" said
Daen, shaking his head again.

# •Chapter Six•

The return trip to the US was uneventful, which made for a good trip by James's standards. He didn't sleep much on the flight. Being in motion prevented him from sleeping well, but being in first class did help tremendously.

When he did sleep, a weird, semi-cartoonish dream about walking around a corner slowly, his hand on the wall, and a red streak following his touch plagued him.

On the first leg of the flight, James had managed to finish a write-up of the trip. Daen concurred that it was accurate and signed off on it. He and Daen had also agreed that James would consult with Daen, and the rest of the group, before taking any further steps involving the Russians.

Now he just had to follow up with calling Calum when he could get a secure line. That was priority number one upon getting to campus, though a good night's sleep was also high on the priority list.

If James was going to continue his work for the group, he needed to come up with a legitimate reason for traveling around the world. The vast majority of his previous missions had been day trips, but this was much more complex than those had ever been.

His medical interests weren't going to allow for immediate world travel, even though his skills were handy in certain circumstances, like the one with Alexander. He needed to be able to travel, have some schedule flexibility, and not have a great deal of co-workers tagging along.

*Problem one is freedom,* he thought, writing it down. *Freedom requires trust, and the most immediate form of trust comes from confidence. Confidence comes from being a subject matter expert.* That meant he needed something in science. He preferred physiology, but biology, chemistry, or physics would do.

He tapped the end of his pen twice against the paper, thinking. The flight attendant asked if he'd like something to drink, interrupting his thoughts, and handed him a tray with fresh fruit and a salad.

"Just water, please," he said.

*Water. Now that was something,* he thought. He wrote down the word.

"Thank you," he said when the flight attendant handed him the water.

*Water is global, and fresh water will soon be an issue for more people than we think. Water is the basis of life and manufacturing, but that isn't helpful unless applied to certain demographics. And I need something that will get me traveling almost immediately.*

He let this thought sink in as he paused to eat the light lunch in front of him. James shook the salad dressing, and poured it on the lettuce, trying to let his mind go blank.

"When you're stuck, draw from the environment, and if you can't, then change the environment," he'd told others in training. It was good advice he'd passed along to the recruits, and guidance that he needed to take now that he was feeling stuck.

He began to look around, thinking, *Travel, distance, speed, time, fuel.* James took a drink of water, scanning the cabin for more inspiration as he thought, *Plane, people, seats, sky, first class, money.* None of these thoughts were helping. He ate some of the salad. *Food, fruit, vegetables, salad, salad dressing, oil.* Pausing, he wrote down oil, before considering it in more depth.

*Oil is a high-value commodity. It requires those in global corporations to travel,* he thought. *Smaller companies tend to pay better, and their resources are more stretched, so duplication in travel is limited. Sales take too much time to build, and you have to start locally. Marketing and management don't. Degrees get you there. The science background fits with petrochemicals, which are carbon-based, and have a biological connection.*

He scratched his head, trying to connect some of his broken thoughts. Then out of nowhere, he got his answer. He spoke it out loud without realizing he was doing so at first. "Find someone with a science background who's in marketing, and let them mentor me without having to get the degree now. Adjunct professors who teach, but have full-time careers are outstanding for that!"

The man across the aisle gave him an odd look, but James ignored him. He allowed himself a smile and finished the food in front of him, having found a path forward. While working, he could do what was needed to advance the investigation into the heroin cartel.

James and Daen split up when they hit Dulles Airport. James was flying into Pittsburgh on his journey back to school in Johnstown, while Daen was heading to the University of Virginia. They were a full day early, but that was all to the good.

Four hours later, James was back on campus, walking into his place. His housemates, freshly tanned, were all back too.

"Hey, James, what's up?" asked Mark. He was James's best friend and roommate.

James's other housemates were playing a video game, and oblivious to his entrance.

"Hey all," James said, giving a short wave before heading upstairs.

John, Steve, Dylan, and Edgar each muttered something. They were in an intense round of 007 Golden Eye, and James knew distractions like saying hi weren't worth their attention.

Mark followed James up the stairs to their shared room. He'd apparently lost his round, and it would be some time before he could get back into the rotation for the game.

"How was the break?" Mark asked, flopping on his unmade bed.

"Not too bad, a lotta work. How was yours?" asked James, making conversation.

James knew Mark's break had been good just by looking at him. Typically, Mark was a rather pale man. Right now, his skin was a light red that might leave a tan. Mark stood a solid six-feet-four-inches and all of 155 pounds soaking wet. He seemed to have gained a few desperately needed pounds that he'd probably burn off in a few days.

"Dude, it was great. I was up at the lake and the weather was amazing. The mommasitas were out too!" Mark crossed his legs and put his arms behind his head.

"Indeed. Did you use your line, 'Hey baby, how about you sit on my lap, and we talk about the first thing to pop up?' with those mommasitas?" James flashed Mark a grin.

Mark blushed but smiled back. "I hate you," he said playfully, as they always did to each other. "Just because I'm on a 'diet' doesn't mean I can't look at the 'menu,' and appreciate it."

James smiled and nodded his agreement. He knew Mark would never cheat on Jamie or anyone else for that matter.

"Only had to help your dad on a water well one day then?" James asked.

"Yup, everything else was pump work," Mark replied. He didn't bother asking how James knew he'd only helped his dad for one day. He was far too used to James knowing things without being told.

"Get back last night?" asked James.

"Yeah, a few people came back, and Jamie wanted to go to a party." Mark looked critically at his roommate. "You look dead on your feet. Did you work the entire time?"

"Most of it. Didn't get much sleep," James answered, sorting through his laundry. Thankfully, Mark wasn't paying attention to the fact that his clothes were dirty, which they shouldn't be if he had just come from spending a week at home.

"Yeah, I bet having two younger siblings in the house, and working second and third shifts doesn't allow for a lot of restful sleep," Mark sighed. "But always exams and papers to look forward to!" He raised his arm in fake celebration. "Speaking of which, can you read my geology paper for me? And I know Edgar needs help with some accounting things too."

"Yeah, when's it due?" James asked, letting out a long breath through his nose.

"First day back." Mark got up to get his paper. Luckily, it was only a few pages, and double-spaced.

James looked at the clock, which read 3:30 p.m. It was getting late in the UK. "I'll look at it after dinner if that's cool. I told Kaleb and Randy I'd be over to review some evolution stuff, but I won't be there long," he said to his roommate.

"Sweet, thanks. You coming back here first before dinner or..." Mark asked, setting the paper on James's desk.

"Meet ya there at 5:30?" James knew Mark hated to eat by himself.

"Yup. Okay, time to go teach these bitches what's up and get some 'Look at my screens' on Dylan, and his gay Siberian Warrior." Mark left the room as James laughed.

Dylan loved to yell "Look at my screen!" right before sneaking up on someone, and using the chop kill in the game. It was the most humiliating way to die in the matches.

James picked up the phone and dialed Kaleb and Randy's number.

"Hello?" Kaleb answered.

"Hey man, you and Randy want to go over that evolution stuff at your place for about ninety minutes at 4 o'clock?" James asked.

Kaleb and Randy were in a fraternity. James spent enough time there that he was like an unofficial brother that had never pledged. It was a convenient connection to have when you needed to explain long absences.

"Cool, see ya in a few." Kaleb hung up the phone.

*That was easy,* James thought.

He gathered his stuff and was out the door. He had one stop first, and that was to call Calum.

The campus lines all ran through a non-descript switchboard, so it was secure enough, as the call would merely trace to an area. This offered more security than he probably needed, but it was there and easy to use.

Ten minutes later, James was in the science building, having gotten past the rather weak locking mechanism and poorly placed cameras the campus used.

"Seriously, this is child's play," he said softly to himself. "It'd be so easy to set up a drug lab and have all the tools we need, and these fools would never even notice."

He dialed into the calling card he had bought at the Washington airport. Then the number he'd gotten from Petior. It seemed to ring for a long time. Just as he was about to give up, there was an answer.

"Who the bloody hell is this? And whatcha calling me for so late?" came a man's voice.

"Sorry for the hour..." James started.

"Who is this? I don't know this voice!" shouted the man.

"I was given this number by a friend of mine named Petior. Is this Calum?" James asked.

"You deaf or just an idiot? Asked who you are, and you turn and ask who I am. Well, isn't that a treat. I suppose this is Stephen then, eh? Yeah, my friend said you might call. He also said to tell you good luck, and he's sorry you didn't take his advice. More like God's luck," the man muttered. "So what you want, lad?" he half shouted.

"I was wondering if you'd be able to help me with a situ..." James started.

"Say one more word, and this conversation ends now, lad. He said you had brains; he was probably soaking up too much vodka. You want to talk? Meet me here in Aberdeen, plain and simple," finished Calum clearing his throat.

"Done," James replied, his brain working overtime. *Scotland,* he thought. Now he needed a real reason to travel.

"Now that's more like it. Take this down," Calum said in a normal voice. He gave James some directions and agreed to meet in a couple of months on James's timeframe. Calum didn't question the delay, and James didn't offer to explain.

"Thanks for the help, see ya soon," James said.

"Aye." With a click, Calum hung up.

*Right. Now it's just sorting out the trip, getting through exams, and securing a good cover, while getting into a new line of work. Well, some of that is just a phone call, so time to focus on school. Almost a mini-vacation*, James thought wryly, throwing his hands in the air just as Mark had done earlier.

Later that night, when he finally got into bed, James wondered if it was all worth it. He could just leave this behind, and get a job, and move on in life. It definitely would be an easier life. Without the group and school, he'd be able to have a relationship finally. Plus, in a year or two, he could spend some money.

He had a lot saved in special accounts, but wouldn't spend it. James had to keep up appearances, and that was starting to get old fast. But this was the life you had to lead to be in the group. Or, at least it was the life he led. He held himself to extremely rigid standards of discipline. He could use the funds he had access to any way he wanted, but it would raise questions, given his family's situation.

He was in the group mainly for the challenge of being the best, helping others, and knowing that at a moment's whim, he literally could do anything he wanted. To him, that was real power and the truest of freedoms. Most people couldn't handle that reality, but James craved it.

"Hey, my mom said she thought she saw you at work during break. She tried to say hi, but you didn't answer her," Mark said into the dark.

"Oh, sorry. I mustn't have heard her," James said quickly from his bed, losing his train of thought.

"That's what she said. She said to say hi, so hi. But you don't miss much," Mark said reflectively.

"I don't know. It was a long week. I was running on little sleep and must have just missed her, sorry. Please tell her hello back," James said.

"Yeah, no problem." Mark rolled over as a shout of "Odd Job!" came from downstairs.

Both James and Mark snickered, knowing what had just happened without seeing it. The guys were playing the game again.

# •Chapter Seven•

The next few weeks progressed quietly for James. The week before final exams, the group had an opportunity to bring a lot of members in the region together. James, with Daen's help, reviewed the Russian trip as a training tool for the others.

Throughout the session, two individuals in the gathering kept signaling their skepticism from the back of the room. It went unnoticed by the others, but James and Daen saw it.

"Tariq and Vic, how would you have handled this?" James finally asked, having explained the incident at the hotel and the capture of Nikolias.

James knew Vic would clam up if directly called out. Tariq, on the other hand, always had something to say.

Tariq looked coolly at James for a moment before standing up to approach the front of the room. "Well, since you both came back in one piece, there's no major issue with how you handled it. But you were careless in the operation for sure."

Tariq was built like a tank, standing six-foot-two-inches and weighing 200 pounds. He had played as a running back in football during high school, and was also an excellent boxer. He'd graduated high school a year early at the top of his class, and his family had money. Despite his talents, he failed to recognize the value of forward thinking and always lived in the moment.

James had missed Tariq's training with the group, but knew Tariq received several warnings about his attitude. It had almost gotten him disqualified several times.

"The extra room should have been on the third floor, above yours, not below. You could've heard people above you, and Daen wouldn't have had to jump around like an idiot. It would have limited their escape options too. You should have also had cameras outside the main door, and a slip mechanism ready to lock it." Tariq pointed at the diagram of the building to indicate where he would've set the equipment.

Daen spoke up. "And the fact that we had limited equipment because this was a gathering operation? Oh, plus the fact that to lock the door with a slip, you need to have someone stationed near the rotating door, or has that 'slipped' your mind, man?" Daen became more indignant as he spoke, mainly because he didn't like Tariq. "Add in the fact that we had no idea of a head count, or if it was going to be kids, or the police, or what. Sitting with all this hindsight is fine, but you ain't been listening."

Tariq jumped right back at Daen, ignoring all he'd just heard. "Plus, you let people escape and kidnap someone who's supposedly a 'friend.'" He put his hands up, and used his fingers to make quotation marks around the last word, then added, "If you knew how to hit someone properly and put them down, you could've stopped all that. Then James almost let someone escape because he couldn't put them down either. Sounds like I need to teach someone how to fight."

Daen stared with disbelief. He was too seasoned to allow his emotions to go any further, but Tariq wasn't. He just kept going on and on. He didn't notice that the reason everyone's attention was on him, was that they couldn't believe he was still talking.

As he continued into his rant about all the mistakes he could've avoided, James walked calmly toward Tariq before interrupting him. "So you're saying you can put anyone down with a single body shot?"

"If they aren't expecting it, as in I distract them with a few head shots." He punched the air, "Or just catch them right like this."

Out of the blue, Tariq landed a vicious shot to James' right lower ribs. The cheap shot hurt. As James dropped to his right knee, he had enough focus to sweep Tariq's knees with his left leg, and Tariq fell onto his back with an audible escape of air. After clearing Tariq's feet, James's leg slammed down on his chest. This knocked the rest of the air out of him. James slid over and put his forearm on Tariq's throat.

"You have a lot to learn. If I want to injure someone, or truly incapacitate them, I do it. I hadn't thought the Russian would recover as fast as he did, but he didn't fully recover, and was easily subdued. Your method has not only proven not to be all you said it was, but it's put you in a much worse position than I'm in. I know you're about to pass out, so I choose to let you up. I suggest you bend your knees and turn to the left. It'll help you regain your breath faster." James spoke calmly, but clearly, even though Tariq's blow had done some damage.

He addressed the entire room as he stood. "When you're in the moment, go with what your logic tells you, and follow your instinct. Keep in mind that intui-

tion is not pure emotion. It's based on your brain putting past experiences together to find a relevant
guidance that is sometimes hard to understand the origin of. We review these operations as a tool." James
paused for a moment to add some dramatic effect to
his words, but also because of the pain coming from
his ribs.

"A way to learn. They aren't rules of engagement.
They are things that have proven successful or," James
gestured at Tariq as he finished, "in some cases not
successful. It is why that sign is there."

He pointed to the sign hanging over the door that
read "*The Life We Lead.*"

"Choices, consequences, learning and utilizing. It's
different for each of us, just like the meaning of that
sign." He felt short of breath, and when he tried to take
a deep breath, he found the pain increased signifi-
cantly.

"Daen, please walk them through the remaining
parts. I'm going to have a seat in a lounge if you need
me," said James.

As he walked out of the room, he could hear Tariq
beginning to gain full control of his breathing again.
Tom, the group's director, walked out behind James
and followed him to the lounge.

"That was a hard hit you just took. Anything
broke?" asked Tom.

"No, but it feels like the punch penetrated deep with
a shockwave," groaned James, lying down as softly as
he could on the couch.

"Anything I can get you?" Tom pulled up a seat
next to him.

"New organs would be nice, but short of that, not
much can be done. I'll make sure I don't bruise irregu-

larly or urinate blood, and I might try a cold bath in Epsom salt," James muttered.

Tom was an experienced director. He had been one of the old school style trainees before the reformation that had taken place four years earlier. He was in his early thirties, with black hair and brown eyes. He looked healthy, and often spoke in a manner that showed concern for the well being of others.

"I talked with Andy about the write-up," Tom said, referring to the regional leader of the group. "He asked what resources you need for next steps."

Though the group was made up of members, not employees, it did have a loosely based hierarchy structure. This structure was essential to allowing them to operate in the shadows the way they did. Tom guided the day-to-day business, while Andy more or less controlled the mutual funds. Andy and Tom had an influence on individual group members, but they weren't directly over them. In fact, only a few people were technically employees of the group, such as Andy, Tom, and the administrative assistant, Korey.

"I've already made contact. I need to get to Aberdeen this summer, and work on a cover. I was going to reach out to Melissa and see what contacts she has to get me into a full-time position in marketing related to oil and gas, so support there would be great," James said through gritted teeth. The pressure and pain were starting to build at his side.

"What happened to the medical field?" Tom asked.

"Too long-term for the travel needed to do this. Can you help with all that?" James asked in return.

"Yes," Tom replied.

"Good. Thanks. Now I need to convince my roommates to do some boxing. This is going to hurt, but I need to have a cover story, so they don't ask about me walking like I'm half dead. They won't refuse some friendly fighting," said James.

James winced as he rolled to the floor. He had thought getting up from the floor would be easier than the couch. He was wrong.

"Tom," he said, but Tom was already there, lifting him.

"You sure you're okay? Do you want a painkiller?" asked Tom.

"Can't. Need to make sure there's no internal bleeding. Just need to chill and sleep. I'm going back to campus and bed. Please tell Daen thanks for finishing the briefing. Good night, Tom."

"James, call me when you get back. Just to make sure you don't pass out and all."

James gave him a thumbs up and shuffled out and said, "Okay."

# •Chapter Eight•

Once on campus, he called Tom, and then shut off his cell phone, which would automatically forward all calls to their house phone on campus. Getting back to his room went smoother than he could've hoped. He wanted to grab an ice pack, but he was happy just to make it back to his room without being stopped. He was swinging his legs into bed when Edgar came in.

"You had a call from Tammy. She asked if you'd like to meet and go over physical chemistry tomorrow." Edgar sat down on Mark's bed.

"Okay, thanks. I'll see her in the morning. I'm beat and calling it a night."

Edgar ignored the obvious hint that James didn't want to talk. "Tammy huh? 'Physical' chemistry, huh? Gettin' a little one-on-one time?" Edgar teased.

"Don't be all jealous just because even your hand rejects you," James coolly replied. He wanted Edgar to leave.

"Whatever," Edgar said, his classic line when he had no better response. He got up to leave, which was also predictable. He was through the door, and almost had it shut when he popped his head back in. "Can I see what you did on the take-home portion of the accounting final?"

"I turned that in yesterday." James tried to get comfortable without showing he was hurt.

"What? Why?" Edgar asked indignantly. "It's not due 'til tomorrow."

"I told you Sunday I was turning it in early for the bonus. You were like, 'Oh yeah, me, too.' You went upstairs, and I figured you did it," James replied.

"You were serious? Shit!" Edgar left, shutting the door, and James shook his head.

It took him a while to get comfortable enough to go to sleep, and he was greatly annoyed when, at 3 a.m., he woke up because he needed to go to the bathroom. His first movements to get out of bed made him gasp in pain. He slowed down and figured out how to raise himself using the wall, and steel beams that made the footing of the bed. He then was able to lift himself into a vertical position as gently as possible. This took a minute. When you need to go to the bathroom, that's a long time.

Having used the toilet successfully without blood coming out, he checked his side in the mirror. *Marvelous,* he thought. The bruises were already a lovely blue, and yellow, and black mix, and he knew it was just getting started.

He made his way to the kitchen and got two zip bags and ice to create a double sealed ice pack. He was getting ready to turn off the light, when he noticed a note by the phone.

*"James, the Fishermen called at 11:31 p.m. for you. E"*

Flicking the overhead light off in the kitchen, James made his way back upstairs to Edgar and Dylan's room. He walked in, and was about to bend over to wake up Edgar when he stopped. *Too awkward,* he thought. It could wait until the morning. James retreated to his own bed.

The unwritten rule in the house was minimal talking in the morning until 10 a.m., with the emphasis on minimal. Pointing and grunts worked just fine in most cases.

Edgar was the last one to slosh into the kitchen the next morning. While he grabbed a toaster pastry, James asked about the message, which got everyone's unwanted and semi-disgruntled attention.

"Hey, what else did the caller say last night?" James asked.

"I told you what she said," barked Edgar.

"Not Tammy, ass, that." James pointed to the note.

"Oh, yeah, what the hell is going on? This douche made a point of saying the time like three times, and made sure I spelled 'fishermen,' and not 'fisherman.' He wouldn't give me anything else. It was messed up. I didn't want to come get you when he first called, but after he hung up, I almost did." Edgar's voice was semi-raising in volume. "You in trouble or something? This is some shit like out of a bad spy movie."

This discussion caused a rumble as all eyes turned to James.

"Everything's fine. It's a group that fishes, and apparently, they wanted to be clear who was calling. You know, being plural for a group, and not just someone calling themselves a fisherman, and sounding like a tool." James knew his reply sounded weak.

None of the guys were convinced, but Edgar spoke up. "Two things wrong with that. One, you don't fish, and two, why would he call at 11:30, I mean 11:31, at night? And why insist on saying the time three times?"

*Because he's a dip shit recruit that didn't know what he was doing*, thought James.

Out loud, James replied, "I'm going with my dad and uncle out West to where this fishing group is, so there's a time difference. As far as being so specific, I can only guess."

It still sounded weak, so James began building a more elaborate version in his head. His friends weren't complete morons, but they knew nothing about the group, or most of what James did, or what skills he had for that matter.

"If you're in trouble, man, say so," came John's hoarse voice.

"We got your back bro," said Dylan, as Mark nodded over his cereal.

James deliberately took a deep breath, and the others knew what was coming. He was about to unleash a string of logic on them that would explain the story he'd just built in his head. Though, in reality, James was invoking a Pavlov type reaction from them. He had done things like this so often that his friends just accepted what he said as he was always right. Most of the time they didn't really listen to all he was saying.

"The fishing group probably isn't a full-time professional organization. The person who called did it after normal work hours when he had the chance. I suspect he realized after you answered what time it was on the East Coast, but he had you on the phone, so he wanted to give you the message. It would also stand to reason that the caller is rather anal retentive and introverted. He referred to the fishing group in the plural to make sure he got your attention. The fishing group is evidently important to him. Since most individuals who fish have limited friends and move in small groups, thus the introvert, they place a rather high value on what social time they have with others. The repeating of the time was more than likely his way of acknowledging the lateness, but also his anal retentiveness coming out to make sure you took a message, as was the spelling of 'fishermen.' I would venture to say he started off with 'May I speak with James?' and not 'Hi, is James there?'"

Edgar nodded. The rest of the room stared for a second before moving to get out the door.

"If I were in trouble, I would come to you guys, no doubt." James said this to give finality to the conversation. He, of course, knew what the message really was about. Something had come up with the police, and the group was letting him know he needed to be in touch.

"Still weird, man, but whatever." Edgar grabbed his food out of the toaster and set off to class.

The day was horrible. The lecture room seats didn't help James's side, nor did taking notes to get ready for final exams. His injury was killing him, but he knew nothing was broken, and he wasn't hemorrhaging. He also wasn't looking forward to that night and getting hit. The anticipation of more pain made everything worse. Anticipation always makes things worse.

In his second class of the day, James found Tammy. She had a soft, youthful face with pale green eyes. She was very quiet and didn't mix with a lot of people, but she was very smart. She also was an extraordinarily caring person, and her boyfriend took advantage of her big heart sometimes.

"Hi Tammy," James said, taking the seat to her right.

"Hey," she returned.

"Sorry, I didn't call you back last night. I was beat by the time I got the message, but if you'd still like to study for P-Chem together, that's cool," said James.

Tammy said, "Yeah, sure. I won't be able to stay too late. I have to see..."

"See Brody, yeah." James gave her a weak smile. *She can do so much better than him, dumb rock that he is,* James thought.

"He wants to go see a movie tonight," Tammy said, opening her bag.

"A movie? Tonight? Doesn't he know finals are starting?" questioned James.

"Yeah, but he doesn't usually like to go out too much, and he wants to go see this movie. He's been having a real tough time at work and is stressed," she said.

"Tammy, you work thirty hours a week, have a great GPA in a science major, and helping with your sick grandma. He works forty hours a week running a forklift, and that's it." James had other things he wanted to say but refrained.

"I know, but he really wants to see it," she said softly.

James knew it was a pointless argument, so he dropped it. He liked Tammy and wasn't happy to see Brody manipulate her like this.

"Library at 3 o'clock?" James asked.

"Yep, lower floor as usual," Tammy grinned. It was their normal spot.

"How was the date?" John asked, as James walked into the living room later that evening.

"Date?" James inquired.

"Yeah, the date Edgar said you had, for some physical stuff," Dylan added with a wink.

Everyone except James laughed, as they typically made fun of him for things like this. Ignoring the question, James had retrieved a single set of boxing gloves out of a closet. Now was as good a time as ever.

He tossed the left one to Edgar and put on the right one. Edgar's eyes began shining like Christmas lights, and the others immediately cleared a space in the middle of the living room, as if this was a scheduled main event. It was rare that they could get James to participate in this type of foolery.

The rules were simple. You could only use the gloved hand to hit with, and nothing below the belt. Shots to the head were to be controlled so that no one got a broken nose or a tooth knocked out.

As they squared up, Dylan stepped in like he was a referee/commentator, and turned his hat backwards. He hammed it up, pretending to grab a microphone from above his head so he could speak into it.

"In this corner, wearing the worn jeans and ugly ass shirt, we have the leanest wonder of the world, James!" Dylan then pointed at Edgar. "Annnnnnnnd in this corner, we have the monster of monsters, the champ of chimps, Edgar!"

Dylan pretended to drop the microphone, and brought his hand down in a swinging motion and screamed, "Fight!"

James immediately switched to a southpaw stance so that his right hand was in front. He threw a few jabs that Edgar easily dodged before he hit James's left shoulder. This wasn't what James wanted. He needed his side to be the main target. He knew Edgar could fight a bit, so he'd just have to bait him. James and Edgar exchanged a few more jabs as the guys screamed at them. James decided to do some flashy worthless crap, and jumped to switch his feet back and forth, while throwing a jab. It worked.

"Ohhh, and the judges have to give the point to Edgar as his Leanest takes a blow to the ribs," Dylan's voice called out.

A few more of those might sell it. James's eyes watered, but he was still on his feet. It had been a solid punch but nothing too hard. They were just playing after all.

"How is James going to answer that? Apparently, with a pop right to the forehead of the Monster. That will make it interesting folks," Dylan continued.

Mark, and a friend who lived off campus, Patrick, came in and joined the others.

They continued to move around each other, and then Edgar slightly tripped on the carpet.

"Looks like James has the Monster so scared he can't stay on his feet!" said Dylan.

"Kiss my ass, Dylan!" Edgar shouted, quickly looking away, giving James a chance to land a punch to his chest.

James deliberately stuck the punch out there a second too long, and Edgar cooperated with a shot to the ribs. This one was true, and James went down on his knees.

"Oh, the Monster says, 'I ain't going out like no bitch' and catches those ribs like he's trying to break crab legs," rang out Dylan's commentary over the roar of laughter from the others.

James flipped his friends off as he stood up. His side was screaming. It was affecting how he could move, so he stood still and rotated. Edgar was a big guy and didn't like to move too much, so James baited him with a few well-placed jabs before stepping with his left foot. This placed his right hand behind him,

and in the power position, and Edgar moved accordingly.

They moved as one, Edgar to his left and James recovered with his own foot motion to minimize the
distance Edgar would have on the upper cut he was
about to throw. James's maneuver worked, and the
blow hurt like hell. He simply dropped and lay there.

"One, two, three..." came the count from Dylan.

Very quickly, James added, "Five, ten. I'm done.
The last one caught me." The room was laughing as
James laid there, his insides in agony.

Edgar came over and pulled him up, which added to
James's pain. They did a one arm hug to show no hard
feelings.

"I'm making a pizza," James said as an excuse to
leave the room.

"Me," came five voices, meaning they wanted pizza
too.

"I'm ordering two pizzas then," James said.

"In," came the five voices. Since James was ordering, and all wanted in, that meant he didn't have to
pay, and the excuse still got him out of the room.

He ordered a plain and a pepperoni before slipping
into the half bathroom downstairs. He was hurting, but
he now had his cover for the injury and could be less
careful about it, but still had to be semi-careful in
showing how bad it was. It would take at least two
weeks to recover from this injury. That was going to
make moving out a challenge.

*Knock, knock.*

"Out in a minute," James said, leaning against the
wall, his butt on the toilet lid.

"You all right?" It was Patrick.

"I'll be okay, thanks," James said, waiting for Patrick to walk off.

Patrick was a short, hairy guy, who looked like the quintessential Italian. When he opened his mouth, you expected him to start shouting and using slang while waving his hands around, but that wasn't his style. He had a pleasant way about him, and often just blended into the background.

Exiting the bathroom, James found Patrick scooping ice into a bag. "That hit looked hard, thought you'd want some ice," he explained.

"Cool, thanks." James took the ice, and the two guys sat at the kitchen table.

"Wouldja want to go over some physics with me before the food comes?" Patrick asked.

"Yeah, cool. Let me grab my, oh, you brought my bag in too. Nice!" said James grateful he didn't have to get up.

They worked until the food came, listening to the guys fighting in the next room. After the pizza, they returned to physics, and Mark joined them. About an hour later, Patrick's mother called. He excused himself and came back a few minutes later.

"Gotta run," he said, picking up his things without looking at them.

"Everything cool?" asked Mark.

"Mmm," lied Patrick. He threw his bag over his shoulder and walked out.

Mark and James exchanged a look. James gingerly got up, and followed Patrick out the door.

"Hey, you okay?" James asked.

"Yeah," came Patrick's soft answer. "Look, man, I know you can see whatever. It's just family stuff. I'm okay."

"Cool, no prob," James said, and they parted.

James knew that Patrick's uncle, also named Patrick, was a piece of work who had ties to the mafia. James didn't let Patrick know this of course, because Patrick went to great lengths to hide it. Besides, his friend Patrick wasn't directly involved, although he could certainly be a potential source for connections with the drug operation later on.

"Ugh." As James turned to go back in, his side gave him a shot of pain to remind him it was still there.

Later that night, James made a secure call to the group from the science building to see what was up. It turned out to be something he'd already taken care of. The police didn't directly know about the group, but the group often fed them information. It was often obvious what they needed, but it helped to have two police officers in the group. The end goal was to have the police indebted to the group, so that they could leverage the relationship when needed.

James also checked on the funding he needed for Aberdeen and made a few connections to set up a job. On top of that, he learned Melissa had worked her magic, and created some other covers for him. Tariq, it turned out, had made the fishermen call. James informed Tom how it had gone, and Tom said he'd address it.

# •Chapter Nine•

Final exams came and went, as did graduation. The guys made fun of James's side for being injured for the remainder of the semester, and laughed as he moved out. They watched him struggle with loading the truck, though they helped him get the stuff down the stairs.

"One degree done, a lifetime to go," he said to himself, as he pulled away to start the summer.

During the drive to his parents' home in Duncansville, James got a call from Tyler, who was also in the group.

"Hey, James, how's it going, buddy?" Tyler said.

"Well, well, well, if it isn't Tyler White. I'm doing great, how are you, man?" James asked.

"Just getting ready for summer. Did all right in classes. Tom said I should give you a buzz about a job connection," Tyler said.

"Yeah, need something related to oil and gas, particularly in marketing, if possible, to allow for easier travel. Trying to find someone who's a professional, with a science background, who also does adjunct teaching in marketing. Figure it will be an easier path than getting an MBA."

James gave a dirty look to the idiot who'd just passed him doing 90 mph. He hoped a cop would pull him over.

"My Uncle does oil and gas. He's an adjunct professor at Pitt, and has degrees in biology, and an MBA in marketing," said Tyler, chuckling.

"No way! He hiring?" James asked excitedly.

"No idea, but he's always looking for talent. Probably can get you an internship at least to start," Tyler said.

James paused and thought a moment. "Whatever you think is best."

"Okay, cool. I'll call the house tonight," Tyler replied.

"I owe you one, man," said James.

"You're on crack. I still owe you like ten for all the stuff you've done for me. Hell, five just for the Epazato thing. Didn't think I was making it out of that one alive."

In an amused tone, James said, "You got yourself out of that. Anyhow, thanks. Let me know what you find out."

"Will do. Later," Tyler said, getting off the phone.

James smiled. This was a great start to the summer. He slowed down slightly when he saw flashing red and blue lights,, and laughed out loud. His wish was coming true. The driver who'd been speeding was getting pulled over. "Ah, whatta day," he said out loud before turning up the radio.

That night, Tyler called James back to tell him his uncle had left for Russia that morning, and would be back in two weeks. His aunt Kathy had described in detail a million things going on at the house, and Tyler hadn't been able to get a word in.

"She was going on and on about the kitchen, and how she wants a television in there. Then she said as soon as Uncle Todd gets home, she's taking him shopping because, God forbid, she buy an electronic for the house without him. Well, that got me thinking. What if you happened to be the salesperson who sold them the TV? I mean, what better way to demonstrate sales and marketing? Plus, you can bring the conversation around to backgrounds and all that. It allows my uncle to think it's his idea."

"That's phenomenal. Now I just need to figure out what store they shop at, and..." James started.

"Easy, I'll send you the address in an e-mail. She's making him go to dinner, and he loves this place on McKnight Road in Pittsburgh in a plaza with an electronics store. She'll make him go shopping before dinner, and he'll want to be close to the restaurant." Tyler laughed, and then gave James a description of his aunt and uncle.

"Excellent. Tyler, you're the best. Thanks, man," said James.

The setup was easy, since it turned out the electronics store was a major chain with a lot of turnover. Melissa, who was a genius with computers and identifications, arranged for James to be a transfer from a different fake store. They used moving for graduate school as the reason for the transfer paperwork. It was a valid reason that wouldn't be challenged, even though James had no plans to attend graduate school.

James set his first day at the store to be the one before Tyler's uncle arrived home. Everything went smoothly, and he was able to get a feel for some of his coworkers as well as the store. Thankfully, he had the early shift that first day, and was working the later shift the next day, which made his commute of 2.5 hours each way doable.

The following day was rather slow at the store. James was working with two of the most annoying people he could think of, both of whom were aggressive salesmen. As the day wore on, he was starting to think that he'd have a problem even getting to Tyler's uncle, assuming he showed up, but he was wrong.

Around 7 p.m., a couple walked in who exactly matched Tyler's description. Todd looked extremely grumpy and tired. The other two salespeople took one glance at him and disappeared. James let the couple walk around for a minute or two. From what Tyler told him, he knew enough to wait for some signal to approach, so that he'd be welcomed instead of being seen as being intrusive.

The couple stopped in the area with smaller televisions to have a discussion. Todd suddenly moved away toward the new, larger screen sets and pointed at one. Kathy shook her head, and dragged him back to the smaller screens. Todd looked around and made eye contact with James, and then nodded, indicating he wanted help.

"Hi, I'm James. How can I help you?" he asked.

Kathy spoke. "We need a television for our kitchen. I like this one, but he likes that one. Can you tell us the difference, besides price?"

"Absolutely, but can I ask a few questions that might help in a proper selection?" James asked.

"Like what? This isn't exactly rocket science," Todd shot back.

James smiled and began to ask questions about how often the set would be used, how much natural light was in the kitchen, what noise level they normally had, where they expected to position it, what the kitchen layout was like, what their appliances looked like, and how many people would be using it. After hearing their answers, James drew a mini-layout.

At that, Kathy slapped Todd on the arm and said, "See, there's more to it than just picking up a TV."

Todd rolled his eyes and asked James, "What do you recommend?"

"Well, I think you have two options. The first is to go with this flat-screen thirteen inch. It should do most of what you're looking for and be okay," James said.

"And the second?" Todd asked, his eyebrows raised in a skeptical look.

"If I may, given what you described with viewing, sound levels, and how things are situated, you may want to consider looking at a new high-definition set, with a surround system."

Kathy began to laugh, and Todd's eyebrows went higher, this time in shock.

"I know it's way higher in price, but hear me out," James began. He walked them through his reasoning, from position and color to the flow of the rooms. This wasn't as big of a stretch as it might have seemed to get them to listen. Todd's initial draw to the high-end sets had given him the opening that he needed.

Twenty minutes later, Kathy was shaking her head. "We came here to buy a TV for $150 dollars, and we're walking out spending $5,000. You talk about me and shopping? Geez."

Todd ignored his wife. "You asked some good questions to make sure we got what we needed, and not just what we thought we wanted."

"Needed? Really?" Kathy said sarcastically, and James laughed.

Todd said, "Quiet woman," which apparently just made her mad, and she walked away. The man continued, "You in school?"

James explained that he'd just finished. He described his background and hopes for a marketing job. After this small discussion, Todd smiled.

"I'm part owner and COO of a small chemical company. How do you feel about interning as a marketing person for me?" Todd asked.

"Wow, really? That's a great offer, but I'm not sure I can afford to leave here and..."

"Your pay will be $25 per hour, and you can work as many or as few hours as you like. There will be some travel involved. Do you have a passport?" Todd asked.

James paused deliberately, but also with a bit of shock, as he hadn't expected the wage to be that high. "Yeah, when can I start?"

"Give me a call Monday, and we can sort it out then. Want to make sure all this stuff you sold me is quality." He winked at James.

James thanked him several times, and proceeded to wrap up the transaction.

Later, he called Tyler to relay the story, to which Tyler replied, "He must have liked you a lot. He's a nice person, and if you do well, he'll support you."

"I think this makes us even, Ty," James said.

Tyler just laughed.

# •Chapter Ten•

That night James reflected back about the Epazato case that he and Tyler had worked a year ago. It was the first mission Tyler had been the primary investigator on, and James had been asked to join after it was rather well developed.

"Hi guys, am I interrupting?" asked Tyler walking into the room James and Andy were in, followed by Tom.

"Nope, we were just finishing up Ty, especially if you're bringing us some drinks," said Andy smiling.

The two men had just finished reviewing James's latest mission. It had ended up with a deposit of over $1.5 million dollars going to the group's account, with some of the funds going to private accounts James held.

Tyler smirked, "I wouldn't drink this stuff, unless you wanted to trip out for a few hours." He set two green bottles on the table, with the label away from James and Andy.

"Absinthe?" questioned James.

"Of all people, how the hell do you know that?" asked Andy.

Everyone's eyes were on James with surprise, because it was well known he didn't drink.

"Oh come off it. That was so simple even you could piece it together Andy. A green alcohol drink that has psychedelic properties? What else could it be? It's a rather known thing, and despite everyone's opinion, I'm not that much of a sociopath not to know that stuff," said James, with a little indignation in his voice.

The others just burst out laughing. James gave them a fake squinty smile and flipped them off.

"Well, funny that you say that James," said Tyler. "That is actually a myth for real Absinthe. You're much more likely to die of alcohol poisoning before you ever would get a hallucination. The real stuff is about 72% alcohol. It's meant to be blended down before you drink it."

"I thought it was made from a green worm or something. Isn't that why you're supposed to see a green fairy when you drink it because it is the green worm hatching?" asked Andy.

Tyler sat down, as did Tom.

"I haven't heard that before about the green worm and the fairy. I mean I've heard of the green fairy part, but no. It's made from anise, fennel, and wormwood. The green color is just chlorophyll added back in after the distillation. It originates from France, and according to legend in 1905, a farmer there killed his family after drinking Absinthe. He said he was hallucinating from the drink. Well, that spawned others to start saying it, and it got banned from a ton of places, including the US. It does have thujone in it, but so do a lot of things we eat every day. Like I said, you'd die of alcohol poisoning before you'd get enough thujone in your system to hallucinate. Apparently, it is a..." Tyler checked his notes before continuing, "GABA receptor inhibitor in the brain."

Everyone looked at James, who sat there stone faced. He knew why they were looking at him, and he was fighting the urge to explain what Tyler had just said.

"We are waiting here human encyclopedia. Explain away," said Andy. Tom frowned slightly at the comment, but Tyler laughed.

James sighed before saying, "If it is a GABA inhibitor is acts on cannabinoid receptors just like THC from marijuana. It can cause the common characteristics of hunger ,and a lethargic feeling, but as Tyler said, it isn't enough to cause a real hallucination like PCP would. So if we know that, why has it been banned? Bacardi 151 has a 75.5% alcohol content, and you can get that."

"Since when do lawmakers make decisions based on facts or real data? They play to the public, not to reason. Hell, it is like asking why marijuana is still banned when we know it has extremely useful properties in medicine. Just political garbage," said Tyler.

"Wait, what is GABA?" asked Tom.

"It stands for Gamma-aminobutyric acid, I believe," said James, and he left it at that. James suspected Tom only asked to feel involved in the conversation.

Tom merely replied, "Oh," before dropping the topic.

"Great, what does this have to do with us?" asked Andy, who was ready to leave.

Tom frowned at him again and looked like he was going to say something, but didn't.

"Well, I was hoping James could help me out. Tom said he thought he'd just finished a project," said Tyler with anticipation written all over his face.

"Perfect. He did, and that also means I'm not needed for the rest of this discussion. Later guys. Oh, Tom, can I talk with you quickly in the hall?" Andy asked as he left the room.

"What do you need help with Tyler? I was planning on taking a few weeks off with summer just starting. Making excuses to get away is a little more challenging right now, as my parents expect me to be around when not in school," stated James.

Tyler handed James the two bottles. "What is different about these?"

James held the bottles and looked at them. From the back, he didn't notice anything remarkable about the clear glass. He held them to the light and still couldn't see a difference. He checked the bottoms and the sealed tops, which both appeared identical. He finally checked the labels. James waited to check these last, as he suspected that that would be the most likely place to see a difference. He found one bottle to have a small green goose on the label and the other didn't.

"The only real difference is the green goose on the one label," he said, putting down the bottles as Tom walked back in.

"That spawn any thoughts in your head?" asked Tyler, with a hopeful expression.

James blinked. "My immediate thoughts, well, I would think that the one with the goose might come from Canada. They don't have an official bird, but the goose is often mistaken as being it. The stamp being green could just be a play on the liquid color, but maybe it signifies a higher alcohol content. Then again, it could represent the green fairy meaning it does have true psychedelic properties."

Tyler and Tom smiled at each other.

"The psychedelic properties right?" asked James. They nodded as he asked, "The lab upstairs confirm which one?"

"LSD," said Tom.

"Your idea on the goose might help explain where it is coming from. I got this one," Tyler held up the one without the marking, "from someone in Toledo, Ohio." He set the bottle down and pointed at the other one. "This one I got in Scranton, Pennsylvania."

"That is a considerable difference in distance, but they're both illegal. This is more of an ATF issue, isn't it? Why are we looking at this?" James asked.

"The stuff from Toledo is on their radar, but apparently there isn't enough volume flowing in that they're concerned. That bottle's $350.00. The one from Scranton was $900.00, and even harder to find. We are looking at it because the ATF, and the DEA, aren't treating it seriously. There has been an increasing rate of people tripping out in the last six months, and that is when the green goose material came on the scene," said Tyler.

"I think if we shut this down quickly it'll stop any chance of it to take hold, and cause serious issues with a lotta people. The incidents seem to be in the states near the Great Lakes mostly, so your idea of it coming from Canada makes sense. We originally though it was being imported via New Jersey," Tom said.

"Is West Virginia the only state listed that isn't touching the Great Lakes?" James asked.

"Yes, how'd you know that?" asked Tom.

"But the green goose bottles aren't showing up past say Chicago, or near the western side of Lake Superior are they?" asked James with his eyes closed.

"Right again, but what does that mean?" asked Tyler.

"They are using the interstates to transport this material. We need a road map, and I can show you what I mean," said James.

Tom retrieved a map, and James explained. "You said you got the one bottle from Toledo right? What if they are bringing it over the bridge from Canada, through Detroit? From there they can use Interstate 94 to get it to Chicago. They can cut down to Indianapolis using Interstate 69. They can also use Interstate 75 to get into Cincinnati. Now that I think about it, I bet if you made a plot of where the incidents of green goose is used, it'll be East of Columbus, Ohio."

They looked at him with vacant expressions, as he went on, "They are using Erie to bring in the green goose material. It has Interstate 90, 86, and 79 right there. Plus it picks up Interstate 80 quickly. If they are getting the material into Scranton, I assumed they could go about the same distance using Interstate 79 into West Virginia. We need that plot, and then to overlay it with this road map. This is how they did it during prohibition when illegal booze was brought in from Canada."

The plot did show the incidents just as James predicted. It also showed almost no incidents of use of either product near Detroit or Erie, Pennsylvania. This looked suspiciously like the smugglers were making a point of not selling in those cities, so that the ATF and DEA wouldn't have a reason to be in those areas.

Tyler asked James to help him verify and maybe gather enough evidence to get the ATF or DEA interested. James agreed more out of curiosity to see if he was right, than an actual desire to participate. Stake-outs are typically extremely tedious activities.

Tyler had figured out the number of incidents tended to spike around the full moon, which would make for a perfect time to unload shipments in the dark. The next full moon was three weeks from then, and fell on the weekend. That would make it easier for James to participate, as he could make sure he wasn't scheduled for work, and tell his family he was going camping for the weekend.

They decided to try Lampra Marina. It had a public dock, was near a campground, and also had railroad loading docks. This was ideal for loading and unload-ing ships, without actually being noticed with all the other traffic.

Keeping watch on Friday afternoon and night, they hadn't seen anything out of the ordinary. There were a fair amount of people coming and going from the nearby campground and marina. There were some tour boats that would go along the coast or to Canada, and even a small festival a block away.

Saturday had started out as uneventful as Friday had been, until Tyler came back to where James was watching the far side of the marina.

"You know that Epazato's charter tour boat we saw yesterday? It just left to head to Canada, with about ten passengers on board," said Tyler.

"And?" questioned James.

"Well, they dock in the US and supposedly had their last run about an hour ago when they got back," said Tyler.

"Now that is indeed odd my friend. Let's go see if we can record some of their activities when they get back," James said, getting to his feet.

It took them a while, with so many people coming and going, but they were able to get two remote cameras placed in strategic points.

They were just there to gather information, not to actively engage the smuggling operation. It was always a top priority for the members to stay in the shadows.

Just as the sun set, the boat returned. It had ten passengers onboard, presumably from the early trip that were returning for the night. After the passengers had cleared the dock, one of the crew hit the main power switch on the shore side of the dock that controlled the dock overhead lights.

Three white cargo vans pulled up and parked near the cameras Tyler and James had installed. The drivers got out and made their way down the dock as the lights came back on. Tyler and James watched as the four men walked down to the boat. The three drivers were handed crates and walked back to the vans. During the drivers' third trip, other people walked down the dock to get to other boats. The three men said "Hello" and went about their business.

"I'm going to go down and see if I can't get the boat's registration number by pretending to walk to the boat on the opposite side of the dock," said Tyler.

"Why not wait 'til they are done unloading the boat and the activity calms down, or just get it tomorrow?" asked James.

"Maybe I can sneak-a-peek at where their smuggling compartments are as I walk past," Tyler replied standing up.

James wasn't particularly keen on this idea. "Dude, it feels like an unneeded risk to me. We have enough information as it is to hand over to get these guys busted."

"It'll be fine. I will be pretending to be taking a leak off the end of the dock, so it won't look as odd when I walk back. Those guys carrying the crates didn't bat an eye as those other people walked past them," said Tyler, now on his feet, just as the driver's started their fourth round of retrieving crates.

"Up to you, but it sounds like a unnecessary risk to me," said James. "Hey, leave the camera. You walk down with that, and they may say more than 'Hello' to you."

Tyler gave James a big grin and said, "You sound like Tom," before he walked away.

Just as Tyler managed to start down the dock, the three drivers were handed crates, and beginning their return trip to their vans. The drivers loaded up the crates, and climbed into their vehicles to leave just as Tyler reached the boat. He slowed his walking pace down and paused, staring for a moment at the back deck area of the boat.

"Don't stop and look you ass," James said to himself.

Suddenly, two men appeared at the stern end of the boat. James couldn't hear what was going on, but was looking through the high power lens of the camera. From what he could see, it didn't look promising, as the three men seemed to be having an argument. Then, a gun was pointing at Tyler, and he boarded the ship.

"Son of a bitch," said James. He grabbed a 9mm pistol from the bag, clipped it to the back of his belt, and swiftly made his way down to the dock as silently as he could. His eyes were looking for anything he could use to shoot through to potentially muffle the sound of gunfire. He hadn't brought a suppressor, but that didn't matter as they don't silence gunfire, but merely drop the decibels down to a safer level without having to use ear protection.

Reaching the shore end of the dock, he stopped at the pay phone. He dialed 9-1-1 and left it off the hook. They'd have ten minutes maybe before a patrol car would get there. James hoped it would be enough to extract Tyler and disappear.

James reached the boat and saw that the windows were all covered. A few remaining boats were making their way in just as it was starting to get completely dark out, and gave James a little cover in terms of sound, and movement, when climbing onto the boat.

The two men who had taken Tyler onboard, were arguing what to do with him as James snuck onto the back deck of the cabin cruiser. James made his way along the starboard side of the cruiser to get to the bow.

He was hoping that this boat had deck ports like his grandfather's did. The ports on his boat opened to a sitting area that turned into sleeping quarters as well. Once inside, he could sneak up behind the men to gain the advantage and rescue Tyler.

He found the ports, and they had doors on them that wouldn't open. They were locked from the inside. James moved quickly and pressed his ear to the glass of the cabin to see if he could hear what was being said.

He didn't catch everything they said, but it sounded like they didn't believe Tyler had a reason to be there, and that he wasn't just checking out their boat by coincidence. Their voices were getting more aggressive and louder. James had to do something quickly.

James could hear what sounded like a few more boats approaching, and decided to use them as cover as he had done with the others. He was going to try to climb to the captain's deck, and hope there was a descending ladder into the main cabin from there. The boats were getting louder just as he managed to get to the top. Unfortunately for James, the only ladder was the one that led to the back deck.

James decided to see if he could lure them out. He undid two butterfly bolts that held a scanner and radio in place. He was going to throw the lighter scanner onto the deck, and hope that the sound would be enough to get one of them to come out to investigate. He could then hit that person with the radio on the head, and climb down and fight if he had to. Hopefully, Tyler wasn't tied down and could then attack the guy inside.

Just as James was about to throw the scanner, the sound he thought was multiple boats coming in, stopped. It had been a single boat coming in, and was coming in way too fast. It was causing a wake. The wake hit the cruiser just as James threw the scanner and he lost his balance. The scanner hit the back deck with a loud smashing sound, just as James slammed into the water in a spectacular belly flop.

With James still submerged, the next wave caused by the incoming boat pushed him under the hull of the cruiser. As James started to move, his feet felt like they were in a cargo net. He thought, *You can only survive three minutes without oxygen.*

This would mark the seventh time he experienced drowning in his life. He wasn't a strong swimmer, and did get a panic attack when in water that he didn't know the depth of. He did know that it couldn't be very deep at the docks, but he was also disoriented. He couldn't see in the dark water, and couldn't see lights anywhere.

He started to get a little frantic, still trying to free his legs as the fourth wake wave hit him. This time he hit the right backside of his head on the hull. His brain went into overdrive as he thought, *I hit the hull on the right back, waves pushing me from the left. That means I'm facing down, feet to the stern and head to the bow. I need to go left and arch my back into a 'U' to find air.*

He tried to kick, but it didn't help. He was afraid to reach back with his hands in case he lost orientation. He was starting to get very dizzy and panic even more. In a last-ditch effort, he started swimming as hard and as fast as he could with his arms to the left, so he wasn't under the boat. He cupped his hands, pulling the water behind him. The combination of panic, frantic muscle use and lack of new oxygen, inhibited James from realizing that, with his legs tangled in pond-weeds, he was actually diving. That is until he touched the bottom.

*If that is the bottom, then I need to stand up!* he thought. He pulled his torso to his knees, and started flapping his arms like a bird. He felt his feet touch bottom, and then he jumped up. His head broke the surface a moment later, his arms still flailing around. He was trying to get some air. His eyes saw something sticking out of the window on the port side of the cruiser.

His feet were still tangled, and he went back under for a moment. He repeated pushing off the bottom, though he blew out all the air he could while under water. As he reemerged, he was able to get a better gulp of air. The second kick off the bottom had freed his legs too. He swam to the back of the cruiser and climbed out, just at Tyler emerged.

"We need to go," said Tyler.

People were peering through their own boat windows or coming onto the dock. James and Tyler, raced along the dock, as people wondered what was happening.

"Grab the bag, and bring it back to the end of the dock," James said trying to capture his breath as they ran.

As Tyler retrieved the bag, James got the two video cameras they had set up. When Tyler arrived back, James took a pair of gloves out of the bag and put them on. He removed the tapes from the cameras, and gave them a fast wipe before setting them on top of the pay phone. James hung up the phone, and dialed 9-1-1 again just to make sure the police would come, and wiped off the receiver. He wrote a fast note and placed it under the tapes before he and Tyler left.

"What about wiping down the boat?" asked Tyler as they ran.

"It's a tourist boat, it'll have all sorts of finger prints that they'll never be able to trace. As long as you aren't bleeding and didn't touch blood, we'll be fine," said James.

About a minute later, sirens could be heard as they climbed into the rental vehicle that they had. They left the tent, sleeping bags, cooler and such behind. They didn't have time to collect them, and they were easily gathered a few hours later.

Tyler later told him that the two men had decided to kill him, and dump his body in the middle of the lake with weights. Lake Erie is one of the most challenging bodies of water in the world, and there was a good chance he'd have never been found. He went on to say that the guy closest to the back deck went to check on the crash, while the other guy looked out the window to see what had made the splash.

Tyler explained that he smashed the man's head through the glass looking at the water, before the other man had turned and came back in. They then fought for a moment before Tyler was able to get him to the floor, and put him in a sleeper hold.

The police found the tapes they left and were able to get a huge international bust. The guys on the boat became star witnesses when confronted with the evidence Tyler and James had collected. Their testimony led to nine other convictions in the US and Canada, along with shutting down the production of both forms of illegal Absinthe.

This had been the first mission involving smuggling James had been involved in. He ended up leading a few more in the following year that were progressively more challenging. The culmination of which was James being assigned the Spara case.

The Epazato case taught him a great deal, and better prepared him for his future missions. One thing he decided was going forward, he'd always have a microphone set, or at least walkie-talkies with him, so that he and his partner could always stay in contact. He also decided to have more devices that he could use in an escape than just a single pistol.

# •Chapter Eleven•

A mere two weeks after starting his internship, James was on a trip to learn more about the North Sea market. The day had been considerably more tedious than he had anticipated, especially with jet lag thrown in. The customer meeting had gone completely in the wrong direction once his colleague Dennis had opened his mouth about the efficacy of the biocide.

When they weren't able to show field data for the North Sea, the customer had begun asking more detailed questions on field trials for all the products. Apparently, Dennis had failed to inform the customer that they were hoping to get a field trial with them. Now it was a mess.

That wasn't the only mess. James had a meeting that night to address some loose ends on the drug ring connections. He was having a difficult time tracking down any additional information regarding this Asian faction Petior had mentioned. However, now that he was in Aberdeen he was hoping Calum would deliver some much needed insight. For some reason, Calum had insisted on meeting on a Friday night.

As James headed north back toward Aberdeen after the ill-fated customer meeting, he looked around at the rolling landscape. The hills on his left, and glimpses of the shoreline of the North Sea to his right, were very beautiful, even with the gray sky that seemed to be a reflection of the buildings below. In many ways, the landscape reminded James of being back home in Pennsylvania, minus the sea.

He found a pullover area on the carriageway, and decided to get ready for his meeting with Calum now, instead of at the pub. Before the trip, he had dyed his hair a very light brown, almost a dirty blond color. He had taken the time to make sure that all hair, regardless of the location on his body, was reasonably matched. Now, he was putting in color contacts to turn his hazel eyes blue. He also added a small scar that started on the left side of his chin, and crossed underneath to the right. Nothing too big, but certainly visible. He also added a small scar on his right cheek. He debated whether to add a mole to his left ear as well. It was the little details that stood out when trying to get to know someone, but he didn't want to overdo it. He was coming in clean-shaven, which was unusual, as it allowed for further feature identification.

In the end, James added the mole to his outer ear, but used some putty to cover the two moles on his left cheekbone. Finally, he made the bridge of his nose seem wider. He then took pictures of himself in case he needed to duplicate the look later.

Pulling back onto the motorway, he quickly found that traffic was backing up near a major roundabout fifteen kilometers or so from Aberdeen. Stop, creep forward ten to twenty meters, stop. Go a few car lengths, stop. And so it went. About 75 meters from his turn into the intersection, he had to stop again.

*Bang.* He'd been hit from behind. The impact wasn't hard, just enough to jar him a bit.

*Great, just what I need in a rental car in Scotland,* James thought.

James hoped that the guy who had hit him would follow him until he could safely pull over. Traffic began to move, and James pulled forward, quickly memorizing the license plate behind him. However, he had no need to worry, as the other driver followed him through the roundabout, and into the nearest parking lot.

James got out and quickly walked to the back of the car. Thankfully, he saw no damage. The other driver emerged, and it wasn't a guy at all. In fact, it was a very nervous woman, who appeared to be on the brink of tears.

"Are you all right?" James asked, in a gentle voice that he hoped conveyed that he wasn't upset, but was instead concerned about her.

He quickly made his way to the front of her car. She dropped her bag, and James bent to pick it up.

"Oh, I'm sorry, thank you. I... I... have it, thanks, oh, I'm sorry. I don't know. I was just goin' and all of a sudden you were stopped. I barely touched the brake as I hit you. I..." Tears began gently flowing from her captivating eyes.

James stared into her face. Even with the tears, she was very pretty. Her shiny black hair was pulled into a bun, that was very elegant, but professional looking. She wasn't wearing makeup and honestly didn't need it. Her complexion was that of the Scots, but on the darker side. Her cheekbones were stunning and her eyes, shimmering with tears, were a light brown.

"Are you hurt?" James asked again.

"I, I'm fine, so sorry. Are you fit then as well? I'm so sorry. I honestly don't know what ta do, but I will find a way ta make this right," she said very quickly, before stopping, and taking a heavy breath.

James feared she was about to hyperventilate. "Aye, no worries, I'm fine." For some reason, he immediately began speaking with a slight Scottish accent. Having an attuned ear was useful for things like this.

"Are you sure you're okay, then?" James added. "I don't think the boot has much damage to it, if any." He gestured toward his car, and then stepped back to look at hers, before speaking again.

"All seems well here for you. No damage to us or the cars, so all is well." He looked up with a reassuring smile, but he could see she was still very upset.

"See here?" He pointed at her bumper. "Not even a scratch to the paint, so no chance of real damage. That and you maybe were going a slow jogging pace, so how much damage can that even make?"

"What about here and here?" She pointed at some chips in her paint, as well as a scratch on the side of her bumper that would have never touched his rental.

"The little pecks are just from driving. The scratch, I can't say, but your front touched the back, not the side. Come, take a look at mine, you won't see it damaged. A little dirty, but no marks," James said, as they walked toward his car.

She peered down at his bumper with her arms crossed as if trying to hold herself together. "What do we do then? Do we need ta phone the police, and get a report, and all of that?" she asked.

"No, I think we're okay without any of that. My name is John Boyd." James smiled and held out a friendly hand. He needed to be sure this wasn't a setup, so he was going about it in a cautious manner. At the same time, he knew that if this was a real accident, it wouldn't matter who he was.

"I'm Carissa Tate." She took his hand and shook it. "I really am very sorry about all this. Should we exchange information, just in case there is some damage that comes up, then?"

"I would rather exchange information with the hope of maybe taking you to a supper," James replied. The words surprised him, and he felt dorky for throwing it out like that, but much to his surprise, she giggled. Her smile made her look like a beauty queen.

"Well, that certainly is the most unique way I have been asked out, and with me looking all tossed," she said, rubbing her hands under her eyes.

"I don't think you look tossed at all. I'd like to take you on a date tomorrow if that's okay," James said, writing down his number.

He passed her a small sheet of paper so she could write down her number as well. It was a good thing he'd gotten a UK SIM card. Later, he'd have to get a combined system to link the phone numbers.

"Well, I feel terrible. After all, I tapped you, and here you are asking me out. And tomorrow I have plans with a friend of mine." She handed him her number.

"I see." James felt a bit deflated.

"I would like ta though, perhaps another time? But I don't want ta go just, I don't know... just because of the accident." She frowned slightly.

"No worries, we can try for a different day. I'm free tomorrow. Silly of me to think you might not have plans. I'll be traveling soon, but perhaps when I get back I can give you a ring, and we can sort it out then? And this accident has been the best thing to happen to me today, to be honest." Smiling sheepishly, James looked down at his feet before looking up to see that she was also smiling.

"That sounds alright, then. Listen, John, I am sorry, but who knows, maybe this will turn out ta be a good thing all around. So you will call me, then? And you will let me know if there are any repairs needed?"

"Yes and yes, but it's a hired car, so no worries there," James replied, still smiling. "I'll be letting you get on, then. Hope you have a good day tomorrow, and we'll talk soon. It was nice meeting you, just wish it had been under happier circumstances, but glad all the same," he said.

"Thank you for being so sweet and, yes, please do ring me. Bye," she said.

Unexpectedly, she half hugged him and walked to her car. She gave a small wave that James returned as she disappeared into her vehicle. She pulled away, still waving, as James finally moved to climb into his car.

He got in and made his way toward the pub to meet Calum, having forgotten that he was having a bad day. In fact, he felt rather good.

# •Chapter Twelve•

Calum was waiting in the pub when James arrived. He was a short man with a potbelly, long sideburns, and a rather withdrawn hairline. The hair that remained was speckled with gray, as were his bushy eyebrows. His rather large legs looked odd against the rest of his frame.

James laughed to himself when he realized the pub had the same characteristics as Calum. Like Calum, it was very wide, but rather short in length. Like his hair, a straw overhang was bald in places, and rather decayed in others. Also like Calum, the walls seemed to have a bowing bulge. The difference was the walls looked this way because a variety of pictures hung on them.

As James entered, an elderly couple was leaving. The old lady bumped a picture near the door on the wall. James caught it and hung it back up. It was part of a variety of different scenic views with the same group of friends in each.

"Calum?" James asked, turning toward the bar.

"Aye. You'd be Stephen then?" came his Scottish accent. "Well, pull up a seat there lad, and have a pint. William, a pint here," Calum said, addressing the bartender.

"Thank you, but stomach troubles today, a pint wouldn't do so good for me," James said quickly.

"Bring the pint still. I'll have it then." Calum picked up his glass, and finished it in a few gulps.

"Can I fetch you anything?" William asked, in his deep voice.

He was missing a few teeth. Tall and bald, with bright blue eyes, he looked to be in his sixties, and appeared in many of the pictures on the walls.

"Just water, please. Oh, and maybe a basket of chips, yeah?" said James, and William nodded.

"So, you're in need of some information, then. Well, what is it z'actly you're looking for lad?" Calum asked this very directly and clearly, and James was taken aback by his bluntness.

"Yes, but is it okay...?" James began. He'd already memorized the room and the exits. He'd read the people in it, and scanned it visually for cameras, but was still unsure this was a place to talk.

"We talk here and now or not at all. I'm not one for doing all the foolery. This place is safe. Now, what is it that you need? I was told you were a man to listen to then, right? So I'm listenin'. What is it then?" Calum let out a belch, picked up his new draught of beer, and drank, his gray eyes staring at James.

"Right, I'm looking for information on drug rings between the Italians in the US, Asia, and Russia. I also want to know how they relate to Aberdeen," said James, recovering quickly.

Calum set down his beer, picked up his knife and fork, and began cutting his shepherd's pie. "A lot, that. Afraid I don't know most of that, then." He took a bite of the pie.

As Calum chewed, James asked, "What bits do you know?"

Calum calmly swallowed, cleared his throat, and continued as if James hadn't spoken. "Seems to be a lot that is none of my concern. I was told you helped my nephew out of a spot. Told I should give you a listen. Maybe the best way I can help, and pay my bloody nephew's debt is to tell you a story. Do you know the story called 'The Stone Wishes?'"

James shook his head as William laid his English style chips and water in front of him. He also registered that Calum was lying about Petior being his nephew. His eyes had dropped both times he'd said nephew. In fact, James would bet Calum didn't have any nephews at all.

Calum took a few bites of food, swallowed, and began. "There was once this wee bit of a lake that people would come and chuck a stone at to make a wish. The lake was on a farmer's land. The legend says, that the farmer had found the wishing lake, and had chucked a stone into it with a wish he had marked with wax. He had wished to be very successful and rich on his farm. It goes that the stone he had thrown came back right at the spot he had thrown it a moon later, but smooth and without the wax. Within the farming season, his wish had come true, so he decided to share the great wishing lake with others."

Calum paused to take a long drink of his beer. "Another pint then, William," he called. "Well, the farmer set up a platform to cast from, and a spot for rocks. He charged a quid to come up to the lake and throw a stone, and another quid for coming back to try to recover the rock four weeks later. He told those who came, it was just a small charge to help with all the traffic and such, you know. He had signs advising how to best write with the wax, and identify the thrown rock. People came, and did as he said. It became so popular that he had to hire a few extra hands to help."

Another pause for a drink, and to finish off his food, followed by more burping, before he continued. "One day, an older woman from the village came. She was loved by the entire town, but rather poor. She paid her fees, wrote her message, and gave her stone a toss. She did this once a week for a month. She then continued to come back, and look for each rock. Each time, she was disappointed to find it was still written upon.

The farmer knew her, and felt bad for her. After she had left on her last throw, he walked down, found her last stone, and read what she had written on it. She wanted to win the lottery for £1,000 pounds." Calum scratched his head as if he was thinking.

"You see, each day, the farmer had been going to the lake, and collecting all the stones that had been thrown. He stored them in a shed, and marked which day he'd have to set them out for the people to come find. The people didn't know this of course. He took her stone, with the winning lottery request, and wiped it smooth of wax. The next day, he made arrangements to have a fake notice sent to the woman in two weeks time with a winning deposit of £1,000 pounds. He also arranged for the local press to find out. He was relying on the old woman to say she had cast a stone into the lake. This would increase business, and the £1,000 pounds was just an investment for the advertising."

James wondered where this was going. The story was dragging a bit.

"A week later, the old woman came back, and found her smooth stone, and was very excited. She cried out to everyone, and showed them the wax free rock. The crowd cheered and congratulated her, but in a half-hearted manner. After all, she was the only one to have gotten a smooth stone back, meaning her wish should come true. Well, besides the farmer that is," Calum added, almost as an afterthought.

"Well, the next week, that dear lady got the notice as designed, and died from a heart attack on the spot. However, the word spread like wildfire, and suddenly there were traffic jams, and more people at the lake than the farmer could manage. There were so many people that they abandoned the normal path, and began cutting through the farmer's crops to get to the lake. The crowd was unmanageable, and certainly had no concern about paying for their turn. The police weren't much help, as the local authorities didn't have the means to address such a crowd.

After the second day of nonstop people, the farmer's crops had suffered a lot of damage, and he hadn't been able to collect any fees. Not that it mattered, as he wasn't able to collect the cast stones either. He eventually had to try to close everything off, just to gain some sleep, and keep people off his few remaining crops."

James noticed William listening and frowning at the story, as Calum continued.

"On the third day, there was a knock on the farmer's door at dawn. The police were there with the local news. This had become such a sensation that the lottery commission had heard about it. Upon investigating, they discovered the old woman hadn't even played the lottery, nor had they sent her any money. The police searched the farmer's property, and found the buckets of rocks with the wax on them."

Calum paused and finished his beer with a smacking of his lips before continuing. "The media exposed the story, and the crowds were gone. The police issued a hefty fine. The fine was double all the funds the farmer had gotten from the wishing lake for all the trouble the fake story had caused, as well as for running a fraud that involved the lottery system. But they didn't arrest him, as he hadn't cost the lottery system any money.

The farmer lost all his money and had no crops at all. He was ruined, and had to move away, because he couldn't afford the bank note any longer. Plus, the local townspeople blamed him for the old lady's death, and were mad in general for the lies, though they'd never really believed in the wishing lake in the first place," concluded Calum.

"So the moral of the story is that greed will be your undoing?" asked James, who didn't think much of the story. Either Calum was drunk, or a bad storyteller, or he was making it up as he went. All in all, it was a bad story that James barely followed.

"Hell, lad, I didn't say that. You can take a fair few things from that about greed, or lying, or just being a bit dumb in leaving discoverable things about, or maybe that wishing isn't enough to make things real. Or, perhaps, pursuing something you wish for might not be the best thing for you."

The last part was the message, and James knew it. It was the same message Petior had given him.

"The farmer wasn't successful because of the wish, just the opposite," James countered. "He made the wishing lake up after he'd harvested a good crop. He wished to be rich, and he got in over his head and lost everything."

"As you like, lad, as you like," Calum said. He handed James an envelope. "This man was an associate of Anthony Spara. They had a falling out, and don't like each other now. As for your other questions, well I don't know'er about that. I assume I've settled Petior's debt. Good luck, and don't lose your farm."

He threw some money on the bar, clasped James's shoulder, waved to William, and exited.

A real lead. James hadn't mentioned anyone's name, but there it was, plain as day. Anthony Spara.

James quickly left. Twenty minutes later, he was parking at the hotel and climbing out of his car when his phone rang.

# •Chapter Thirteen•

"Hello?" James answered.

"Hello, John, this is Carissa. We uhh, bumped into each other earlier," she said.

With a slight chuckle, James said, "Hi Carissa, how is your evening going, then? All well and no car troubles, I hope?"

"Oh no, it's fine. I wanted ta call and say sorry again. I feel really bad, and you were so sweet and all. Didn't care for the cars until you were sure I was fine, then asked so nicely about a supper. Listen, you're free tomorrow, right?" She said all of this fast, as if she had practiced.

"No problems, and yeah, I'm free." James smiled widely, completely unaware that he was doing so.

"Would you fancy going ta a football match? My friend isn't able ta go, and I thought maybe this would be a good way ta apologize and say thank you, as well as have that date. If you don't want ta go, that is understandable. I know this is last second. I told Jessica she was putting me in a spot with the extra ticket, but she said her mum needed help with the dog. The dog had surgery today for something on its leg and is in a sort. Sweet dog, but as I say, I have an extra ticket."

People thought James talked fast, but he had nothing on Carissa.

"Thing is," she continued, "it's at Paradise, with the Celtic."

"Yes," James said. "I'd like to go with you." This was a new sensation, being asked out by a woman.

"Seriously?" Carissa sounded relieved.

"Aye, but I think I should drive. Don't want you bumping into another guy whilst out with me."

Carissa said, "Cheeky! At least you have a sense of humor. I have ta be in Glasgow a wee bit longer than the match, I'm afraid for a few days, you know. Well actually, I live here as I finish university, but may move soon. Can I meet you there, then?"

"Sure, sure. What time should we meet outside the stadium?" he asked.

"The match is set for 1 p.m., so quarter past noon would be good, you think?" she asked.

James replied, "Sounds great. See you tomorrow, and thanks for inviting me."

"I think I owe you at least that much. Glad you're coming. Bye," said Carissa.

James hung up the phone and walked into the hotel. He felt good, and he didn't want to spoil it. He decided he was taking the rest of the night, and tomorrow off just to be happy. The letter from Calum could wait until tomorrow night, and work wasn't going anywhere. He was going to have dinner, and then relax by the pool before ordering a movie in his room.

The next morning slowly passed until it was time to start the three-hour drive across Scotland. At noon, James parked. Ten minutes later, he found Carissa at the gates.

She had her hair in a ponytail that suited her. The smile on her face and absence of tears made James note just how very good looking she was. The smile seemed to span her entire face. That, along with her twinkling eyes, made for an extraordinary effect. James had a positive feeling; a tingle he couldn't explain.

Reaching Carissa, he held out his hand and said, "Good afternoon, you look fantastic."

She blushed and shook his hand. "Shall we go in then? I'm very happy you came and all."

James started to walk toward the entrance and Carissa stopped him.

"Oh, we are in the club, this way," she said, still blushing. "How's the saying, 'I ain't no cheap bitch ta date'?"

This was priceless in her Scottish accent, and they both started laughing.

"Now who's cheeky? Lead the way then." James grinned from ear to ear, as they made their way to the proper entrance. "Thank you again for inviting me. This should be a great match."

"It really should, yea, but you know the Celtic should win," Carissa stated as they reached the door.

The hall was very well done with a great combination of tile and brick. The history of the football club covered the walls, and the displays showed the accomplishments the team had made throughout the league.

"May I help you?" asked the man at the desk.

As Carissa got the tickets, James started to take in more details. The elevator was to the far left, near the doors they'd come in. Everything appeared to have a fresh, updated look, even the surveillance system. There seemed to be a good bit of dead space that visually wasn't accounted for when you thought about the outside of the building. Before James could think about that too much, Carissa had the tickets and grabbed his hand.

"This way," she said, letting her fingers slowly slip away.

James smiled and gestured as if to say, "After you."

They had a few flights of steps to walk up. As they did, James found himself at eye level with Carissa's backside. *Nice*, he thought to himself as they hit the second platform.

As if he'd announced what his eyes were doing, Carissa smiled and said, "I do a bit of running, and a day of squats and lunges to get that shapely bottom."

James felt himself instantly flush, which was rare, given his level of control over his emotions. "I... I um, well, I umm... I wasn't trying to... we are going up the steps and all... it was just kind of right in front of me," he finished lamely.

Some people nearby snickered.

Carissa smiled. "You look like someone painted you red. I will take it as a compliment. At least you didn't try ta steal a touch. Had ta give the last bloke I saw an imprint of my hand for that. Wanker that he was." She winked.

They had reached the proper floor for the club seating. They walked through two doors, and into a rather large open gathering area. The first thing James noticed were two stands where wagers could be placed about eight feet from the door he and Carissa had entered. Immediately to the right were the restrooms.

They took a few steps on the hardwood floor toward the general area. Several large televisions suspended from the ceiling were showing a variety of sports. Beneath the televisions was a buffet style layout of lunch foods.

"Fancy a wager on the match?" Carissa asked.

"Oh, yeah. What do you think, a few pounds on the Celtic to win?" James played along, though he hadn't expected the question.

"A few pounds on them ta win, then? How about having some stones and put the quid on a scoring match and get the odds?" Carissa was smiling, but serious at the same time. The fire in her eyes was irresistible.

"How about a twenty pound note? You pick the score." James dug the money out of his pocket after handing Carissa the betting sheet.

"Hmm, well, what ta pick, what ta pick? Want a good return on the money, which I, of course, get half the winnings if it comes through." She threw James a sly sideways glance, and he chuckled, nodding. "How about the Celtic win by two goals?" she asked.

Without thinking, James said, "Well, if you want to play the odds and get the best bet, then make it the Celtic win 3 to 1. Still have your prediction, but you get a 2.5 percent better bet."

"Oh! Done this once or twice then? A few pounds, he says, like this is his first time." Carissa put down the pen and glanced at James with her eyebrows raised, a smile on her face. She was sharp and fast.

"That was some of the fastest calculating I've ever seen," said the lady taking bets.

James found himself at a loss as to how to follow up without exposing too much. In the back of his head, he processed the slip-up. "Old trick with the numbers, you know, based on her prediction of a two-goal win margin and all." James handed over the money and the wager sheet.

The lady processed the request and gave Carissa the slip.

"That solves that on who is holding the winning piece," James said with a grin.

"Have ta start this date off right. You pay, and I collect. A yin and yang system, right?" Carissa said this with as straight of a face as anyone could before laughing out loud. "Want a spot of food?" She gestured toward the spread, and James agreed.

He felt hungry and something else in his stomach that he couldn't explain. All he knew was this date was all of ten minutes in, and he was having a blast.

They collected some fish and chips, and went to find a table after a mini-fight over who was going to pay. They found a table and James went for drinks. A few minutes later, he returned with a beer for Carissa, and a cola for him, when he discovered an older couple had joined them.

As James set down the drinks, Carissa said, "This is Mary and Joseph. Very cute name combination, eh? Most of the seats are filled, and they asked if they could join us. It seems they make all the home matches."

"Nice to meet you," James said, shaking hands with them both. "Can I get you drinks?"

"Oh no, deary, that won't be needed. We have some water. I don't take the drink any longer, and it gives Joseph the winds something terrible," Mary said.

Joseph merely held up his water and muttered, "Yes, dear," before returning his attention to the monitor showing the horse race.

The group ate and chatted, with Mary and Carissa speaking the most. Carissa, like James, was enjoying the flow of the day, and saw no reason to alter their circumstances. Besides, they'd be taking their seats for the match soon.

It soon transpired that Mary and Joseph had three children, two daughters named Antoinette and Alice, and a son named Terry. Mary had been a schoolteacher until the summer before last. Joseph was a master plumber, who apparently was the world's leading expert in designing below-ground-pitted systems.

"What is that, exactly?" James asked, having never heard of such a thing, but with a high level of interest.

"Well mate, the best way to explain is an example, you know. So take an old system, without the plumbing in, with a well feed, which has no pumps. Like an old castle without proper electricity, you know, hard to put the systems in the walls. Well, you typically have all sorts of issues, but the easiest way to get around that is to put a sub-level pit in that has the water feed off the well. As the water feeds through, it drops and creates the flow to climb, and pressure the pipe properly." As he described this, Joseph crudely drew on the back of a napkin.

"Now," he continued, "if you're so industrious as to want heated water, you put the boiler down too. That has its own issues, mind, like the need for an exit that is proper, and nearby at the base level because..."

Mary interrupted, "Joseph, dear, I'm sure that was more than a satisfactory answer, and the match is about to start soon. Shall we take our seats?"

Joseph immediately said, "Yes, dear," got up, and started shaking hands.

Mary continued, "It was lovely having a chat with you both. Please enjoy the match, and hopefully the Bhoys win, eh?"

After they left, Carissa turned and said, "Well, shall we go too, then?"

James immediately got up and looked Carissa dead in the eye, mimicking Joseph, said, "Yes, dear."

Carissa let out a loud burst of laughter, before covering her mouth. Recovering, she said with a dazzling grin, "I don't think we are quite at their level yet."

They passed through two side-by-side doors into what looked to be a proper restaurant, on their way to their seats. It looked vaguely familiar to James, but after a while, a lot of places began to blend.

The seats were great. They offered a spectacular view of the pitch at an angle to the goalkeepers net. The whole stadium seemed to open up to them. The seats were comfortable too. They were wide and with a fair amount of legroom, and certainly nicer looking than some of the seats in the other sections.

Adding to the atmosphere were all the people around them. Everyone was carrying on like it was a large party. Conversations spanned several rows, and everyone kept jumping in and out of everyone's conversations. James thought it was like being with his family, only slightly larger with drunken Scottish accents.

James had never really followed soccer in the US. The best he could do was to avoid saying soccer in place of football. He'd just go with the flow as best he could, but even his keen ears were having issues following the Scottish.

"Where do you hail, lad?" came a booming voice from behind him.

"Me?" James asked.

"Aye, you. Certainly not this bell of a lass with ya now, so where you from?" the man said. "And what is your name, or did ya forget that too?"

James felt a ton of people suddenly look at him. It was as if someone had turned off the noise of the crowd all at once.

"My name is John, and I hail from Aberdeen. Might I ask yours?"

"John from Aberdeen, you say! Well now, what brings a man from the eastern parts all the way to Tom Burns' stadium then?" said the man.

James always found sports enthusiast to be slightly annoying by some of the claims they made like 'we won' or 'my team.' James thought this was another example of that, but James didn't know that Tom Burns was formerly a famous player for the Celtic.

Before James could answer, Carissa jumped in. "Perhaps this bell, who is named Carissa, wanted an outing ta see the Bhoys demonstrate how the game really should be played."

The crowd, including the inquiring man, laughed. "Too true that, too true. Well, this will be a match for sure. Us lot," and he made a vague gesture with the pint of ale in his hands, causing it to spill, "we all come to most of the matches, and the seats you have there are not held on for the season, but just for single matches. Always like to know we have the right sup-porters in the group, eh lads?"

The crowd gave a loud cheer of "Stripes!" and the original babble broke out again.

As Carissa and James sat down, she didn't seem very disturbed about the exchange. "The Glassies, you know, we are friendly folk." She changed the subject. "Now, when the match starts, until the first shot on goal for us, we will stand and jump, and show our backsides to the other team as they come down our end of the pitch."

"Literally, as in pull a moony?" James asked.

"Nah, just turn our back ta them, ya know, and jump. You'll see," she replied.

With the player introductions completed, the match began. Inverness, the opposing team, was moving up the pitch with the ball. As one, the crowd stood, turned around, placed arms over each other's shoulders, and began to jump and chant. James went along as best he could, though he seemed to be the only one out of the rhythm of the jump.

The announcer said that Celtic had possession, and again as one, everyone sat to watch. This happened two more times, and James concluded this was a lively bunch. As drunken as they were, he was surprised people weren't falling while turning front to back, and back to front again.

"That was a good set then, no idiots tried ta climb onto the field, n' doesn't look like anyone took a hard fall," Carissa said, as if she'd heard his thoughts.

Another ten minutes passed, and then one of the Celtic players had a break. He moved quickly to the position as fast as he could. The goalie wouldn't have time to recover if the kick were true, hard, and at the right angle. The ball was there and the kick thrown...

"Oh, what the bloody hell was that shite? You dirty, flat eyed bastard!" came the pre-adolescent voice of a boy, who looked to be about nine years old directly in front of Carissa. He was standing between two grown men, both of whom looked down at him.

"How the bloody hell do you miss that?" the boy continued. "Maybe if you opened your eyes and looked at what your worthless arse was supposed to be doing you could make the goal! Bet ya if ya had a bit of meat between your legs, like a proper man, your yellow gook of an arse would be making that play. Stupid dumb bastard!" hollered the boy. "Get him some rice!"

"You tell 'em, son," said the man to the boy's right, looking down with pride.

After the initial shock had worn off, James laughed so hard he was practically in tears. Never had he heard a child speak with such a foul mouth, let alone be encouraged by a parent to do so. He turned his head to semi-hide the fact that he was laughing, as he didn't think the racist part should be encouraged with laughter, but the torrent of words had been impressive.

Carissa looked at James and said, "Ah, well, you know, the match and all, and the wee Glassie lads."

The boy turned and shouted, "What of the wee Glassie lads, Risa?" giving a special accent to the abbreviated version of her name.

"Now that's enough of that, lad," said the boy's dad. "You treat the lady with some respect, as she didn't say nothing bad ter you. Besides, she looks like she could tan your hind end for good, and I won't be able ter stop her neither."

The neighboring crowd laughed, as did the boy and Carissa.

The match was scoreless until five minutes left in the first half, when the Celtic scored on a long shot right off the post. The stadium exploded in cheers, and a great chant broke out as fireworks went off near the opposite end of the stadium.

The remainder of the first half had some great shots on goal, and spectacular saves, as the teams battled it out, but the first half ended 1 to 0 for the Celtic. A player from Inverness was given a red card just as the half ended, apparently for being too mouthy with the referee.

They went back in the area with all the monitors to eat, and found it had been refreshed with different foods, and different seating arrangements. Once again, James felt he should pay.

"Carissa, are you sure I can't help with the costs? I don't want you to be put out or anything," he said.

"No worries. Care for a bit of these cakes then?" she answered, pointing towards some small cakes in the buffet area.

They gathered some snacks and found seats to watch two horse races. They became so engrossed in conversation that they found themselves among the last to return to the match.

Returning to their seats for the second half of the match, James stumbled. He'd been too focused on his thoughts, and had almost fallen down the steps, but he managed to catch himself at the last second.

"Oh, you all right then?" Carissa asked, reaching down to help. Regaining his feet, his heart racing, he caught her eyes. Those big eyes were staring into his face with a look of worry and relief.

"A pint too many then, lad. You Aberdeen lads need to learn how to hold your drink." The crowd near enough to hear gave a roar of laughter, as the uncle of the nine-year-old spoke to James. The boy was grinning from ear to ear.

It seemed to happen rapidly, but the match was suddenly over, and James and Carissa were back out in front of the stadium. James wondered where the time had gone, and had to think to remember the Celtic had won by a final score of 1 to 0.

# •Chapter Fourteen•

"Suppose we should have gone just for the Celtic winning the match, then? At least we would have made twenty quid instead of losing it."

Carissa was looking at James almost apologetically, or was it in a happy way, but very soft? Not being able to read a person was unnerving and exciting for James.

"No worries. Best money I've spent in a long time. But what would be an even better spend of money is to take you on a proper date, if you'd let me." James tried not to speak in a clumsy manner.

"That is sweet, but I..." Carissa began.

"Ah, ah, no worries, I understand. I just..."

Carissa placed a finger to James's lips to stop him from speaking.

"As I was saying, I'm here in Glasgow for a bit more, but would love to go to supper with you, very soon." She said this softly while removing her finger.

"Tomorrow?" James blurted.

"Did you not hear me?" she asked, eyebrows up.

"I don't mind that it's here. Please, let me take you to supper tomorrow. I will be traveling the day after, and don't want to wait so long. Please?" James finished, deliberately trying to create what he thought 'doggie eyes' would look like.

It must have worked, as she said, "Yes, fine then." She took out a pen and paper, and wrote down her address. "Want to pick me up at 7?"

"Sooner," he retorted.

"Sooner, is it?" She laughed. "We will be having supper with the likes of Mary and Joseph. But that's fine, let's say 6." She put the pen back into her bag.

"Perfect. See ya then, and be dressed to impress." James regretted saying this the moment he said it. *Wait, did that sound bad or maybe will she take it as I don't find her attractive? Damn, why I'm so bad at this?* He wondered if he should clarify.

"Sounds like you are a good listener about taking me someplace proper. I like that. I will be ready, no worries. Bye, John." She smiled as she walked away, and James almost melted with relief.

*This girl was different. Most women didn't react like that. She might be a keeper,* he thought excitedly.

Then another side of his brain kicked in, *Maybe she was just really well trained.*

The last thought didn't make him happy, but it was reasonable. Still, he had gotten a second date, and if it were as genuine as it felt, any suspicions he had would be easily dismissed later.

James was right on time the next day. He pulled up just as the clock showed 6 p.m. to find Carissa walking out of her building.

Dressed to impress was an understatement. She looked phenomenal in a royal purple dress that hugged her figure, with matching shoes. Carissa had done her hair differently too, and it flowed around her beautiful face in a way that seemed alive. She also had gone very light on the makeup and perfume. James was particularly happy about this, as he preferred a natural look and hated heavy perfumes.

He quickly got out to open the door for her. "You look amazing!" he stammered.

"Thank you, my good sir, you look handsome yourself," Carissa replied smiling.

"I think you're going to enjoy this place tonight. A mate of mine made the arrangements last night. He said it was the best place in the city." James climbed back in the car and started the engine.

"I'm sure it's lovely," she said.

They made small talk and laughed for the twenty-minute journey to the restaurant.

"How'd you get us a table for tonight?" Carissa asked, when they parked and he opened her door. "It takes weeks to get a reservation here. Who's your friend?"

"Ah, just like your tickets, this is my treat, and so is how I came about it." James answered her question with a playful sense of mystery.

Carissa just smiled and offered him her hand to help her out of the car.

Neither remembered the food, environment, or anything about dinner later, just that it was one of the best evenings they'd ever had. Saying goodbye three hours later at Carissa's apartment seemed to take a long time. James was terrible at goodbyes anyway, but this didn't feel right. He stood for a moment, setting his weight in his heels, and just listened as her words washed over him. His eyes fixed on hers, as each word rang in his ears, but nothing registered. He focused his breathing because he knew what he wanted to do, and needed to be in control for it.

Slowly, he reached forward and took her hands in his. She peered down at his touch. It wasn't an aggressive move. It was the opposite, a gentle and calming touch. He wrapped his palms over the back of her hands, allowing his fingers to wrap around her wrists.

Slowly, they looked up at each other, and he stared at her big, beautiful eyes.

He had his proof at that moment.

"Risa, I've had more fun than I can remember having in, in, well ever. I would like to see you again please, and as soon as I get back if you're willing," said James in a slow voice.

Carissa blushed, her fingers grasping his fingers now. She leaned forward to kiss him. It wasn't a long, hard kiss like you see in the movies. It was soft and just long enough to be a full kiss. The kind of kiss you would give a lover who was nearly asleep. She pulled away for half a breath before they kissed again, like a newlywed couple that has just been pronounced man and wife.

She stepped slowly back, smiling, and then turned, and began walking up the sidewalk.

"I will take that as a yes," James called after her. "That, or I'm going to have to ask that Glassie lad to supper, as he was by far the second most entertaining person I've been near the last few days."

She turned, smiling. "I was going ta say the same thing if you hadn't asked, don't ya know. Cute lad. A wee bit too dirty for my taste, but cheeky calling me Risa as he did."

James smiled. He loved her dancing eyes and accent.

"Call me tomorrow before you leave, and we'll sort the date then," she said, starting to wave.

"First thing," James said, then felt his brain recoil as if to say, *Too fast and desperate sounding, fool!*

"I would expect nothing less." She turned and walked away, humming a light tune.

James went to turn and almost fell. He'd forgotten he locked his legs and restricted blood to them. He felt something surging through him that was beyond adrenaline. It was love, and he knew it. He knew it just like everyone always said you would. What's more, she felt the same. He had needed to be sure, and now he was. This was no setup. This woman was into him as much as he was into her.

Her pulse had quickened when he had held her wrists. Her eyes had dilated, even though there'd been no change in the lighting. Her reaction had been purely chemical and unmistakable. What's more, her eyes had responded the same way when he'd almost fallen down the stairs at the football match. This was impossible to fake.

James was happy and smiling like he'd never smiled before. In fact, by the time morning came, he'd have a sore jaw from smiling so much.

The following morning, James rolled over to see the clock blinking 6:30 a.m. just as the alarm sounded. He hit the off switch and flopped back onto the bed. He'd been having a fantastic dream in which he was dancing with a laughing Carissa.

He rolled toward the phone.

"Good morning, sleepyhead. What happened to the first thing, then?" came Carissa's answer.

"Good morning, Risa, how did you sleep?" he asked.

Carissa chuckled. "So I see the lad's take on me name has stuck, then. You know, I will have to come up with a right nickname for you too, I suppose. Hmm, I will have to have a think on that, I will."

James laughed.

"What's so funny about that?" Carissa asked.

"Nothing, it's just that I'm happy is all, and hearing your voice makes the joy come right out as rain from the sky."

"Well, now, who would have thought you were a poet? A good on-the-spot one at that. That was very sweet and lovely of you. Ah, that is your nickname."

"What? Spot?"

"No, 'love,'" Carissa said, and James could tell she was smiling and probably blushing by her voice.

"Can't argue with that, can I?"

She giggled.

James went on. "I will be gone for a bit, but should be back in a few weeks. I'll know a more specific date soon. Would it be all right then, if we just managed to talk until I can get back? Shouldn't be more than four weeks, with the training and visits and such."

The previous night, they'd both talked about their jobs, his in marketing and all the travel, hers as a bank teller up for a promotion. The promotion was why she'd been in Aberdeen, and she was looking to move there after graduation if she got it. They also talked about living in different areas growing up, which easily explained their faded accents.

"I think that is perfect. When do you fly out?" she asked. Carissa's voice sounded fainter, and James had a feeling she was getting ready for work based on the background noises.

"I leave for the States in about three hours. Shall I let you go? I hear you gettin' ready," he said.

"Oh sorry, I wasn't bored or anything, just..."

"No worries. I know how it can be in the morning. I'm just glad we could talk before I left. If you'd like, I can give you a quick ring when I land, should be about tea time for you."

"Yes, please, that would be lovely. Okay, got ta run. Thanks for calling and safe travels," Carissa said.

"Talk soon, Risa. Bye," James said, and they hung up together.

She called him 'love.' He knew it was just a nickname, but it reminded him how little she knew about him. Though he had recognized the feeling yesterday, hearing the word so quickly was making him second guess things. He wasn't good with strong emotions within himself.

He thought a moment, then stood up with the phone in his hand. He knew what he needed to do. He needed a conversation with Master, who helped him when he felt his emotions might get the better of his logic.

"So, what is the question exactly?" asked Master.

"Should I tell her that my name and appearance aren't real, and that I wasn't trying to lie to her?" James answered.

"No, that is not the question," Master stated.

James paused. "Do I love her?"

"No, wrong," Master stated.

"Okay, all things simple." James paused again. "Do I trust her? Can I trust her?"

"No, wrong, but closer," said Master.

"Can I trust myself?"

# •Chapter Fifteen•

James showered and packed, but deliberately left the envelope Calum had handed him unopened. He could pass along the letter and let someone else take it from there, but it sounded like this connection in Asia would advance him a lot further down the line. Even so, Calum, with Petior's insistence, had told him not to go down that path.

If James had been anything his whole life, it had been someone who recognized the wisdom in others' mistakes. On the other hand, other individuals seldomly had his skill sets. This wasn't a vain or prideful thought, more an affirming one. He wanted to move forward for the good of taking down something evil with no thought of self-reward, aside from conquering the task itself.

*No harm in opening the envelope*, he decided. He didn't have to do anything if it was too horrible. He grabbed the note and sat on the bed. There were two sheets.

The first page read: *"Osh, Kyrgyzstan, entry point. Noi Rasa is the contact (phone number on next page). Two weeks' notice for approval. No more than two people accepted. Don't bring a negro. Don't bring electronics that can't be shut off. No weapons. ID will be required with copies presented ahead of time as instructed."*

James moved to the second page. *"STOP"* was written in large bold writing taking up half the page. The letter continued, *"If you call, state the following: 'I was calling about A S pirit.'"* The phone number mentioned on the first page was given below, followed by instructions, *"Call at 1:32 a.m., eastern standard time."*

James was intrigued. He'd have to talk with Tom when he got back to sort this out, and figure out how to get to Kyrgyzstan, but that didn't sound like the final destination. Lots of questions were popping into his head. James got up and placed the note in his bag. It was time to head back to the good old USA.

Later at the group headquarters, it took Tom about thirty minutes to shed some light on the note James gave him. "The city and country are what the note says. As for Noi Rasa, that's Laotian n' means 'little king.' We have no records on him. The requirements seem straightforward. I'm guessing the negro part refers to Daen."

"I thought that, too," James answered. "An English speaking person wrote this. A native English speaking person, by the way, the letters are written. Probably Calum, so it's specific to me. Odd that they said about the on/off switch for the electronics though."

"It is. So, you're going into a Russian-speaking area, to meet a Laos-named man, who is supposed to be an Asian connection. The town is near the China border, but outside of the city that area is deserted. It has nothing, literally." Tom unfolded a map with satellite pictures.

"Anyone else speak Russian, and both dialects of Chinese and Laos?" asked James.

"Actually, yes. Rain Man." Tom looked serious. "You know that."

"Don't call him that. He hates it. He knows what it means," James said.

"Sorry, Tim. But you can't be thinking about taking him in with you." Tom stood up and placed both hands on the table, peering at James. "You have no idea what's out there. He'll slow you down tremendously, not to mention he'll blow the cover if someone asks him even the slightest direct question we haven't thought of first."

"I don't know the languages, and that's more dangerous to me than anything," James replied. "I've repeatedly been warned not to go down this path, so I'd rather rely on knowing what others are saying, and having his eyes, than to go in deaf and blind. I'll work with him and give him specific tasks. He's not my biggest worry."

"James..." Tom started.

"Can we get him the needed cover and ID? I'll need a new one made, as it looks like I'm going to have to burn the Stephen Lewis identity after this."

"Melissa can do it, and you know it. That isn't an issue. There are too many unknowns in this. Maybe the 'STOP' in the note is a last ditch effort to save you." Tom's voice dropped. He knew he wasn't going to be able to stop James.

James thought a moment and said, "The concern is noted, and I'll make every effort to be safe, and come back with Tim. I haven't failed yet."

"No one does until they do," Tom said quickly.

James waited patiently in the long silence that followed those sage words. After all, knowing when not to talk could be a powerful tool. Finally, Tom got up to leave.

"You'll have to work out how to get Tim for that long, and a name he won't mess up. He isn't used to this type of thing, and you're about to mess with his schedule and time. He solves puzzles for us," said Tom with a pleading tone, "and I think this is way beyond him." He didn't want to allow this, but at the same time, he had faith that James would handle it.

James knew Tim would be excited about doing fieldwork, and that was a problem. Tim was truly schedule oriented. They usually had to give him a few days' notice just to make sure he'd be calm and focused when it was time for a meeting. Tim needed to associate a distinct time and place to be comfortable.

The trip to Osh would be unpredictable, cross over time zones, require Tim to be around a vast number of people he didn't know, and require a cover story. The trip was essentially the opposite of how Tim lived. However, James had to explore this option, or go back to the drawing board.

"Hey, Jake!" James called as a man walked past.

Jake paused and stuck his head into the room. "What's up?"

"How'd the bust go last night?" asked James.

"Smoother than silk. That information about the audio set up was great. We had that thing going full swing, and it really did sound like we had a solid extra eight people. The sergeant in charge didn't want to proceed, but the captain himself called, and said to do it. No shots fired from the buyers, the sellers, or us. Plus, it's all on tape. I talked to Shane, who talked to the three suspects last night. They all confessed, and are all turning state's evidence. This was a slam dunk. Thanks again for all the help."

James waved, and Jake disappeared down the hall.

Jake was relatively new to the group, and had been one of the people James had mentored. He was smart and even-tempered, and could make choices, but he lacked the natural ability to actively engage others in making things happen. He was also a lot older than most new recruits at the age of 22.

James had spent time with him thinking out plans, and developing reasonable scenarios, and showing him that people were like any other resource. Though Jake took a common cookie-cutter approach like the CIA or FBI would, at least he was open to new unconventional methods, which the federal agents couldn't do.

Having openness to new ideas was an essential characteristic of the group members. The CIA/FBI/DEA types were good at what they did, but they had the wrong mentality. In fact, that was exactly why this group existed. Its members did the things the others couldn't, all because of their unique approach, and lack of desire to get the credit. It was all about playing the game in order to achieve the result, with the result ultimately helping those who couldn't help themselves.

Korey, who was the general manager of the facility, and assistant to Andy and Tom, came in the room and said, "Tom said to tell you Tim is here and in D1."

Korey was a kind lady who never asked too many questions, and was utterly trustworthy and loyal. The mother of three, with a husband who had been a drug addict, she had a remarkably upbeat personality, though the lines on her face, and general manner of moving, told the true story of the stress she experienced.

"Thanks," James said, pulling himself out of his seat. He was surprised Tom had moved so quickly. No doubt, it was to prove a point about how poorly Tim was going to take this operation. What was more surprising was that Tim had responded so quickly.

James paused. He felt a little uneasy. He needed to sort this out first in a logical way, and for that, he needed a quick talk with Master.

"Everyone is going to be against this idea," James stated.

"Really?" asked Master.

"Well, aside from Tim and me, that is."

"Assuming you're right about Tim, that means the two people who are the most affected are okay with this. What's the problem?" asked Master.

"Aside from everyone else thinking it's a bad idea, ya mean?" asked James.

"Since when do you concern yourself with what everyone else thinks of a situation? You see a path, and you go for it. As things come up, you adjust. Tim is as safe in your hands as anyone. If he wasn't, would you consider taking him?" asked Master.

"I..." began James.

"This sounds like self-doubt and emotion. You walked through a decision tree, and exceeded 50 percent. You have a path," said Master.

Still thinking about the logic Master had just reminded him of, James walked down the hall to room D1 and entered. At a glance, he saw Tim was in rare form, pacing along all four walls as if doing laps, and talking nonstop in a rather disjointed way. He did this when he was nervous, and felt like he was out of control.

"She was trying to make an appointment, she said. Well, that doesn't make sense. Who needs to make an appointment? You simply add the acid. It's not a hard thing to remember, and of course, if you don't, you get complications. Complications that cause harm. Harmful burning that is very bad and painful, yes."

Like Tom, Tim was in his early thirties, with brown eyes and hair. He looked a great deal like Larry from *The Three Stooges*, though without the baldness.

Tim's eyes found James. "James needs sleep. He has been up for too many hours and also needs to eat today. Those pants are new, though. Only washed once or twice, but the shirt is old. Very old. The excuse she made, well, I do not see why she said it. The lies are obvious, and she will have to go to jail for a long time for killing her husband and son. This is very irregular, very. We didn't have a time set up to meet."

"Hello, Tim. I'm happy to see you," James said, stepping into Tim's path.

Tim dropped his head slightly. "Hello, James. I'm sorry I commented on your clothes. They are nice, I'm sure."

James allowed a moment of silence to go before he spoke. He wanted Tim to get his own sense of things. "Tim, thank you for the help on the code for the Rose operation. It made everything work. We couldn't have done anything without your help. You're the man with the plan."

Tim looked up, smiling. "Yes, obviously, the encryption, it was just a number system. Like the telephone hierarchy, of course. It was very obvious once I saw it. You caught the bad guys, and they're not coming back, right?"

"All thanks to you, buddy. You're the man, as always," James said, taking a seat.

Tim copied him and also sat. He was making prolonged eye contact, something he rarely did. James knew Tim loved receiving praise, and being called 'the man.' Apparently, his parents had never praised him, which didn't help his introverted nature.

"Tim, I was wondering if you could help me again, please," James said.

"Obviously, yes," said Tim, his legs bouncing. James wasn't sure if that was out of excitement at the thought of a new project, or out of nervousness at having his routine disrupted.

"We have a problem that is very far away near a town called Osh, in K..." began James.

"Kyrgyzstan, yes, obviously. You don't speak the language or do so poorly. It's how your tongue and lips move together. You can roll your tongue, so it makes it harder for you. I can speak in Latin and Spanish and French and Italian and Thai and Cantonese and Mandarin and Vietnamese and..."

James held up a finger. Immediately, Tim dropped his head and was silent. This was a Pavlov-style response instilled by his parents in his childhood.

"Tim, you're awesome at everything. I wish I could do things like you, but I can't. I need your help," James affirmed.

Tim looked up and began frantically looking around the room. "Well, where is it?" he asked impatiently.

"This time, we do not need to you translate something on paper for us. This time, I'll need help in the field," James said, slowly and clearly.

Tim's response was mixed, but very literal. He froze, and a moment later he started to shake. He then froze again, his physical response reflecting the battle that was going on inside his mind. He had continually insisted he was as capable as anyone to do fieldwork. In fact, Tim felt he was more than capable, but it went against his need for routine. For him, it was truly two worlds colliding.

They waited in silence for a minute, Tim's response becoming more and more drastic.

"Tim, you don't..." came Tom's voice, but James moved so quickly to keep Tim's field of vision and attention on him, that Tom had to take a step back. James held out his left hand behind him to signal to Tom not to talk.

Tim was starting to calm down, except for his bouncing left leg.

"What do you think, Tim? Will you help me?" James asked.

"Obviously, yes, but it's my operation, and I call the shots?" It was a question filled with anxiety, not his usual, matter-of-fact tone.

"No, Tim. You and I will review, and I will give you instructions that I need you to follow, no matter what. Can you do that?" asked James.

"Obviously, yes," Tim replied, dropping his head.

"Tim, goin' on the trip means you will be very far away. You will have a different name, and your schedule will be mixed up. You will miss all your activities while you're gone," Tom said.

"Tom, I am not stupid!" Tim screamed. "What is my new name?" he asked James with a hungry look.

"What do you want it to be?" James asked.

"Tim Ferguson," Tim said instantly.

"I like the last name, but do you think we should change the first name, too?" James knew it was better to ask Tim than tell him.

"Fine," he replied with a roll of his eyes. "Jim Ferguson."

"We will call you Jim for the operation, but your documents will say James Walter Ferguson, and you will have to remember that if someone says 'James,' they are talking to you the same as if they say 'Jim,'" James said.

"What is your name, then?" Tim asked. "Obviously, it is confusing if we are both James."

"Grant Mathers," James answered. "Grant Adam Mathers. I'm the son of a rich multi-chain gas station owner. You will be my cousin on my mother's side, but also with a wealthy father who is an investment banker. No need to change our ages or birthdays. You will get all new documents for the trip from Melissa, and you'll have to stay in character the entire trip from the moment I pick you up until we're back."

James paused a moment to let Tim digest this. Then he continued, "I will have to ask you to speak as little as possible to others, and when others are around, as little as possible to me. Even pointing or making noises to get my attention will have to be minimal. You'll have to pretend you can't speak unless asked a very direct question by someone in security or something like that."

Tim nodded. He still looked anxious, but was no longer shaking. He took a deep breath and asked, "Obviously, I need a new background with degrees, addresses, pictures, contacts, friends, and things like this. When will I have those? Then there are the trip details we need to discuss, obviously. When are we doing that? When are we going? When will we be back?" He began to shake again.

Tom stepped forward. "Tim, are you sure you want to do this? It is very dangerous and difficult."

Tim paused and gathered himself. "Yes."

James smiled at Tim. "We will have all that information very soon. Melissa will need a day, or maybe two, to get us new documents. Then, I will set up the plans as quickly as I can, and tell you the moment I know. I hope to have all of that sorted in the next three days, but if I don't, I will at least give you an update by then. Sound good?"

"Yes, but what about cell phone numbers, and rooms, and packing? I will obviously need to know the exact place we are going, so I can pack the right clothes," said Tim.

"We will figure all that out in a few days. If I could answer it now for you, I would. We just have to go step-by-step," James said.

"Just like the song. I like that song." Tim began to hum to himself.

"Thanks, Tim. I'm glad you're coming along. It will be an adventure!" James said.

Tim nodded his head in time with the song he was humming. In many ways Tim was brilliant, and in others, he was like a child.

James clasped Tim on the shoulder as he got up to leave, and Tim reached up and touched his hand. Tim didn't care for physical contact, but he had learned that some touch was what 'normal' people did, and he tried hard to participate in 'normal' people activities.

Tom caught James in the hall. "Wait."

James stopped.

"You're creating a new ID for this trip? Won't they know who to expect or have some clue?" Tom asked.

"No," James said. He turned to walk down the hall.

"No? You're just gonna leave it at that?" asked Tom, apparently not following.

"You worry too much, Tom," James said. "Petior is former KGB, and went to the trouble of having a fake uncle write, and give me that note. His real uncle was there as the barman. Petior was protecting me, and gave me an out, remember? He wouldn't set an expectation with the connection by giving them a name. That way they couldn't try to find me. A new name is fine. Bye, Tom."

Tom stood there a second, then walked away.

# •Chapter Sixteen•

"Hi Melissa," James said, knocking before opening the door having just left Tom.

Melissa was an expert at identities. She could create anything he needed, and had the ability to get into most systems to set up verifiable information. She had some limitations on accessing the human resources files of certain companies, but she had over 100 she could use.

She was bright, pretty, and well liked by those she met. It was part of how she'd been able to build her network to establish full cover stories. She also had a mole on her left ear that had been James's inspiration in Aberdeen.

Melissa was an old classmate of Tim's from their high school days. She had introduced Tim to the group. She had always been a defender of his and saw him, in a sense, like a little brother, even though Tim was older.

She peered up from her screen, and smiled, as she rose and gave James a brief hug. "Well, if it isn't Mr. Enigma himself. You've been busy. How are you?" She stepped back and looked at him.

"Doing well. Thank you for all the help lately on the documents, and connections, and everything. You're always so awesome," James said. "How are you?"

"Doing okay myself. Got that software I was working on done finally, you know, for Steve. Also made a choice on a house finally. Now I just have to fill it. And most importantly, thank you, thank you, thank you again. Mom is recovering from the stroke. We would have lost her if it weren't for you. Still, don't know how you recognized that." Melissa looked back at her screen as she finished speaking.

She didn't like eye contact when personal things were discussed. This was one of the reasons she wasn't in field operations. She wore her heart on her sleeve.

"I'm just glad I happened to be there," James said with a smile, though that wasn't completely the truth of the situation. The complete truth of the situation was that he hadn't planned to attend Melissa's party at all, but had decided he needed to be there as the day had progressed. He'd dreamt of it months earlier. It was one his semi-cartoonish style dreams and one he remembered ahead of the event. This one showed Melissa's mother falling into a pool dead.

During the real party, she did fall, but not into the pool. James figured a second fall would take place, unless he found out the cause, or got her out of there.

"I just had a feeling. You know, she isn't exactly young. She'd eaten twenty minutes before and was happy and active. It wasn't too hot, and she didn't seem to trip, so I just thought it would be worth running her through some easy tests. That was the lifesaver. I didn't do anything anyone else couldn't have done" James said, trying to be modest.

"Yes, you did. I wouldn't have thought twice about her little spill. No one else paid attention to all that stuff. And they didn't ask her to smile or roll her tongue or even who the president was. You did. You saved her life by getting her to go to the hospital. That in and of itself is a miracle. She is so stubborn. Without you, Sammy wouldn't know his Grammy. And, you're the best, and our family is eternally grateful."

She turned her head the moment she finished speaking. James pretended not to notice, but the crack in her voice gave her away.

"How is your nephew?" he asked, changing the topic. "That kid is a bundle of energy just waiting to explode. Made me tired just watching him run around that day."

"Sammy never stops. He's even like that when he sleeps. It's like watching a dog having a dream, the way he moves and kicks. He stayed with us last weekend and crawled in bed with Isaac and me at some point. I didn't know he was there, and neither did Isaac, until he kicked us both awake at the same time!"

She and James laughed.

"Isaac and I woke up, and both said 'Ow' and 'What was that for?' and 'Are you okay?' at the same time. Sam just kept on sleeping. Isaac grumbled something, scooped him up, and flung him over his shoulder to take him back to the guest room. Two seconds later, I heard him go 'Ugh.' Apparently, Sammy left a big old drool on him. Crazy kid."

Melissa had been facing him during this funny recall and now looked James over more critically. "You sure you're okay? You look, I don't know, different somehow."

"I couldn't have gotten that ugly since you saw me last," James quipped.

"No, smart guy. I don't know what it is."

"Tired looking?" James offered.

"No. More alive, or happy, or a mix. I don't know." She shook her head briefly. "So, how can I help you?"

"And how do you know I didn't just stop by to say hello?" James smiled with raised eyebrows.

Melissa turned back to her screen. "Because you knocked as you came in, and asked me how everything was going. If it were just a social visit, it would have been you just coming in and asking how I was. You aren't the only observant person in the world who recognizes patterns to human nature."

James laughed and said, "Someone has taught you well."

"Blah, blah, blah. Don't break your arm patting yourself on the back. So what's up?" Melissa said, making it evident it was time to get to business.

"I need two identities made up," James stated.

"My God, you have more IDs than everyone else combined. How on earth can you need two at once?" Melissa asked, with a combination of sarcasm and disbelief.

"I need one as Grant Adam Mathers, and Tim will need one as James Walter Ferguson. Use our actual birthdates and..."

"Tim? Tim who? You can't mean Tim Smithfield, who I actually saw come in today." She looked aghast at James.

"The very same," James said calmly.

"No, you can't be serious." Melissa looked at James with incredulity. "Come on, you know Tim can't go into the field. I can't go into the field, let alone Tim. He'll fall apart. How the hell is Tom allowing this? And what are you going to tell the people at his residence?"

Melissa glared at James. She stood up, her tone changing. "Now I see why you got me in a good mood before introducing this. You can't do this, James, you simply can't."

James's expression didn't falter. He wasn't happy or sad or mad.

Melissa, on the other hand, went through a variety of emotions, ending with anger. *Slap!* Melissa struck James across the face, and he had to admit Melissa had a great left hook. Her finger caught his ear canal just right, increasing the pain for James. After a moment, she took two deep breaths and puffed both out. Then she sat down and began to access records.

"What are the names again?" Her voice was grim with disapproval.

James gave the names to her and the backgrounds he'd given Tim. He was so detailed that she knew he'd somehow gotten Tom to go along with it, but that didn't stop her from making it clear she disapproved, as they sat there going over potential background builds with educations and the like. As they finished up, James explained that it would be essential to hide all of the languages Tim could speak, and she should only list Spanish in his education transcripts.

"Are you sure? I mean, really sure? Have you considered the 51 percent values? I know you have great consideration for people, and place extreme value there, but we are talking about Tim. He's limited. I've seen him struggle so much. I know he wants to do this, and he's really good with you, but James, please." Melissa's finger hovered above the final keystroke that would send the information to the needed databases to generate fake documents overnight.

"I'm as sure about this as I can be. I will take every measure to protect Tim. You know that. As long as I do the set up properly, we'll be fine. This is an information retrieval mission, nothing more. I just need his language expertise. There is no one else who can do it, or I would take them in his place in a heartbeat."

She hit the key.

"Thank you, Melissa, for the help." James turned to leave.

"Hey," Melissa called. "I still think it's a bad idea and not sorry I slapped you."

"That's why I thanked you." James gave her a smile as he backed out the door, closing it with his left hand, and Melissa gave a deep sigh.

# •Chapter Seventeen•

The alarm sounded at 1:21 a.m. James clicked it off, and switched on the light. Two minutes later, he was calling the number on the instructions he'd gotten from Calum.

"Hiiooo," came the answering voice.

"I was calling about A S pirit," James said, slowly and clearly.

"Oh, you wish to talk about the A S pirit. This is a very hard vehicle to find. Lucky we are only people to have this, sir. We have to make arrangements for you to come get the vehicle. When will you come for the vehicle, sir?"

James caught on immediately. The time of day and the phrase meant the right person would get the call, and if, by chance, someone else did, it would look like he was calling about a Spirit brand car. Using the time of day a call was placed was a trick the group used.

"What is the earliest I could come with my partner to collect it?" James asked.

"When do you wish, sir? We will need to make sure we have all documents, and things for you to collect before your trip. You will, of course, have the $300,000 US dollars for the vehicle. It is a rare one, and hard to get, yes?"

"Yes, and as soon as possible. Is two weeks from tomorrow too soon?" James asked.

"If you get us the documents tomorrow, sir, we can do two weeks. Payment needs to be in appropriate bonds, yes?"

"Yes, that sounds great. What documents will you need? How can I send them best and to whom?" James asked.

"We will need evidence of the bonds, as well as a clear fax of passports, and travel itinerary, sir. I will get them, but you may call me Noi. I suggest a planned visit for two full days at least, and I am sure you want to leave some free time. Do you need a recommendation for lodging, or perhaps I arrange for you?"

"I appreciate you offering to make the arrangements. My friend who recommended your services to get this vehicle clearly knew what he was talking about. Thank you for all the help," said James.

"You are most welcome, sir. Are you ready for faxing numbers?" said Noi.

When the call ended, James went back to bed, but had a hard time getting back to sleep. He was worried about Tim. James would have to think of rules for him, and knew that Tim would take the rules rather literally.

The next day, after gathering the documents from Melissa, and the secured bonds, which Tom grumbled about, but Andy didn't bat an eye at, remarkably, James visited Tim. Tim lived in an assisted living community with other individuals who needed a bit of looking after, though they were high functioning. It wasn't an institution by any means. In fact, it was a pleasant little community. It had originally been built for the elderly, but had lost funding about halfway through development. The state had picked it up, finished the units, and was using it to better the lives of people who saw the world differently than most.

James went to the front gate, and asked for Scott, the coordinator for the house Tim lived in with two other roommates. Scott was, in a manner of speaking, Tim's caretaker. Scott was in his late thirties and easygoing, with a love for art and music. James felt this was why he was able to relate to the individuals in the facility so well. He looked at the world differently too. James suspected Scott used pot on occasion, though not when on duty.

Scott waved as James approached, causing Tim and his housemates, Dan and Byron, to look up and wave too. Their home, yellow with red shutters, sat on a corner lot, and you could see the street from the back area.

They were working in the garden with a roto-tiller. Scott was supervising, and the guys were enjoying expanding the garden they had started.

"Hey, dude, how you doing?" Scott said, in his slightly slow, mellow voice, much like a surfer's. "Long time no see."

"Doing really good, man. You guys got quite a project going on here." James shook hands with Scott, Dan, Byron, and then Tim, who had been taking his turn with the tiller.

"Yeah, good stuff. Trying to get that healthy green vibe going with my main dudes here. They have a real gift for it," Scott said.

Byron nodded vigorously. He tended to carry things out to the utmost, regardless of what he was doing. James always feared Byron would give himself whiplash if he kept nodding like that for too long.

Dan, who was musically gifted, had obsessive-compulsive disorder, and occasionally did things in increments of seven. James suspected the disorder was linked to music, because when he did act upon it, he had a rhythm to it.

"It's true, yes, we have grown all our peas for a year successfully, yes. We are very good at this, yes. We will do the others well, too," Dan answered, almost singing.

Tim chirped in. "It comes down to understanding the correct growing conditions, obviously, for the plant. We give each the right amount of water, and monitor the pH each day per plant section. Also, the rows and angles are set for the right amount of sunlight, so obviously we are good at this."

James smiled, "Maybe on my next visit I can have a fresh salad from your garden."

"Yeah, yeah, yeah, yeah, yeah, yeah, yeah," answered Dan, and Byron started nodding.

"I would like that," James assured them. "Please, don't let me interrupt what you're doing. Scott, while they work, can we talk a moment?"

James gestured to the white plastic chairs around a small table in the corner of the yard next to the house, and the two men sat down.

"How are things going here?" James began. "Everyone doing well?"

"Yeah, dude, everyone's good. Haven't had any issues. You know, just keep them on a schedule, and having things planned out keeps the residents happy. Especially these guys."

Scott pointed at the three guys. Tim was still doing his section, and Byron and Dan, walked on either side of the freshly tilled earth with aerator shoes on.

"I spoke with Tim a few days ago about going on a trip for a few days," James said. "He seemed excited, but I could use all the help I can get to get him ready.

We leave in two weeks. Do you think that's enough time?"

Though Scott didn't know everything about the group, he knew Tim did some secret undercover stuff. In fact, Tim had gotten Scott off a murder charge a few years before, because of his abilities to recognize patterns. Tim had successfully proven the blood splatter pattern at the crime scene meant the killer had been at least six inches taller than Scott, despite all the evidence indicating he had killed his ex-girlfriend. Tim was also the reason Scott had the job at the assisted living community, so Scott tended to be rather flexible with Tim's work with the group.

"Oh, is that what he's been so anxious about? He wouldn't say. Yeah, dude, that's cool. We can set up daily schedules, and review it with him each day until you leave. He should be okay, as long as we give him lots of details. Where are you going?" asked Scott.

It was a natural question to ask. After all, Scott did look after Tim, but Scott also knew he didn't have the authority to stop Tim from going if he wanted to go.

"We're taking a road trip. I thought he'd enjoy seeing how farmers work in cornfields, and I have a business meeting in Indiana, near Evansville," said James.

"Whadda you going to do with Tim during the business meeting? You know how he likes to voice his thoughts," Scott said.

"I could use your help on that," James answered. "I need to make sure he doesn't do that, if you know what I mean. He's super excited to go on this trip, and I know you're always encouraging them to try new things. I think he can do it, but he'll need some rules to help drive his behavior."

The guys shut off the tiller, but Dan wanted to take a turn, and finish the last part.

"Dan, keep it upright when you start it, dude. That's it," called Scott. "Yeah, we can work that out," he continued. "It's only like an hour, right? All we should have to say is during the visit he shouldn't talk, needs to sit still, and pretend he's asleep, while keeping his eyes open, and being awake."

"That's just it. I don't mind if he speaks if someone asks him something. You know, I want this to be a trip where he feels like 'normal' people, as he puts it. If someone introduces themselves or whatever, I don't want Tim to just zombie out," said James.

"Oh yeah, good point. This will take some work. Let's make a small list of do's and don'ts. Then we can work on adding specifics. Dan and Byron will help as actors. They did really well in Hamlet last year," Scott said.

"Okay, I have a few things written down already." James pulled a small list from his pocket, and handed it to Scott.

"Nice, dude. Good start. I like the phrasing. *'If an adult asks you a specific question, smile and try to answer yes or no. Then, if you can't answer yes or no, just give a simple answer, as you would try to give someone who is seven years old.'* He does well with kids. That should be easy for him to relate to."

Twenty minutes later, when the guys were finishing up in the garden, James and Scott walked toward them.

"Hey dudes, what do you think if we do a play-acting exercise?" Scott asked just as James's phone rang.

It was Carissa.

"Can you explain the idea while I take this call?" James asked.

"No problem, dude," replied Scott.

James walked away as he answered the phone. "Hi! How are you, Risa?" His slight Scottish accent was in full swing.

"I'm doing just fine, thanks. How's you, John?" she asked in a cheery manner.

James imagined her smile as she spoke. "A lot better, now that I'm talking to you again," he said, and immediately thought, *Lame!*

"Oh, well, that is sweet, Love. That makes me smile, then. I was just calling ta see what was happening with your day. Has it been good?" Carissa asked.

"Well, today has been good. I'm just visiting with some friends at the moment, and one is a co-worker, who will be going on a trip with me whilst I'm traveling, you know, and just going over some details in the back garden here. The rest of the day was just getting some reports and stuff on the market together," James said. "What did you do today?"

"Oh, I won't keep you from your visit, you know. I just fancied a small chat ta talk with ya," Carissa said quickly.

"No, honest, it's okay. Please tell me about your day. I would really love to hear about it," James said, with such sincerity it all but gushed from him.

"Right, then. Well, I actually got a small bit of good news today. Remember that promotion we discussed? Well, they said that I am up for it now that I finished at university, so I will be moving to Aberdeen," she said proudly.

"Risa, that is brilliant. Well done! I'm sure they've finally started to see what I saw from the first moments," James said.

"Oh? What is that now? A greetin' lass having a bad hair day that has a decent chest?" She started laughing. So did James, though he made a mental note to look up what she meant by 'greeting,' as it sounded like she used it to mean crying. It turned out, she did.

"Those are some fair attributes, you have to admit, yeah?" James asked playfully.

Still chuckling, she said, "Too cute, Love, but thanks, that was very nice. Got ta run a bit with Judy, a friend of mine that I may not have mentioned before. She is a good girl, and does a lot of sport. She should have been a boy, and kicked everyone's behind. Anyhow, we had a run, and then just finished supper. Just made a pizza is all, but now she has dish duty, since I prepared everything whilst she showered, you know."

"Sounds like a fair day, then," James said. "So what kind of pizza did you make?"

"Just a ham, and onion, and cheese pizza. Nothing special. Why, you hungry?" she asked.

"No, I'm just trying to judge your culinary skills, and if it's worth having dish duty for your level," James replied.

Laughing, Carissa said, "Cheeky, well played, sir. So, listen, I'm going ta let you go because you're having a visit, and I have no idea how expensive this call is going ta be, but it was worth just ta hear ya."

"Definitely. And it will be my turn to call you next," James said.

"That it is, and you best, you know," Carissa said.

"Talk soon. Bye, Risa," James said.

"Yeah, bye-bye now, Love," said Carissa.

Before she could hang up, James heard a distant female voice say, "Who are you calling 'Love'?"

James was pretty sure she hadn't told her friends about him yet, but it seemed like the cat was out of the bag now. James stood there a moment, enjoying the thought, before going back to the guys.

As he reached them, he found them all eagerly awaiting his return.

"Scott has told us the plan. This is going to be great. Dan is already thinking of music we could write for the play," Byron said, while Dan nodded.

James glanced at Scott, who said, "Hold on. Remember, it's just an acting thing, not a full play."

"Yeah, but plays that don't have music as part of the play can still have music, can't they?" Dan said, slightly crestfallen.

"Obviously, yes, of course," Tim said.

"Dan, how about you come up with some music, and after the last rehearsal we can add it, and see how it goes. I think your music is always so good. It might make the play look bad in comparison," James said quickly.

"Yes, it's true. I've written good pieces. They have been played at the best places in the world. By the best players in the world. They only play the best. It is very good. Yeah, I see what you mean," Dan said, almost singing again.

Scott whispered, "Nicely done, dude."

James nodded. *Everyone falls to flattery,* he thought.

"So when do we get the script?" Byron asked.

"Script? Uhh, tomorrow," James said.

"But today, you visited unplanned, you know. To-morrow doesn't have a visit scheduled either. That is very unusual. Ver..." Dan began.

"Dan, it's okay for the plan to change sometimes." Tim was shaking slightly as he said this. "We can put it on the schedule now for the next two weeks. What time will we start, and what time will we end each day? Of course, we will need to cancel other things. Margaret will..."

Byron started to shake his head, and James spoke up. "Byron and Dan, what if we start rehearsal in a week? Get it on the schedule properly, but still get you a script tomorrow to learn?" James said, hoping this would help calm Tim too.

Byron started nodding, as did Dan and Tim.

"That settles it then," James said, and everyone was smiling.

Scott and James worked out a schedule that didn't interfere with daily things, such as meals, before James set off. He was encouraged by Tim's efforts to support the idea.

James then called a friend in the group on his way back home. Sharon was a good writer, and worked for a major network for late night news. She was familiar with creating scripts based on boundaries with short notice, so James filled her in on what he needed.

The next weeks passed with ease. The guys learned their parts, and Tim learned to stick to his rules in a variety of situations. It was almost time for the real test. The real life adventure that was unpredictable, and not surrounded by friends. The test would be hard for Tim, and it would involve people who weren't like him. But in his heart, those were the people Tim wanted to be like.

# •Chapter Eighteen•

Two days before James and Tim were set to leave, Daen called James.

"Hello?" answered James.

"James, man, what ya doing?" came a serious sounding Daen.

"I'm driving home from work. Why? What's up?" asked James.

"Can you come down to 7995 Tuckerman Lane in Rockville, Maryland? Zip code is 20854. Just take Interstate 270 toward Washington, DC. I'll meet you there," said Daen.

"What? I mean, yeah, do you need me there now? That is a good 3.5-hour drive." James was confused but trusted Daen. If he said he needed help, James would be there.

"As fast as you can get here, but yeah man, I really need your help tonight. Something came up, and I would, you know, feel better with backup on this. It involves a weapons dealer," Daen said, using a serious tone.

"You got it. Anything I need to pick up?" asked James.

"No, I have everything the two of us need. Thanks," and Daen hung up.

James made it home about ten minutes later. He printed out some directions and grabbed some clothes.

He told his parents he was going to be out playing night basketball with his friends and may stay over at John's.

Three and a half hours later, James parked near a CVS in the shopping plaza that matched the address Daen gave him. He was about to get out and switch license plates, when a tapping on his window made him jump. It was Daen.

Daen opened James's car door and said, "Your car will be safe here, let's go."

They walked a few spaces over, and jumped into a 1991 New Yorker town car, with tinted windows and oversize wheels.

The moment they got onto Interstate 270 heading South, Daen started to talk. "Look, man, I appreciate you coming down, and without really any notice. I think I have tracked down a weapon's dealer that has been operating for a long time. His name is Sylvester Craig. I got a write up of him in the equipment bag in the back seat there if you want to read it."

Daen didn't continue to talk, so James took the hint, and reached into the back seat to get the folder. The equipment bag was full of different scanners, laser sound monitors, microphone packs, a camera with zoom lens, a taser, a few pistols, flashlights, smoke bombs, and a few other things.

James grabbed the folder and began reading, just as they started on Interstate 495 East. It turned out that Daen had been researching this guy for a while, though James never recalled him talking about it. He had almost a year of notes in the back pages of the dossier, but the important information was on the front page.

Apparently, Sylvester specialized in getting ghost guns, which were untraceable firearms. The remarkable thing was, according to the file, he was a one-stop shop. That meant he was the buyer, serial number remover, parts exchanger, and seller. It cut down on the number of people that could give him up if they got busted, but if he got busted, he was going away for life.

He ran his operations in some of the rougher neighborhoods of Washington, D.C. It looked like he was the preferred dealer in Washington Highlands, Columbia Heights, Mount Pleasant, Park View, and Brentwood. There were statistics listed for each area by the number of armed robberies, homicides and other acts.

James put the file on his lap. "So what is the plan for tonight Daen?"

Daen drove on for a few moments before saying, "I need to get him on tape. He is slick, but I need to have something convincing. Something that is beyond a shadow of a doubt. I need this to stick. I know it's him, and need to prove it."

Daen sounded like he was almost talking to himself as he said all of this. James thought, *I wonder if that is what I sound like sometimes.* However, he didn't press Daen on why he sounded so determined to bring down Sylvester.

"Right, well, what do you want me to do tonight? Or am I just an extra set of eyes and ears? Given the neighborhoods we are going into, I imagine that's why you wanted me," asked James.

"Yes," was all Daen said.

James was feeling uneasy. "You alright? You seem almost pissed off?"

"Sorry, man. I am just really focused on this tonight, and don't feel like talking much. It isn't you, and

I do appreciate you coming down tonight, man, really," said Daen, without unlocking his eyes from the road.

"Alright, final question then. Why are we taking this big, slow, dressed up old man's car? If things go wrong, we need to get out quickly, don't we? I mean, I know you are a phenomenal driver and all, but this thing won't perform like we need it to in that situation will it?" questioned James.

Daen had taught James some high-speed driving and maneuvering techniques. In the course of their training as recruits, Daen had demonstrated some of his talents during an exercise that had impressed James. Though, in that particular exercise, James used a clever trick to win the event.

"It'll blend in. It's one of the most common cars you'll see tonight. Plus, the tinted windows will hide the fact that we're in the car, unless they're looking through the windshield. You'll be sitting in the back, so they don't see me sitting with a white boy, and instantly assume we are cops," Daen said.

"Fair enough," replied James.

They drove to the Brentwood area, and parked about a third of the way down a street that had triplex housing on both sides. The narrow street had a lot of potential objects around it to hit as he backed into the spot.

James climbed over the seats, and into the back asking, "Okay, what is the game plan?"

"Now we wait. His car isn't here yet, but the birds have already flown the coup, so he must be on his way," said Daen.

"I am assuming you mean the neighborhood corner watchers. I was wondering why there seemed to be no one out. Are there any rooftops bird's nest that we might need to worry about?" asked James.

"Not tonight. Sylvester won't do business if watchers are out. He deals with as few people as possible. Whoever he is dealin' with has to have the area cleared up for 30 minutes before, and 30 minutes after they meet. Transactions always take place in the car. It reduces the risk of being recorded. He even runs a bug detector over them to make sure they aren't wearing a wire. Hand me the laser monitor please, man," said Daen, his eyes fixed on the end of the street.

The laser monitor measured vibrations on glass. When people speak in a vehicle, it is as if they were speaking in a glass bowl. The vibrations from their voices can be detected and recorded. The recording could then be analyzed, and synthesized, into the actual conversation. James and Daen won't be able to talk while using the laser monitor, as their voices would cause interference.

James handed Daen the device while putting on the headphones. He thought it would be less conspicuous if he had the headphones on as people couldn't see him.

"Gimme the headphones too, man. I want to hear this go down, but keep the recorder back there. I just need you to keep your eyes open," said Daen.

James handed up the headphones and asked, "Do you have binoculars in this bag? I don't see any, and I don't want to turn on any lights."

"Check the side pocket," said Daen.

They sat there for about another ten minutes without any activity, besides a couple that walked past the end of the street walking a dog, but had no way of seeing them in the car. Then Sylvester arrived.

He pulled up in a Camry that was as average as could be. It wasn't new or flashy, and nothing about it looked suspicious. The car parked on the other side of the street from Daen and James, before the driver turned off the engine. Maybe a minute later, a slender man walked out of the house a door down from where the Camry parked, and got in the passenger side.

"Okay, man, here we go. Keep your eyes open," said Daen.

James was diligently watching as best he could. He was trying not to move too much, so that he didn't cause sound, while Daen used the laser monitor. This went on for about three minutes before Daen said, "Shit. Something ain't right. They aren't giving me what I need to hear."

James stayed quiet but was wondering what was going on. He started to watch the Camry, but caught himself, and began to watch actively around them again.

"Damn, man," said Daen.

The two men got out of the Camry, and started to walk inside the home the slender man had come out of. Daen took off the headphones, and set down the laser monitor. He sighed. "This isn't what I needed. Do you think the laser monitor will work on the windows of that place?"

"No, it won't. Not unless you are talking directly to the pane of glass. What now, just calling it for the night?" asked James.

"Can't man, I need to do this tonight. Hand me a pistol, and the recorder that is in the other side pouch of that bag," said Daen, spinning around to face James.

"Dude, are you sure? This isn't a controlled environment, and I'm..."

"You mean like Russia? Was that a controllable environment? Just back me up. Damn!" Daen was clearly frustrated.

"Okay, sorry. Here," said James, handing him the gun and a recorder.

Daen spun around, and just as he opened the door, he said, "Stay here man. I'm gonna go in through that top window using that ladder the neighbor has out. Just make sure no one sees me, or comes up on me with that ladder up."

"Hey, take this too," said James handing him a microphone pack, while putting on the other one.

Daen looked at it, but hooked it up as he got out. "Hear me?"

"Yeah, I got ya," said James.

Daen crossed the street swiftly, moved the ladder into position, and climbed up onto the porch roof. He slipped through the window and said, "Ow, shit."

"You alright?" asked James quickly.

"Yeah, man, I'm fine. This is the bathroom, and I thought the toilet was a counter, and my hand went into the bowl," said Daen.

James wanted to laugh, but didn't out of respect for his friend. "Can you hear them?"

"Not with you talking in my ear. I'll be fine, just stay there, and keep an eye out if anyone else comes up to the house," Daen snapped at him.

James heard some faint sounds like the bass on a car stereo, but then he heard a door squeak, and the bathroom light came on. Sylvester had come in.

"What the fuck you doin' here mother fucker?" asked Sylvester.

"Look, man, I don't want any trouble, I just..." Daen started.

"You just what? What the fuck is this shit? I told you last time to back the fuck off!" said Sylvester aggressively. James saw Sylvester grab hold of Daen by the neck. When he did that he found the microphone pack. "What in the fuck? You fucking wearing a wire? You little son of a bitch!"

"Wait, no it isn't..." was all that James heard from Daen before it went dead. Sylvester apparently had taken it off him.

James wasn't sure what was happening now that he lost audio. From what he could see visually, Daen was being manhandled. Sylvester dragged him out of the bathroom, and into the bedroom that was next door. James was watching through the bedroom window now. Daen freed himself from Sylvester, and the two men separated. They appeared to be arguing. James was confused as Daen should be able to take this man in a fight, but he wasn't engaging him so he could get out.

Through the bathroom window, he saw the slender man's head, then torso, and then body appear in the hallway. He was coming up the stairs.

James didn't even think. He got out of the car, sprinted to the ladder, and climbed as quietly as he could. He could hear the three men arguing, but nothing was making sense. He successfully climbed in through the bathroom window, and could hear more clearly now.

"I don't know how to make this clearer. You got nothing here. Nothing to do with us," shouted Sylvester.

"Hey, we ain't doing this in my house man," said the slender man.

"I don't see why you just won't let me do it. What could it hurt? I don't want anything from you, or from you. Just want..." said Daen, before his voice was muffled like his mouth was covered.

James sprung around the corner. He saw that the slender man had grabbed hold of Daen from behind, and he was covering his mouth. James grabbed the man by the back of his belt. This surprise attack did get him to release Daen.

James fell backward, bringing his knees to his chest, so that he could roll on his back. He brought the slender man with him. The slender man's back hit the bottom of James's feet. As the men rocked backward as one, James kicked out sending the slender man over his head, and tumbling down the stairs.

"Who in the hell is this?" shouted Sylvester, just as James kicked.

"Nooo!" scream Daen, and a single gunshot rang out followed by two loud crashes. One came from the bottom of the stairs, and one from inside the bedroom.

James got to his feet to see Sylvester lying on top of Daen. Sylvester was shaking, but Daen wasn't moving. He rolled Sylvester off Daen, who was covered in blood, but Sylvester didn't resist or point his gun at James. A horrid gurgling sound was coming from Sylvester. His breathing sounded like a stuck air pump. Daen got to his hands and knees as James looked down at Sylvester.

The gun shoot had gone through Sylvester's neck just at the collarbone.

"Help him, please!" cried Daen.

At this, James heard a low bubbling noise, and then the death rattle. It was the unmistakable sound of the lungs completely emptying all the air from the body.

This particular death rattle was accompanied by blood spurting out, and made it sound even more eerie.

James bent down to try, but before he could even apply pressure to the wound, it was obvious Sylvester was dead. Daen knew it too. He picked up Sylvester's head, and cradled it to his chest, hugging him.

James could see the exit wound just at the base of the skull. The bullet had ripped the whole way through the neck before hitting the spinal cord and exiting.

Sounds were coming from downstairs. The slender man was starting to stir.

"We have to go," said James, but Daen was crying, and still holding Sylvester.

The slender man appeared and said, "No, no, no, no!"

He joined Daen on the floor. Then James saw it. They were related. The slender man and Daen could easily be brothers, while Sylvester could be their father. Aside from Sylvester being white, the facial features of the three men were extremely similar.

It sounded like some people were on the street, and James was starting to think about the cops coming.

"What the hell, man? You couldn't just leave it alone could ya? He was just starting to accept me as a son because of the guns. He would have came around to you. Why didn't you just chill the fuck out and leave it alone?" screamed the slender man through tears.

James thought he understood. Sylvester had been absent from both of his son's lives. Daen had tracked him down, but Sylvester was going slowly. He had just started to build a relationship with the slender man. The brothers knew of each other, and apparently had accepted one another. James suspected that they were only half brothers.

"Leave. Leave now. Just get out. I don't want to know or see you again. Get out of my house, and you never show your face in this hood again. And go to hell while you're at it," said the slender man, starting to become angry.

"It was an accident. He went to shoot my friend, and I stopped him, and it went off," Daen started to explain.

"I ain't blind bitch, just leave before I take that gun, and shoot you myself fucker," said the slender man, with a building rage.

James grabbed Daen, and got him to his feet. He pulled him through the bedroom door, and they went down the steps. As they walked outside, there were a few people out, and a lot of people looking out of their windows. James opened the passenger side door as Daen got into the driver's side and started the car.

The slender man came out of his door and screamed, "Hit them fools until they Swiss cheese!"

Daen shifted into gear and hit the gas. Bullets started flying at the car. James and Daen ducked down as two shots hit the trunk. Daen was going as fast as he could. His expert driving skills came into play as he fishtailed around the corner without hitting anything or slowing down. He raced ahead, and ran a red light. Another driver barely tapped the tail end of their car as they speed on. For a moment it felt like Daen was losing control of the car, but he countered perfectly.

"You alright?" asked James.

"Yeah, man," Daen answered.

"Well, how about you slow down then before we get hurt or hurt someone else. They aren't going to be able to hit us any longer," said James in a calm tone, though his adrenaline was pumping.

Daen did slow down. It was as if he hadn't been aware of what he was doing, but just doing it.

"Do you want me to drive?" asked James.

Daen shook his head. "No, I feel better driving. Look, man, I, I don't even know what to say."

"I screwed up. If I had just done what you told me to, and stay in the car, none of this would have happened. I am sorry Daen. I should have just trusted you knew what you were doing, and just did what you told me to," said James with his head down, meaning every word.

"No, man. I should have been honest with you. I mean I was, he was a weapons dealer, but that wasn't what I needed you for. I needed you tonight to be the cop. I was trying to set him, and my brother up to get a DNA test. I was going to blackmail him to do the test for both of us. But then in the car, he started to admit to being my half brother Davis's father. Then he said there was no way I was his son. That's when they went inside the house. I'm sorry man, I should have just leveled with you, but I thought that plan would work. I know he was getting ready to jump the country too. He thought the police were starting to get onto him, but it was just me," said Daen, then, he started to cry again silently.

James didn't know what to say. Daen hadn't said much about his childhood, but that was typical of the group members. No one disclosed much, as it was a mechanism to protect themselves, and stay semi-anonymous.

The rest of the car ride was quiet. Reaching James's car, he gave Daen his basketball clothes, so he could change out of the blood-soaked ones he had on.

Daen explained, even before James asked, that his brother's neighborhood would take care of the body. They wouldn't bring the cops in for that, and risk Davis getting blamed for Sylvester's death, when it was clear a self-defense issue. James wasn't feeling overly confident about this, until Daen reminded him of the statistics he'd just read about the crime in that area, and how many crimes went unsolved. He decided to follow Daen's lead. Besides that, they both could come up with an alibi by calling the group if they needed it.

"He was never around when I was growing up. It was just Momma and me. If I am being honest, man, he was a terrible person. I don't know. Maybe this is for the best. I think, I just wanted him to admit he was my dad, like so I could have that. That is all I wanted from him," said Daen, with his head down.

James waited to speak. He wanted to make sure Daen knew he was listening, and there for him. "Daen, that shirt can be tested. It has his blood. Maybe you could use that to help repair things with Davis."

"Yeah, man. You're right." Daen looked up at James, and gave him a weak smile. "Thanks for saying that. I'm not sure I would have thought about it until it was too late. I was going to just torch it with the car." Daen seemed to be recovering a little more as he said, "Thanks for coming tonight, and sorry for all this bull-shit. It wasn't supposed to go down like that, but thanks for having my back."

After Daen had changed, they hugged briefly and shook hands. They decided not speak about it again unless they had to. Daen felt it was best if they treated it as if it never happened. It would be difficult for both of them to do so, but James did have a pressing matter with Tim in two days that he needed to focus on.

# •Chapter Nineteen•

James and Tim were sitting in the airport, waiting for the announcement of their flight, and Tim was clearly nervous.

"I researched this, and looked at it from each airline. I do not see what this extra trip accomplishes. Why do we need an extra day? When are we getting there? What if the tomatoes need watering, and Byron or Dan forget?"

James wondered if the whole trip was going to be this way, despite all the preparation that had gone into getting Tim ready.

"Tim, we are following the plan. We are on schedule. The extra trip to New York City is to verify the itinerary we provided to our contact, and to make our backgrounds more valid. Remember, to make it believable, we need to make it real." This was the fifth time in the last two hours James had explained this.

"If that is true, why do you keep breaking the rules? You set the rules. The rules need to be followed, right?" Tim started to shake a bit. "We need to make the whole thing real. The whole thing, but you aren't following the rules, so how do I know what rules should be followed?"

"Tim," James said, with a bit more force in his tone, but not in volume, "What rules am I breaking?"

Tim's shaking intensified. "You said once we start, we follow the rules. You keep calling me Tim. Isn't my name Jim for the trip? What about that? I... I... I..."

"You're right. Very right, sorry. We will follow the rules, Jim," James said, catching Tim's eye.

Tim stopped shaking. He sat up and was quiet.

*Really?* James thought, *That's what's been wrong this whole time?*

James chastised himself for the slip-up. Tim was right. He'd made the error. This was going to be harder than he thought. He wanted to focus on keeping Tim safe, not on the minor issues, and the task of playing nanny. However, for this operation to go properly, he'd have to do what was necessary, and more or less baby-sit Tim.

James was still thinking about Daen, and the incident with his father. It was distracting him, and he needed to focus.

"U.S. Airways Flight 3957 is now boarding," came a voice over the speakers in the airport.

"Okay, Jim, that's our flight. Ready to go?" James asked.

"Why, yes, of course!" Tim answered in a voice that sounded like he was a pompous actor out of a Monty Python movie. He had assumed this voice consistently over the last few days. Scott had thought it was out of nerves, but apparently, that was what Jim sounded like in Tim's mind.

They found their seats and buckled in. As the other passengers settled themselves, Tim pulled a coloring book, and crayons out of his backpack.

"Jim, where did you get those?" James asked, in a low voice.

"They are allowed and I like them," Tim answered rather loudly, with some attitude in his voice. "In the van, we have Stow-n-go tables, and can use them. This is just like the van, and it's not against the rules, Grant."

James paused a moment, his brain racing. "You're right," he said. He sat back. It wouldn't be worth the fight or potential scene to argue. Then he remembered the takeoff and landing, and carefully chose his words. "Jim, you'll have to put them away for a short time during takeoff, and then again when we land. You'll be able to use..."

"Obviously, that is the rule," Tim said, handing James the safety card in the seat pocket, and pointing to a picture.

*Damn. I should have made Tim a set of flashcards with pictures. Apparently, that solves everything,* thought James to himself.

Aside from Tim getting overly excited about having a Coke on the plane with a small bag of pretzels, the rest of the short flight went well. Thankfully, the airport hotel was a mirror image of the picture they'd seen in the magazine on the plane. Tim drew four pictures of what he thought the rest would look like, but he wouldn't show James until they had checked in.

"Jim, this is an incredible drawing you've made of the lobby." James stood at the window in the room they were sharing, gazing with astonishment at Tim's pictures. "How'd you know what the 360-degree view would be like from just one side of the lobby in that picture?"

"The magazine had an outside and inside picture. I see it, and draw it from my internal eyes. It's all there. You just have to see."

Tim was trying to organize his bathroom supplies, and seemed to be confused by the toiletries already there. James explained that it was okay for these toiletries to be there. Tim didn't seem to agree, and he put them in a bag to give to Byron and Dan as a present. He kept the mouthwash out of the bag, as it was a 'cool looking' color.

A short while later, James discovered that Tim snored. Correction. It wasn't just a snore, it was a snore with a gargling sound. James sighed. He was a poor sleeper, to begin with, so this was going to be a long night, and an even longer trip than he'd expected since he didn't sleep on planes.

That night he dreamt of Daen, and how his father died. It was if his subconscious was trying to point out his mistakes. Throughout the dream, he kept hearing the death rattle sound that Sylvester made. Later that day, James would attribute that to Tim's snoring.

"The lights aren't on. The lights aren't on. The lights are not on!"

James's eyes snapped open, "What's wrong?" he asked.

"The lights aren't on. Why aren't the lights on? It's time to get up, and the lights should be on." Tim was speaking fast.

"Right. One second," James fought the entanglement of blankets and pillows for a moment, before freeing his right hand, and turning on the lights. He saw the clock flashing 6 a.m. Tim's internal clock was apparently set for that time, and the lights in his room were probably set to automatically turn on then too. James sat up, and ran his fingers through his hair.

"Oh, wait, what time does Jim get up, we didn't discuss that?" Tim peered at James while sitting upright in bed with a perfectly contented expression on his face.

James chuckled a little.

"What's so funny? Are you going to answer me on what time Jim, I mean me, I mean I... I... I..." Tim began to shake.

"Jim gets up when he needs to," James said. "He doesn't have to have the lights on. Jim doesn't have to eat at the same time each day. He eats when he's hungry, or can eat. He showers if, and when he can, or wants to. Jim doesn't shake, or talk fast when he's scared, or nervous, or unsure. He sits still and smiles. Until we get back to the house with Dan and Byron, you're Jim." James said this with a deadpan voice, looking right into Tim's face.

Tim stopped shaking, and adopted the voice he seemed to have created for his alter ego. "We have to get going then. I'm hungry, and want breakfast, but I want a shower first." He gave a small shudder and stopped. He got up with a smile, and went to take a shower.

The rest of the morning went perfectly well. Tim mostly smiled. Aside from checking his watch repeatedly, he acted perfectly normal. They left the hotel, and boarded the plane for the first leg of the journey without any major issues surfacing. In fact, the only problem was when the flight attendant had asked what Tim wanted to eat.

"I'm not hungry yet. I would like to eat in about fifteen minutes," Tim said to the stewardess.

James turned to look at him, and let out a small sigh.

"The chicken pasta, please," said Tim, winking at the stewardess. He made a small discrete face at James as she looked away. The flight attendant handed him a tray across James's body and waited, but James was lost in thought, wondering what just happened. "She is waiting to hear what you want, dumb-dumb," Tim said, organizing his tray of food.

"The s-s-same, thanks," stutter James. The stewardess gave James a slight smile, and handed him a tray. James looked back at Tim, and tossed his hands up as if to say, "What was all that?"

Tim smiled slyly. "I sometimes have to eat when I can. It is the rules."

"Obviously," James said, and they both laughed.

In Istanbul, Jim had to have a hat, as apparently, that was his thing according to Tim. After finding the moneychanger, they got a hat, and caught the second flight.

The human body had always amazed James, and the control the brain had on it. Tim functioned perfectly well as Jim. He even caught and corrected small glitches he occasionally made. It was a little scary to see how efficiently he was able to make the switch, but it was a little comforting too.

Tim liked the baggage claim area in Osh. "You can see how it works at some points. Very cool," he commented.

It was an older conveyor system, and very different from more modern ones seen in the US, or in newer airports.

James stepped closer to Tim to explain that fact. He finished with, "I still prefer my bags to be handled by the valet." He'd figured out that Tim, as Jim, was pretending to be a spoiled rich kid.

"Indeed," said Tim. He started moving in what he apparently thought were 'rich people' motions. As long as he was consistent, that was fine. In fact, had the situation not been what it was, his accentuated motions would have been rather funny.

# •Chapter Twenty•

They got through customs easily, walked outside, and saw a number of individuals standing around with signs. There was a man in a suit holding a sign that said *Ferguson/Mathers.* James waved at him.

The man spoke, "I am Noi. My car is this way, sirs."

Noi led them to a large black SUV that had a driver waiting for them. The interior had soft, white leather, and the windows were tinted. The center consol was a mini-bar that had a selection of high-end magazines.

Noi sat in the front passenger seat, and turned to engage them in conversation as the driver pulled away. "All of the arrangements for your stay are made based on the itinerary," he said in a professional tone as if he were a concierge. "Tomorrow, we will depart very early at 6 in the a.m., as we have a long drive, sirs. Please dress comfortably, but you may wish to bring a coat. We will have a vehicle exchange for the last part of the journey that will be a slightly less comfortable ride. Please feel free to help yourself to the refreshments in front of you, sirs."

He gave them a wide grin, exposing a gold tooth, among a lot of yellow teeth. He also had a rather dehydrated, ashy look despite his expensive clothes, which showed hints of yellow at the brim of the collar. He was a heavy smoker, judging by his rather pungent and honestly gross smell.

He continued in his slightly annoying voice, "If it is acceptable, sirs, we will need to make a stop at my office. I apologize for this, as I know that you are tired from your travels, but it is needed, please. We can take care of the transaction and paperwork, yes?"

James said, "That is fine," as Tim was happily drinking another Coke. After a quick look at James, Tim nodded too.

The office turned out to be a car dealership. This was, by far, the leading car dealership for a significant distance around the area, and it offered a variety of high-priced vehicles. As they drove around the lot, James noticed several cars in the back that didn't seem to fit with the rest. They were newer vehicles, but lower end cars. Then, James saw a Spirit with writing on the windshield. The left side said, 'SOLD' in English, and the right side appeared to be in Russian.

Immediately to the right of the Spirit was a large fenced area, with other vehicles that didn't appear to belong. James didn't have a clear view, but they looked to be older sport utility vehicles, some of which had been used by the military force, judging by the paint.

Noi took them to his office, located at the back of the building, and down a long hallway. The door to the hallway had a key code security system, and mounted cameras. The hallway itself had barren stone walls, a low ceiling of perhaps two meters, and an unusual floor that was a mix of tile for about a meter, and then floorboards. This pattern repeated itself for the length of the hall. The baseboards along the hallway had notches as each floor type alternated.

The sound of their footsteps echoed loudly as they walked on the tile, and the floor creaked when they walked on the boards. The creaking reminded James of Roman's place. He allowed his eyes to follow the baseboards, and suspected sensors were hidden at the notches.

After graciously ushering James and Tim into his surprisingly lavish office, Noi shut the door and hit a button. Locks could be heard clicking into place, and a small monitor illuminated on Noi's desk that James and Tim couldn't see.

"May I offer you refreshment, or perhaps fresh fruit?" Noi asked, walking toward a bar area.

Before Noi finished the word fruit, James spoke. "Thank you, Mr. Rasa, but no, we are fine."

James deliberately reached into his coat pocket, and removed a few documents and the bonds. Tim also removed his documents. One of the rules was for Tim to do whatever James did when it came to showing documents. Another, wasn't to accept food or drinks if James had refused them, and didn't turn to ask Tim if he wanted some. The expectations set by the rules were working great so far.

Noi gave his yellow smile, and sat at his desk. Looking in a drawer, he found his tobacco and a lighter.

Tim spoke up in his rich person voice. "Please do not smoke near me. It's rather gross and poor for your health. And it's stinky."

James didn't visibly react, but his insides froze for a split second.

"Very sorry, sir. Very sorry. Please, I mean no disrespect, and yes, I will not smoke," Noi said quickly. "Thank you for reminding me of manners to you, sirs."

James was relieved as he thought, *This might just work out perfectly. If these people are used to being spoken down to by rich jerks, then Tim's small quirks will be easily dismissed.*

They sat for a moment as Noi gathered two sets of documents. They were the faxes of the passports James had previously sent.

"Please, sirs, is this you?" he asked.

"Yes," James said.

"Obviously," said Tim.

James moved his right hand to Tim's knee. They had worked out a signal of James tapping his knee with three quick, but light taps, as a signal to be quiet unless very directly, by name, asked a question.

Noi smiled, held out his hands, and said, "Yes, sirs. May I, please see the originals?"

They handed him the documents. He compared them, made a note on a piece of paper that they couldn't see, and scanned them before handing them back.

"Please, sirs, come with me," he said.

He had them stand against the far left wall before taking profile pictures of them. As they finished, he took them to a countertop near the bar, and slid a portion of the counter back to reveal a fingerprinting station.

Luckily, this older method of fingerprinting would take days, if not weeks to verify. Tim's prints could link him to the assisted living institution, and reveal his true identity. Though the probability of this group being able to access that information was minuscule, as it wasn't part of a database even accessible by agencies in the US. As for him, he was wearing a false set of fingertips, so it wasn't a problem.

Tim had wanted a new appearance like James, but Tim didn't like the feeling of makeup, scars, or contacts, so they'd given him some highlights in his hair like he'd seen in a movie. It didn't change his appearance much, but it made Tim feel like it did.

James had made his own ears appear pushed out, and put putty across the bridge of his nose to make it appear wider, and his eyes appear closer together. He wore contacts to give himself brown eyes, and added a burn type scar to cover the back of his right hand and wrist.

Noi provided rubbing alcohol to help remove the ink, and they washed up in the sink to the right of the bar. After getting cleaned up, they returned to their seats.

"Please, now the bond payment for the 'car' sirs." Noi used his hands to make the symbol of quotation marks like Tariq did.

James presented him with the bonds, deciding he must watch a lot of American TV and movies.

"Thank you, sir. Yes, this is all in order. I have documents for you to sign, please, and we will have your car ready for you in a few days' time." He pulled a stack of papers out of a drawer. "If you can please sign at each of the tabs, we will be all set, sirs."

James pulled the stack of papers to him, and began reading each of the documents.

"Please, sir, they are standard agreements that I am sure you have signed before," Noi said, noticing James was taking the time to read them.

"I understand, but I read everything before I sign it," James answered abruptly, without looking up.

Noi was taken aback. "Oh yes, sir, of course. I mean no disrespect, sir. I know you must be very tired from the journey."

"Yes, you have said that," James said, slightly impatiently. He was following Tim's lead on acting pompous. Noi became quiet, and began entering some information into a computer. Tim absentmindedly hummed some Michael Jackson music to himself, mixing the songs.

The documents were all in English, and truly were documents for a car sale. James quickly got through them.

Noi placed several documents in a small carrier with a picture of the bonds he had taken as James finished signing. "Very good, Mr. Mathers, sir. Very good. Would you or Mr. Ferguson care to use the restroom before we depart?"

"No, we are..." James began.

"Yes," Tim said. He stood up, and began doing the pee dance.

"Have to pee, cousin?" James asked.

"Obviously," Tim said, as Noi unlocked the door, and they walked into the hallway.

Twenty minutes later, after Tim had relieved his bladder, they pulled up to a rather beautiful home.

"Welcome, please, to my home, sirs. I trust you will be happy with your stay. We have a jacuzzi, and sauna, if you like. The cook will make you any foods you would like. My wife and mother will be happy to greet you. Your rooms share a bathroom if that is acceptable, but all the plumbing works," Noi stated, turning in his seat to face them.

The night went well. They enjoyed a nice dinner, before heading upstairs for a good night's sleep. Noi reminded them that they needed to leave at 6 a.m., and asked if they would like to join him for breakfast at 5:30. They agreed and headed to bed.

When they got to Tim's room, James noticed Tim was rather quiet, and looked a bit put out.

"Jim, are you okay?" James asked.

"Very tired, Grant, very tired. I miss my bed, and want my pajamas," Tim replied. He was doing his best to stay in proper character.

"Let's get to bed, then," James said. They did just that following quick showers, and all of the rest of the normal habits that gave Tim a sense of normalcy.

After Tim was settled in, James went to his room, and checked his voicemail messages. The first message was from his buddy, Mark. "Dude, where are you at? Want to play some basketball with everyone tonight? Call me back."

The second was from his mother wanting to know when he'd have a day off, because his dad needed some help. He felt a twinge of guilt at not being able to help them out immediately.

The third message was from Carissa. James listened to the message three times, letting her words roll over him. "Hey, saw that you called me, then. Not sure where you are, or what time it is, but I hope you're happy, and doing well. Can't wait ta speak with ya. Oh, and I told Judy about us. Anyway, talk soon, Love. Bye."

James called his mom and Mark, reminding them that he was traveling for work, while telling them nothing of importance, but assuring them he was fine. When he called Carissa, he was slightly sad to get her recording. He didn't leave a message, as he always felt he sounded terrible in them. She'd at least see that he'd tried to call, and that was what counted, or at least he hoped it did.

# •Chapter Twenty-One•

The next morning was rough when the knock came at the door. James was exhausted but got up. It was Noi himself.

"Sorry sir, but it is 5 in the a.m. I thought you may want time to prepare, sir," he said through his stained teeth.

"Yes, thank you. Have you woken Jim?" James asked.

"He is already awake, sir. His light is on, and there are noises from the room he is in," Noi said.

"Okay, thank you, we will join you for breakfast." James shut the door and went to check on Tim through the adjoining bathroom. He shook his head, thinking it would help clear the prior night's bad dreams of fire, death and tears.

"Good morning!" Tim said, when James peered into his room. He had just finished getting dressed and was putting away his pajamas.

"Hey, Jim. You're up and ready today, I see," James yawned.

"Yes, well, it's obviously five and time to be up. Plus, the bed is very soft, and it was great to sleep on. I will have to get one like it when we are home. I mean we can afford it." He said the last part as if he'd just remembered to be extra flashy.

"Okay, please finish getting everything set, and we will go eat and start the day. Remember, I'm not sure what will happen today. The only scheduled thing I know for the rest of the trip is our flights back. So far, things have been very good, and we need to keep it that way. Noi said we will be driving a long time today. It's fine to bring your music, but please leave the coloring books and stuff here in your bag," James said, setting some expectations.

Tim nodded and went back to his packing.

They departed on time and headed south. Four hours after their departure in the black SUV, they made a sharp turn while going around a bend. It looked like they were going over the edge of the road into a sudden drop-off. Noi warned them a minute before they took the turn, but that didn't prevent the feeling of shock as it happened. Tim started to shake, but the transition was remarkably smooth, aside from that little drop feeling in the bottom of their stomachs. James was fairly certain Tim would have wet his pants if he hadn't gone to the bathroom when they'd made a stop to refuel and have a small snack. He leaned over and asked if he was all right. Tim merely nodded and went back to his music.

Two hours later, they stopped in the middle of a path in the midst of what appeared to be nothing but a wasteland.

"We are just waiting for the next vehicle, sirs. It should be here any moment as we are right on schedule," Noi said, and the driver nodded. "Sirs, if you might wait in the vehicle until I ask you to step out once the other arrives, I would be most happy. Look, here it is now." Noi pointed.

An old green Suburban, probably from the 1960s, was coming towards them. It stopped alongside the black SUV and Noi got out. The driver of the black SUV stayed put, but locked the doors with Tim and James inside. Noi approached the new driver and gave him the soft leather briefcase he'd placed the documents in the day before. They spoke for a moment, and then Noi walked toward the black SUV. The driver unlocked the doors and got out, and James and Tim followed.

"Please, sirs, right this way. This is Joe. He speaks some English, but we ask you don't speak too much as he is not supposed to. If you do need to stop to make toilet, he understands. From here you have about one hour drive. We will see you when you return, sirs." Noi was showing that yellow smile he had.

The driver had taken two very large gas tanks from the back of the luxury SUV to the Suburban.

Joe was a short man, but very muscular. He had a Chinese look to him mixed with something else, perhaps Italian. The hair and eye color certainly spoke to this, as did the skin tone. He looked very young, possibly in his mid-to-late teens.

After a quick glance at James, Tim made his way to the green vehicle with his headphones on over his hat.

"Oh, sirs, I forgot, very sorry, the electronics. If you have them, you may wish to leave them here with us. You can take them if you want, but only if they truly can be shut off,, and maybe the batteries come out. Same for electric watches," Noi called.

"But my music," Tim said, sounding and looking like a disappointed child.

"I agree, but it sounds like it might get broken, and I didn't see a store in the airport that could fix it, did you? I mean, this place, ugh," James said, conveying their rich snob act.

"Seriously," Tim said, winking at James in a rather obvious way that the others, fortunately, didn't notice.

They removed the electronics and left them in the SUV. As they did this, Joe came up behind them and said, "Must search."

"Oh, yes, sirs. If he can quickly search, just for safety on weapons," Noi said from the front seat.

"Whatever," Tim said, throwing his head back.

After a quick pat down, Noi and the driver of the SUV waved goodbye, and the Suburban was off. They drove for about sixty minutes, but it seemed much longer. The wasteland seemed endless, and there was little change in the scenery. Suddenly, Joe came to a stop.

Tim leaned over to James and whispered, "Why are we stopping?"

James shrugged and whispered back, "Maybe he has to pee."

Tim giggled.

Joe removed the battery from his satellite phone. When he finished, they set off again.

Suddenly, Joe hit the gas hard. His foot was down as far as it could go as they started up a slight incline. Just before they passed a large rock on either side of the Suburban, Joe took his foot off the gas, shifted to neutral, and turned off the ignition. Tim started to shake violently.

"What the hell are you doing?" James demanded, taking off his seatbelt and reaching over the seat.

Joe pushed him back easily, as if he had expected the reaction. "It okay. Sit. We start in minute. We pass shut off place," he said in his broken English.

Joe made no motions to jump out of the vehicle and seemed rather calm. There were no visible signs of danger, so James, reluctantly, went with it. Tim, on the other hand, didn't handle this extreme disruption well. He was shaking very badly and didn't seem to know what to do. James placed his left hand on Tim's right knee to see if the contact would help. It didn't.

A few moments later, as the Suburban was starting to lose speed, they passed another set of rocks. Joe applied the breaks until they stopped, popped the battery back into his satellite phone, started the engine, and they continued driving. A few moments later, they crested a ridge that opened up to show a magnificent stone building built into the side of a cliff.

Based on the land layout, James hadn't expected to see a cliff, much less this building. It looked like a fortress with an exterior wall and battlements. A tower seemed to come from about the center and reach upward, almost touching the underside of the overhanging cliff slope.

The sharpness of the angle of the cliff seemed to defy gravity, but that wasn't the only remarkable thing about it. It seemed to hug the fortress and hang over the top. James suspected that if you were on top of the ridge, you could peer down and the fortress would be invisible.

As they approached, the stratification of the layers of the cliff became more and more pronounced. James's eyes scanned them as Tim commented, "This is very pretty how the layers look!"

James tapped him on his leg, and he quieted down.

A metallic line in the stratification made a large, upside down 'U' shape. The top of the tower seemed to be designed to be at the peak of the crown of the upside down 'U.' James wondered if it was made of lead, but that didn't seem likely.

They pulled up to a gate. Someone on top of the wall could be heard calling out, and the gate lifted with a rattling sound of chains being drawn. As they proceeded through, they found another wall that seemed wider than the first. The stones used on this interior wall were more like bricks, and the wall was only about three meters high, with several visible doorways. This made James think it was hollow inside.

They drove right as they entered, and James could see an Indian man, or perhaps a tall boy, on top of the exterior wall. Two other teens, a boy and a girl, both with dark skin, seemed to be controlling the gate. They all wore ragged clothing that didn't quite fit.

Looking up, James saw two other vehicles parked that were in various stages of disrepair. One was a military truck and the other a Suburban. They showed extensive signs of rust and were missing different engine parts.

Joe stopped the truck, got out, and opened the door for Tim. The dark-skinned girl rushed to open the door for James. As James exited, he looked at her and said, "Thank you."

She dropped her eyes, and James saw what looked like scarring on her neck and parts of her back. Strangely enough, now that he could see her properly, she appeared to be more indigenous to the Amazon region than Asia.

"Come," came Joe's voice, and James and Tim followed him to a door in the inner wall.

James had been right that it was hollow inside. It seemed to be about fifteen feet wide and used for storage. The light inside was poor, and the doors cast odd shadows down the length of both sides as far as they could see into the curves.

Exiting the other side, they found a large area with several small, shack-like buildings in front of the main building. A few touched the inner wall at the end of the circle-like curvature.

Standing at the main door was a man wearing a suit and white shirt. He smiled as he walked down the three long steps that led from the door. If there was any doubt that this man was Chinese, it was dismissed the moment he spoke.

"Oh, wercome wercome. I Tan, Lien. Very prease to meet such fine men. Prease, come, come." He was motioning them inside.

James knew he wouldn't have to explain to Tim that the man's first name was Lien, since introductions began with the family name in Asian cultures.

Tim and James passed through the doorway and heard an exchange of words between Joe and Lien. Lien seemed to be yelling at Joe, who was trying to explain something, until Lien struck him on the head. Joe just stood there, eyes down, and listened as Lien yelled some more.

James grabbed Tim, who was starting to shake. Tim became very upset at shouting and physical violence. He took off his hat and began spinning it in his hands.

"Jim, we can't get involved. We don't know what it's about, and it's not our concern today," he said quickly and quietly.

"I know what they are saying. He said Joe should have used proper manners, and taken a bonus with him. Joe was saying it was for a different thing, and then he got hit," Tim said, still shaking.

"Jim, you're able to deal with violence, remember? It's a rule, and Joe is okay right now. It's a rule," James said. He then asked, "What do you mean 'bonus'?"

Tim stopped shaking. He looked sad. "I don't know, but it is what he said. Grant, I would like to go home soon. I do not like this place."

"Soon," James replied.

# •Chapter Twenty-Two•

Lien finished yelling, and Joe went back outside. Upon joining them, Lien began to speak as if nothing had happened while ushering them down the corridor that had a vaulted ceiling.

"Here we are in main front area. Different area of our home reached from here," said Lien, spreading his arms wide.

As they reached the end of the corridor, they found a grand opening. It looked like an interior courtyard, with magnificent mirrors and tapestries on the walls, large carpets, and soft leather couches. A bar area in the corner had a suited Caucasian boy with large ears, and red hair manning it. He looked extremely out of place.

Looking up, James saw that they were under the tower, but the interior chamber of the tower also had a variety of angled mirrors intermixed with steps leading to the peak. James quickly realized the mirrors were used to harvest natural light, though electrical lighting was present too. He also recognized that cameras were everywhere, and not just the obvious ones in the corners.

Lien spoke again as if giving them a tour. "If come with me to right, find most eregant rooms for guests to try before taking home." They followed him down the right-hand corridor.

James was confused, but Tim seemed happy to be on this little tour, and didn't appear to think anything was wrong. James wasn't about to upset the peace, so he kept quiet and smiled, as Lien showed them a well-furnished bedroom inside the second door on the left as they entered the hall.

The king bed was set on a hand carved frame with posts that ran to the ceiling. The royal purple curtains on the bed were pulled back, and the walls were painted a soft lavender color. On the ceiling directly over the mattress was yet another mirror. James's eyes denoted a small line running from the edge of the mirror at the headboard toward the wall. It was perfectly straight, and could easily be a line for a hidden camera that had been patched over. A door on the far left of the room led to a very nice bathroom, with a shower and tub. Everything was tiled and looked modern. The plumbing seemed to have been added after the fortress was built.

Stepping back into the hallway, they met a woman who looked very much like Lien. It turned out to be his sister, Bik. She was very gracious and said, "If hurry, seeing them at bathing room."

Tim spoke up, "We just saw the bathroom. I liked the shiny green tiles."

Lien interjected, "I giving tour. Bik, Go!"

She gave him a look and walked away.

"She as bad as her bastard, Joe," Lien spat. "Qiang right to treat her as cousin not sister anymore. Prease, this way. Show more."

James gave a dismissive shrug of his shoulders to show his lack of concern. He understood that many cultures of the world had different views and this was one of them. He didn't personally agree with it, but at the same time, he felt that Grant wouldn't care too much and acted accordingly.

They saw another room similar to the prior one, and then a third room set up like a classroom. "This teaching room. For pray teacher, and bad student," he winked.

Suddenly it clicked in James's mind. This was a brothel. The teens working out front were probably all bastards of the prostitutes. Lien thought he and Tim were potential new clients, and Joe had tried to tell them they weren't. The bonus he mentioned must have been a woman to keep them company on their journey to the fortress.

James stepped forward to speak with Lien. "Sorry, I think we should..." but Lien cut him off.

"Okay, okay. I take you now. I show you. Normar the rast room, but go see now," Lien said, still flustered. "Bik's ruin surprise."

James tried to engage him again, but Lien waved him off and said, "Come, come."

Tim followed Lien, clearly eager to see more of the castle, and James followed them, trying to think of how to tell him they weren't there to visit prostitutes. All the while, he kept processing what he saw. *This is a rather out of the way place to set up a brothel,* was a thought at the front of his mind.

Lien took them through a few more passages and turns, then stopped outside a room, and opened the door for them. They could hear voices and splashing coming from inside. Tim walked in, and James paused to try to explain.

"Mr. Tan, I think we need to speak. Jim, my cousin, and I are here to gain some information," James started.

"Yes, yes, to see what we do training. Make some picks, yes?" He gave a prolonged wink and a smile. He was missing several teeth, and had atrocious breath.

"No, Mr. Tan. We have come for other information. We called and spoke with Mr. Rasa about the A S pirit information," James said.

"What that? Oh, mean stuff? Or Sirff, or how say?" He paused. "Sruff. No, snuff!" Lien exclaimed, clearly thinking he had found the right word. "We train, but you do as wirr. Pay is yours."

"Snuff? No, we don't want to kill anyone or have sex. We are here for information..." James began again.

"Ohhh, but your cousin, he showing other intention," Lien said, laughing and pointing.

James turned to see Tim stepping out of his pants.

"Tim!" James cried out, and there was an echo. He called, "Jim, stop!" getting the name right this time.

Tim looked up as James raced toward him. Steam issued from the huge bath, but that wasn't the only thing in the two to three-foot deep pool. It was filled with what looked like at least thirty children.

James paused. He couldn't believe his eyes. James had expected to see a variety of women, and perhaps some men, but not kids. Now he understood the warnings about coming here.

"They asked me to play. I like to swim, and they said I didn't need swim trunks. They don't have any, and they said adults swim with them all the time," Tim said, looking innocently at James.

James focused, speeding up his thought process. He couldn't tell Tim these kids were slaves and being abused. He'd freak out. Tim's very nature was child-like and innocent. He was great with kids, and enjoyed playing with them, but he couldn't join them.

Perhaps a second went by. James could hear Lien's approaching steps. "What if one of the kids peed in the water?" he whispered quickly.

"Oh, that isn't good, sometimes that happens. Yeah, good point," Tim said thinking.

James turned back to the pool. In the blink of an eye, he counted twenty boys and fifteen girls. They seemed to be every age, size, and skin tone imaginable. They certainly weren't all from this part of the world. As they splashed around, James noticed they all seemed to have a similar scar somewhere just below their waistlines. Each scar was about the size of a nickel, and looked like a burn mark.

"See, have finest here," Lien said into James's left ear. He turned to Tim and said, "Prease feer free to do as rike. They very friendry." He clapped twice.

A white boy stood up from the center of the pool from a crouched position, and faced Lien. He was about eleven years old, but hadn't entered puberty. He was one of the older kids, if not the oldest, but that wasn't the remarkable thing about him. It was his blue eyes and straw colored hair. They struck James, as did the boy's scars. Three were very distinct. One was on his inner right thigh near his groin, one at his pubic symphysis, and the other was on his center-left upper thigh.

The boy started scurrying around, and ushering kids toward James and Tim.

Just then, a young man about James's age, rushed into the room, and pulled Lien to the side. He had a determined look on his face and spoke rapidly.

The kids swarmed James and Tim, chattering away, and pawing at their clothes. Only the blue-eyed boy remained in the water, but he was right at the edge, watching the other children.

About two minutes later, the stranger finished speaking and left. Lien came over, and clapped his hands twice. The blue-eyed boy called the others back to the pool.

"Why are they going back? I thought we were going to play a game. She said we were going to play hide and seek." Tim pointed at a little girl about nine years old, with long black hair who was waving at him. He waved back.

"So sorry. My nephew instructs me not suppose see. Here for other thing. So sorry," Lien said. "Prease, come now, this way."

"Wait, just one moment." James held out his hand to stop him. He quickly decided to exploit this mistake, and Tim's innocent desire to play with the children to their advantage.

"Why can't we discuss both?" James asked. "As you said, my cousin is interested, and so am I." In his head, he finished with the thought, *Interested in freeing these kids, and burning this hellhole to the ground, hopefully with you and your partners in it.*

James knew he needed to secure the trust of his host a bit more in order to see the best way to help these kids. He also knew he needed to see more of the layout.

"Please, finish showing us around before we conduct our other business." James looked into Lien's face, trying to conceal the rage burning through him. Thankfully the room was hot, and covered up how red he had to be turning.

Lien laughed and wiggled a finger at James before bowing slightly. "Oh, oh, oh, I knew. I knew. Good, yes." He turned and called "Seim!"

A young man who looked about seventeen years old appeared out of the dark corridor. Lien said something to Seim, who vanished. He then called "Fang!" and another young man about the same age appeared. Lien spoke again, but this time pointed at the children, clearly telling him to round them up, and get them out of the pool.

"Prease, this way," Lien then said to Tim and James.

Tim looked a little sad to leave the kids, but he followed.

"Seim terr them wish to finish tour, then join for tarking," Lien said.

Finish the tour they did. They saw the dormitory-style bedrooms for the kids. They also saw a real classroom where, according to Lien, some of the children were educated as requested by their to-be-masters. There was even a nursery that seemed to be empty of inhabitants at the moment. They saw areas that made James want to vomit, and hurt Lien at the same time. They passed at least two rooms with a variety of equipment clearly meant to train the kids for a variety of things. The place seemed to operate in a made-to-order style for the clients' requirements of the children.

Most of it went over Tim's head, but when he saw the whip in one room, he asked James, "Why do they have that? Those are used to hit horses to make them run faster."

"I don't know, Jim, maybe they have horses," James answered quickly.

"Strange place to keep it, near where children play, and sleep, and go to school. They aren't teaching the kids to hit horses, are they?" Tim asked loudly.

"No," James said.

"Probrem? What is hitting horses?" Lien asked.

"Nothing, Jim was mistaken." James turned quickly, and bumped Tim's leg to signal him not to talk, because Tim looked like he was about to start an argument.

They exited into the same courtyard area they'd begun in, but from what would have been the central hallway. The original corridor they had gone down was now on their left.

"We go now finish other business," Lien said, leading them down the last remaining hallway, now on their right, from the interior courtyard.

This hallway had a different feeling from the others. It felt more like a home, but for those not enslaved. It was decorated with paintings and pictures. It, too, had a variety of doors that presumably had grand bedrooms behind them.

James couldn't help but wonder what they were getting into now.

# •Chapter Twenty-Three•

They stopped at the last door on the left. Lien knocked, and they entered into an impressive looking office space with twenty-five televisions on the wall, and high-end computer equipment. The right-hand wall hosted an impressive surveillance system and server equipment. There seemed to be some major circuit breakers for power there too. As the door shut, James heard a powerful locking system engage. Clearly, no expense had been spared in this operation.

While James and Tim checked out the room, Lien whispered something to the stranger who had come to the pool room. He then introduced a woman. "This Jie, wife of brother Qiang."

There were a total of four extra people in the room now, Jie, Seim, the stranger, and another man lurking in the corner. James saw no mirrors in this room, but there were cameras.

The woman, who looked to be in her early sixties, stood to welcome them. She was dressed in a mix of Chinese and American clothing that suited her very well. Her eyes were set firmly on James, and then shifted to Tim, and then back to James. James knew instinctively, she was shrewd and calculating, but he felt something else about her, something protective.

"Welcome," Jie said. She turned and walked to her desk, sitting in a high-backed chair, as though she were royalty.

"Prease arrow me to introduce my nephew, Yan. He very bright young man, speaks ten ranguages fruentry," said Lien.

The stranger from the pool shook Tim's hand, who seemed to be doing fine with all this contact. When he reached James, he briefly locked eyes with him. James's eyes swept over Yan, and he quickly realized this wasn't someone to underestimate. Yan's energy and demeanor radiated confidence and power, and he had the body of a trained fighter. His clothes were new and looked to be of European design. James thought it likely that he had been educated there, probably in France or England.

Breaking the handshake, Yan went and stood on his mother's left side, allowing Lien to finish the introductions.

"This Seim," Lien pointed, "that Hanser from children's book."

Hansel didn't look German, James noted. He looked more Egyptian.

James noticed that Tim was fidgeting slightly too.

Yan began to speak, and James noticed that his mother looked straight ahead at them, but the others' heads dropped ever so slightly.

"Yes, welcome. My family is honored to receive you. Please have a seat." Yan motioned to the chairs in front of the desk. As James and Tim moved to sit down, a cart was heard being pushed toward them. "May we offer you refreshment?"

A rather nice selection of fresh fruit, cookies, and cheeses appeared, with a variety of drinks. Tim glanced at James before selecting pineapple, and a bottle of water. James took two small cookies, and a bottle of water also.

"Thank you," Tim said, excitedly eating the pineapple, his favorite fruit.

"It is our pleasure to have you as our guests," Yan said with a gracious smile, but his eyes were as calculating as his mother's, who was watching with great interest.

She said something to Yan in Chinese. He went on, "We have gotten a note from Noi Rasa saying your identities were verified. He says the requested bonds of $300,000 US dollars have also been collected. He goes on to say, our security measures of fingerprinting, and photo taking are also complete. His final note is that you, Mr. Ferguson, and you, Mr. Mathers, are related, cousins."

"We are. Our mothers are sisters who married into very wealthy families," James said with pure confidence. Tim nodded with a mouthful of fruit, his right leg beginning to bounce a little.

Yan presumably translated that for his mother, who gave a small nod. "Always good to have family, is it not?" he said rhetorically, looking at them. "We have my family here, my mother, my uncle, my aunt, and all of our 'children.'"

On the last word, he spread his arms as if to say everyone in the compound was part of the family too.

"The missing part of my family is my father. He isn't here, and hasn't been for five years now." Yan leaned forward on the desk with both hands. His tone and speech were steady, but his body language reflected barely tempered aggression.

Tim was thankfully still occupied with the fruit, but James focused on the son and his mother. She sat as if made of stone.

"You come here seeking information on a man most hated by this family. By my mother," Yan stood up, and swung his right arm toward her, before pointing his thumb at his chest. "And by me."

"Anthony Spara, and his family are why my father is dead," Yan declared. "They took away the business my father helped build, and gave it to the pukes of Russia and Afghanistan. They took away our great border connections that allowed us to operate freely, with our business ventures. You see what extremes we have to go to. My mother wants to know exactly why you want this information, and what you intend to do with it?"

The mother gave no response, but Lien now wore an angry look on his face.

James spoke in a matter-of-fact tone, but with great conviction. "We feel the information you have on Anthony Spara might allow us to bring his family down, and send them all to prison for life. We also think it'll cause massive disruptions to the Afghan, and Russian drug trafficking markets. That should result in a few key people losing their lives for not being able to move the material. In short, we want to ruin all the people you hate."

"That isn't answering why," Yan said, in the same stance he had taken when talking about his father.

"That is simple. He did the same thing to our fathers." James made a motion toward Tim, who looked up from his third serving of pineapple and nodded.

Yan translated what James had said to his mother, but it didn't sound like Chinese. Then he asked, "How?"

"The Spara family also cheated our families out of our share of money. My father is a rather successful gasoline chain owner in the US. We have a lot of distribution capability, access to refineries, and that sort of thing."

James took an opportunity to glance at Tim, whose leg hadn't stopped bouncing. By the state of his chin, he wasn't going to stop eating pineapple until the tray was empty.

James continued, nodding towards Tim. "His dad is a rather well-known, and respected investment banker. He can move a lot of cash as he needs to." James was adjusting the background slightly on the spot to make it more appealing to the Tans.

Yan opened his mouth to speak, but his mother said something sharply. Yan turned, and translated what James had said. She said something back to him.

"That is interesting, but how does it relate to moving drugs?" Yan said.

"The investment banking allows for easy money laundering. I think you can see how it can be useful. Besides the apparent logistics associated with the gasoline, there's another factor. My uncle and father invested a great deal of money in figuring out how to dissolve the heroin into gasoline to transport it, undetected, and then process it to get it out quickly and purely."

Yan had translated all of this before James went on.

"Anthony Spara saw the operation, had his people trained on how to do it, and cut my father and uncle out. He's been working with a different laundering agency for years, and lied to us about the rate of exchange he was getting. He also decided it was easier to start bribing gasoline truck drivers across the nation, instead of waiting for my father's fast-growing business to get out of the northeast part of the US."

Again Yan translated, but he seemed to be speaking a different language than before. The accents weren't the same. There was a moment of silence. Yan gave a tiny nod to his mother, who gave a much larger one back. Yan turned to face them.

"You have purchased the file, and we are happy to give it to you, friends," Yan said. "However, my uncle informs me that we may have other business to discuss. Is this true?" he inquired.

Tim was fidgeting so bad that it was hard to ignore, and Yan certainly had noticed. "Are you all right, Mr. Ferguson?" he asked.

Tim stood up, and James realized what was wrong before he said it.

"I really need to go make," Tim said.

"Make? What do you mean?" Yan said, taken aback.

"He has to use the bathroom. And while he does that, we can discuss further business," James said.

"Oh, yes, I see." Yan motioned to Seim. "Seim will show you where you may use the restroom," he said to Tim.

James watched them move along the corridor on the monitors, his mind racing. This was his chance to set something up without Tim overhearing the conversation, and potentially blowing the cover. He needed an excuse to come back.

"So how do these arrangements typically work for your organization?" James asked. He had no clue how to begin something like this.

"Very simple. What would you like? We have a wide variety as you have seen, and getting something special isn't too much of a problem, if you do not care for our inventory," Yan said.

James thought, *Variety! Inventory! These are kids, not wines or fruit!* James could feel his anger growing, and fought to contain it. James took a deep breath quietly through his nose, and forced himself to calm down. For him, taking control was thinking in an extremely logical way, and actively ignoring emotion. This topic, however, was proving difficult to be solely logical about.

"I think your current inventory will meet the needs of my cousin and me," James said, returning the smile that Yan was giving him with an effort. "Where would we be on pricing?" he asked.

"I see that you are excited, my friend," Yan laughed. "Your ears are burning with desire. Price depends on what you want, and how you want them trained. We can accommodate anything you want."

"Jasmine catch Mr. Ferguson's eye, she fond of him in bath," said Lien. "And prease correct Mr. Mathers, you fond of X."

"Another for X. No, that will not do," Yan said, shaking his head. "He is old and used. Should have gotten rid of him, but he is good for the others."

"But Mr. Mat..." started Lien, but Jie stood, and began to shout at Lien, who instantly quieted. She then turned on Yan. When he looked at her, she lowered her tone quickly, as she finished her words with him.

"I apologize, Mr. Mathers, for my uncle speaking out of turn. And I shouldn't dismiss a desire of yours, as my mother rightly pointed out. Would you care for X, and do you think Jasmine would be suitable as a starting point for Mr. Ferguson?" Yan asked all of this in a flat, but polite, tone.

Two things registered for James. First, Jie spoke English. No one had continued to translate for her. Second, Yan was in charge, not her. She was a cover. That was the extra feeling about her he'd sensed earlier.

"What would be the cost, and when could we arrange for all of this to be done?" James asked. He knew he was getting short on time.

"What preparation do you require? We can train them in..." Yan started.

"No, no additional training, aside from education in studies such as math, science, English, and other basics," James said. He caught site of Seim and Tim reappearing in the first monitor. "Also, I want this to be a surprise for my cousin. So if we can just refer to 'the package' when he comes back, that would be appreciated."

Yan nodded. "The cost will be $40,000 US dollars for X, and $65,000 dollars for Jasmine. This is a special deal for you. It is because, you're going to take care of Spara, and, also, to encourage you to come back to us for future needs." Yan gave what he felt was a charismatic smile and wink, and James fought the urge to get up and beat him silly.

"That is fine. I will have to make arrangements to get documents to take them with us, and to get back here for them. That may take some time. Plus, we would like them to be fully fluent in English. Say less than a year, hopefully, closer to six months?"

"So long?" Yan said, as Tim and Seim returned.

"There are a lot of moving pieces, and I want to do it right. Besides, by that point, I may have news for you, on how we are doing with taking care of Spara." James stood up. "And it gives you time on your end, as well."

Yan recognized James's standing as a take it or leave it proposition.

"We leaving?" asked Tim.

"I believe we have finished all our business. I assume payment in the same way as before, and that you will inform Mr. Rasa, and he will be the connection point again?" James asked.

"Yes, very good. Very good," Yan said.

He whispered something to his mother, who rose from her seat. She pressed on the molding at the corner of her chair, and a small click sounded. She apparently had triggered a small, secret vault room. She entered, and took a few steps that could be heard on the stone floor of the room. James imagined she must have a stride of about eighteen inches. If so, the vault was at least a few feet deep, which meant it could hold a lot of files and objects. She returned quickly, and handed a thick binder to James. She then bowed, and said her second word in English. "Goodbye."

Promptly, Hansel and Seim steered James and Tim out of the room, followed by Lien. A few paces down the hall, Seim broke away at a run.

"We thank for time. Good to meet. Joe will return you to Noi," Lien said at the main door, as Seim reappeared, closely followed by Joe. Lien handed Joe Noi's carrier and returned inside.

While they walked with Joe back through the inner wall, James tried to mentally capture all the points he could on dimensions, cameras, and the like. It was a lot to take in, especially when he was still fuming inside. He wasn't paying attention to Tim, but he should've been.

# •Chapter Twenty-Four•

Outside, they climbed back into the Suburban, and began the drive, and James reminded Tim that Joe would shut off the vehicle in a few minutes, but it would be okay.

Tim replied "Obviously," with a small burp.

As they approached the stone markers, Joe didn't stop to take the battery out of his phone this time. He just cruised up, placed the vehicle in neutral, and killed the engine. He managed to remove the battery as they drifted. It took them about the same amount of time to get through as before, as the slight decline of the ground helped.

Just before Joe stopped on the other side of the markers, Tim turned to James and said, "My tummy hurts."

James asked, "Hurts how?"

Joe stopped the Suburban to restart it, and Tim quickly got out. Joe started to protest, but Tim vomited. It was almost impressive, how much pineapple came roaring up. James and Joe got out to join Tim, who was shaking.

"I want to go home now, please. I want to go home," Tim said, almost crying.

"We are. We are going home." James gently grabbed Tim on the sides of his head, and looked him in the eyes. He could smell the rancid odor of fruit mixed with stomach fluids, and almost vomited himself.

"Here," Joe said, handing Tim his thermos of water. Tim took it, and rinsed out his mouth.

James turned and said, "Thank you, that was very kind."

Joe nodded and climbed back into the Suburban. After one more rinse, so did Tim and James.

The rest of the ride back was uneventful. Tim curled up against the door, and wiggled his toes in his shoes. James assumed this was a relaxation technique, and didn't question it. He was trying to keep his focus on all that had transpired so that he could write it down. James kept running everything through his head to keep it fresh.

Noi greeted them, holding open the back passenger door with his high-strung, crackling voice saying, "Hello, sirs. I am glad to see you again. I trust all went well with your business?"

"No," said Tim, clearly impatient and grouchy. "I want to go home now."

"Sir, is there anything I..." Noi said, apparently offended.

James stepped between Noi, and the door to the vehicle. "Everything is fine. My cousin's just sick. We need to get back as quickly as possible, please." He climbed in, and Noi shut the door.

Joe came up to Noi, handed him the small carrier, and walked back to the Suburban.

James opened the window just in time to say "Thank you," to Joe. The man paused, and gave James a small smile and wave.

Noi climbed in, and they were off. Noi turned to strike up a conversation, but Tim had already turned on his music, and moved to the back to lie down.

"Sir, are you sure he is okay? No disrespect, sir, but, it would be most bad if he is sick in here," Noi said.

James adopted his pompous tone. "He is fine. Just let us be."

"Oh, yes, sir." Noi turned back around, looking very put out.

James opened some sparkling water, and poured a small amount into a glass. He moved to the back to give it to Tim, whose face was pressed into the seat.

"Jim. Jim. Hey," he said, gently touching Tim's shoulder. Tim just shook his head.

James took off Tim's right headphone. "Jim, please drink this. It will help your tummy. Here now," James said.

Tim didn't move.

"Please. We are almost done, and you have been the best field partner," James whispered.

Tim turned. He looked miserable, and had puffy eyes. He sat up, drank the water, made a face of disgust, and lay back down without a word.

On the journey back, Tim didn't want to stop to eat. He used the bathroom when they got fuel, and came back a little shaky. He told James he had 'the poopies,' but he didn't have any further episodes.

About an hour later, Tim sat up, and leaned forward so his head was next to James. "You know, Grant, she was saying some odd things," he said quietly out of the blue.

James glanced toward the front of the car. Noi made no response. He clearly hadn't heard Tim.

"Not now, but I'm glad you remember. Let's talk later," James said with a wink.

"Okay," Tim winked back, looking as though someone had hit him in the eye.

He now seemed perfectly fine. *Must have just been way too much fruit*, James decided.

After dinner, James confirmed that Noi would take them to the airport about 10 a.m. the next morning.

James waited in Tim's room until he was fast asleep before leaving him. He had to hand it to Tim; he had pulled off some really difficult things. James was proud of him, and was looking forward to hearing what he had to say, when it suddenly struck him. Tim could draw everything he saw. He could make a perfect map of the place. James turned to wake Tim, but then thought better of it. Tim would remember, and he deserved a restful sleep.

James returned to his room, picked up his phone, and called Carissa. Even hearing her voice on the recording would be fantastic.

"...ello?" came a female voice. The line had a bad connection.

"Um, Hi Carissa," James started.

"Oh, nae, one mo', t'is Judy. Carissa, it's John! Her' she comes now," Judy said.

"Hi," came the sweetest voice in the world, according to James at least, slightly out of breath. "How's you?"

"At this moment, I couldn't be better," said James, and he meant it. For the first time in the last few days, he was only thinking about one thing, and it was the one thing he most wanted to think about.

"Long day?... t... ma...," Carissa said in a garbled way.

"Sorry, can you repeat that?" James said.

"What'd ya say?" came Carissa's reply.

James quickly made his way to the window, hoping that would improve the quality of the call connection. "I asked what you said," James said.

"Love, I can't get all... what you're sayin... me. We have..."

"I was just calling to say hello. I'll ring you back when I have a better connection. I hope you hear me say this." A bit sad, James enunciated each word slowly and clearly.

"Yer, alright. Tal..., Love," came Carissa's reply before the phone went silent.

James sighed. He wasn't sure what he'd planned on talking to Carissa about, but he felt disappointed anyway. He rubbed his head, as he was starting to get a headache. It was time to call it a day.

The journey home went smoothly. Their flights were on time, and they had plans to debrief the next day with Tom. They were able to fly home without stopping in New York for a night. James knew the Tan family wasn't tracking them closely. They didn't have to, as the Tans had video, pictures, and copies of documents to keep them in line.

The first thing Tim did when he got home was to check the schedule. He then walked back to James and said, "I think I like being Tim better than Jim. You can be Jim or Grant, but I think you should just be James from now on. I'm going to go watch Discovery Channel now. See you tomorrow." He stuck out his hand with a huge grin.

James immediately shook it and said, "Well done."

Tim gave him another long wink, and was off to join Byron and Dan. It wasn't like Tim to initiate a handshake. Tim had learned how to do another 'nor-mal' thing. James was proud.

# •Chapter Twenty-Five•

James stayed in a hotel near the group to get a good night's sleep, before returning to his family, and the chaos that reigned at home with two small children. He was planning on moving the following weekend to Pittsburgh for his internship, as a two-hour commute was less than ideal, but first, he wanted to help his dad with a few things.

At 4 a.m., James was wide awake. He wanted to go back to sleep, but he knew that was about as likely as sitting next to a quiet toddler on a plane. With a deep sigh, he threw his legs out from under the covers and sat up, before falling back on the bed again. It was going to be a long day if he continued feeling this sluggish.

After taking a shower, he felt better, and thought he'd try giving Carissa a call.

"Good morning, Love," she said in a greeting.

James felt a tingle in his toes. "Good morning there, Ms. Risa. How's you?"

"Brilliant, thanks. What time is it there? Why are you up so early? Everything all right?" she asked.

James chuckled. "Well, it's clear, then, isn't it, why I'm up half past 4? It's to talk to you, and that always makes everything perfect." He hoped he hadn't sounded too cheesy. He always scoffed at the illogical fluff so many couples spewed at each other.

Carissa loved it. "You are always so sweet. I was telling Judy that the other day, and she said it was just a ploy ta get a little somethin' somethin'. I told her ta stop being so jealous, and go for a soak. She had gotten pure bleezin', you know, the night before and was a bit turned out ta start. Well, after that she gone and got a bug up her..."

James took in each word eagerly and awaited the next. He didn't have to think, process, or act on anything. Just listen to her sweet voice with her rather sexy Scots accent, that many found to be less than pleasant.

"Here I am, rambling on and on. You must be bored silly. Tell me about your days," Carissa said a good while later.

James's brain, which had just been idling, slipped abruptly back into gear. "It's been a lot of travel. Switching hotel rooms each night is rather wearing, to be honest. Not sure why I thought traveling for business would be fun. It really isn't, you know. It's nothing like personal travel. I get to see a lot of offices, airports, and hotels. After a bit, they all run together. I will be here in the States for about a month for additional training, before heading back to Aberdeen."

"Wow, that is a bit of time away." Her voice held a soft hint of disappointment.

"Aye, I didn't find out about the additional training until recently. Very sorry on that, truly. But, when I get back, I would love to see you, and go out to dinner, and a movie, and to a club if you would?" said James.

Carissa's voice was normal again. "All in one night?" she laughed. "Well, I like ta hear you want ta make up for lost time, but one thing at a time, John, or I'll have ta start callin' you Jack Flash then, eh?"

James laughed. He wished every day could start off like this.

Later that day, James was at group headquarters when Tim and Tom came in.

"Hi, Tim," James said with a smile. "Hey, Tom."

"Hi ya, James," said Tim, grinning. He was excited to be debriefed. Usually, he was just called in to examine various puzzles that others couldn't decipher.

"I was just informing Tim how we'll be proceeding today," Tom said.

"Which was completely unneeded, obviously. I know how these things go, Tom. I am not dumb," Tim said, in an incredulous tone.

James decided to move things along before Tim got too aggravated. After all, this was why Tim got so annoyed around the group. He felt like he was treated like a little kid.

"Tim, I'm interested in knowing a few things." James stood up. He walked over to the whiteboard, and wrote three questions:

*1. What did the individuals say when they were not speaking English*

*2. Can you draw the fortress, its rooms, and passages*

*3. How did you feel about the trip*

Tom sat back, aware that James had taken control, even though he was technically being debriefed too.

Tim studied the list. "Do you want me to do them in that order?" he asked. "And why didn't you use punctuation?"

James laughed, and corrected the punctuation. "You can do them as you want, but how about we do the drawings last?"

"Oh, good. Those will take a long time, and just the stone fortress? I can do the airports, hotel, Noi's house, and the office too." Tim tried to mask his excitement. He did it poorly, and it just made him look like he was sitting on a bottle shaker.

"Well, how about the whole fortress and Noi's office?" James suggested.

Tim made a fast transition to the last question. "Right, well I feel that it was long. Very tiring. My sleep is off, and I have this weird feeling at the top of my head. On my brain." He touched the upper part of his forehead as he spoke.

"It's called jet lag," Tom said.

"Obviously, he asked me to describe how I feel, not define things, Tom," Tim fired back.

James interjected, "You can also say what you thought about everything, too."

Tim paused. He had a rather reserved look on his face. "It was exciting, but very scary sometimes. I think I like doing my work here more, and not so much in the field, though the kids looked like they were having fun. That made me smile. Oh, and drinking all the Coke was good too. The tummy ache was terrible. And I think some of those people were bad, and said weird things. I'm happy to be home, and see my shows. That's it," he ended, looking at James and then over to Tom as if to ask if it was okay.

"Got it, Tim. I think you did great. I know it was a rough trip, and you did as well as anyone could've."

Tim smiled from ear to ear as James went on. "What were people saying that you thought didn't make sense?"

"Oh, that. Well, it was just Jie and Yan. They kept switching languages, obviously, but they didn't even answer each other in the same language. They used Mandarin and Cantonese and Thai and..."

"Why were they switching languages like that?" Tom asked, interrupting him.

With a dramatic flare, Tim stood up, shaking. "I was talking, Tom!" He seemed to be expressing a lot more emotion lately, but like a six-year-old who didn't know how to do it properly.

"Sorry, sorry. I'll be quiet." Tom motioned with his hands to get Tim to sit back down.

"Tim, I thought they were switching languages too. I'm glad you could understand all of them. That is excellent. What were they saying back and forth?" James asked calmly.

Like flipping on a light switch, Tim was calm again. "Well, at first it was just making fun of someone for overpaying. They said they would have given the information for free, and they didn't even have to negotiate. They never said who that was, but it couldn't have been us, because we didn't give them any cash." He paused and blinked with a puzzled expression.

"What else?" James asked.

"Well, it didn't make sense. Jie was the boss, but she kept saying things like she was suggesting them to Yan. Once she said," Tim tried to mimic her voice, "'Do you think we can take his spot? Maybe we can get the fields going. The kids are worth more in the field, don't you think?' Then she said something, if they got far enough, they could take all the operation over by replacing the top. Yan liked that," Tim recalled. "He got excited, and got more excited when he started talking to you."

James nodded. He knew better than to discount what blind revenge, and greed could do to people.

"Anything else, Tim?" James asked.

"No. Nothing they said," Tim replied.

James's eyes narrowed. Tim was a literalist after all. "Did anyone else say anything I didn't hear?"

"Oh yeah. The kids were all talking. A lot of them can speak a lot of languages, you know. They mostly were saying, 'Pick me, play with me, I am soft, or come join us.' Things like that. Some of them had marks on them. Like bad hurts and scars. I think they need to watch them more carefully, so they don't get hurt." Tim said the last part with determination, and then went on.

"When Seim and I walked past the kitchen going to the bathroom, I could hear a lot of voices talking. They were talking about getting food ready for a feast the next day, and someone was talking about needing extra help on the roof. Then two people, close to the door, were talking about something with getting her feet ready, and they laughed, but it was two men. They sounded like older people," said Tim.

"Any idea how many?" James asked.

Tim thought for a moment. "Obviously, I don't know how many, but I heard four different voices, and it sounded like a lot of people in the room. One of the voices was a woman, and the other three sounded like men."

James asked, "Any idea what they were talking about?"

"No, it sounded like general talking about things they needed to do," said Tim.

James registered there were probably a lot more people than he had seen. "That it?" he asked.

"That is all I can remember. Seim didn't speak. Just pointed. Oh, the bathroom was very old. It had boxes on the walls like the fancy ones, but wasn't very nice. It was clean, though. That is it," Tim finished.

"I can't thank you enough, Tim. Honestly, you were great, and did more to help than I could ever have expected."

Tim just smiled and said, "You are welcome. Are we done? Can I work on the drawings now?"

"Yes, sir, you may. Tim, for the fortress especially, a map style drawing would be helpful, as well as what the whole thing looked like as we pulled up. Each of the walls in the office with the monitors would be great. Same for Noi's office area," James clarified.

"Not a problem. I like drawing." Tim walked over, and shook his hand again, in the same stiff manner as the night before, and James smiled.

Tom walked Tim out, and James sat a moment before pulling out the file on Spara. It sounded like more adults were in that place than just the Tan family, and that Yan had taken over for his dad, with his mom acting as the figurehead.

He wondered about the younger adults in the place. *They are probably 'leftovers' nobody had bought and had little choice about what they do. It's sad, the traps people are in through no error of their own, due to the selfishness of a few, and the blind eye of many.*

He put the folder away. Somehow, this matter with Spara seemed to have taken a backseat to the unexpected issue with the Tan family. He felt fired up, and decided to go work it out in the combat zone training area.

# •Chapter Twenty-Six•

Walking through the solid double doors to the training portion of the building a minute later, James found a few people on the floor moving the standing bags and sparring equipment. He could see others working out in the weights area behind the etched glass, but he couldn't make out who they were. He walked into the locker room, and greeted his friend Gary, who was heading toward the other exit to the aquatics section wearing a wetsuit.

James changed into shorts and a t-shirt, before grabbing his gloves and feet pads. Just before he closed the door to his locker, he heard his phone ring.

"Hey, Mom, what's up?" James answered.

"Nice to see you're actually talking, Mr. Quiet. Where is the thing your dad uses outside on his thing?" She could never remember what his father's tools were called.

"Outside," James said, in a smart-alecky way.

"Don't be funny. He's looking for it, and can't find it," his mom said.

"Mom, you have to tell me a little bit more about what he's looking for. And why didn't he just call?" James asked.

"I don't know. He's running around trying to get some of the road leveled back down because he doesn't like the taper or something. The pavers are coming, but have already said it's fine as it is. Told him he'd better not mess it up, and end up costing us more." She said this calmly, before screaming, "What?"

James pulled the phone away from his ear a mo-ment before saying, "I hope whatever that was, was worth my ear drum bursting."

"Stop whining, or I'll give you something to cry about," she retorted.

His mom was a very caring person, but that was easy to miss due to her rather hard shell. Often there wasn't a lot of sympathies spared on 'life's bumps and bruises,' as she called them. As kids, getting a swift blow to the head was a daily occurrence. So much so, that all four of the older children instinctively flinched when she walked by. A determined woman, she didn't believe in wasting money, and rarely did things for herself. She had overcome a lot, much of it so that her children were fed and clothed.

The family wasn't exactly poor, but they certainly didn't have a great deal of money. Many nights, dinner was a bowl of oatmeal, or a peanut butter and jelly sandwich. The older children didn't have brand name clothing growing up, unless they bought it themselves. The age span of twenty-five years between the oldest and youngest helped a bit regarding living expenses, but there were no funds to send anyone to college. Even if there had been, chances are they wouldn't have been given, as it was the family belief that if you wanted something, you had to find a way to get it. This was a lesson James had learned many times, and one of the first he could recall.

"Your dad says it's the boom pin for the bucket," she continued.

"Oh, it's in the truck box, on the left-hand side, on the middle shelf. Or it was the last time I saw it. If he reorganized again, then I have no idea," James said. He added, "'The thing your dad uses outside on his thing,' really? That was the best description you could give me?"

"Shut up," his mom said, before hollering, "Check the middle shelf on the left, he said in the box!" James assumed she was yelling to his dad.

"And now both of my ears are bleeding," James complained. "So much for being able to hear for the rest of the day. You know the phone is cordless, you could've walked over, and told him that instead of yelling it." James rubbed his ear again.

"Very funny. What time do you think you'll be home?" his mom asked.

James smirked, and said, "I should go, as I can't hear anymore if you're saying anything. Just sounds like the ocean in my ears."

"What do you mean 'like the ocean'? If you were deaf, you wouldn't hear anything, smarty. I thought you studied the body in school?"

"What?" said James, letting out a little laugh.

"Don't be cute." Her tone was changing quickly to annoyance.

James decided not to push his luck. "Around 8, but I can help tomorrow with whatever."

"Good, I have an appointment in the morning to see the doctor about my stomach. You can watch the kids," she said.

They said their goodbyes, and James put the phone back in the locker, and left the locker room.

The training session he had seen before had ended. The only people left on the floor were Sharon and Amber.

Amber was a tall, and extremely athletic instructor. James particularly liked her smile, but it came at a price. If you saw her smiling it was because she was kicking your butt.

Sharon was a bit shorter, and an expert at being accepted into groups quickly. She could get people to talk and gossip like no other. She was a gossip, which came in handy as a news writer, and had a very sassy manner at times. She also had a genuine desire to do better in life. James suspected her desires and ambitions weren't in line, as she didn't stick to too many things very long. Her new ambition was to be a better physical fighter because, as she said, "I can already fight with my mouth."

"Hey, ladies," James called out with a wave.

"Hey," they chorused back.

"I'm getting better at fighting, James. You're going to be next," Sharon said.

Amber immediately jumped on board. "That's a great idea James, spar her."

James shrugged, and walked over.

Sharon protested. "Now? We just did all that stuff for, like, an hour. I'm exhausted, and just want to crash."

"You'd better get ready, or you're going to get beat," James shot back, smiling.

"I already have my gloves off," she said, holding up her taped hands.

James smiled, "I'm well warned, here we go."

Sharon narrowed her eyes and scoffed. James noted her right eyelid closed more than her left, meaning she was left eye dominant. He recalled from earlier interactions that she was right handed. James would use a southpaw attack for a few moves. Then, he would switch feet, and stance, knowing she wouldn't be able to respond in time. Sure enough, within fifteen seconds James was landing each of his strikes with ease, and dodging all of hers.

She puffed a little and said, "This isn't fair. I'm tired, and he's faster, and stronger, and better."

"Excuses are like assholes. Everyone has one, and they all stink," Amber shrugged. Sharon rolled her eyes, and Amber went on, "You think in a fight anyone cares? Deal with it or don't fight, but you never know when a fight is coming to you, so you'd better be ready. Now fight!" Amber was no-nonsense kind of person.

Sharon lunged at James, who honestly wasn't expecting it. He quickly sidestepped her, and delivered an uppercut to her lower ribs, and two jabs to the head. He didn't hit her hard, and she had on equipment, but she was still enraged. When she came back in, she was throwing everything she had at him, and in poor form. James sharply maneuvered her into a bind, so that he could stop her and talk.

"Don't swing like you have a hammer in your hand when you punch." James released her as he spoke. "Create a tight fist, and hit with these two knuckles." He grabbed her hand, and balled it into a fist, before pointing to the index and middle knuckles. "When you punch, do it from the shoulder, and have hip rotation in it. The fist is the delivery, but the punch comes from the shoulder. To move the shoulder, move the hip."

Amber nodded to show she agreed with him.

James and Sharon sparred three more minutes. He let her get in a lot of body shots, encouraging her to hit him as hard as she could. There was a lot to be said for actually learning what it felt like to hit someone. She couldn't go anymore after that, but Amber was ready.

With Amber, James was going to have his hands full. He was skilled, but Amber was an authentic martial artist. She had the speed and power to clean his clock, but he also knew that if he kept the fight tight, he'd eliminate half her offense by stopping her kicks.

They sparred. Amber came out aggressively, as she always did. James stayed on his feet, and moved in semi-circles trying to get in, but her feet were keeping him at bay. They went at it for about ninety seconds. Amber was kicking butt, but James was finally able to move in, as she threw a back leg turning kick. He pulled his punch, but it landed true as he blocked her right leg kick. She went down.

"Oh!" Sharon called, as Amber attempted to leg sweep James.

He stumbled. She didn't get it off clean, but it was enough to get him to back off while she got up. Amber smiled. Quicker than a snap of the fingers, she used a scissor-kick on him, taking him down. *Wham!* He hit the floor, where he took a heel kick to the thigh.

"It was fun to use that," Amber said smiling.

"You kicked butt!" Sharon said clapping.

James, still on the ground, rolled his eyes at Sharon.

"You fight so well with your hands. You need to get some more legs in there, James," Amber commented, extending a hand to pull him off the mat.

"I won't ever have your legs," James said, gaining his feet.

"If you worked at it, maybe you could have my legs under you faster than you imagine," Amber said.

James's eyebrows went up, and Sharon giggled.

Amber rolled her eyes and said, "Get your minds out of the gutter, ya pervs," which just made them laugh harder.

Tariq walked out of the weight area, as she added, "In a fight, you would take me, James. I know in sparring you're pulling the power instead of giving it to me."

"Can't even handle a woman, eh James? Maybe, I should teach you how to handle women right, and give her the 'power' where it matters," said Tariq, with a smirk.

"You can't even handle your hair, let alone a woman. Come back another time, little boy," Amber shot at him.

He ignored her. "What about it, James?" he asked.

James looked at him. "You going to teach me the finer points of punching? I seem to recall us going through this little exercise before, and you on the ground."

"That was bullshit, and you know it. I bet I can throw a better control punch than you. Amber here can be the judge. What do you say?" Tariq asked, with a swagger to his motions.

"What did you have in mind?" James asked.

"A walk-up punch to the nose. The one that does it the fastest without actually hitting the other one wins. The forward motion will make it harder to control," Tariq said.

"Oh, that's so dumb," Sharon said.

"Okay, you can go first," James said quickly.

Sharon threw her hands up dramatically and sighed, "Men."

Amber stood to the side as Tariq took about six steps back. James stood waiting.

"Don't be a little bitch, and flinch, or close your eyes," Tariq laughed, but no one else did.

A split second later, Tariq threw his punch. It was very fast, and had power to it, and stopped a hair from James's nose. James blinked, but that was the extent of his moving.

"My turn," James said, as Tariq took his prior position. "Ready?"

"Born ready," Tariq said.

Amber rolled her eyes. "What a douche."

James laughed, "Right."

Instead of punching towards Tariq's nose, James deliberately hit him square in the forehead, and he went down. Sharon and Amber roared with laughter as Tariq lay there, grabbing his forehead with both hands.

"Looks like you win, Tariq," James said, attempting to restrain a smile.

Tariq was mad. "What the hell, man?" He got to his feet. "You gotta hit when a man isn't ready for it? That is a total bitch move."

He swung at James, who ducked under it, and punched him squarely in the armpit. Besides hurting a lot, a punch to that spot makes the arm numb for a few moments.

Tariq let out a gasp of pain.

"You can thank my older brother for that trick, and the armpit punch," James commented, with a slight bitter undertone.

"Looks like you're the bitch now. Best stop while you can, and while I'm inclined to let this situation go unreported," Amber said, in a serious tone.

James nodded, and Tariq stomped off with a "Whatever!"

"Hey, didn't he sucker punch you a few weeks ago?" asked Sharon.

"Indeed he did," James said.

"Nothing like the stove calling the pot black," Sharon said.

"Kettle," James corrected her.

"Huh?" Sharon looked at him.

"Never mind," James said, as she had the saying wrong.

The women left, and James worked the bags for about thirty minutes. He considered Amber's point about kicking, and decided that once he was in Pittsburgh, he'd learn some Taekwondo. Besides being fun, it would offer a ready made excuse for any potential bruises from activities for the group.

# •Chapter Twenty-Seven•

That night, though it was good to be home, he didn't sleep well, as his schedule was still slightly off. Morning came quickly, but his mom had taken the two younger kids over to an aunt's house, instead of waking him. The house was quiet. That is, until his dad got home.

"James, get up!" his dad barked at him. "Can't lie there crushing that bed all day."

James's eyes reluctantly opened. He was still tired, and a bit surprised he hadn't heard his dad's truck coming up the lane.

"Yeah, okay," was all he replied.

His dad ran a salvage yard. He was a simple man who tended to be hard to read. He could be overly blunt, and short with people, though not on purpose. Often, he seemed abrasive and inconsiderate, and his drinking didn't help. He saw the world one way, and believed any variation to that was just wrong.

Though James was a few inches taller than his dad, his old man was still of average size with a lean build for his age. He tended to wear his hair on the long side, and because of that, James had grown up with his hair longer when he was little. James used to joke that when his dad came back from getting a haircut, it was still longer than James would ever let his grow once he was an adult.

"That's because you don't know how to work. Out in the sun all day, you want your hair just like mine. Keeps the sun off your ears and neck, and protects you from bug bites," his dad once told him.

"What about the winter, when the bugs are dead, and the sun is nowhere to be seen?" James fired back.

His mom heard the exchange, and promptly smacked him as his dad answered. "Keeps you warm, dummy. Geez, and you're supposed to be smart."

James decided to cut his losses and not reply.

It turned out the help his dad needed wasn't so bad. He just needed assistance with the tractor, and hooking and unhooking chains. Small things like this just went a lot faster with help. James was walking beside the bucket with one hand on a tree to stop it from swinging, when he got a call from Carissa.

"Hey Risa, how's you?" James asked in a loud voice.

"Good. What is all that noise?" she said.

"It's a tractor. Listen, can I call you back later?" he asked.

"Well, I called ta let you know I won't have me phone for a few days, but I will be thinking of you, and will call again as soon as I can. It's for a team thing with the bank. I have ta do it as part of the program, and promotion then, you know," she said.

"Aye, right, then. Well, we'll talk soon then. Looking forward to it," James said, a little louder to make sure she could hear him over the tractor.

"Brilliant, Bye, Love," Carissa said.

"Bye," James said.

A minute later, when they were unloading the tree, his dad called out, "Who is Risa?"

James paused. Normally his dad was half deaf due to all of the loud noises that he dealt with day in, and day out. He typically had the TV so loud you could hear it anywhere in the house.

"I said sister," James said, without looking up.

"Oh," his dad replied. "Why were you talking like you're British or something?"

James thought, *Don't let the Scots or Brits hear you say that*, but only said, "Just keeping it interesting."

James glanced up to see his dad shake his head. Predictably, his father went into a lecture about how not being normal was bad if you wanted to be success-ful, because people wouldn't relate to you. This wasn't the first time James had gotten this lecture, and it wouldn't be the last. It did end differently this time, though.

"James, your mother and I are worried about you going to Pittsburgh and all. We're proud of you gradu-ating from college. Not many in the family have done that. But working with others in an office and all, just hard to understand. We want the best for you."

"I know, Dad, but you guys need to trust that I know what I'm doing." James spoke with the right in-flection in his voice to let his dad know that he was listening, and appreciative, but James had thought this through.

"I sure hope so. I know you got all them loans and stuff. Don't agree with all that debt, but it's your prob-lem to solve. You need to get out of it as fast as you can..." The lecture that followed took a solid five min-utes.

Recognizing when you're five years old that you're more intelligent, but less knowledgeable, than your parents makes for a difficult childhood. He also understood the distinction between knowledge and intelligence. James's parents simply had difficulty thinking beyond their everyday lives. It was part of the reason he didn't care to spend too much time at home, as life there was way too slow for his taste. It did, however, teach him patience, and how to operate silently from the shadows.

James had an early start the next morning at group headquarters, where he managed to get through the file on Anthony Spara. It was all there. The family tree, the structure of the organization up to about five years prior, the distribution chain, the location of the fields, the cargo ships, and the names of the partners needed for the operation in foreign countries. It even mentioned Spara's sister's tragic death, but without details. This was enough information to not only indict Anthony Spara, but about fifty other people in multiple countries once confirmed.

James glanced again at a letter he'd found in the file. It had been stuck between pages seven and eight, and he had a feeling it wasn't supposed to have been there. The note was from Yan's father, Qiang, and written in English.

*"My son Yan, I am very proud of you. As I join my fathers in the eternal life, I know that you will bring my spirit honor, as I was unable to do before leaving you. You have been critical in keeping up on what the enemy has been doing these last few years, and that will be of much use in destroying them. Remember the lessons from Sun Tzu, and do not let them see you acting. Use another that is equally injured, and control them as we have gone over many times. Below is information for your eyes only, and I trust you will find it most advantageous.*

*You know, of course, that Joe is the disgrace of my father's daughter, and a bastard to the family. His father is Anthony Spara. Spara does not know of the boy's birth. He will value this, and you can use this as leverage, if things become out of control, and linked to the family. Your aunt was very drunk the night she lay with Spara, and does not remember who the father is. I know as I caught them. But at the time, he was my business partner, so I sacrificed her virginity for the business. I know your mother always questioned why I would not let the bastard join the others for training and auction. She thought it a weakness for my sister. It was not. In fact, I could have sold him several times, and refused very good offers, but in business, you must make decisions to guard the future.*

*When things fall for Spara, stay out of the way. Do not get involved directly or indirectly. The fallout will be very large and widespread. It could take three to four years to settle, as the world will have a vacuum of power. I have made preparations to safeguard the family, so keep things as they are for the external world, but vigorously maintain internal protections. I know that you will, as you have designed many of them, especially the greatest one's surrounding protection. I am very proud of your genius. When it is clear that dominance has been reestablished, you will still be able to reenter the market. Your mother remembers all the details from the fields.*

*You must sit with her, and map it out in case she passes too. You have the key with X marking the spots of real power. That is all the protection you will need outside."*

The letter was simply signed *"Father."*

James was curious about the steps Qiang and Yan had taken to maintain internal protections. James wondered if the internal protections were the cameras, and the very high tech computer system. The system, though impressive, wasn't genius. It just required the right hook ups, as all the material was available on the market. James was still curious as to how they had gotten all the equipment in. Nothing could pass without a battery removal. Unless, maybe, that was the genius part, getting past the force field, or whatever it was, with everything still working. He needed to learn more about Yan Tan to see what this was all about. He made a note to dig deeper, and hopefully find a connection to Yan.

He started to think about the reference to the X key, as no map or code was included, when there was a knock on the door. "Come in," James called.

Korey, the administrative assistant, poked her head into the room. "Can you come with me, please? There's something you should see." She had an astonished look on her face.

"I'm about to leave. I've got to get to work," James said, which was true. "How long will this take?"

"Trust me. You want to see this." She turned and left.

James closed the file and grabbed his bag. As they walked, he stuffed the file inside. She led him into the largest gathering room, and when he looked around, his mouth hit the floor.

Tim was standing in the center of the room. Covering the bulk of the light green walls were drawings. Incredibly detailed drawings. It was as though Tim had begun snapping pictures with a camera when they'd arrived at the fortress, and had simply printed his pictures in blue and black ink.

The drawings contained details James had forgotten, like the two standing plants on either side of the bar. However, the level of detail went far beyond that. Tim had even put in the hanging glasses over the bar, and James suspected he had the correct number of glasses.

James understood Korey's expression now. Gaping in amazement, he found the main corridors and layout. This was better than any simple floor plan. It even appeared to have rooms James hadn't seen that Tim had written *"Guess"* on. James recalled their conversation in the hotel on the first stage of their trip.

"I think this is okay. Is it okay?" Tim asked. "I mean I know I didn't draw each brick from each room. It would have taken me much longer to do so. Obviously, I can do that if you want. The detail is the easy part." Tim was speaking very fast, and starting to get nervous.

"Tim, no. This is just freaking awesome. My God." James was still looking at the drawings when Tom and Andy walked in. Tom apparently had already seen them, but Andy was speechless. He looked around while James continued talking to Tim. "I can't even begin to tell you how impressed I am. That isn't even a strong enough word. This is just incredible. You did this in just three days? How?"

Tim smiled so big you could see the bridgework on his back molars. "Obviously, yes, I did all this. But I also finished the office building, and the car lot like you said." He pointed at a large stack of sheets on the table. "I would have done more, but that is all you said to do. And my hand started to hurt too." Tim cradled his right hand in his left.

"Can I see you in my office, please, James?" Andy asked.

James nodded, and turned back to Tim. "This is great," he repeated fervently. "Thank you so much, Tim. I owe you big time for all of this. We'll have a pizza party soon! I'll organize it with Scott, and get it on the calendar."

"Oh, can I pick the toppings?" Tim asked excitedly.

"Of course! Whatever you want, buddy," James said, matching Tim's tone.

"Well, obviously pepperoni, but we will have to try a lot of different ones. Can I invite anyone I want?" Tim asked.

"Yes, we just have to organize it with Scott. I have to run now. Andy needs me, and I'm going to be late for work, but we'll do it soon," James said.

Tim paused a moment, and then shook James's hand with both of his, still smiling.

"Korey, can you let Scott know." James said, breaking free of Tim's grip.

"I'll take care of it," she said with a smile.

Andy wasn't a heavyset man, but he certainly had a massive top to him. His broad shoulders and little neck, sat upon what had once been a very built chest. It appeared that Andy had neglected to work on his legs, as they looked like spindles that could crack at any moment. He had dark grayish eyes, and jet black hair that was just starting to gray. His dimpled chin suited his rather round head, and he apparently suffered from eczema, given how his skin always looked.

"Tim is excited, James." Andy gestured for James to have a seat as he walked into the office. "You did well with him."

"I can't stay. I'm running late as it is." James wanted to make it clear that he wanted Andy to get to the point, and save the accolades for a different day.

"I see. I'm not going to fund any side projects involving that fortress," Andy said, getting straight to the point.

James's mind exploded with thoughts as it always did. He had his comment ready, but he literally bit his tongue to prevent himself from voicing it. He knew that silence was better.

Andy knew what he was doing. "Keep your silence, hoping I'll rethink what I just said. I won't. I know you had Tim get those drawings together, so you could front some type of attack, or siege, or whatever."

James remained silent, and stared into Andy's eyes.

Andy went on. "The objective is Spara, not this trafficking thing. At least not right now. I need your focus on Spara. This is the biggest thing we have going, and you've been phenomenal, as always. Finish this, and then we move on. Okay?"

James's mind raced along its spider web-like paths, recalculating his answer. He came out with, "Okay, Spara is the focus. Got it. I have to run."

Andy had clearly expected some resistance. "Oh, okay. Thanks. I'm glad we're on the same page."

James headed for the door, but stopped. "I'll be taking Tim's drawings for safe keeping, as this is still my case. Unless, of course, you're going to give it to another team that hasn't been there, or established any relationship. Speaking of, I don't think Tim would be willing, nor would he be a smart bet to send back."

Andy gave a curt nod, and James closed the door.

James stopped to gather the drawings. The room was empty, so he made short work of it.

He was a solid fifteen minutes behind schedule for a drive that would take at least ninety minutes. He made it to Pittsburgh in seventy-three minutes with a bit of high-speed driving, and luck that no police were on Route 22 that day.

# •Chapter Twenty-Eight•

Things were coming together. James made arrangements to see Carissa while doing some upcoming customer visits, and finishing his training at the Aberdeen office. His colleague Dennis had spoken highly of James's ability to turn around a critical field trial, and that customers had specifically requested that James be involved from here on out.

James couldn't help but reflect that he'd only given the customer what he wanted, a simple enough concept that apparently got lost in the day-to-day flurry of activity for most businesses.

He'd also gotten some preliminary information about Yan that required a trip to the UK. Yan had spent three years at the University of Cambridge studying magnetic fields. It just so happened that the leading researcher in the field, a professor Yan would no doubt have had, was giving a lecture the first week of James's trip back to Scotland. Attending it would be a great way to gain some insight.

Now it was moving day from his parent's home to the "big city," as his dad called Pittsburgh. His buddy Mark agreed to help. They loaded up James's rusty Ford Tempo, the trailer on his dad's truck, and a few things into Mark's car and set off.

The day was hot. The hottest of the year, and the air conditioning in the Tempo wasn't the best. Combined with hitting a traffic jam before the Squirrel Hill tunnels made for a long journey, though it was only a hundred miles. When they arrived at the apartment on Brown's Lane, and walked inside, it felt like an oven.

The studio apartment was on the top floor of an old brick building. Sunshine poured in through two small windows, and the air conditioning unit was shut off. James immediately put down the box he was carrying, and turned on the unit to try to cool the place down. That wouldn't happen until fourteen hours later, around 6 a.m.

"You would pick the hottest day of the year to move, into the hottest damn apartment, you could find," Mark commented, dripping with sweat.

"Whatever. I don't want to hear about heat from you. You had the heat in the freshmen dorms so high it felt like this year round," James retorted.

Mark flipped him off in a lazy sort of way, and walked out to get another load.

James's dad was unstrapping the bed, couch, computer desk, dresser, and two small tables. He worked quietly until they got the first things up to the apartment.

"How much is this place a month?" he asked, but before James could answer, he said, "Never mind, I don't want to know." He then sat down on the air conditioner. He'd do this for a minute after each load of things they brought up.

Since James didn't have much, the unloading went quickly. When they finished, they could've all used a shower to cool down, but that wasn't in the making since all the towels were being used as packing blankets. Besides, Mark and James were hungry. Mark planned to stay the night, and James was taking him to dinner.

"We're starving. Want to grab some food, Dad?" James pointed to his own wallet to indicate he was paying.

"Not really, no. I want to get back on the road, and home. Besides, the A/C in my truck works a lot better than this thing." He patted the unit he was once again sitting on. They said goodbye downstairs, and his dad was off.

Then James and Mark walked to a small shopping center next to the apartment building. It was a place James would come to know extremely well. Entering the mall doors felt amazing as they got a blast of cold frozen air. They both gave a sigh of relief, then laughed to see the other one doing the same thing. They had spent so much time together they were as much brothers as friends.

James began to memorize the mall immediately. Each corner, where escalators and elevators were, and distances between exits. Two different episodes in malls in the last few years had made him a little hyper-sensitive to knowing their layouts very well.

They grabbed some pizza from the café, and talked about a lot of nothing for about an hour, enjoying the well-earned break. They then decided to buy some fabric to cover the windows. That turned out to be a disaster. They had no idea on the size and guessed. Since they didn't know how to hang curtains, they did some 'on-the-spot engineering,' until the windows were mostly covered. It took them well over an hour, and the sun beat directly on them the entire time.

"Can it get any hotter?" Mark kept asking.

James snapped back, "Yes, every time you say something."

This merely started an argument. After getting the windows covered up, they decided to go to the grocery store to get refreshments, and cool off again. When they got back, the apartment was slightly less hot. Then they got to work, unpacking.

Mostly they worked in silence with the radio in the background. It was too hot to sleep. They ended up working through the night until everything was done, and even James's computer desk was in place. They both grabbed quick showers, and crashed as the sun came up. *It's been an irritating sort of day*, thought James as he dropped off to sleep, but he recognized that Mark was a true friend to stick with him until the job was done.

As he often did, James had some had weird dreams. One of the dreams was about running on a treadmill through a fire trying to get to a toy store. Another involved walking around endless corners trying to escape people chasing him. One involved failing between two choices, over and over again, and the result was one of his brothers dying. The last one however, felt very real.

*He was dropping to his knees, and reaching for something in dim light. He felt happy, but shouldn't. There were footsteps coming as he grasped what he needed, and started to come out from behind the curtain like cloth.*

After a few hours of terrible sleep, James and Mark got up. They fixed the window coverings properly, and went out for breakfast, and then Mark headed for home. Alone, at last, James called Carissa, who had tried to call him at least twice since he'd left his parents home.

# •Chapter Twenty-Nine•

"Well, hello there, how's you?" came her comforting voice on the other end of the phone.

"Brilliant. How are you, beautiful?" James was melting at the sound of her voice.

Carissa gave a small giggle James hadn't previously heard. "I wager not many have seen how adorable you are."

"I'm not taking that one. The odds are stacked against me, and as far as I'm concerned, you're the only person deserving to see it," James said, in a sheepish tone.

"Love, you have no idea how that makes me feel ta hear you say that. And I truly believe that is how you feel, too. Thank you." She made a kissing sound over the phone.

James paused for a moment, letting that feeling he was starting to associate with her to wash over him. It was a sensation like a slightly too warm day, but with a gentle breeze blowing over him, creating that perfect feeling of contentment and relaxation.

"I'm sorry I wasn't able to take your calls. I hope it wasn't anything urgent," he said.

"Actually, John, I do need something, and it is a bit urgent," Carissa said.

James snapped immediately to attention. "Risa, what's wrong?"

Carissa laughed, "Nothing is wrong, Love, but ta be honest, it is nice ta hear you almost spring through the phone ta help. You know I've the opportunity and such with the bank, yeah?"

James relaxed slightly, "Aye."

"Well, they want me ta move a bit faster than I thought they would," she said.

"I don't blame them. They don't want to lose you now that they have you. Smart lot," James said.

Carissa paused a moment. "Makes this easier ta ask you now that you say that. Would you want a flatmate for a bit until I can find something else? I will pay the full rent for the time I'm with ya, and me stuff can go ta storage. I know you travel all the time so I thought this would be all right, all around, you know." She said all of this without taking a breath.

"Wow," James said, to give himself extra time. His brain had already spider webbed in its decision path, and he was surprised at his extreme emotional response. To make this work, he needed to establish a place, and the utilities under John's name. That part was simple. Paying for it was another matter, as he tried to avoid tapping into resources he had access to for non-operational things. He was entirely free to use the funds as he saw fit, but still exercised caution. However, if she were covering the rent, then he just had the other bills.

He wanted to say yes with every inch of him, and for all the right reasons, but she still thought he was John. *This doesn't seem the right time to tell her, but if not now, when?* James thought. The longer they saw each other, the harder it would be to tell her, and for her to accept it.

"I'm sorry if that is ta much. No worries, I will manage something. Just thought... Anyhow, how is your..." Carissa had taken his three seconds of silence incorrectly.

Interrupting her, James said with a frog in his throat, "I think it's a brilliant idea, and I truly would love for nothing more."

"John," she said slowly, and James cringed. He felt guilty that she didn't know his real name. "Are you sure? I don't want ta pressure you. I understand if you're not comfortable with this," she said.

"When are you moving in?" James asked.

Silence followed this question for a moment, then a slight sniff.

"Are you crying? There's no reason to cry," James said.

Carissa laughed and said, "No, I'm not having a cry. I was having a think for a mo' and me nose itched. I'm not a basket case type. Is that the kinda of girls you like?"

"Cheeky. Well then, my fair lady, I think we are in agreement. When are you moving?" James asked again.

"I was thinking on that, and want ta do it whilst you're home over a weekend. If you can help that would be just about the best thing ever," she said.

"Of course. Want to do it the first weekend I'm back, early Saturday morn'?" In the background, James heard a door slam.

"Perfect. I have ta run, Love, but we can get the smaller stuff out of the way later. Judy doesn't normally slam doors, but she just returned from hospital, so I don't think it was good news."

"Right, talk soon then, Risa."

"Bye, Love," Carissa said, gently before the line went silent.

James was glad to end the call, as he would've had to do some fancy talking to avoid giving the address he didn't have yet. This was one of those times that being a member of the group was extremely useful. James placed a call to Korey, and explained that he needed a one-bedroom apartment, furnished, with a few basics, in a decent part of Aberdeen, preferably new construction, under his alias of John Arthur Boyd. He also asked her to specifically select places where the neighbors kept mostly to themselves.

Korey called back asking for birthplace information for John, which caught James by surprise. He said to list his birthplace as Glencoe, but to say his family homestead was at Inverbervie. He explained John would have traveled a lot as a kid.

The next night, he called Carissa, and gave her the address. He wouldn't see the apartment until he arrived himself, but he'd have a few days to get whatever he needed, and make the place seem reasonably lived in. With the essential details taken care of, James finally began to relax. *Yes, things are falling into place*, he thought.

The next day at work, James was speaking with his boss, Todd, about how to position two new thermodynamic fluids. They ran through a few different points, including the current market, how the company's current chemicals were perceived, and where the value add was from the customer's point of view.

The two men had differing viewpoints in this area. James was trying to stay respectful in the discussion, but his argument was logical, and it was frustrating arguing against phrases like 'I feel' or 'In the past'.

They had just finished talking about pricing, and had agreed it should be done on the market, not cost, when Todd gave a deep sigh.

"I think it's time we terminate this internship," he said.

James sat up, rather shocked. "But wait, why?"

Todd raised his eyebrows, and began to speak just as James quickly cut in. "I have to say, that seems harsh. I realize this is your business and your call, but you asked what I thought. And it isn't like there were others in the room as we talked. I will do what you think is best, but..." James was surprised to hear Todd chuckle.

"I want to hire you full-time, right now. But I can't hire you, because of the potential merger, so I'm making you a consultant. Same principle as the internship, but it looks better on the resume, and you get paid more. Just no time and a half," Todd explained.

"Oh," James said, rather confused, but regaining his normal thought process in the blink of an eye. He found himself analyzing why the thought of losing this job had caused so much distress. Yes, he'd have to re-work a lot of preparations he'd already done, but then he realized he wasn't distraught about that at all. It was the thought of Carissa, and maybe not seeing her. This worried him, and the worry must have shown on his face.

"Sorry, that was a bit mean. I was just teasin' for a moment. You have a lot of talent. If you didn't, I certainly wouldn't have you going all over the place," Todd said with a smile, that asked for forgiveness, and delivered reassurance at the same time.

"Yeah, no problem. Just caught me off guard," James said, with a small laugh.

"I don't mind you and me discussing things openly one-on-one. I assume that if others are around, you'll follow my lead unless I ask for your opinion. People are going to talk about you. They already do," he said.

James frowned slightly.

Todd continued, "Not because you've done any-thing wrong, but because you're doing a lot right. That means change, and people don't like that. So a target will be painted on your back 'til they get used to you. Just keep it low key, do what you need to, and let me handle the rest. Come on, let's grab some food, and hash out a deal." He clasped James on the back as they walked out.

James felt better. He was getting a considerable amount of money for his first post-college job. More than most people with more experience, and an ad-vanced degree. No benefits, but he was still young and healthy, and on his parent's health insurance. He also had a lot of responsibility for strategy, market research, customer needs, and cost analysis. It meant a lot of time in the field, and at the plants, and not so much behind a desk, which was exactly what he wanted. Plus, he set his hours, and technically didn't have a boss.

# •Chapter Thirty•

The next few nights brought weird dreams about corners, being chased, fire, toy stores and more. On Saturday morning, James got up, and walked over to the mall. He knew the dreams had to deal with malls, because those situations all happened at different malls, and James thought walking through this mall might stop the dreams.

He strolled through the doors he and Mark had first come through, and lazily went to his left. He found himself comparing this mall to the one where he had been chased by two CIA agents years ago.

James recalled that day. He had just finished a de-briefing at the group, and was heading back toward his college. As he was getting near his exit, he thought he had someone following him, but thought that wasn't likely. Being the cautious type that he was, he decided to take a detour just to make sure.

He got into the left lane, and passed a car. The po-tential following vehicle did the same. James then got back in the right lane to take the exit ramp, and so did the other vehicle. James made a left that would take him back to school, but would also lead him to the mall.

James aggressively got over to turn into the mall at the last moment, but the car following him just drove on. James felt a little foolish, but decided that now he was here he should get another pair of jeans. He was down to one pair, as he had recently torn his other pair playing flag football with his friends.

The mall had over 100 stores and restaurants spread over two levels, with five large anchor department stores. It was only a few years old, and had a very steady crowd of people there daily. Though it was basically a long rectangle, the layouts of the first, and second floor differed because of a few courtyards.

James parked on the backside of the mall, on the third of four levels in the parking garage. He'd go in on the second floor, as that was the fastest route to get to the store he needed. James wasn't much of a shopper, and preferred to be in and out. He picked the third floor in case his car wouldn't start, as it was having battery issues. This way he could get a battery jump if needed, without having to worry about blocking other cars in near him while he did this.

After backing his car into a spot, he got out of his car and walked to the trunk. He was going to change his license plate back to the plate that was registered to the car. James always changed his plate when he went to the group if he wasn't using a rental car. One of the advantages of his dad having a salvage yard was there were always a lot of old plates lying around. James took this extra step as a precaution. It was one of a few precautions he had taken with the group since day one; after all, they were spies.

He opened the trunk, and started to shift the stuff he had around so he could lift the panel covering the spare tire. He had just lifted the spare tire to grab the hidden license plate, when a car quickly parked in a space one over from his.

James glanced over to see the vehicle that had been following him parked on his left. Two men got out quickly, but calmly. James dropped the tire, and grabbed a wrench he used to adjust the terminals on the car battery from the truck before closing it. He slid the tool into his back right pocket.

The driver, who was nearest James, said "Casey Rosas?" and before James could even say "Who," he slammed James's head into the trunk of his own car. James didn't have a glass jaw, but this sudden attack, and the force of the slam did stun him for a few seconds before he could react.

The passenger held open the back driver's side door as the drive pushed James in. James pulled the wrench out of his pocket, and just as they went to shut the door, threw it into the door jam as he sat up. The wrench stopped the door from closing. The passenger took a step forward, but the driver that had pushed James in, grabbed the doorframe with his right hand to shut it again. The wrench clanged to the concrete of the parking garage. James quickly pulled the door, and smashed the man's hand between the car door jam and the door. The other man made a move toward the door, and James kicked it as hard as he could. It caught him hard in the knees, and knocked him down, screaming in pain like his partner.

James got out, and the man with the injured hand swung a left hook at him. He missed, and his fist hit the car. James threw a sharp left jab that made the man stagger slightly, followed by a powerful right uppercut. The uppercut landed squarely under his opponent's chin, and he fell backward bouncing off his car, before hitting the concrete face down.

The other man rolled over to get to his feet, and James's thrust the car door into his head. With both men knocked out for a moment, James had to check them for weapons. Neither man was carrying a gun, which James thought odd once he checked their wallets. The man with the crushed hand, and potential broken jaw, was Elliot Varga. His counterpart was named Brock Jones. The amazing part was both men's identifications said they were with the CIA.

They were starting to come to, and James decided he wouldn't be able just to drive away. He needed to inhibit these men for a while. He took their wallets and made for the mall. James kept his head down, with his chin almost touching his chest, as he quickly walked toward the stairs that would lead to the second-floor entrance of the mall. He was fishing his phone out of his pocket as he walked. The men were on their feet, and moving as fast as they could together to catch up.

James was in the mall just before they started down the stairs. He dialed *-6-8-9-1-1, and hit send. He wasn't sure if this would prevent the emergency center from seeing his phone number as being the caller, but it couldn't hurt to try.

As he rounded the first corner on his right, there was a hat store followed by a toy store. The hat store had several hats just outside the doorway on display. They had flashing lights that said 'Love,' 'Fancy,' 'Sweet,' and 'Sassy' on them. James grabbed one as he walked by. No one noticed as there were a lot of people at the toy store that day. There were so many, that the people were spilling out into the corridor trying to get the latest Beanie Babies.

The hat would do two things for him. First, it would hide his face well enough to make identifying him difficult by any witnesses. Second, the lights on the front would create a halo effect in case his face was captured on a camera; again making it difficult to get a positive identification on him.

"9-1-1 dispatch, what is..." came a voice on the phone.

"I'm being chased by two guys that just tried to mug me in the parking garage. I'm currently on the second floor of the Galleria mall just passed the toy store. Please send help," said James, still walking away. He put the hat on, and looked around.

The agents had just made it to the intersection and spotted him. James knew if they were CIA agents, they wouldn't jeopardize the kids.

"Sir, remain calm, are you in the mall?" asked the dispatcher.

"Yes, they are too. They are still following me. What should I do?" asked James, playing the role of being a victim.

"Sir, they won't harm you in front of people. Just remain calm, and on the phone with me. We have officers nearby. You should..." said the dispatcher.

"They are getting closer. I'm afraid they're going to jump me, and there're all sorts of kids around. I'm going to run for it," James said, cutting the dispatch officer off.

He was still walking away at a fast pace, but not running. The CIA agents had just gotten past the toy store area and the crowd. They too were walking at a rapid pace, though one was doing it while visibly in pain.

"No sir, do not do that. Please go into a store and behind a counter. Get near people. The officers are almost there," said the dispatcher, in a louder voice.

"I can't. I'd have to turn around to do that. I'm going to exit by The Ground Round restaurant on the front side of the mall. I need to be able to run. I have a blue hat on that says 'Sassy,' they both have sports jackets on with black pants," said James, in a desperate-sounding voice.

"Sir, no..." was all the dispatcher could say as James hung up.

James took the left corner, knowing the agents would lose sight of him for about five seconds. Through the double set of exit doors in front of James, he saw a police car. James began to run as the two officers made their way inside.

James ran until he passed the officers who were rushing toward him. Once he was on their other side, he called out "they are right there in the jackets." He then began to run again.

The agents had just taken the corner. They didn't have time to get away, plus the agent named Brock couldn't run normally with his knees all banged up. They were body tackled from what James could see through the doors. He didn't wait around to see anything else.

Since he had their identifications, the cops weren't going to listen to anything they were going to say in a hurry. At some point, they would get cleared, so James didn't feel bad for them.

He ducked into a small area outside next to the restaurant where they kept the trash. He took off the hat, and threw it out. James then took off his outer shirt, and threw it away too, before walking around the perimeter of the mall to get to his car.

He took a twenty dollar bill from each wallet to cover the cost of the shirt and the hat. In a few days,

James would come back to pay for the hat, while replacing his shirt. James then wiped down the agent's car to remove his fingerprints. He did the same to their wallets before placing them on the gas pedal, so they were easily found.

James checked out Brock Jones and Elliot Varga in the group's computer system. The system wasn't exactly complete, but neither name showed up. James mentioned it to Tom, and he said they would look into it further. James had volunteered to do it himself, but Tom insisted that someone else do it so that they were impartial. James thought he was being a little dramatic, but he did understand the logic of following that rule, so he let it go.

The next time James had come to the group's building, he noticed a few new cameras hidden in the tree line. When Andy saw him, he explained that they add those to make sure people weren't being followed from their location. He also said the agents had mistaken him for a man named Casey Rosas. Andy showed him a picture, and he had to admit it looked like him to a fair degree, except that Casey was ten years older, and had a larger chin.

James found himself outside of a barbershop in the mall near his apartment. He had been aimlessly walking around while reminiscing. It reminded him of the barbershop that his dad had taken him to occasionally at their hometown mall. He decided to get a haircut.

While he sat in the barber's chair, he thought about the other mall incident. That incident had changed his life forever. He learned a lot about fire from that event, but it was how he had met Ian Doyle. He'd soon have to contact Ian to ask for help, and he wasn't looking forward to it. He hated calling in favors, and this was going to be a big one. However, saving Ian from that mall fire probably would make him more willing to help.

# •Chapter Thirty-One•

Over the next few days, James got everything set for the trip to Aberdeen, but there was one last thing he needed to take care of in person before he set off. Tim's pizza party.

James pulled through the community gates, and headed for the central complex. It looked like a ghost town until he got to the building. Tim had invited the entire community to the party, and as they had nothing better to do, they all came. James laughed to himself as he walked in the door, and saw the crowd. *Good thing I'm getting a raise so I could pay for all this*, he thought.

Byron greeted him enthusiastically as he came into the main area, and pointed to Tim, who was wearing a suit and sunglasses. When he saw James, Tim lifted the glasses off his face, gave him a wink, and put them on again. Laughing a little to himself, James waved and winked back, before turning to find something to drink. As he walked away, he saw Melissa and Isaac dancing with some of the other guests. He ran into Scott at the drink table, who was trying to regulate how much soda residents were having, and failing miserably.

"Hey, man, this party was a great idea. Everyone is really excited and having a blast. Tim is definitely the man of the hour tonight. Everyone has been going up to him, and talking to him. Normally, they just keep to themselves, but I don't know, tonight everyone is just jazzed. Must be Dan the DJ doing his thing," Scott laughed. Once again, James pictured Scott holding a surfboard on the Californian shore.

Korey came over to James and Scott dragging her daughter, Heather, behind her. Her son, Lance, was by her side. "Hi guys," she said.

"Hey, Korey, how you doing, little man, and little chick-a-do?" Scott asked in his mellow way.

Heather hid behind her mom, but apparently Lance thought he was being spoken down to. With a roll of his eyes, he said, "Fiiiiiinnne" in a drawn out, sullen way.

"That's enough, Lance," Korey said, throwing Lance a dirty look. She redirected her attention to James. "Don't worry about the party tonight. It's been taken care of. Tim got a bit carried away, and Andy..."

James stopped her quickly with, "It's all good. Glad everyone is having a good time. Thank Andy for me, please." His voice started a little loud and gradually softened.

Lance sniffed audibly at James's comment, with a scowl on his face.

"Knock it off, Lance," Korey said in a deep under-tone, and James recognized the growl of an irritated mother. He had heard it many times from his own mother, usually because of something his older brother had done.

Trying to keep the peace, James asked Lance, "How'd school finish for you?"

"Okay," he said, in a bored way.

"What's okay? Like all A's and B's?" James asked.

"I'm not an idiot. Seriously, who gets B's in any class that matters?" Lance shot back.

Korey grabbed her son by the shoulders and said, "Boy, you better be respectful."

"I was," Lance said, slipping her grip. "It's not like I asked him about that stupid haircut, or if he has a decent game at Mortal Kombat."

"Lance, no one cares about those damn video games. I swear to God I'm going to toss that whole thing when I get home." Korey was starting to get loud.

Scott walked away, clearly wanting to avoid a confrontation, but James decided to take the kid on.

"What system?" he asked.

"N64, what'd you know about it?" Lance asked back.

"I like Mario Golf," said Tim, who had just walked up.

"Now that's a good game. I like playing with Bowser," Lance said to Tim, his whole expression was changing as they became engrossed talking about the games.

Korey and James talked separately, Heather still hanging on to her mom for dear life. Releasing a deep sigh, Korey began to apologize. "I don't know what to do with him. If it isn't about video games, he's sarcastic, and mean spirited. His father is no help. His skipping a grade, I think has also caused some issues."

James felt his whole body tense up. He dreaded these conversations. He never knew what to say. He found such experiences draining, and the things he did say sounded ridiculously cliché and boring.

He also thought people preferred to complain about their lives, instead of just figuring out how to fix them.

When offered a solution, people typically reacted like it was the best idea in the world, and as if they couldn't have come up with it themselves. James often felt bad, because, half the time, he was replying in a sarcastic manner, and felt people could see right through it. But they didn't, and they kept coming to him for advice. It made social interactions a task.

He liked to socialize, but he also valued alone time so that he could recharge. He knew this was a characteristic of being an introvert, but he didn't really care. Personal conversations like this were just daunting, though he didn't seem to mind the ones with Carissa, and a small select number of others.

Korey had been going on for nearly thirty minutes with James giving mere "Hmm" and "Yeah" answers, when Lance came rushing back. In a soft, but determined voice, he asked his mother, "Where's the bathroom?" James pointed behind him, near the patio doors, and Lance took off running, holding his bottom.

"Lance? Lance! What's wrong?" Korey chased after him, dragging Heather with her.

Tim walked over, smiling. "Well, it's obvious, isn't it?"

"What's obvious, Tim?" He was attempting to see what was happening in the direction of the bathrooms.

"Why he ran off," Tim calmly replied, selecting a Dr. Pepper.

James glared at Tim.

Tim took off his sunglasses, rolled his eyes, and said in an almost bored voice, "Well, obviously, we were having a farting contest. He lost. It's supposed to be you just pass gas."

It was a good thing James didn't have any liquids in his mouth, as he would've spat them out. He gave an initial roar of laughter, before covering his mouth. Tim merely giggled a little, though James suspected he was laughing at him, and not Lance.

"He likes that Mortal Kombat game like the other kids," whispered Tim.

James, regaining control, whispered back "What other kids, and why are we whispering?"

Tim gave James a confused look. "Should we not whisper? I thought others weren't supposed to know about, obviously, 'the trip.'" He made quotation marks with his fingers as he said the final words, a habit he had picked up from Noi.

"We shouldn't talk about that, but tell me quickly in general what you're talking about please." Tim now had James's full attention.

"It was what some of the boys were asking me to play, you know, at 'the place.'" He made the finger quotes again.

"Why didn't you mention this before?" asked James.

"I did. I told you they kept asking me to play," said Tim, putting his sunglasses back on.

"Oh, right, got it," said James quickly.

"They said if I won I got a happ..." Tim began, but James placed his hand over Tim's mouth, and then quickly released him.

James gave him a wink and said, "Got it."

Scott called out "7:54 group." About ten people stopped what they were doing, and made for the door.

"What's happening?" James asked Tim.

"The party ends at 8 p.m. We can't all fit through the door at once," Tim said, now waiting for Scott to call his group.

"But it started at 7 p.m." James was confused.

"Yeah, how long does it take to eat pizza? People have shows they want to see, obviously. They are leaving, based on how long it takes to get back to their place, to see their shows at 8 p.m.," Tim explained.

Scott called "7:55," and Tim walked out the door with Byron and Dan.

Apparently when Scott said "man of the hour," he meant it literally. James shook his head in wonder. It was so simple, and it worked for this crew. He just wished more people operated this way.

# •Chapter Thirty-Two•

The day after the pizza party, James went over his notes in preparation for an important phone call. He stalled a moment by pondering his three goals.

The first, was to get all of the kids, and any cooperative young adults out safely. Second, was to level that place with the Tan family in it. That meant taking out Noi Rasa too. Last, he needed to see what information he could extract from the Tans' system. He'd possibly be able to leverage information on previous clients, before allowing justice to find them too.

James had his own set of rules for life. One of them was never to be in debt to anyone, without a plan to pay them back tenfold. This meant that before calling in a favor, he tended to have a rather large bank of favors already rendered. He knew he'd need a full squad to accomplish his three goals, but he only trusted one individual to take on something like this.

James took a deep breath, and hit send on his phone.

"Hello, this is Major Ian Doyle," came a voice.

"Major, now? Last time we talked, you had just made captain. Must be sleeping with the right people," James said.

"Son of a bitch, you have some timing!" the major said in a boisterous voice. "How you doing, James? Damn, it's been a while."

"I was just thinking the same. So what's his name?" James asked, laughing.

"Kiss my ass. You know damn well I don't swing my bat that way. But yeah, I just got this promotion last week. And you're right. Last time we talked, you were calling to congratulate me on making captain. Knowing you, calling today isn't a coincidence, ya son of a bitch," the major said.

James smiled, and set the record straight. "In all honesty, my friend, this is pure coincidence. Before I forget, congrats on the promotion. I'm sure it is very well deserved."

"Well, aren't you a sweet talker n'at." The major typically was very good at hiding his origin from Western Pennsylvania, but occasionally it slipped out as he spoke.

"How are your parents doing, and how is Melanie?" asked James.

"Oh, Melanie is good. Enjoying work, but we're still having issues having a baby. Mom is doing all right. Cancer still in remission, thank God. Dad is ornery as ever 'cept now, with him retiring a month ago, he's driving Mom up a wall. She kicked him out of the house the other day, and locked the door for four hours." Major Doyle started to laugh.

James was laughing too. "What? No, she didn't. Why'd she do that?"

"Said he was getting on her nerves, so she tricked him to go get the mail, and locked all the doors. You know the old man. He bitched up a storm at the door through the mail slot. Mom turned up the TV to drown him out, so, he went in the backyard, got out the chainsaw, and cut down a tree."

"Was it falling over?" James asked, still laughing.

"Shit no, he did it just to annoy Mom for locking him out. Cut the whole thing up too." By this point, the major had regained control, and was telling the story as he normally did, with his fake angry voice, which just added a dramatic, and funny edge to the whole thing.

"What did your mom do?" James asked, playing right along into the storyline.

The major continued, "You know Mom. She came out when he was finished and said, 'Good, now we have something to burn, you can build me that fire pit you promised me fifteen years ago. Let's go find some bricks and materials.' Then she tossed him his keys."

"Oh my God, your parents. What did your dad do?" James asked.

"He bitched about five minutes about spending money, and then they got in his truck, and picked out supplies. I got them both on the line at once, and told them, 'Yinz guys aren't right. No wonder you have three messed up kids.' They just laughed. Then I told them about the promotion. They were pleased. Mom wanted to send me a check for some reason, and Dad said he was proud, but not proud enough to send money," finished the major.

They both laughed.

"Look, James, always good to talk with you, but I have a thing in about ten minutes. So if you didn't call just to congratulate me, you called for a different reason. What's up, and how can I help?" The major was back to his normal tone, and James recognized the authoritative, non-time wasting style he adopted.

James took a deep breath and began. "Well, Ian, it's like..."

"The last time you called me Ian, you were saving my life. What's wrong? And don't give me the bullshit version. Spill it out, and we'll fix it." The major used his voice to full effect.

"I need a black bag task force to help me take out a human trafficking operation in China, not too far from the Kyrgyzstan border. Looking at an unknown number of children at this point, but more than thirty-five. Also need a special assembly of people, who can deal with this, preferably those with experience with the juvenile system. The place is an old fortress that has some kind of electric shield, and it sits under an overhanging cliff."

Silence followed his words.

"Ian, I realize I'm asking a lot. You know if I had other means to deal with this, I would, but you're the most realistic chance I have of doing this, and getting the kids out alive. I can cover the costs for the guys and..."

"First, stop calling me Ian if you're doing it to gain a psychological advantage," said Major Doyle.

James smiled. That was exactly why he was doing it.

"Second, how many men, and when do we need to roll out?" asked the major.

James answered quickly. "Not counting either of us, I think ten will do. I don't have a date yet, but probably four to six months from now. We can set the date with a two-week notice. Are you sure this is easily doable?"

"Easy? No. Doable? Hell ya. You wouldn't ask if it weren't needed. My family owes you. A lot of families owe you. And the fact that we're going after kids makes it the right thing to do. Get me a general profile on what you think we need, and the men you want. I can cover the rest with this much notice," the major replied, snapping his fingers.

"And the military use?" James questioned.

"Don't worry about it. I am where I am because of you, and because I run these types of operations. We'll clear out other rats' nests in the area n'at. It's not like they're scarce. Gives us a reason to be there," he said.

"Thank you, Ian." James said this not only as a friend, but also as someone who truly recognized the issues this could cause.

"I still owe you, even after this, but it's cool, James. Get me a dossier, and we'll go from there. Got to run. Talk soon." Major Ian Doyle hung up.

James sighed in relief, as he hadn't had a backup plan.

Writing the plan for the major to review turned out to be more complicated than James had anticipated. He was reluctant to disclose his goals of extracting the children until the last minute, but he also wanted extremely skilled soldiers, who would have an emotional connection due to their past. James knew this would help ensure the mission stayed a true black bag operation. There is no motivation like revenge, cloaked as justice, especially when partnered with the instinctual desire to protect innocent children.

On the plane to Aberdeen, James accomplished two things. First, he did some layout work for what he was now calling Operation Joshua, as Operation Jericho seemed too obvious. He felt it best to have several variations worked out, until he and the major knew the crew going in.

Second, he created a plan for getting some current information on Anthony Spara. As was customary for him, he'd start at the bottom, on the street. Then he'd try to get a meeting with his friend Patrick's uncle. He needed to keep the Spara investigation moving forward to keep the group happy, in a manner of speaking.

It was different, the way the group operated. If he wanted to, James could literally stop what he was doing, and walk away. Technically, he didn't even have to give up the file on Spara, but that would be highly irregular, and didn't fit with how he felt anyone should operate. It was that last trait of fulfilling promises that made it all work.

Individuals were internally motivated to accomplish their tasks. They didn't do it for glory, or recognition, or money, though money often accompanied the end results. It was all about the challenge of doing the right thing when others couldn't, or at least it was supposed to be.

In Aberdeen, the apartment Korey had secured was exactly what he'd asked for. The property manager, a short, grouchy looking man with sideburns that flowed into a full beard, met him on site. He had a bit of a waddle that James instantly recognized as a bad right hip.

"So, you be John, then, eh? Well noew, me name is Michael, you know, and I have ter say, that lady that rang me, then, she said I were ter get you all fancied up on livin'," the manager said in a low pitched voice.

They shook hands.

"Noew, this be the Baker Building we have you in," said Michael.

"Why is it called the Baker Building?" James asked.

"Oh, it's me family name, and I be looking after it, so it's called that," replied Michael.

They walked up two flights of steps to the second floor, where they took a left, and walked down the hall. They got to the corner, and stopped in front of door

221. James laughed silently, as he often did, thinking, *If only it had the letter 'B' after it, it would be perfect.*

Growing up his family had often called him Sherlock, because of how he could just piece things together so quickly. With the apartment number, and the building being called the Baker building, it reminded James of Sherlock Holmes' address of 221-B, Baker St.

"Well noew, yer should be okay ter do fae a bit, yeah? The misses went ter the shops, and me son helped get yer situated. Need to sign those papers, exchange some quid, and yer set. That Korey lass, said yer might be doing some remodeling, and 'tis fine just as long as yer don't block any windows, and don't be extending into the neighbors' spaces." Michael kept speaking as James looked around quickly. "Plus yer have space, you know, in the lowers fae anything yer want stored."

They took care of the paperwork, and Michael gave him two sets of keys, and his phone number, telling him to give him a call if he needed anything.

The apartment was great. The bedroom occupied the corner of the building. The layout allowed for privacy, and the cement floor soundproofed the place. Should it come up, this layout would help explain why James didn't know his neighbors.

James made a list of things he needed to make the apartment look lived in, such as sheets, clothes, bathroom items, and food. After laying on the twin bed, he decided that it needed to be replaced. He felt tired from the flight, but doing the necessary shopping would be a good way to avoid napping, and extending the effects of the jet lag.

He didn't manage to find half the things he needed, since many of the local shops, once he found them, were closed on Sunday. He did manage to get some basics at a shopping center that would get him through until the next day. By the time James returned to the apartment, he was exhausted. It didn't help that he'd nearly had two accidents on the way back, because he'd forgotten to stay in the near lane when making a left.

He was happy to crawl into bed. He soon remembered that the mattress was extremely firm, so much so that he might as well have slept on the floor. The bed had to go, but that was a problem for the next day. He gathered a blanket and two pillows, and crashed on the sofa, falling asleep quickly.

*Everything hurt, and there was no sound, or just one constant sound, he couldn't tell. An intense heat was coming from a roaring blaze to his left. As he rolled to his right, his blurred vision saw someone on the other side of an old iron gate pulling a chain.*

It was 3:37 a.m. when his eyes opened. James felt extremely uneasy, as he always did with those types of dreams. Still, it was better than the hallway dreams that were almost cartoonish, and had the red streak, or climbing burning ladders in a mall.

James decided to get up, instead of trying to force himself back to sleep, which rarely worked anyhow. He was still feeling the effects of the travel, and decided he'd better eat something. After breakfast, and a rather good shower, he revisited the list of things he needed to buy, and tucked it in his back pocket.

For the time being, he decided to work on the list of requirements for each individual in the operation. James wasn't sure how the major would go about searching for the right members, so he felt he'd better error on the side of caution, and list requirements only. It took him two hours, and several versions to get it where he wanted it to be.

*1. All members need to be highly trustworthy to keep the operation black bag. They will not be informed of the target until the operation has started.*

*2. Individuals on the ground need to come from an abusive background, foster care, or child protective services.*

*3. Individuals on the ground need to have experience in extracting people.*

*4. A few individuals need to be marksmen with shooting handguns and assault rifles.*

*5. All individuals need high intelligence, and a plan to pursue academic development.*

*6. Need one explosives expert, one electrical expert, and one communications expert.*

The first one went without saying, but James didn't want to leave anything to chance. The other items, if filled, would give him the working crew he needed, assuming everything fell together as envisioned.

James got up and stretched. He felt achy, and wasn't sure if it was from sleeping on the couch, or the jet lag. Then he dug the paper out of his pocket and added, *"Find a gym"* to his list. There was nothing like a good workout to flush the system with endorphins, and help reset the circadian rhythm.

He normally would have headed to the office, and gotten a jump on the day, but he didn't have access to the building. He doubted anyone who knew him would be in that early, so he did some work from the apartment. James also decided to ask Michael about internet access. Hopefully, all he needed was a router, and maybe a modem.

# •Chapter Thirty-Three•

That day and the next passed with ease. James was able to get everything done except finding a gym. He also managed to talk with Carissa about moving in. She asked again if he was sure it was okay, and he answered, "Yeah, I've already spent next month's rent because that's your problem now." She'd laughed.

On Wednesday morning, James set out for Cambridge to attend the session with Dr. William Watterson. The journey went well, and he had plenty of time to find the building and lecture hall. The crowd was larger than he'd expected, but that was all to the good. He'd be able to blend in, and observe more discretely.

James repressed a chuckle at his first glance of Dr. Watterson. He looked like a modern version of President William Howard Taft, complete with the large belly and mustache. All he was missing were the round glasses.

The lecture began, and James soon realized the material was intended for a more advanced audience. He knew some basics, but this hardcore physics was beyond his understanding, at least at the rate Dr. Watterson was speaking. Glancing around, James realized he wasn't the only one struggling. A lady on his right, asked the person on her right, if she understood what Dr. Watterson was saying, and that individual admitted she was puzzled, too. James felt better knowing he wasn't alone in being lost. He decided to interrupt, so as to have a semi-reasonable excuse to talk with Dr. Watterson later, in private.

"Excuse me, Dr. Watterson. Dr. Watterson?" he said.

The entire room, including Dr. Watterson, turned as one. Dr. Watterson was clearly irritated by the interruption, while the people near James seemed to lean away from him.

"Yes?" said the irritated professor in his Welsh accent. "What is it?"

"Sorry to interrupt..." James began.

"Ah, well, I accept your apology and will continue. Now as I was saying..." Dr. Watterson began speaking again.

James kept his tone pleasant, but increased the volume. "Dr. Watterson, could you please perhaps review the last few points again? I wasn't able to follow the jump from interperpolsion forces, and the skin effect, as you were describing it."

"Perhaps, young man, you shouldn't be in this room if you are unable to follow the material. This is my lecture, and I do not allow others to speak while I'm speaking. If you are unable to keep up, I suggest you start at the beginners' course, and come back when you have mastered that material." Dr. Watterson gestured toward the door.

"I see. Well, I think you will find that I'm not the only one exiting the room. Not to mention, I don't believe that a simple request of..."

A red-faced Dr. Watterson cut off James by shouting, "First, I doubt there are any original thoughts rattling around in that storage compartment atop your shoulders. As far as others not following, they too can depart. I can lecture to an empty room as well as a full one. Calvin, see this individual out!"

A slim, young graduate student in the front row stood up. James had already begun making his way out of the room, and Calvin fell instep beside him. When the doors shut behind them, Dr. Watterson began to lecture again, but Calvin stayed outside the lecture hall with James.

"You must be new here, or hate the program, to stop him in mid-lecture like that," Calvin marveled. "Surprised he didn't take your name down. He must be getting soft in his old age. The last person to do what you just did got tossed out of the school completely, but then again, he had a full-blown argument in the middle of the lecture. This was a few years ago, but everyone still talks about it like it was last term." Calvin spoke with a lot of hand motions and weight shifting.

"Right, well, I won't keep you from returning." James turned to leave, still peeved. Now he needed to rethink how to get information on Yan.

"Oh, no, I can't go back in. He'd kill me. Besides, I know the material, as it is me research. I can explain what you were asking about. I think that's why he had me escort you out to answer your question," Calvin said smiling. "The head of the department has been on him, about being too abrupt with pupils, but there's no way he is going to lose his reputation, so out you go." He pointed his thumb over his shoulder, and stuck out his tongue, and blew a raspberry.

"Sounds like a great boss you have there," James said, in a rather sarcastic tone.

"He isn't so bad, once you get to know him. Oh, and as long as you don't disagree with him in public, or private, really. Best to just let him think it was his idea all the time. But then, it still has to go along with his theory." As an afterthought, Calvin added, "That's where Yan messed up. Well, if you want to go..."

"Sorry, who?" James stared at Calvin.

Calvin looked back at him. "Who what?"

"Who did you just say?" James asked. He suddenly realized his entire demeanor had changed, and consequently put Calvin on his guard. James forced his body to relax and said, "Something about someone disagreeing with Dr. Watterson."

Calvin's eyes got wide for a second before he said, "Oh, yeah, Yan. That was a fight, that. Shame, too, Yan had brains. He was me brother's flatmate the first term we were here as freshmen. We thought we'd try a little separation, so we just lived next to each other, but with different flatmates. Didn't work out too well, so we ended up swapping the next term. Things were better after that. Well, not for Yan. A few terms later he got tossed out." Calvin jerked his thumb, and made the raspberry noise again.

As they began to walk, Calvin started to ask James questions like, "So are you new here?" and "Where do you come from?" and "Are you majoring in particle engineering?"

Before James could answer any of the questions, Calvin was onto the next. It was rather annoying.

They walked down the hall, and into a lab area that had a lot of equipment running in a very large space. The room held an enormous circle of tubing, with a variety of wires and transducers hooked to it, which made it a little challenging to walk around the crowded space at the edges.

There was only one other person in the lab as they entered. James saw a blond ponytail lying over the back of a white lab coat. When they were a few feet away, the woman looked up and smiled. *Wow*, thought James. Just as it registered how pretty she was, she walked up and kissed Calvin, as though he had just singlehandedly saved her family and all her friends from a fire. As the passionate kiss broke, her hand disappeared down Calvin's front. Based on his reaction, she must have grabbed something she shouldn't have, at least not in public.

Turning to face James, and putting his arm around the girl's shoulder, Calvin said, "This is Regan. Regan, this is uhh..."

"Hi, I'm James," he said, reaching out and shaking hands. Immediately, he realized he should have gone with John, as that was the identification he had on him, but it didn't matter, as he was certain no one was going to check it.

Calvin began to explain what had happened during the lecture, but James wasn't sure Regan was listening, as her right hand was groping Calvin's backside. James didn't understand her physical attraction to him, but then again, beauty is in the eye of the beholder.

When Calvin got to the part where James questioned Dr. Watterson, Regan gasped, as if Dr. Watterson were going to walk in, and somehow associate her with James's evil deed.

"See, told you, mate," Calvin said smugly.

Not sure what to say to this, James merely smiled.

Just then two more people entered the lab, and James did a double take. It looked like Calvin and

Regan had just walked in. Either this was the twilight zone, or someone had figured out cloning, or had created a time warp. Not only were the newcomers identical to Calvin and Regan, but the new Regan was also walking with her hand in the new Calvin's back left pocket.

"How'd it go?" the original Calvin asked.

"Fine. You know how he is. Got through the rest of the material, announced he was heading to the pub, and that was it." The new Calvin made the same raspberry tongue sound, and did the same thumb jerk, while the new Regan giggled.

"James, this is me brother Raymond, and this is Regan's sister Regina. We're all twins. Though Regan and I are the cute ones," Calvin said with a big smile.

Regan gave a small "Aw," and proceeded to kiss him.

"Calvin tells me you were flatmates with the last student to interrupt Dr. Watterson," James said, as a way to introduce the topic, and break the ice.

"Yan? Yeah. That was a bad day, wasn't it? Well, he had it a lot worse than you. Always banging on about creating an artificial zone for sustained electromagnetic pulse, remember that?" Raymond said to the room in general.

"Well, he did sort of demonstrate it on the accelerator," said Regan, turning her head to look at the encircled area.

"Right." Raymond said, looking disinterested, but James looked at everyone, in turn, silently asking "And?"

They failed to pick up on it. James felt he'd better not push it for now. He'd have to circle back to it later.

"So can you explain the lecture to me, please?" he asked instead.

"Oh, yes, of course," Calvin said with a smile.

"Have at it. I have to go check me video feeds," Raymond said, walking away with Regina.

Regan kissed Calvin on the cheek. "Go be brilliant!" she told him with a giggle.

Calvin blushed. "Sorry," he said, as he led James to a room just on the side of the lab. "She can't keep her hands off me. Pure animal magnetism. Get it? Kind of appropriate, since we work with magnets." He had a huge grin on his face, but then looked serious. "Actually, it can be a bit annoying. She's bright and all, but she wants me all the time." He shook his head as they sat down at a desk. James felt like shaking his head, too, but he resisted the impulse, as he didn't want to insult Calvin.

Over the course of the next few hours, Calvin walked James through the finer points of the lecture, and what they were doing in the lab. The focus was on creating a better power source for batteries through magnets. They were making a lot of headway from the traditional 60 to 1 ratio, to having a few tons of magnetic force into the size of a baseball. The drawback was that the temperature had to be extremely low.

"This is similar to superconducting ceramics, where there's essentially no loss of efficiency in conducting electricity over any distance in a cold enough environment, but" James paused, "that isn't seen naturally, right?"

"Exactly, yes. It's just that we're storing the energy for release as we see fit, not just transporting it." Calvin leaned back in his chair.

"So what happens when that energy is released from a high capacity substrate? Say if it were to come out extremely rapidly?" asked James.

"You'd get a rather large electromagnetic pulse, then. Funny you say that. It's exactly what Yan kept pushing. Kept asking about sending electrical fields through a high conducting substrate to generate a sustainable EMP. Dr. Watterson said it couldn't be done, not at normal temperature at least. Yan seemed to think it could."

"What do you think? Could it be done?" James asked.

Calvin paused. "I think it might. Yan seemed to be getting some results, but he never shared his methods. I would like to believe it could be done. It could accelerate what we've been trying to do here by years and years."

Later, driving back to Aberdeen, James thought about how he was going to get Calvin to evaluate the fortress, and tell him how to dismantle the system. It seemed the logical thing to do to get Calvin involved, given his level of understanding, but it was also risky. Simply telling him about the setup would create a firestorm of questions, not to mention the fact that Calvin was very much a part of what James called "the herd." That meant he could get loose, and talk about things he shouldn't.

James reminded himself that he was putting the cart before the horse. Until he and the major worked out the plan, it was impossible to say if expertise with the EMP was even needed. His instincts, however, made him believe that it would be.

# •Chapter Thirty-Four•

Moving day came, and James stood inside the flat Carissa shared with Judy. Judy wasn't speaking much, so James took his cue from this, and concentrated on getting the truck loaded. After they finished, James left the ladies to say their goodbyes.

Carissa came out a few minutes later, her eyes shiny with tears.

"Listen, I'm sorry, she seemed down, you know. Just had a bit of family troubles of late. She really is a sweet person, and has always been there for me." Carissa paused and bit her lip, clearly trying to decide whether to say more.

James gave her a weak smile. Usually, he wouldn't truly care about Judy's problems, but as it was Carissa explaining it, he had some interest. "No worries," James said.

"It's just hard for her and all," Carissa said, feeling a need to explain, but not wanting to violate her friendship with Judy.

"It must be hard to have a mum who is ill with her dad passed on. I'm sure the treatments at hospital will help the cancer," James said.

Carissa took a step back, puzzled. "How der ya know that then?"

*Oops,* he thought. "Ah, well I saw the papers on the counter in the flat for cancer treatment from two weeks prior. You had talked about her coming back from the hospital the day you asked about moving in. Just put it all together," James said in a humble, but sort of dismissing way.

"Doesn't explain how you knew it was fer her mum, though," Carissa said.

"Aye, that is true. Well, the photos on the wall show Judy with her parents each year on her birthday. The last two are missing her dad, so I thought he had already passed. Judy looks rather healthy, and she wouldn't, if she'd just had chemo a fortnight ago. So I just guessed her mum had breast cancer, because that last picture shows she had a breast removed based on how the fabric was on her chest," James said.

Carissa just stood there. This didn't make James feel any better. He should have just said he'd guessed instead of trying to explain everything, but he didn't want to lie. He felt guilty enough about all the lies he'd already told her.

Finally, she spoke. "I knew yer ta be brilliant, but can you go on pretending not ta know, please? Just in case Judy was ta say something ever. She doesn't want others ta know."

"Of course," James said, relieved. He was happy that Carissa didn't dwell on things like that.

Three hours later, Carissa and James walked through James's apartment so Carissa could get her bearings. James had done most of the packing of the vehicles on the front end, and had strategically placed most of the things he felt would make it into the apartment where they could easily be off-loaded.

After looking around, Carissa turned to him. "Well now, John, what lass did you last have in this place 'sides me?" Her tone was serious, but she had a mischievous twinkle in her eye.

"Ohhh, you got me. There're half a dozen a week, you know. What gave it away then?" James asked, smiling.

"Simple," she said, walking over to the table, and setting down the box she was carrying. "Never seen a lad that had a place in order like this before. And this wasn't a last second dash ta clean, neither." She gave him wink. "I pay attention ta things meself, you know."

They both laughed.

They walked through the rest of the apartment, discussing what they should bring up. When they got to her queen sized bed, Carissa thought it would be too much trouble.

"Well, I can just kip on the couch," she said.

"If anyone is sleeping on the couch, it's me. I sleep there a fair amount of the time as it is. Didn't you notice the bed was made? I never make the bed." The last part was true, but given the rest of the apartment, Carissa didn't believe him.

"John, this is your place. I can't be having you put out like that in your home, now. And this is just until I'm able ta find me own place, you know. Honest, Love, that is sweet, but I can't," Carissa said.

"It doesn't make sense. I travel, and you're paying the rent. No, I'm bringing up your bed, and setting it up after I take the other down to storage." James began to dismantle the bed.

Carissa paused a moment, then walked over, straightened James up, and kissed him. Two hours later, they returned to unpacking the vehicles, a bit exhausted, but invigorated. From the moment of that kiss, her bed became their bed, and his apartment, their apartment. Carissa was there to stay, and they were a couple.

# •Chapter Thirty-Five•

Walking out of the major's office in Pittsburgh, carrying the folder labeled 'Operation Joshua,' James couldn't help but smile. The prior months had been some of the most confusing, inefficient, and frankly illogical of his entire life, yet somehow he was still moving things along, and managing to everyone's satisfaction. For once in his life, that included his own. He knew he could keep it up for a while, but he wasn't sure he wanted to.

Work was progressing as it needed to. He found he didn't have to try too hard, and was still ahead of most of his colleagues. In fact, Todd had told him it was his goal to find something James couldn't do.

James was involved in some regulatory work for new product development that just so happened to require him to be in Aberdeen a great deal. The North Sea restrictions for chemicals were some of the most stringent in the world, and took a lot of time and effort to work through. Todd thought this would be great experience for James to learn the business.

For her part, Carissa was getting used to the idea that James would be gone for weeks at a time. She, too, was traveling for business for the Royal Bank of Scotland, or RBS for short, but not nearly as much as James. She was very sensible, and didn't complain about the time they were apart. She also didn't feel the need to talk to him every day while he was gone about a lot of nothing. Her view was to enjoy the time they had together, and work hard when they weren't. Every time James thought about this, he grinned.

The Anthony Spara operation was progressing slowly. To explain why, James used the excuse of work making things difficult. In part, working a real job was why most individuals stopped participating in the group after graduation. Another reason most stopped, was to take care of personal interests they'd developed using the skills they'd acquired. That, and they'd been trained to get out while they could before too many 'coincidences' developed. Besides, as members grew older, it made it easier for others to accept that they could have advanced skills, and that removed a useful tool for members of the group.

After securing the file on Operation Joshua, James picked up Daen from the group complex in a rental car from a pay-in-cash place that he liked to use. They were on their way to see Patrick Scalpini, the uncle of his friend Patrick from his college days.

It turned out it wasn't too difficult to get a meeting with him. James didn't even have to contact his friend Patrick to do it. He'd simply walked up to a few individuals who looked rather strung out, and had visible track marks at a fast food restaurant. Their dealer was there, and had taken them to get some food. James thought it was a smart approach to retaining customers. At least they didn't starve to death, and they'd remain loyal to him, as he kept them alive.

James told the dealer that he was trying to get a supplier so that he and a partner could arrange a new distribution arm. Patrick Scalpini had called him personally two hours later on the throwaway phone number ber James had given the drug dealer.

James filled Daen in on the conversation as they drove to the meeting location.

"So you're telling me, man, this dealer just called Scalpini, and Scalpini accepted what you said, and agreed to see us?" Daen asked.

"Yup." James prepared to make a left turn.

"That is crazy. What if you were a cop?" Daen asked in a confused manner.

"Seriously, that crossed my mind. If we can extract enough information on the Spara target, I'm thinking of letting Jake take this guy down," James said.

"Nice man, nice. Why didn't you just bring him instead of me?" Daen asked.

James shrugged.

"I'm calling bs on that. You have a reason, man. Don't even try to play me like that. I've worked with you way too many... Oh, I know. This Scalpini thing feels too easy. You're on your guard, and you need someone you know, and who knows how you operate." Daen smirked at James, who gave no reaction, but drove on.

"No reaction huh? So I'm on the right path, but there's more. Hmm, Spara is a reason, but not a major one." Daen's eyes narrowed. "I'm just guessing, but you're thinking of saying Virginia and D.C. for the distribution, right? It will give enough distance, and I know the area, right, man?"

James remained silent, but was impressed with his friend.

"I'm right," said Daen.

A few minutes passed, and then Daen turned to look at James, not satisfied he had found all the reasons.

"It's simple. It always is with you. What is this music?" Daen turned the radio off as some annoying song came on. As he did, he glanced at his hand, then at James.

"That's good. Real good. Ha, ha, ha, man, I didn't think of that. Bringing a black guy to a drug deal, like that's a rarity." Daen laughed, and James smiled. He knew full well that Daen wouldn't be offended, but his race was one of the reasons he wanted him there.

They pulled into the parking lot of an Italian restaurant. "Talk about stereotypical, but I guess that's why it's a stereotype," Daen commented.

James slowly turned his head to look at Daen.

"What, man? You're banking on stereotypes," Daen said defensively, throwing his hands in front of James' eyes.

James gave a slight tilt to his head as his eyebrows went up to acknowledge the fact. "That's true," he said.

Walking in the front door, James prepared to do his usual scan, but was amused by the décor. It was like something right out of a gangster movie. That is if gangster movies went out of their way to have checkered tablecloths, wax candles in wine bottles, shabby curtains, and a speckled tile floor.

Daen leaned into James and whispered, "There's your stereotype."

"Indeed," James whispered back.

"Can we help yous?" a man said, approaching them. There were three other men besides the greeter in the restaurant. They all looked like they could use a shower, and possibly a pacemaker, given the state of their sweat-stained shirts, beer bellies and forced breathing.

Daen gave an extremely brief snicker that sounded like he was stopping a sneeze. *There's your stereotype*, thought James, knowing that was what Daen was snickering about.

"We have a meeting with Mr. Scalpini." James spoke in an even, but non-threatening, tone. He didn't want to give them any cause to feel disrespected or threatened. He tried to get his brain to stop noting the stereotypes, but it was just too easy.

"Oh, Mr. Scalpini, is it? I'm sure he is 'specting yoos." The man did a weird bow and motion with his arms. He and his cohorts laughed at this.

Daen and James stared ahead, silently waiting for the man's next move. He checked both of them for weapons, and presumably wires, as he ran his thumb hard down their sternums.

"Sit there." He directed them to a table, to their right, in a corner. "I'll get him for yoos."

Daen and James took a step as the man turned around and shouted, "Yo, Patrick, yoo gots some guests and whatnot out here. What do yoos want I should do with 'em?"

The other men looked in the direction of the back, too, which was a good thing, as James and Daen both cracked wide grins, as they walked to the table.

"Yeah, I'll be there in a minute," came a voice from the back.

A teenage boy walked out carrying a video camera, and a stepladder. He looked familiar. He spoke to the man who had greeted them, saying, "C-c-can you not yell all the time?"

"Hey, Albert Einstein, do the fancy video stuff, and mind your business." The man raised his hand as though to strike the teen, who was clearly out of reach.

The boy just shook his head as the man sat down with a grunt.

They waited about a minute before the same man yelled again. "Yo, yoos gonna make these guys sit out here all day or what?"

A string of swear words flowed from the back, followed by, "I'll be there in a minute."

After a good five minutes, the faint sound of rushing water could be heard, and out came a middle-aged man, with a rather bad hairpiece. As he rounded the corner, he nearly tripped on the stepladder, mainly because, he wasn't looking where he was going as he adjusted his pants.

"Why yoo gots this out? Could hurt somebody with this thin' here!" Patrick Scalpini said, yelling at the teenager on the ladder.

"You asked me t-t-to install this now, so that's what I am doing. How else do you th-th-think I can get up here?" the boy asked, through gritted teeth.

Patrick looked at him, and shook a finger. "Don't get too smart there, genius boy. You're my nephew, and I love yoos but I will kick this ladder right from under yoos."

The man hitched up his pants one more time, and then put a fake smile on his face as he walked over to greet James and Daen.

They stood up to shake hands and introduce themselves. Daen used Bryan Douglas, but James had changed to Christopher Macker, because he'd burnt the Stephen Lewis name.

Patrick pointed to the other men in the room. "That there's Fat Tony, next to him is Nicky, then yoo have Big Tony, and his brother, Bobby."

Bobby turned out to be the man who had greeted them.

Patrick swung around and said, "And the genius with the video camera is my nephew, Andrew. His mother is my sister, but she did right, and had him with an Italian named Sebastino."

"P-p-perfect, glad you approve of my dad for being Italian, even though he's in p-p-prison for beating my mom," Andrew growled at his uncle.

James confirmed the teen's identity in his head. Andrew was his friend Patrick's little brother, based on the last name.

"Yo! Don't talk about the family like that, ever. Yoo hear me? Just do your magic, video wizard," Patrick barked, as he turned to face his guests.

"I k-k-keep telling you, I don't know how m-m-most of this works. I'm into computer graphics, and gaming systems. This is j-j-just hooking up wires," Andrew told his uncle, rather exacerbated.

"One more word, and I swear by the Holy Mother and her son, Jesus, I will break that pizza paddle over yoos head!" Patrick said, making a motion toward his nephew.

"Mr. Scalpini," James said, drawing Patrick's attention to him and Daen, "we have a long drive ahead of us, so perhaps we could start?" He couldn't believe how this was turning out. It was almost surreal.

"Yeah, right, sorry. Yoo know kids, gots to keep them in line." He adjusted his pants again, and sat down. "How can I help yoos?"

"As you may recall, we are in need of a supplier. We don't like to source locally, as it tends to lead to complications if the network is somehow breached. I'm sure you understand," James said.

Patrick nodded. "Yeah, 'course. Yoo don't play too heavy in yoos own backyard. Smart. I like smart business associates."

James laughed in his head, and Daen jumped in.

"We are looking for a reliable source. Looking to do five kilos a week to start. If the business is..."

"Hold on, let me stop yoos right there," Patrick said. "I don't do black tar like that."

Daen stared at James, and James stared ahead, his mind working ferociously. *Italians don't like black people. Still, Scalpini's body language didn't indicate it was a racist comment. In fact, his body language, tight muscles, and dilated pupils, indicated he was fearful.*

"Mr. Scalpini, we discussed what we're looking to buy over the phone. I don't understa..." James started, before being interrupted again.

"Yeah, and I don't move that kind of volume," Patrick said, in a more casual voice. "I thought yoo wanted a few kilos a month or somethin' like that."

Daen kept quiet, still staring in a deadpan way at James. This was why James liked to work with Daen. He didn't overreact. At the moment, Daen needed to play the role of a cold drug dealer, who was holding James accountable. The stare he was giving James signaled that loud and clear.

"I indicated we would be looking for substantial amounts. Perhaps you can facilitate a connection. We would certainly be willing to share in the profits." James followed up his words with a hard smile.

"No, I ain't gots those kindsa connections. The little I do I get from a guy that sometimes pays me with it to feed his coke habit. No way he can get that volume, and besides, he ain't zactly professional if yoos know what I mean." Patrick sat back in his chair defensively. "Now if yoo want coke or some pot source, we can do that business."

Patrick was lying for some reason about his connections, and James knew it. Perhaps this explained the previous fearful reaction. Daen, however, made one last ditch effort.

"You sure you don't have that connection? I can pay a month in advance. We would be selling into the D.C. area," he said firmly.

"I said no." Patrick's physical reaction of fear was even more pronounced. "How many times yoo need to hear that?" Patrick stood, and put both hands on the table, staring them down.

"We'll be going, then," James said quickly, standing up. Daen followed, but lifted himself using his hands on the table.

"Get the fuck outta here!" Patrick suddenly blazed at them.

There was a sudden scraping of chairs, and the four other men stood.

"This is my place of business! Who the fuck do yoo think you are? Get out, get the fuck out!" Patrick was furious, and his friends held him back.

Daen and James made for the door while Patrick's tirade of screaming and foul language trailed them. Once outside, they picked up the pace until they made it to the car and were off.

"What was that? Damn, man, he just freaked out!" exclaimed Daen.

James took a few quick turns to get out of the immediate area to make it harder to be followed. After a moment, he answered, "I think it was two things. One, he was lying about a connection to heroin, and we pressed the topic. The second was your hands."

Daen looked at him, puzzled. "What do you mean my hands, man?"

"When you stood up. You placed your hands on the table. I think he took it as a challenge or something. I don't know, I'm not looking to go back and ask," James said, heading back toward the group's headquarters.

"Well, shit," said Daen.

The two men sat quietly for a moment before Daen asked, "Man, did you get the sense like they were trying to be all mafia in there? Like, they were making a point to be like that?"

"Yeah, or maybe they're just really stupid, and have no idea how to operate. Let's face it, Andrew was by far the smartest in the room. But that's not what concerns me," replied James.

"What'da mean? It was a little scary, the way he acted." Daen pulled out his sunglasses as they went west into the afternoon sun.

James nodded. "Exactly. He was scared, dude. That had all the makings of a bully overreacting like a scared little kid."

"Let me guess, man, his breathing went up, or his hands turned red?" asked Daen, his voice cracking slightly.

"Those probably happened, but given his general health, that wouldn't be singularly detectable by the catecholamine rush. No, his muscles tightened, and his eyes dilated. Or I should say his pupils. But there was no detectable light change," said James.

Daen just shook his head, but James didn't see it. A moment later, James interpreted the silence as Daen making fun of him, and said, "Smart ass," in a joking tone.

Daen took a deep breath, and James knew he interpreted the silence incorrectly.

"James," Daen said, as he removed his sunglasses, "what happened with my father, well, that wasn't your fault. I know I said it before, I just wanted you to know that I meant it that night, and I mean it now. I just... I don't know man. I wanted you to know I have thought about it more, and nothing has changed between us. Hell, maybe you ultimately did me a favor. I just..." He stopped talking.

James didn't know what to say, but felt he had to say something. "Daen, I should have listened, and followed your lead." James looked over at Daen, who had a few tears running down his cheeks. He pulled over.

"I trust you, man, and I hope you know that," Daen said, wiping his eyes with the back of his hand.

James nodded and said, "Daen, I trust you too, and promise I will follow your lead the next time you ask for my help. I'm still very sorry, and I won't try to make excuses for my actions, because it won't change the past. But thanks for still trusting me, and for forgiving me." It would be the last time they spoke of the incident directly.

Later that day, with their most immediate potential connection to the Spara situation virtually worthless, James and Daen informed Tom and Andy, that they'd have to exercise other options. Other options that would take time to develop. Tom and Andy were okay with the set back on Spara.

Tom asked if James or Daen planned to do anything with Patrick to destroy his operation. Both said no, but they'd circle back to it later, and bring Jake into help.

Andy was fine with this. Tom grumbled a bit, but in the end, he agreed it could wait.

# •Chapter Thirty-Six•

Now that James had some extra wiggle room, he wanted to focus on Operation Joshua, and take care of the Tans once and for all. It would certainly help some of the stress that he was carrying. In fact, even though he was happier than he'd ever been in his life, thanks to Carissa, the stress from Operation Joshua, Spara, work, and all the other things he did for the group was getting to be a lot, even for him.

He was still getting everything done, and doing it well, but he also was being a lot more direct with people. Some of his co-workers took this as arrogance, and thought he was just showing off.

The truth was he was trying to help others along by giving them logical suggestions. They interpreted it as him telling them what to do. James knew he processed things more quickly than most people, but he didn't have time to slow down to their speed. With everything going on, he didn't feel that correcting any co-worker relationship damage was worth the time.

Instead, he wanted to focus on the next steps he and the major had put together. They were setting up a facility near Pittsburgh where they could train for their number one task of evacuating the children. That was simple enough. The more challenging part was going through a variety of scenarios, as kids could often be unpredictable.

That wasn't the only unpredictable thing. They didn't have an accurate headcount on the number of kids or adults/older teens in the compound. On top of that, they didn't know what kind of resistance they would face, aside from the fact that they were attacking a fortress. This spawned a debate that played out between James and the major about two weeks after his and Daen's encounter with Scalpini.

"Look, I understand. I really do, but that doesn't change the fact that we're going into an operation with a high number of unknowns. Worrying about motivation is the least of our problems," the major said, with a lot of animated movement from behind his desk.

James was leaning on the other side of the desk, his fingertips on his forehead. He let his fingers run through his hair before saying, "Keeping this operation as secret as possible is paramount. I've no doubt your team can execute, and keep things to themselves, but this is different. We need the right guys."

"Just how is it different? And before you answer that, I have other things I want you to answer first. What is the main objective?" The major asked.

"Safely removing the kids from that hellhole, and getting them to the safe location I'm arranging," said James, in a low voice. He had made contact with what seemed to be a very decent organization in Kyrgyzstan. He couldn't transport the kids too far, but given the resources he thought would be available after the operation, he felt confident about the plans he was making for them.

"Right, is that the primary?" asked the major standing up.

"I just said it was, Ian," said James, in a reserved voice.

"Good." The major walked around the desk, and stood over James before continuing. "My primary objective, which is only superseded by yours, is to get my troops and myself home alive. I know my team. They know me. I would follow any one of them into hell and back if they asked. Just like I would with yinz. You have to trust me. My team doesn't need any extra motivation to stay quiet. They're all on board, and have no idea what we're extracting. They are doing it for me," the major stressed. "I may not have the exact best individuals for the field, but damn it, I have the best team, and I'm not going without my team."

James sat looking at him for a moment, as tension filled the room between the two individuals, who both were rarely wrong. James then said, "Lame finish. I was expecting something a little more awe-inspiring than that." He cracked a big grin.

"You son of a bitch," the major laughed as the tension broke. "You try coming up with something to convince a hardhead like you that sounds all inspirational, without sounding like a douche n'at on the spot." He turned to go back to his seat, adding, "Still leaves open what to do about this EMP thing. My guys are good, but this sounds like something we haven't ever faced."

"Yeah, I know. I'll work something out before we enter training." James still didn't know how he was going to do that. His last contact with Calvin had been positive, but he needed to find a way to get him involved without knowing exactly about what.

James returned to Aberdeen the next day. Just in case something happened, he was glad he'd arranged to spend a few weeks working from there, and, consequently being with Carissa, before leaving for training, and the operation. He didn't have a fear of dying, though he had to admit it had crossed his mind lately.

This was his life, planning for the 'in case something happened.' He'd often been made fun of as a child, and even as a young adult, for his ability to anticipate scenarios and plan for them. It made him different and weird, something he'd decided to embrace a long time ago. Carissa didn't seem to mind. In fact, she seemed to adore the fact that he could do that.

"You know, Love," she said to him, the night before he left for training, "what if you don't make it back in time, then?" She was lying on his chest as they watched television. She'd been rather cuddly and provocative that night. It was nice, but James was also appreciative of the fact that she wasn't constantly 'touchy feely' most of the time.

James momentarily froze inside, but played it cool. "Is that a question or a wish, Risa?"

"Don't be a prat. I mean if you aren't back in time for Judy's party," she said, poking him in the ribs playfully.

"Ah, right, the party," he said, as she nuzzled his chest. He felt the tension leave his body in relief. "Well, if I end up staying longer, we can arrange for the surprise to be held at the same place a week later. I actually think it'll come as more of a surprise if we do it then, but it won't tie into your announcement for her moving to your branch. Unless you just wait to make the announcement. Plus, if the party was later, we should be able to give her the puppy at the party, as it will be old enough. Should make for a better time for her."

"Why didn't I think of that? Wonder if I can get the transfer delayed any longer?" Carissa said thoughtfully, more to the room than to James.

"Just tell them you'd rather do it during the middle of the month than at the end with closing," said James.

"Oh, right, didn't even think about that. Always thinking, you. And you definitely were thinking about something else when I brought up the party," said Carissa.

"Not really too much, just that the program was back on," he said, trying to be dismissive.

She gave him another poke, and he grunted.

"But you did think something. Heard your heart beat faster I did just then." Her voice was muffled as she spoke into his chest.

He didn't even think, just blurted, "That's because my heart will always race with fear at the thought of never seeing you again."

Apparently, James hit a chord with those words, and the television program was forgotten. They made love twice before Carissa fell asleep cuddled up next to him.

# •Chapter Thirty-Seven•

The next day, he headed off without waking Carissa, though he left her a little note. It was going to be a long four to six weeks before he could see her again.

Before his flight left, he headed to Cambridge to see what he could extract from Calvin, or maybe Dr. Watterson, about how to dismantle this EMP force field.

He arrived at the university with about an hour in which to get the information he needed. Calvin and Raymond were in the lab, along with Regan and Regina. Luckily, as James walked in, the ladies were saying goodbye, though it looked like they wanted to take the guys' tongues with them. They giggled as they passed James, and both pinched and then slapped him on the butt.

James was astonished. He certainly hadn't encouraged that. Calvin just shook his head, but Raymond spoke.

"Ah, sorry about that, mate. They are a bit frisky. Me bum has a permanent red look to it as often as they do that. Not always so sure it's Regina doing the grabbing. They kind of sneak it at you."

"Ah, right," James said, mainly because he didn't know what else to say.

Calvin took off the safety goggles he was wearing and turned to James. "How's it going? Need any more information on how the fields work or such?"

James hesitated a moment, wondering if he should just be direct or not, but time was pressing, and he had nothing to lose. "I wanted to ask, how you would disable an EMP?"

"What EMP?" Raymond asked, but Calvin dived right in.

"Good question, but you can't disable an EMP once it starts. You can prevent it, but once it goes, it goes until it becomes too weak to be detected. It follows the laws of energy, mate," Calvin said.

James was stuck. He didn't want to mention Yan again directly, but he needed to get the twins talking about his experiments. He decided to play stupid.

"Wait, you were talking about creating an extended EMP?" He used his hands to make a big arch in the air.

"That?" Calvin said with a small chuckle. "Nah, mate, told you. Can't be done. Least that's what Dr. Watterson says unless it's really cold."

"If that's your situation, remove the cold." Raymond returned his attention to the circular test ring, but continued, "That will stop the sustained EMP."

"You said someone had done it before and got the boot out," James said quickly.

"Not quite, said he was trying to do it. Never got it to go for any real length of time." Calvin moved to turn a switch for his brother, even though Raymond hadn't given an indication he wanted him to do so.

"Oh, Yan's stuff," Raymond said, followed by a *click* as Calvin turned the switch. A faint humming could be heard.

"Brilliant," they said as one, looking at an oscilloscope.

James had no other option now. He needed them to be interested. Telling them the truth, or part of it, was the best way to generate that interest. "What if I told you that an extended force field is possible? And more importantly, that it can be done in open conditions on a massive scale?"

They laughed. "I would say that the girls hit the wrong end, and you need some sense knocked into ya, mate," Calvin said.

James grabbed a sheet of paper, crudely sketched the layout, and described passing through it. He described the issues with the batteries and electronics. He even told them about the use of older vehicles.

Calvin spoke first, "You are barking mad, mate. First, you need to have a conductor capable of that. It would be extremely expensive and have to be rather thick and run right along the perimeter to start. And then how are you keeping it...?"

James cut him off. "Wait, there is a natural layer of some metal. Very visible." He drew the cliff with the layer of what he originally had thought was lead. "What if that goes underneath the...? What are you staring at?"

"Look a bit familiar, Raymond?" asked Calvin.

"Just a bit. Looks like that antenna Yan used two weeks before getting thrown out. Made out of iridium, weren't it? Thought Dr. Watterson was going to have a heart attack when the invoice showed up a month later. Had a total of fifty grams of iridium, a small fortune it was." Abruptly, Raymond got up and left.

His brother's departure didn't strike Calvin as odd. He merely commented, "Right, Yan was here a lot those two weeks, and then had that row with Dr. Watterson about his idea. And you say this exists in an open environment?"

James nodded as Raymond returned with two videotapes in his hand, proclaiming, "Got 'em."

It turned out Raymond had cameras set up to automatically record any activity that went on in the lab. The tapes he'd recovered filmed the two weeks Yan had experimented with the iridium wire.

It took a few minutes, but they'd found a section where Yan was alone in the lab and conducting an experiment. Sure enough, any electronic object he placed over the circle failed. However, the equipment inside operated just fine, as did the equipment outside.

They did notice that the antenna portion that extended out like an arch was starting to glow toward the end of the experiment and that Yan slowly powered everything down.

"Wow, brilliant," said Raymond in a hushed voice.

"That's an understatement, brother," said Calvin in an equally awed voice.

James was starting to run short on time. "Listen, how would you eliminate the EMP force field?"

They seemed to come out of a trance. "No idea," they said together.

"We still have that wire, though," said Raymond.

Calvin nodded. "Yeah, we're going to have to give that a go. But you said this is out in the real world. Do you know where? Can you take us?" He was getting excited.

"No, I mean, yes. Yes, I know where it is, and no, I can't take you. I just need to know how to dismantle it in a quiet fashion." James spoke a little firmly. He needed to get transport units in to rescue the children, and that required the force field to be down. Taking out the fortress would probably take down the EMP, but the kids needed to be out first.

"We have to study it. We might be able to figure it out. Seeing it operate is the only way to know," Calvin said.

"Listen, I think I've set you on the right path. No doubt this will leapfrog your research. If you can figure out how to dismantle the EMP, call me." James handed him his number. "You at least owe me that."

He paused, knowing he needed more of a guarantee that they'd take action. "I'll see about getting you out to see the real one operate, but you need to act quickly. I need a response in ten days." James offered this just to tempt them, but had no intention of taking them into the field.

He turned to walk away but stopped and then went back, pulling all the cash he had out of his wallet. "This," he held up the cash, "is for whatever you want, but I need you to keep this to yourselves and not anyone else. Not Dr. Watterson, or even the girls."

The twins nodded and took the cash. Students always needed money, and James was going to wager that, that stack of pounds would go a long way.

"No worries, mate. This is with us. It will make our careers, and we want to see it operate in real time. We'll ring you as fast as possible," Raymond said.

James shook hands with them and walked out. He then ran to the car and drove a bit recklessly to the airport. It was a good thing Daen had taught him some high-speed driving techniques because he needed every second he could get.

At the airport, he screamed down the hall for them to not close the door to his flight, but he made it.

# •Chapter Thirty-Eight•

James, the major, and his team had been together for three days. They finally had the training course completed to give a reasonable mock version of the fortress where the kids were being held. He was pushing himself and everyone else hard on getting it finished. His instructions had been very clear, and James had double checked every detail to make sure they got it right.

After securing funds out of a private account the group didn't know about, James had just made final arrangements with Noi. Simultaneously, he was dealing with work-related problems, and keeping projects going on that front as well.

On the fourth morning, the major sought James out and pulled him aside. James knew something had to be up, and it had to be personal, as this wasn't how Ian Doyle customarily did things.

"What's wrong? Everything okay at home?" James asked.

"Home is fine, but since you asked, you are what's wrong," the major said flatly.

James did a double take, "What?"

"You're ordering the team around, and haven't earned the right to do so," the major said. He wasn't a man to mince words. "This is my team. 'Team' is the operative word. Each man here respects the others.

331

Each man can step up and take the lead, and each man knows when to follow. You haven't demonstrated any of that to them. You're barking orders without giving them the full vision of what's happening. How can you expect them to work if they don't know what they're working toward or why?"

"Look, we don't have time to..." James started, but the major raised his hand.

"I've said my piece n'at. You take the action you feel best, but I can tell you, I wouldn't want these men walking into this operation thinking this is how you're going to lead them. I've had to stop Jason and Kevin, from grabbing hold of you more than once. They're staying in line out of respect for me, and because I'm vouching for you. Don't make me look like a fool. Fix this." The major walked away.

Ian's tone had stayed even the entire time, exactly how James would have said it. No emotion, just logic, and James recognized his friend was right. He needed to become part of the team.

That day, he let the team get on with learning the passageways. First, in the light, then with night vision goggles, then in the dark. The guys outside the training exercise could see everything on monitors, and it was funny, and a bit disconcerting, watching guys stumble around a bit, or doing the same hall twice by mistake, or just walking into walls. James stayed away until they all finished, then approached the group. The men were huddled together, looking at a clipboard.

"Hey, guys, what's up?" he asked, in a lighter tone than he typically used.

Everyone was silent except the major, who said, "We're reviewing times. We have a standing bet that those who finish last buy the beer at the next bar. It looks like Jason, Kevin, and Ben are buying tonight."

Everyone laughed, even Jason, Kevin and Ben.

"Still have one more person to make the runs," James said.

They got quiet and stared at him. The silence grew uncomfortable. James shifted his weight and smiled. He felt like he was back in school, and the last kid to be picked for a team again.

"Yeah, I still need to go," James affirmed. He hoped he sounded confident but pleasant.

The men crossed their arms and stared at him. Finally, one of the guys, Rocker, made a flip with his hands as if to say, "Get on with it if you must."

"Right." James took his time. Doing a run in the construction was different than just studying the map. It felt real, just like the halls had felt on his and Tim's tour.

When he finished his first try, and walked back out, Paul announced, "Ooh, looks like Ben isn't paying dontcha know."

Everyone let out a great burst of laughter. It was clear they were laughing at James, not with him.

"Double or nothing. I'll do a lot better with the next round," James said, smiling.

The major just stared at James as if to say, "This is your mess."

In fairness, they'd all taken three practice runs per round before doing it timed. James knew this, but winning wasn't the point.

He did this round in the goggles, again slower than the others, but faster than before.

"Guess this means I ain't got to pay, either," Jason roared.

"I have one more round," James said.

"Not worried," Kevin said, to more laughter.

As James emerged the final time, having executed the run as effortlessly as if he were strolling through the park, silence again reigned. The difference this time was that it was born of amazement. James had beaten the best time by more than two minutes, in the dark. Little did the team know that on his first two passes, he'd counted his steps, and taken his time to learn the halls. It was a trick he'd learned when he was nine, and had lost his vision for ten days due to eye surgery.

"Woah, looks like he isn't buying tonight. After that performance, I feel like buying him a beer for sure. That was awesome. We watched on the infrared, and ya made no mistakes," said Paul, who was generally good-natured, and liked everyone to get along.

"Got lucky," James shrugged.

"Lucky, my ass," said Kevin.

"I told you guys, he has skills. Besides being a jagoff that is," the major said, and everyone laughed, and began to head toward the chow hall.

The major knew James was able to move well without sight only because of how the two men had met. For a moment, James wondered what Ian had told his men about how they'd come to be acquainted in that mall fire. James was certain they didn't know the full story by any stretch of the imagination.

"Wait," James said. "I think I still owe you guys some beers."

"You just kicked everyone's ass, and it was double or nothing. Means you owe nothing," Matt said.

"We didn't bet on the last round, just the first two. So tonight is on me. There's a place in town we can go to after dinner," James said.

Again, silence. Rocker, who had said maybe ten words in the last four days, gave a shrug, and made his way to dinner. The others followed, and talking broke out. The major caught James's eye for a second, and gave him a wink, as they carried on.

After dinner, James and the major volunteered to stay sober and drive, and everyone else was more than happy with this arrangement. They ended up at a rather nice sports bar that had multiple large screen televisions, pool tables, darts, and even a shuffleboard game. The bar itself was large, and made a flat bottom 'V' shape. James appreciated the quality oak wood, with a highly polished brass rail that ran the length of the bar.

He was starting to win the guys over one at a time. He'd learned that Rocker was the lead singer for a band back home. James had commented, "Yeah, I could tell by how much you talk that you have a great voice." This got some laughs, and a bird flipped his way by a smiling Rocker.

He'd learned that Haiden and Keegan were cousins and talked about fishing every chance they got.

Paul was the explosives expert, and had apparently started at a young age, which explained why he was missing part of a finger.

The master of arms was Jason, who knew more about weapons than the rest put together.

Kevin wanted to go into podiatry, but was serving as the medic, and communications person for the group.

Matt was an amateur pilot, but also had broad-spectrum vision that came in handy as a marksman.

Ben was also a marksman who had grown up in a family of hunters. He practiced every day to be the best, because he wanted to fit into his family. It turned out he was adopted.

They were having fun, and no one drank too heavily. The men were on their third round of beers when the evening took a turn. James had just passed the last of the beers to Paul, and turned to grab his water, and pay the bartender when a bald man standing six-feet-four-inches, and weighing a solid 270 pounds bumped his left side. As James had grabbed his water with his left hand, it spilled a little, and a drop landed on the man's hand.

"Watch what you're doing, asshole!" the man said aggressively.

James glanced up at the man, slightly disgruntled. Clearly, the guy was drunk. He decided to move on and let it go.

The man leaned into James's face, saying, "I said, watch what you're doing, asshole. You could at least apologize."

James's forehead scrunched up, as he said, "Sorry?"

"That ain't no apology, wrinkle face. Say it like you mean it," said the man. The man's friends, who were all large as well, chuckled.

Paul, having just made it back to the table, let the rest of the group know what was happening. The major held out his fingers to signal the group to hold tight for now. James did his normal thing, and within a blink, assessed the individuals and situation. He decided to take the high road.

"You know what, you're right. My mistake. Sorry, that drop of water hit you. Have a good night." He gave a false, close-lipped smile, and handed the bar-tender the money for his team's beers.

"That sound sincere to you, boys?" asked the man. The group shook their mullet-covered heads. "Nah, didn't to me either. Try again, boy," he said in a growl.

James knew this guy was looking for a fight, but he didn't feel like obliging him, and couldn't risk getting entangled with the cops, and causing a delay. "Look, man, sorry about that. Let me buy you and your friends here a round of beers. What will ya have?" James spoke as politely as he could, but he had a feeling this was still going to end badly. He set his glass of water back on the bar.

The bartender quickly said, "What'll it be for yinz? Another round of Iron City?"

"Nah, I think his offense is worth more. Like one of them imported fancy beers. Gimme a Blue Moon," said the man, with a determined look in his eyes. The bartender poured the beer quickly and set it down. He then turned to the others, and asked what they wanted. Before they could answer, the bald man said, "Hold on, let me see how this one does first."

He picked up the glass. Looking James in the eyes, he slowly brought it up to his mouth with his right hand. Just as the glass touched his lips, the man made a fast motion, and dumped the contents over James's head. He shook the glass to get every drop out before setting the glass on the bar with a loud slam.

"Now that hit the spot!" he exclaimed and laughed.

The live band that had been playing fell silent, as did the other patrons in the bar, but the bald man and his friends roared with laughter. James couldn't see what his group was doing behind him, but he heard the scrape of several chairs, and the sound of men getting to their feet. The bald man's friends suddenly stopped laughing.

James turned his head visibly to the left, but not so far that he could see his companions. He paused a moment, then turned back to face the man. The major sat down. After a moment's hesitation, the other guys followed his lead.

The bald man let out a great burst of laughter. "Looks like your little friends know what's good for them, too." He and his friends laughed again, and so did James. "Getting your ass kicked funny to you, boy?" the man said, spurring on the laughter from the others.

James shook his head, spraying beer everywhere, but the bald man somehow ignored this shower. "No, but the fact that you think they stood up to help me is funny. The truth is, they stood up to protect you and your friends from me." A moment passed in which the energy of the room shifted. James was taking control, almost through sheer willpower.

The bald man and his friends laughed. The sound was defiant, overly confident, and held an element of surprise to it. James's response clearly was unexpected by all, but especially by the bald man, who had five inches on James, and more than a hundred pounds.

James shifted his left foot behind him and said, "I think we're going to call it a night so no one gets hurt." He turned abruptly as if to leave, but the bald man grabbed his left shoulder with his right hand.

*Idiot,* thought James. At moments like this, time seemed to slow down. In reality, and James knew it, his focus was so sharp he reacted as if he saw every-thing a move ahead. This just made more things happen in a smaller space of time.

Given his would-be attacker's position, James had deliberately placed his weight on his left foot, so he'd have better pivot control. As the bald man pulled him around, James brought his right arm up, and around the bald man's arm to break the shoulder grab, and secure the offending appendage. He followed that with a swift turning kick with his right leg to the man's diaphragm, causing him to double over. Still holding the man's right arm, he used his right leg to kick the man's right knee before releasing his arm. He then quickly stepped in with his left arm, and grabbed the man's head. He banged it into the bar rail, allowing his own hand to follow through the motion, so that the bald man fell to the floor.

In the highly polished brass, he saw two of the man's friends coming toward him. The one on James's left was slightly closer. As he turned to the left, he grabbed his water with his right hand. Swinging around, he blocked the hand of the closer man with a wide sweeping left forearm block, while throwing the water in the other would-be attacker's face. He continued turning, smashing the empty glass into the left temple of the dry attacker, and knocking him out.

The wet attacker didn't stop, but he did hesitate slightly when the water hit him, giving James the time he needed to hit the dry man with the glass, and gain better position. The position change forced the wet attacker to throw a wild swing with his right arm. James promptly blocked it with his own right arm, and kicked him in the stomach with his right leg. Turning into the man's arm that he still held in his right hand, James crushed it with his left elbow, causing the man to suffer an extreme hyperextension. James then slid under the attacker's arm, and stood up, while bringing the injured man's arm down hard onto James's own shoulder. The man's shoulder dislocated. When James saw a knife fall from his hand, he finished him off with a leg sweep, and a stomp to the chest.

James prepared for the other man's friends, but they were moving away, not attacking. The room was so quiet you could hear the ceiling fans between the grunts of the man on the floor with the broken ribs. The other two men were still unconscious. The whole fight was over in seconds.

The major walked up behind James and said, "Time to go, I believe."

"Right." James turned to the bartender, and handed him twenty bucks. "That's for the beer, glass, and mess. I suggest calling at least two ambulances." Pointing at the men, he said, "These two have concussions, these two have broken ribs, he has a knee out of place, and he has a shoulder out of place. Maybe an elbow, too, not really sure. This is my number if the cops want to talk." He wrote down his number, and handed it to the barman.

The barman shook his head with a grin. "I'm ninety-nine percent certain they won't need to talk to yinz. My cousin-in-law is the sheriff, n'at is self-defense if I ever saw it, plus it's all on tape."

James shook hands with the bartender, and walked out with the team behind him.

"Dude!" Rocker said, as James walked by.

"Does he ever shut up?" James asked, grinning. Everyone laughed.

James felt rather good. It had been a while since he had a rush like that, and he felt lighter. Reflecting, he had to admit it had been a great release. He did feel slightly guilty for causing so much damage, but it was nothing life threatening, and hopefully those guys wouldn't be such idiots again.

Just before James turned in for the evening, the major came into his room. He let out a deep sigh as if he was going to give a speech, and then said, "Well, that was the most extraordinarily unique way of building the team's confidence that I've ever seen. Paul was all about getting up to help you. I had to order him to stay seated. Afterwards, he was saying they should start calling yinz Leonidas."

James laughed. "That's an entirely inaccurate analogy. Now, if I'd..."

"Not the point, you nerd," said the major, in an elevated voice.

James squinted and shook a playful fist at his friend.

"It was impressive, but I can still kick your ass." The major winked and walked out.

The next morning, having thought it over, James decided to tell the team their objectives. He started with the list he and the major had discussed, and then told the guys the story of his and Tim's trip, and the discovery of the children. He didn't disclose why he and Tim had gone, but merely said they'd gone to secure intel. The men didn't question this, but they did ask other questions.

Paul was first to raise his hand. "Why are they out so far in the middle of nowhere? How can they get customers way out there?"

"Customers? Really? Customers?" Ben challenged Paul's choice of words, clearly angry.

"Ooh geez, well, what do ya call them? Visitors?" Paul asked, almost apologetically.

"I think the term you be looking for is deranged sickos," Keegan said, which was immediately followed by a "Mhmm," from Haiden. The two cousins did this almost every time the other spoke.

James took command of the room. "The children are valuable. The location isn't an issue. In fact, it's a fortress we're attacking and bringing down."

Ben stood up with a determined look on his face. Everyone looked at him as he stood there. Finally, he spoke. "How many?"

"At least thirty-five when I was there six months ago. Not really sure now, and not sure how many adults are former abused kids that want out, too," James said.

Ben paused, every inch of his face showing hatred as sweat began to roll off him. "I was abused as a kid. No kid dies, and we never speak of this. Ever. Sorry, Major, but James, you have full command," he said, through gritted teeth.

As he sat down, all of the other guys stomped their left foot, then right foot, and clamped their hands once, including the major. Later, the major explained to James that the stomps and clapping was the way they sealed a pact.

For the next few hours, James walked them through the potential plans and they listened. They didn't speak unless, James paused and asked if they had suggestions or questions. The answer was always the same, "Not today, sir!" James was the leader now, but he recognized he should follow each individual's expertise and suggestions. Over the next two days, they ran through scenarios, and made modifications.

He particularly liked the sticky bombs Paul had brought. Essentially they were a spear on one end, and a sticky material on the other. This would allow for bombs to be placed just about anywhere. A timer or detonator could be used to set them off.

Ben was training with James on some additional hand combat. Ben and Matt decided Matt would play sniper from a distance. Matt and James had a very specific discussion on Matt's abilities to take out individuals, and Matt laughed.

"Please, I can take the weapon right out of their hands at three hundred yards without scratching them. That isn't a problem," Matt said, chewing on a toothpick.

It reminded James of Val Kilmer in Top Gun, and James hated the character in the movie. On impulse, he ripped the toothpick out of Matt's mouth, but in a playful manner.

"Good thing that one was dead. I have more," Matt said, undisturbed, as James walked away, shaking his head and chuckling.

# •Chapter Thirty-Nine•

Six days before the Operation Joshua team was due to set off, Calvin and Raymond called James. They exchanged hellos quickly before Calvin dived in.

"So, we think we have a way to maybe solve the problem," he said excitedly.

Raymond jumped in. "Yeah, we went back through the tapes, and watched most of what Yan did. Parts were out of frame, but we think we figured it out."

"How are you managing to get the parts out of frame?" James asked.

"Well, it's quite brilliant, if I say so meself. We went back, and looked at old invoices that led us to look at old power consumptions. We put it together from there."

James wasn't sure who had just answered him, because they sounded alike, but it didn't matter. "So how do I take it down?"

"Well, we aren't exactly sure, mind."

"Right, but we do think we can."

"Guys, how?" James asked firmly.

"Ummm, right, well, we need to run a test to make sure we're right."

James took a short breath before saying, "Then run it and get back to me."

"Has to be a field test," they both said, extremely fast.

"No," James said. "Just tell me what the test is and how to read the results."

"Can't, mate. You had trouble understanding some of the math with me walking you through it. You won't be able to get it in time," Calvin said.

"This is not a joke or a vacation. This is a serious operation that may cost some people their lives. You have no idea what's out there, nor do you have the skills needed for this. I can't risk your lives," James said, frustrated.

The truth was, he needed the information. The alternative was very risky, and chances were not everyone would make it back if they had to use that option.

"What do you think, Raymond?" Calvin asked.

"I think he needs us. We have the answers he needs. Besides, we don't have to enter into whatever all this is about. In fact, we can be of use. We can be eyes and ears if you guys wear cameras, unless you have that worked out. What exactly are you doing?" Raymond said.

This idea intrigued James. "What about accessing a closed monitoring and computer system on the compound?" he asked.

"Easy, just need to splice in, and we can see everything," replied Raymond.

James processed this quickly, but thoroughly before consenting. He gave them a breakdown on the basics, and what to bring. He'd arrange for their flights, and told them how to get their equipment to a safe point.

James would fly commercially, as he'd given Noi his itinerary for the whole trip, but the twins would finish the journey with the major's team, joining them in

Istanbul. This would give them six hours with James and the rest of the team before James left.

The major wasn't happy when he learned of the addition of the twins. The discussion went on for over an hour, and resulted in James playing a card the major usually dealt.

"What's the alternative? If you know how to take down the EMP force field, and get the kids out, let me know, and I'll cancel their tickets," said James.

The major scowled and walked away, saying, "Son of a bitch."

Introducing the twins to the guys in Istanbul didn't go smoothly. In many ways, it was like introducing two hyper dogs to an old folks' home made up of veterans who jump at loud noises. James hadn't seen the twins act this excited, or talk so much before, and he assumed they were nervous. He wished their girlfriends were there to occupy them. After about the third hour, Ben was starting to lose his patience with them. Keegan and Haiden brought this to James's attention.

Keegan tapped James on the shoulder and said, "I think Ben is going to go all rice crispy on your boys."

"Mhmm," said Haiden, with a vigorous nodding that reminded James of Byron.

"What are you talking about?" James asked.

"Well, Ben is about to 'snap' and we are going to hear some bones 'crack' as he 'pops' 'em," said Haiden, followed up by Keegan's "Mhmm."

James got it. He walked over to where Calvin and Raymond were chatting at some of the guys.

"Dude, seriously, can you stop talking for five minutes?" Ben was asking Calvin, who had just been explaining to an uninterested Rocker how the magnetic poles had changed over time.

"But it's important, and it's relevant to the situation. We believe that the..." Calvin had shifted his attention to Ben.

Ben looked at Calvin and clearly stated, "Raymond, I don't care."

"Right, I'm Calvin," said Calvin.

"I'm Raymond," Raymond said.

"What if we were to tattoo your names on your foreheads?" Jason asked.

The twins gave him a nervous look, before Raymond picked up where Calvin had stopped. "You see, it's the iridium that..."

"I do not care. Please shut up, whichever one you are," Ben said, through gritted teeth.

"But..." Calvin said.

Most of the guys looked like they wanted to silence the twins with a good fist to the mouth, but James figured that would dampen the operation.

"Calvin and Raymond, please come here," James said. "Do it quickly, and more importantly, quietly."

With the twins in hand, he reviewed the processes they needed to be aware of. They were to sit with Matt on the cusp of the hill overlooking the fortress once they figured out how to dismantle the EMP force field. They would have a vehicle with monitors, so they could relay information to the team as well. However, Kevin would still have master communication responsibility for the field. They were to take no additional actions, and to stay with the vehicle and Matt at all times.

After making the twins repeeat back what he expected of them, James took them over to see the major.

Then asked them what he'd been wondering for some time. "What's the leading theory on taking down the EMP?"

"Ah, right, that. Well, we think it needs to be done from the inside," Raymond said, cautiously.

"Okay, so what needs to happen? How'd you break it in the lab from the inner part of the circle?" James asked.

The major listened intently.

"No mate, from inside the thingy, you know, the fortress. Um, you need to cut the power," Calvin said, timidly.

The major flashed a look at the twins and then James. James was looking down at the general floor plan on the table. When he looked up, he selected his words carefully.

"Are you telling me that all I have to do is cut the electrical power?"

"Well, it isn't that simple." Calvin made a motion as he spoke. "It will be a rather high voltage you have to stop. Imagine a few breakers, actually."

"It is that simple." James rifled through the drawings until he found the one of the office with the monitors. "You see this?" He held up the drawing and tapped aggressively on the eight master circuit breakers in the room. "Is this all I need to take care of? This is how they bring in all the equipment isn't it? They just shut off the power, bring it in, and power it back up? How long have you known about this solution?"

The twins looked down and didn't answer.

"So it isn't a stored EMP like you study that is triggered by crossing some line? It's just constantly on?" James asked, in a condescending way.

They didn't answer again.

The major pressed clenched fists on the table. He spoke to James as if the twins weren't there. "We could just leave them here, and let them wait until their flight back n'at."

James seriously considered this before taking a different path. "You will go with us," he conceded. "You will follow every instruction you're given. You will conduct whatever test you think you can, but your time frame will be restricted to whenever the major decides to engage. You have no say in it. You will monitor what happens, and speak in the fewest words possible to inform the team of movements. For the rest of the journey, you're to speak only when spoken to. After this is over, you will never speak of it again, even to each other. Make up whatever story you need to in order to gain validity for your research. As that research brings forth results, I reserve the right to call in favors that could be monetary."

"Anything you don't understand or don't agree to?" asked the major.

The twins were looking down like they were two little kids who'd gotten in trouble, and couldn't face their parents, but they shook their heads.

James dropped his voice and said, "Look at me and speak!" He did this for effect, knowing it would help seal their silence.

They looked up, almost in tears. "We understand and agree."

"Fair enough," said James, in his normal tone. He walked away, and the major moved on as well.

Paul came over a short while later. "They're really upset." He gestured at the twins. "They're not so bad. Kinda funny. We should get Keegan and Haiden started on fishing, and see if the twins can keep up with."

"They'll be fine. It's not like we hit them," said Ben.

"Yet," added Jason.

Matt and the major laughed while James smiled.

"Why do they keep looking like that at me, like they're about to run?" asked Jason. From his waist, he pulled what was essentially a hand cannon of a gun, and set it on the table.

"Maybe because of that, dontcha know," said Paul, pointing at the gun.

"What?" Jason apparently didn't think that could be the problem.

"They're British. They ain't all that big on guns. Probably ain't never fired one," Haiden called from his seat about fifteen feet away.

Right on cue, Keegan nodded, adding, "Mhmm, everyone knows that."

"They're probably against the second amendment, too," said Jason.

Ben stared at him, blinking, while James shook his head.

"Dude, they're British. They don't believe in our entire constitution, dontcha know," said Paul.

That was too much for James, he picked up his bag and said, "I've a plane to catch. See you all soon enough. Have fun with them, Major." He gave Ian a rather sarcastic pat on the back. In response, the major flipped him off.

# •Chapter Forty•

The morning dawned brisk and bright. A light fog-like cloud could be seen in the distance as the sun rose. As the sun continued to peak over the horizon, it created different colors within the fog, almost like a low Aurora Borealis. *That's unnatural*, James thought, watching it during the journey to the fortress, attempting to distract himself from what was about to happen.

Most people would be continuously going over the plan in their heads, but not James. He'd never been a person that studied at the last minute for exams, and this was no different in his mind. He knew if he focused on relaxing, he'd perform better, have more energy when it was needed, and have a more pronounced reaction to the adrenaline if it came to that. Wasting energy on the emotion of the moment didn't help when studying, or now. Understanding conservation of energy was a key to how he suppressed his emotions.

He understood why people had this emotional response, but he'd rarely experienced it himself. Maybe that was why today felt unnatural. He was slightly worried. He felt semi-justified because of what was at stake, but at the same time, he was frustrated with himself because it was illogical. He needed to rely on logic to do what needed to be done. Being emotional could result in hesitation, and hesitating could cost someone their life.

They made their trip over the embankment. *Two hours to go before reaching Joe*, James thought.

James glanced at the driver and Noi in the front seat, and then took off his hat, pretending to scratch his head, then placed it on his lap. He carefully extracted the two tiny tracking devices, and battery he had brought. He triggered the second tracking device, and set it under his seat, and shut off the first tracker while replacing the battery. The semi-spent battery, and the tracker went back into the inner brim of his hat. Also in the hat was a splicer Raymond had given him that would allow them to see the video feeds in the fortress, once the EMP was disabled. There was also a CD, plus a hard drive with a cable.

The twins had assured James the hard drive would be fine, because it wouldn't be turned on. With it being new, there was little chance of it being damaged, and there was no data to scramble. James wasn't as convinced, but he didn't have a simple backup plan.

James was betting Joe wouldn't check his hat. He hadn't checked Tim's last time. This was a risk, but a calculated one. Humans have deep-seated behaviors, and Joe had a basic friendliness about him. James had treated Joe well last time, and figured that if he made the transition from the vehicles smoothly, it wouldn't be an issue. If he was wrong, he had a plan for that, too.

James was starting to unwrap a Kit-Kat bar, when Noi looked back at him.

"Doing well, sir?" asked Noi.

James looked at him, slowly closed his eyes, and nodded twice. Earlier, he'd told Noi he had a headache and didn't wish to talk. In response, the driver and Noi had been rather quiet.

As they swung around to meet Joe, James deliberately looked for, but saw no signs of other tracks. The wind probably blew away the dusty tracks each day, which only made it more challenging to find the fortress. He didn't recall seeing them last time either, but hadn't made a point of looking for them.

Joe pulled up in his old Suburban. Noi jumped out, and the driver locked the doors while Noi spoke to Joe. James watched as they exchanged the carrier, and Noi pointed to his head. This made James slightly nervous. Joe and Noi started to walk back, and the driver unlocked the doors.

James climbed out, removed his coat, and held out his arms, ready for Joe to search him. He'd deliberately worn tight fitting clothes so it would be apparent he wasn't carrying anything. He gave Joe a slight smile that Joe returned. After a quick pat down and search of the coat, they were off, Noi having already assured him that he'd be waiting for him upon his return.

As they started driving, James removed his hat, intending to trigger the tracking device. At that moment, Joe looked back. James froze inside. *Has Joe been waiting for this? Had Noi suspected something?*

Joe merely grabbed his water container and offered it to James. "Help with head aching?"

James smiled slowly as a wave of relief crashed over him. "Thank you, Joe, but no. I will be okay."

Joe smiled and went back to driving.

James calmed down, and told himself he needed to stop over thinking. It was obvious Noi had pointed at his own head to tell Joe about the headache James had.

Working carefully, James triggered the tracking device.

About forty minutes later, he cracked his window. He didn't want it to look like he was doing it just as they hit the stone marker. Joe glanced up but otherwise didn't react.

Almost fifteen minutes later, Joe said, "Ready?" and looked at James in the rearview mirror with a big grin.

James chuckled and said, "Yes."

Joe slammed on the gas pedal, and James readied his hand to drop the tracker out the window. As Joe shifted to neutral, James dropped it. *Come get me, boys*, he thought as he and Joe coasted along.

They parked a few minutes later. James noticed the courtyard area looked a bit different. The old trucks were gone, and the place seemed more open. He also noticed some newer looking cameras had been installed along the ramparts.

As they reached the doors, Lien and Bik greeted them, both smiling largely. Bik held a tall glass of ice water, while a girl behind her held a pitcher on a tray.

"Oh, wercome wercome. Very happy see again, Mr. Mathers, wercome," crooned Lien.

Bik nodded as her brother spoke, and offered the glass of water to James.

"Thank you for the kind welcome. No thanks, I'm not thirsty right now," James said, walking up to them, and stopping just shy of the threshold.

Lien stayed behind to talk to Joe. Bik, still smiling, walked with James down the hall, with the girl holding the water pitcher walking behind them. James hoped Joe would tell Lien about his headache, as this would cut down on the chatter. Sure enough, Joe did just that.

"So sorry hear your head hurting. Can offer any-thing?" asked Lien, catching up a moment later.

In a bit of acting, James slowly said, "No, I will be fine. I could use a restroom for a moment, though, please."

"Yes, yes, this way!" Lien and Bik each gestured to the hallway on the right. James approached the door to the first suite, but Bik stopped him. "Sorry, not empty," said Lien. "Prease, this way." He took James to the second suite instead.

"I will just need a few minutes," James said, shut-ting the door on their smiling faces.

He paused a moment and glanced around before re-calling that the ceiling mirror probably had a camera hidden behind it. He made his way to the bathroom. The bathroom didn't have any visible cameras, and James didn't see where one could be hidden, unless it was in the light fixture. He hoped to find a rather visi-ble camera line to splice into for the video feed.

He carefully removed his hat, and splashed some water on his face before making use of the toilet. After washing and drying his hands, he grabbed his hat, and returned to the bedroom. The straw color haired boy was standing there.

James stared at him for a moment, and the boy stared back.

"Umm, do you speak English?" James asked.

"Yes, sir, Mr. Mathers," said the boy.

"Right, so what are you doing here?" James asked.

"I was told my new owner is here, and that he has a headache," the boy answered. "I was sent to do what I could for you. I hope I have not displeased you, Mr. Mathers, sir."

"Are you X?" James asked.

The boy averted his head slightly, as if unsure why James had asked him this, but said, "If you want to call me that, yes, sir. I am called that here by many."

"Right." James took a deep breath to give himself a moment to think. *What if I can get this kid to help get the others ready? He'd helped gather them before in the bathing pool. But no, too risky. Too hard to say how he'd react.*

"No, you have not displeased me," James responded, to the boy's earlier statement. "I'm just surprised to see you. May I ask why they call you that? You do not seem to like it," he said.

The boy continued to stare at him, but answered with some shame in his voice. "They say my name is Xavier, but that is not why they call me X. How do you know I do not like it?"

"You frowned when I said it, and you used a dismissive voice when you answered," James said quickly.

"I am sorry if my voice was offensive, sir," Xavier said.

James adopted a gentle voice before saying, "Tell me why they call you that, and if you do not like it, I will be sure to call you Xavier."

Xavier said nothing, just stared at him for a moment.

"It's okay if you don't want to tell me." James placed a reassuring hand on Xavier's shoulder. "I was just curious. But if you would like to tell me, I will listen."

The boy lowered his head until his chin touched his chest before taking two audible breaths. James slowly lifted the boy's chin. He was crying silently.

"Look, kid, I mean Xavier, I didn't mean to make you cry. I was just asking. You don't have to tell me. Your life is going to be a lot different after today, I promise." James gave him a warm smile, and wiped away his tears.

Xavier regained his composure quickly, and gave a small smile back.

"Let me get you some water," James said. He picked up a glass from the table in the corner, and started to fill it from the water jug. He heard a small sound, like fabric hitting the floor. James turned back around, and was about to ask Xavier if he enjoyed sports. He saw the boy was shirtless, and had undone his pants, and was pushing them and his underwear to the floor.

James dropped the glass. It smashed as he half-shouted, "Hey! What are...?"

The door opened, and Lien and Bik entered quickly. Lien made his way over to James, while Bik grabbed Xavier, and shook him harshly.

"So sorry, if not doing as you prease. We thought fix him," said Lien.

James closed his eyes for half a heartbeat, and then took control of the situation. "Take your hands off my property," he said in a stern voice.

Lien turned to look at his sister. He said something, and she released Xavier.

"He didn't do anything wrong, he's perfectly fine. What were you doing outside the door listening?" James asked, in an incredulous voice.

"We listen, make sure okay. Help with boy," Bik answered, looking angry at being yelled at.

"Do you think I can't handle a boy? Is this how you treat a customer? I'm not sure I'll be returning after today. Where are your sister-in-law and nephew? Let's talk to them." James needed to move things along, as the cavalry would be arriving in five to ten minutes.

He walked out past the others, but stopped at Xavier for a moment, and tousled his hair. "I will see you in a short time, okay?"

Lien followed him and said, "Stay here."

James wasn't sure if Lien had addressed Xavier, or Bik, or both, so he said, "I would like Xavier to join the other children, and when he has done so, for Bik to join us."

As he walked off down the hall, he heard the sounds of two children crying coming from the first suite. He felt himself flush a little, before calming himself down.

"Very sorry for mistake. We make thing better." Lien was groveling.

"Mr. Tan, I have a headache. Can you please stop talking so much? The echo is making my head hurt more."

They walked in silence, back through the courtyard area with the bar, and to the hallway that led to the office. James noticed a camera just out of view of the main corridor, as they turned a corner toward the office. This would work to hook into the video feed. Now he needed an excuse to get back to this spot, plus something to stand on.

Just then, Yan Tan met them in the hallway. "Hello, Mr. Mathers. I'm sorry to hear of your headache, and that your visit isn't going well so far."

*Looks like I'm definitely right about the camera's being in the bedroom*, James thought, as that was the only way Yan could've known what had happened.

"Perhaps we could get things moving along?" James said in a bored, arrogant tone.

They entered the office to find the same cast as before, plus Bik, who joined them about a minute later. Yan's mother seemed not to have moved, and James was fairly sure she was wearing the same outfit as before. She was staring at him oddly.

"We had begun to think you weren't coming back, Mr. Mathers," said Yan, in a sly voice. His uncle laughed lightly.

"I needed to make sure everything was in order for myself, as well as my cousin," James said.

"Mr. Ferguson, yes. We hear he was a little sick on the return trip," Yan said, with a slight bow of his head, before speaking to his mother in a different language.

"Too much fruit. He does love pineapple. Anyhow, that isn't what we're here to discuss, is it?" He again spoke in a bored, arrogant voice.

Jie spoke harshly to her son, still staring at James.

"So sorry, my mother wishes to know why you disrespect her house by wearing that hat?" Yan translated.

James deliberately glanced up as though he'd forgotten he was wearing a hat. Slowly, he removed it, giving a small bow to the elderly lady. "My apologies. When I have a headache, wearing a hat sometimes helps. I mean no disrespect."

She nodded slowly.

"I trust all is in order for today?" James asked.

"Yes, we have done as you have requested. They are both healthy, and have been diligent in their education." Yan answered proudly.

James nodded. "So I believe that leaves us with an update on the Spara family."

The energy in the room intensified. Even the old lady seemed excited as Yan presumably translated James's words.

"You will be pleased to know we have isolated an area where we plan to bring him down. It will take some time, but his underboss, or regional boss, or whatever he's called, is a little greedy. We've started to gather some leverage on him. It turns out he uses cocaine and likes to talk loudly at strip clubs. His entire crew has been recorded bringing him drugs. Hell, he travels with a kilo of blow in his trunk hidden in a spare tire."

James paused a moment to rub his temples, and Fang brought him some water. Without drinking it, James set it on the table beside him just as a loud siren went off. "What is that noise?" James demanded, holding his ears. He assumed it was a warning system, and knew perfectly well what had caused it. The cavalry had arrived.

"Please, Mr. Mathers, don't worry. Nomads sometimes attack our walls. They have never been successful and our people will subdue this quickly. They have been more aggressive lately, so we have had to increase security with new cameras, and warning systems." Yan spoke in a reassuring way. He clicked his fingers, and Seim and Fang left.

As the door shut, a second blast of the siren went off. This didn't sit well with the Tan family. "Nothing to worry about," said Yan, helping his mother to her feet. "My mother, like you, doesn't like this loud noise. She will be going to, ah, a private bedroom, until this passes."

What Yan was really saying was that his mother was going to the vault that must serve as a panic room, as a third blast of the siren was heard, along with the faint sound of gunfire.

"What is going on? I thought this operation of yours was safe!" James shouted, still holding his ears, and pretending to be angry.

"Nothing to worry about. I will personally tend to the situation."

Yan gave his uncle a look, and they also left. Now it was just James, Bik, and Hansel. Hansel shut the door to the panic room Jie had just entered. A fourth long blast sounded, and Bik jumped nervously.

"You wait here, understand? You safe here. Come," she said, motioning to Hansel, and they were gone too.

# •Chapter Forty-One•

That had worked out better than James could've hoped. Never had he imagined that he'd be left alone in the office with just Jie behind a panic room door.

He sprang into action to take down the power grid. The major, the twins, and Paul had reviewed which main boxes they believed to give power to the EMP force field. They'd decided not to take out all the breakers, because James wouldn't be able to retrieve any data, and the camera system wouldn't work, so he started at the ones furthest from the computers, and began switching them off. The twins believed even a partial reduction in power would do the trick, but James wanted to be certain. He tripped the furthest six of the eight, and didn't lose any of the cameras or the computers. He wanted to trip another, but decided not to press his luck.

He quickly accessed a cable that led to the monitors, and was about to snap on the splicer from his hat, when he heard a loud La Cucaracha horn blast. *Yes!* he thought. That meant the guys had made it past the EMP force field with their equipment. James snapped the transmitter into place. Now the twins, Matt, and Kevin would have visibility into the fortress cameras.

He quickly tried to get into the computer system. He removed the hard drive from his hat, took the disc from on top, and placed it into the drive. Hopefully, it would be able to bypass any security, and allow him to make a copy of the hard drive.

He pulled the side panel off the tower of the desktop, and plugged in the hard drive as the CD worked to break the security. It was hard to focus on aligning the pins to the hard drive, as he naturally wanted to see what was happening on the monitors. Finally, they snapped in place, and James found he was in their system.

He wanted to copy the main information, but he found incredible amounts of data, most of which wasn't stored on the computer's main hard drive. The files were all in Chinese, and he couldn't read the names. He needed Tim for that. He decided to sort the files by size, and grabbed those that would fit on the drive. A ton of video must be stored on the drives, and those would be massive files he didn't need. This process, even with high-end technology, would take a good fifteen minutes to transfer. He couldn't wait for the entire data dump onto the new drive, so he turned off the screen, placed the cover back on the tower, and searched the monitors for the kids.

He found them amassed and huddled in the largest dormitory. It looked like there were at least fifty of them. He had to secure them until the removal team was ready, which meant he'd have to come back for the hard drive.

Running out of the office was like turning up the volume on a TV or radio. There was a lot of screaming and shouting, but it wasn't completely audible over the gunfire outside. As James scrambled down the stairs to the main entrance, he heard a crashing of glass from the tower as some explosives hit their mark. He paused a moment to avoid the rain of mirror shards.

He dashed down the middle corridor to the biggest dorm room. When he got there, he found a lot of frightened children, and two young women standing over them. Either they were going to help him, or he was going to knock them out. He didn't have time to be a gentleman.

He was anticipating the second blast of the horn to tell him the explosives were in place to create the main exit to get the kids out. When it sounded, the explosives would go off in five seconds. They had to be ready to go, which meant he had about five minutes to move the kids toward the bathing pool.

"We need to move right now. Everyone to the bath area hallway," he said. The kids just stared at him. "We have to go now!" James shouted.

Little Jasmine stood up, and screamed something, and the two young adults started moving the kids. Just as they began filing into the main corridor, he heard the La Cucaracha horn. He'd underestimated the time needed to move the kids.

"Everyone down, cover your heads!" James dropped to the floor, hoping they'd mimic his actions, and they did. A huge blast went off and shook the fortress. Small parts of the walls and ceiling fell near them, but didn't injure anyone.

James stood and told Jasmine to get everyone to the bathing room fast, and that they'd find men there to get them to safety. She followed his instructions. The kids were moving too slowly. James knew they were scared, but they didn't have time to waste. He tried to push them along. Some seemed to want to stay in the room, and clutched the bed frames, but with help from some of the older kids, he and Jasmine got them all moving. James stayed with them until he caught sight of Ben and Paul.

"You've got ten minutes!" Paul yelled, and James gave him a thumbs up.

Earlier, they'd worked out that once the kids were safe, that they would detonate the exit they created. That way, those who fought for the Tan family would be trapped inside. However, James would first sweep the rooms to make sure no kids were left behind. He wouldn't have time to do that and grab the hard drive, which meant he had to leave it. James didn't give the hard drive a second thought, but began sweeping the rooms visually, quickly sticking his head in, and checking each, his instincts guiding him as much as anything.

He made it to the furthest distance from the opening in less than three minutes. He didn't expect to find anyone, as he hadn't seen any kids outside the main dorm on the monitors previously, but he wanted to check anyhow. Sure enough, on the return path, he found a girl and boy, who could've been siblings, barely clothed.

He got them up and moving. He still checked rooms as he went, but it going was slower now, as the kids were practically fighting him to return to their hiding spot. Luckily, there weren't as many rooms to check going back. James did find a pitch-black hallway with a few thick pipes emerging from it. He figured it was near the back end of the bathing room, but it hadn't seen it on the map, so, he couldn't be sure. There was a faint sound coming from hall, but not a sound kids would make. He decided to move on.

As they reached the intersection that would lead to the newly created exit, Lien appeared. They had about a minute left, and James knew Paul and Ben had already vacated the building. James told the two kids to go to the baths and hoped they understood. Lien was running at him with a gun. Apparently, he thought James was protecting the kids, as he hadn't pointed the gun at him.

"Thank for herp with them. We need secure you," Lien said.

As soon as Lien was within arm reach, James took his gun. It wasn't difficult, as Lien wasn't expecting it. In the blink of an eye, James made a logical choice, one devoid of emotion, and shot Lien center mass three times. He didn't hesitate, nor did he wait to see the body hit the floor.

He chased after the two kids, scooped them up, and ran out the exit. They saw one of the transportation vehicles, and Paul grinning.

James picked up a headset, after handing the kids off, and ignoring Paul's celebratory antics. "Major, this is James. Where do we stand?"

"No losses. We've taken out a fair few of them. They're mostly forced back inside the main hall entrance, but are still keeping up fire," answered Major Doyle.

A voice crackled over the headsets, saying, "East sector, upper torrent has fire coming from it."

A vehicle was racing towards James's position.

"We were waiting to hear from you before calling in the heavy fire, and bringing this bitch down. ETA of 26 minutes. I called it in when you emerge n'at," said the major.

Matt and Calvin were in the approaching cargo van with the monitors.

"This is Calvin," came a voice. "We have a problem."

"What?" James asked flatly.

"It's Raymond. He, he, he went inside," Calvin stammered, as the truck approached.

"We got them pinned, moving toward point B," came a different voice on the headsets.

"Oh, you have got to be shitting me!" said Jason, on the headset.

"Silence!" James commanded. "Not you, Calvin. You better start talking fast."

Calvin and Matt had reached them. James opened the side door to the cargo van, and Calvin tumbled out.

"We were watching on the monitors." Calvin pointed inside at all the screens, and James could see what was happening. Raymond was in the office, snapping the hard drive into his cargo pants.

"Jason, behind you! Never mind. She's down. Some insider's got your back," said Kevin's voice.

"How'd he get in there?" James pulled the headset slightly off his ear to hear Calvin better.

Jason was saying something faintly on the headset.

"The old woman, she had a back door to the room she was in. When you threw that last power switch, it opened a door for her. We watched her go out, and he thought you were in trouble, and wouldn't have time to get the disk. So he went, look out, Raymond!" Calvin called, but Raymond wasn't wearing a headset or camera.

Yan had come in, and had him at gunpoint.

"Damn it," James swore.

"We have to save him!" Calvin pleaded.

Jason spoke again, but James didn't catch what he said.

James was on the verge of saying no. He wanted that hard drive, and he wanted to save Raymond, but the risk was too high. Raymond had acted foolishly, and disobeyed a direct order given to keep him safe.

"James!" screamed Matt, "answer Jason."

"What?" James yelled, sliding the headset back on.

"The guy who saved me seems to be trying to sub- due the others one-by-one, but is losing a fight. Do we help?" asked Jason.

"Does he look like he could be Italian mixed with Chinese, about seventeen years old?" asked James quickly.

"Could be, yeah," Jason said.

"It's Joe. Get him out," answered James.

"Rocket launcher comin' up the steps!" screamed a voice, and they heard a loud bang right next to them.

"Got 'em," came Matt's voice, calmly on the head- set. He had been sniping out of the cargo van.

"We have to go," called the major. "Everyone else is in the clear and maintaining perimeter fire. I do not like leaving a man behind more than yinz, but we have a ton of kids to get to safety."

# •Chapter Forty-Two•

Then James saw someone on the monitors. It was Xavier, and for some reason he didn't have clothing on. He was running up and down the hallway, doing what James had already done, looking for the others. Ben saw him too.

"Major, we have not completed all objectives, and certainly not critical ones," Ben said. "We have one more in there."

"Son of a bitch," said the major. "If we call off this air strike, we won't get another. This is a low flight mission, and they won't risk another pass into an un-sanctioned air zone."

Calvin was watching the progress of his brother. Yan and two others had taken him to one of the staged rooms, stripped him naked, and tied him to an X-shaped cross. They were hitting him with a cattle prod. Calvin was crying almost as much as Raymond was screaming.

James closed his eyes. Two deep breaths later, he snapped them open. He had a plan.

"No one speak for a minute. This is what we're go-ing to do." James was already in motion. Taking off his coat, he grabbed a utility belt, rope, two explosive sticks, two clip grenades, and two loaded 9mm pistols.

"Keegan, take your transport unit, and get back to the major to add some limited support. Paul, I need you to switch the explosives over to timers, and set them for," he glanced at his watch, "sixteen minutes. Then watch the monitors for us. Matt, give him cover from the side as far as you can see. When that exit blows, evacuate, regardless of who is back or not. Major and everyone else, continue to provide fire on the main parts for nine minutes, set up the torrent guns on auto fire, and evacuate. Make no exceptions. Evacuate! Calvin and Ben, you're coming with me. Ben and I are switching to channel two on the headsets if you need me. Matt and Paul, monitor both channels."

Silence had met James's words, before the major said in a hoarse voice, "We have the orders."

James grabbed the general map and flattened it. "Calvin, strip down. Ben, I need you to get to this point with..."

"What? What do you mean?" Calvin was still sobbing, clearly confused.

"Listen to me. We don't have time for you not to listen. Follow my exact orders, or I swear to God I'll leave you and your damn brother here. You want to save his life, then do what I said now!" James was furious with focus, rather than anger. There was no wiggle room in the plan. Calvin did as he was told, and stripped off his clothes.

"Ben, you need to get to this point in the corridor. We can travel together until here. On my mark, you will hear a grenade go off. Count to five, pull your pin, and throw past this door. Then hurry back to this intersection."

James turned to Calvin. "Calvin is going to run past this door." He pointed to the central corridor near Raymond's location. "Calvin, you keep running and meet up with Ben at this intersection. Ben, if he's being pursued, take them out. No matter what, Calvin and Ben, once you meet up, get out. Any questions?"

Both shook their heads no.

They were off, Paul following so he could adjust the explosives.

Ben and James moved quickly, securing the hallway to get where they needed to with Calvin in the rear. Then they split, with Ben heading on a path toward the office, and James and Calvin using back paths to get toward the middle hall.

"Looks like they're all at point A," called Matt over the headsets.

"Calvin, sprint down that hall. When you get to this opening," James indicated the small hall that led to the room Raymond was in, "pause for a moment or two. I'm hoping you'll have someone coming to investigate. If they see you, they'll mistake you for Raymond and give chase. The path winds enough that they won't have a clean shot until you meet up with Ben. You just keep going until you're out with Matt and Paul. Matt, don't shoot Calvin as he comes out."

"Copy," said Matt over the headset.

"Ready, Calvin and Ben?" asked James.

Calvin nodded as Ben said, "Roger that."

"Here we go."

James tossed a grenade as Calvin took off. Calvin hit the small hallway about five seconds after James's grenade went off. Within two seconds, Seim and Fang were barreling down the hallway after him. As they did, a second distant explosion could be heard, though it was louder over James's headset.

"Transport units one and two, headed out," came Kevin's voice on the headsets.

James had planted one of the two stick explosives, and timed it to go off just as the major and others should be pulling out completely. He sprinted down the main corridor, then slowed as he approached the room Raymond was in. He entered and did a fast sweep. He saw a door ajar on the other side of the room, near where Ben's grenade had gone off. James had underestimated the size of the room, and everything in it. Apparently, the cameras had just a central focal point on the X-shaped rack.

"James, they're clear, two down. No eyes. Repeat, we have lost visual," Paul said.

Calvin and Ben were out, but Ben's grenade had apparently done enough damage to lose the video feed, though James didn't know that was the reason it was now off.

James didn't wait to hear more. He made his way over to Raymond, holstered his gun, and removed the wrist restraints. Raymond undid his waist restraint with trembling hands, while James released his ankles.

James spoke into the headset. "Ben, can you come back to the intersection where you just met Calvin? I'm sending Raymond out."

"Copy," said Ben.

"No activity on the outside perimeter," came a voice on the headsets that sounded like Kevin's. He apparently was giving small updates on the progress that James appreciated, even though he hadn't thought to ask for them.

James stood, pulling out his pistol as his stomach felt like a roller coaster. His instincts were telling him he'd been here before, and it had been bad. James saw the door open wider out of the corner of his eye to his left and fired. Yan, also firing, took cover behind some barrels, while Raymond hit the floor, and crawled toward the exit.

James pulled out his other gun, and kept up blind fire. "Go, Raymond! Follow the hallway and make the first left you can, and then run 'til you find Ben. Ben, get him and yourself out. Do not come back in. This is going to plan!"

That was a lie. This wasn't going to plan at all. Yan had come back too soon.

Raymond fled. James managed to get some cover on the other side of the X-shaped rack. He saw another exit on the other end of the room, but there was a lot of open space in between. Just then, an explosion went off in the hallway, signaling that the major and team should be moving out. James needed to get moving too, as he didn't know where Xavier was.

James decided it was all or nothing time. He was out of ammunition, and an explosion was as good a distraction as anything. He pulled the pin to his last grenade, and stood as Yan fired his last bullet. It grazed James's left arm, causing him to spin slightly, and he saw that Yan had something in his other hand. Both men threw their objects at the same time, and dropped to the ground. As Yan went down, he hit a button on the wall. This released an iron gate, blocking James's escape.

*Boom!* Yan's flash bang collided with James' grenade, and they went off together. The force of the shockwave acted like a huge hand, slamming James into the iron gate, and the explosion blocked the door he'd originally come through. Yan hit the far wall, and was pinned under a barrel, knocked out cold.

Everything hurt. There was no sound, or maybe it was just one constant sound. James couldn't tell. An intense heat was coming from a roaring blaze to his left. As he rolled to his right, his blurred vision saw a shadow on the other side of the iron gate.

Just as James began to come out of his daze, so did Yan. All James could hear was a ringing sound, as his eyes struggled to adjust. He felt a vibration to his right as he watched Yan. Visibly gushing blood from his torso, Yan managed to stagger out the door he'd come through. He couldn't use that door. The team was blind to whatever Yan was doing. He could just be lying in ambush.

The vibration behind him was becoming annoying. He rolled to his right to see that the gate was rising. Xavier was pulling a chain rope, raising it.

*A boy*, he thought still regaining focus. James corrected himself. *No, the boy*. He rolled under the gate, and staggered to his feet, and Xavier came over to brace him.

"We have to go, now," James said, and they made their way to the door.

James was quickly recovering, but his ears were still buzzing. "Guys, we are coming now. Do not blow the exit. Repeat, do not blow the exit."

James couldn't hear his own words. The explosions in the room had blown out his headset, but he was too disoriented to realize it. He had also lost a sense of how much time he had.

"Repeat, do not blow the exit. Anyone copy? Hello? Do not blow the exit!" he shouted.

James's shouting attracted attention in the hallways. Distant voices approached as Xavier pushed James on. They reached the intersection where Ben had retrieved Calvin and Raymond. They'd taken two steps down the path to the exit, when the explosion went off.

"Damn it! I said do not detonate the exit!"

James was emotional. He was about to die. Xavier was shaking, and he had been so brave. James closed his eyes and took a deep breath. He needed to focus, not react, but fear flooded him. Fear meant death. He had faced death before, and hadn't been afraid except when he almost had drown those few occasions. *I don't fear death, so why am I afraid now?* James thought.

An image of Carissa came over him. He had that sensation of a warm breath of wind on a slightly hot day that he always associated with her. His mind flashed on how they'd met, and their first date, and...

James's eyes snapped open. He grabbed Xavier and went left. The voices were getting closer, but James knew he was right, or perhaps he was praying that he was. He found the small dark side hallway behind the baths, and hit the mini-light on his belt.

"Stop!" the boy said. "We can't go that way. It is a bottomless pit that has a howling monster!"

"Xavier, trust me. It isn't, and we have to go." James pulled the boy behind him. He took his last remaining explosive stick, and placed it in the ceiling arch of the hallway. He quickly tied an end of the rope he had brought onto the large pipes on the floor at a bracing bracket, and fed the other end into his belt loops.

"Xavier, I need you to do what I tell you. Go stand at the edge of the pit," he ordered the boy. "When I come, I need you to climb on top of my chest, put your arms around my neck, and bring your knees as close to my shoulders as you can. Then hang on tight. Do you understand?" James asked.

The voices were right on top of them. Whoever it was would be hitting the main intersection any second.

"Yes," the boy said, and hurried to the edge.

James set the timer for twenty seconds. He hit the start switch to begin the countdown and ran. He got down on his knees and leaned back like he was trying to limbo. As Xavier climbed onto his chest, James found the edge of the pit with his heels, and slowly leaned back, before turning off the light on his belt. He began moving gingerly down the wall of the pit, just as the individuals chasing them appeared at the end of the small dark hallway. He rushed to slide out of view and slipped a little. He regained some steadiness, but Xavier had started to squeeze harder, his body covering James's mouth and nose, so that he couldn't inhale or exhale.

James's brain, still a little out of whack, processed that he couldn't breathe. As in the past when he'd almost drowned, he thought, *You can only survive three minutes without oxygen.*

Suddenly, he recalled that the airstrike was coming. They had to go faster.

The explosive went off. James slipped again. This time, he didn't recover. He used the momentum of the slip to swing his weight to try to land and roll, as he let go of the rope. This sudden motion created a small breathing space, and James turned his head into the pocket of air, with a deep exhale.

They fell about ten feet. James landed hard on his back and tried to roll, which was difficult with the boy on his chest. Xavier's head knocked into James's, giving him a double impact, but adrenaline was doing its job. James got up, and pulled Xavier to his feet, and spun around. There it was, partially blocked by the boiler system. The exit door that Joseph had mentioned at the football match was framed in light from the outside. The small gap around the edge was creating the howling sound Xavier described.

James grabbed Xavier and ran at the door as hard as he could, intending to bust it open. It opened easily, however, and James fell flat on his face. Xavier helped him up.

"How..." Xavier started, but James said, "Come on!"

They sprinted around the corner just in time to see the taillights dip down, driving away from them.

"Damn, Come on!" screamed James, now moving perpendicular to the fortress to get away from it. They had moments before this place was going to meet two F-14s. He doubted they could run far enough, as beat up as they were, but they had to try. The sound of an engine came from their right.

"Run!" James screamed to Xavier, thinking the jets were early, but his hearing was still off, and he was wrong. It was Matt in the van. James and Xavier changed course, and raced toward the van. Matt swung wide and came alongside them while slowing down. James and Xavier jumped in the open cargo door without Matt stopping.

James fell to his side in the back of the cargo van next to Xavier and closed his eyes, breathing heavily. Slowly, he opened them. He'd have time to feel the satisfaction of completing this challenge soon. Right now, he needed to tend to Xavier, who was shivering uncontrollably.

James grabbed his coat, and sat up against the side of the van with his legs crossed. He called Xavier over, and gave him the coat to put on. He had the boy sit on his lap, and began to vigorously rub him down, hoping to minimize the chance of him going into shock.

"Ooh geez, James," said Paul softly. "Why is this kid naked? I mean none of the others were." Paul handed Xavier some pants that were way too big for him, but that at least covered him up.

James looked at Paul as if to say "Really?" He gestured toward the twins, pulling attention away from Xavier, as he rubbed Xavier's back and shoulders to create heat. "The real question is, why are they naked?"

"They haven't stopped crying yet. We tried to get them to. Just started to treat some of Raymond's burns, when we swung back to get you," said Ben.

"I gave you all strict orders to leave, why did you come back?" James wasn't being stern, or a jerk about it. It was a sincere question, and the guys knew it. His tone was laced with gratitude.

"The twins delayed us slightly in setting off after sealing the exit, dontcha know. Matt spotted ya in the mirror just as we came out of a little dip. We thought it was still fair game to rescue ya, and be the big heroes," said Paul, and the awkward tension broke.

It wasn't funny, but it was good enough to relieve the intense emotion everyone was feeling. Even the twins managed to smile between sobs.

They were just passing the outer marker for where the EMP force field would become ineffective, when they felt a vibration beginning to intensify.

Matt hammered the gas as hard as he could. "Here they come, boys!"

The two F-14s came in hot and heavy above them. Their speed shook the van as they passed, and then a phenomenal explosion sounded. Through the back windows, they could see huge flames shooting up as the van raced away, unharmed.

"Here ya go," said Paul, handing a headset to James.

It was the major. "My boys say it was a clean hit. They dropped two sets on the fortress itself, and another set right into the cliff, which cracked right off, n' buried the whole thing." His voice rang with triumph.

"Any signs of survivors? And is the other problem handled?" James asked.

"That's a negative on survivors. Besides, where are they going to go? It's an hour or two drive to anything, and without any supplies n'at, that isn't happening. And a big affirmative on the other problem. Glad we got yinz out," the major said, in a softer tone.

"Thanks, Ian. See you and the others at the safe spot," James said, removing the headset.

James wasn't worried about the enemy somehow surviving in an unrealistic way. That was garbage you found in the movies. The major was right, no one could've survive that blast.

During the forty-minute drive, and with Paul's help, Ben addressed various medical issues with Raymond, Xavier, and James. James's lower back was messed up, and he probably had a bruised rib or two, along with a concussion, but the bullet had just nicked him, and could've passed as a scratch. Xavier was doing fine, once the cut on his forehead was attended to. The twins were the biggest mess, mainly because of their emotional state. When they finally got dressed, James realized something.

"Raymond, those are your clothes!" he exclaimed.

Raymond looked down at himself, and said indignantly, "What the bloody hell is that supposed to mean? Course they're me clothes."

"What I mean is, they're the clothes you had on earlier. The ones they made you strip off," James said, looking at him eagerly.

"Right, did you think I would run about naked for the rest of me life?" Raymond asked, in the same indignant tone.

"Leave him alone!" Calvin glared at James fiercely, protecting his twin.

Paul tapped James on the left shoulder. "Looking for this?" He held up the hard drive.

"Yes!" he all but shouted.

"Apparently he grabbed his clothes as he made a run for it," Paul said. "Who would've thought he'd bring it with?"

# •Chapter Forty-Three•

As they joined the others around the black SUV, James saw everyone else for the first time since the mission had begun. No one looked the worse for the wear, aside from some scratches Haiden, Keegan, and Rocker had endured from some of the kids in the process of moving them. The kids were very shaken up, obviously, but no one was hurt.

It was almost time to address the other problem, but some important things needed to be handled first. James wanted to make sure they had enough room to transport the children semi-comfortably, that everyone knew where the location outside of Osh was, and that Joe was all right.

James found Joe with Jason and Kevin. As he peered inside their cargo van, Jason told him, "He was fighting with two guys. By the time we got cleared to extract him, he was cut bad. We gave him some morphine to stop the pain."

Kevin slid back so that James could see Joe's stomach. It was drenched in blood. Joe was very pale, and taking short rapid breaths. James knew he didn't have the time or tools to save Joe's life.

"Kevin, can you go look at the twins, please. Thank you, Joe, for your help." He grasped Joe's right hand in his left.

"You saved my life, man. I can't thank you enough," said Jason, in a mournful voice.

"Help children," Joe gasped. "Save their life. Kill evil people that hurt them. He know." Joe pointed accusatorily at the black SUV with his left hand. "He have other pouches with papers. He know," Joe said, fainter. He slowly closed his eyes.

"Thank you, Joe. The children will be looked after, and Noi will answer for his role," said James.

Joe gave an audible grunt and James left. Within two minutes, Joe was dead.

The team had brought a number of extra vehicles with them on the operation. After securing Noi and his driver, they'd left these extra vehicles with the black SUV as part of an emergency evacuation.

James got the kids loaded up, and sent everyone off to the home he had arranged for the children. Just before the vehicles left, he caught Xavier's eye and waved. The boy smiled and waved back, still wearing James's coat.

The major and Ben stood at the black SUV as the others departed. They were holding Noi and his driver inside the vehicle. The kids didn't see this, nor did they see Joe's body removed from the cargo van, and placed on the ground before it left.

Ben and the major dragged the two men out of the SUV, and released their mouth gags. They were still tied with their hands behind their backs, and were on their knees, when James walked up to them with a pistol in his hands.

"If you tell me the truth, I won't kill you. Lie to me, even slightly about anything, and you die. Understand?" His voice was flat and emotionless.

Both men nodded.

"Did you know they were trading children for cash?" James asked this question first. Obviously, they did, but this admission of guilt was a great way to break them down, and get additional truthful answers.

"Please, sir, Mr. Mathers, please. I have a family and..." Noi began.

James placed the gun to his head, and chambered a bullet. Noi began to cry.

"Before I pull the trigger, how about you?" He addressed the driver.

"Yes, I was just the driver, though," he said, with an accent that sounded like he was from South Africa.

James addressed Noi again. "One last time. Did you know?"

"Yes, yes I know, yes, but I have no choice." He began to cry harder.

Multiple questions later, it turned out that Noi did have a choice. He collected a ten percent commission, plus the car sale, for each of the transactions. Noi was initially reluctant to give up key codes and passwords, but after being promised that no physical harm would befall his family, he complied.

"You had a choice. Greed or the innocence of children. You made your choice, and now have to deal with the consequences of those choices," James said, in a condemning tone.

"Please, sir, I had to provide for myself and my family," cried Noi.

James lowered the gun he had kept pointed at Noi during the questioning. He grabbed Noi's carrier bag and noticed, it had a yin and yang symbol burned into the leather. He snorted in disgust.

Joe had been right, in a sense, about the pouches. Noi used his carrier bag to exchange only parts of his records with the Tans. The Tans, in turn, did the same. This meant that neither side had a complete record of any transaction at any one time, and that neither side could operate truly independently of the other. If one side somehow got busted, it allowed a reasonably talented lawyer a way to get the other party off.

During the questioning, the part that got Ben worked up was finding out about the training videos, or visit videos potential masters could log into at their leisure. This explained why certain cameras were in place, and why the servers housed the video files. Noi explained most of this, but when he messed up the servers, the driver jumped in.

"No, you idiot. Those servers were a 2048-bit encryption, and cycled the IP addresses to proxies. They told us to tell the truth, and I'm not dying because you can't explain a simple set up. You ordered all the parts, you should know!"

James gazed impassively at the man. *So much for being just the driver,* he thought.

When they were done answering questions, Ben walked over with two shovels and commanded, "Dig."

The driver and Noi weren't used to physical labor, and the ground was rather hard due to the temperature. Ben, the major, and James took turns supervising the digging of Joe's grave, with James taking the final shift. As Noi and the driver finished, James reached into the SUV to retrieve the wrapper of the Kit-Kat bar he'd eaten earlier. He placed a hair sample from Joe in the wrapper, and put it in his pocket. He then ordered the two men to gently place Joe in the grave and cover him. When the body was decently buried, Noi and the driver both slid to the ground near Joe's grave, breathing heavily.

James, in full view of his captives, released the magazine from his pistol, removed the chambered bullet, and placed it back in the clip. He gave the pistol and magazine to Ben, who had a steely look in his eyes.

"Thank you for answering my questions," James told Noi and his driver. "As I promised, no harm will come to your families." He started to walk toward the SUV.

Ben didn't move, however.

"You, you are too kind sir, thank you, sir," said Noi shakily.

He and the driver went to stand up, but they were very weak. James stopped and gave the two men a stare that clearly indicated they weren't coming with him.

"You'll take us back with you then, sir?" Noi stammered.

The major was on the driver's side of the SUV, as James turned and said, "I'm afraid that's out of my hands. I promise your families will meet no physical harm."

"But you said you would not kill us as long as we told the truth!" said the driver. Noi looked on, scared.

"That is true, I did." James opened the back door on the passenger side. "I'm leaving, and not killing anyone."

James climbed in. As he shut the door, he heard the sound of the clip he had just handed Ben being emptied. *Bang, bang, bang*, pause, *bang, bang, bang*, pause, *bang*, pause, *bang*.

Ben joined them a moment later in the black SUV, and they were off.

# •Chapter Forty-Four•

Arriving at Noi's office, James found the men had been truthful. Thanks to the pass codes they'd revealed, he found a lot of funds in several currencies, as well as bearer's bonds. James logged into the system and quickly found the information he needed. He searched for himself and Tim first just to see how much was out there. A lot, it turned out, and he was impressed, once again, with the detail Melissa had supplied to give them outstanding back-stories.

He eventually accessed about $86 million in funds, once he was able to get into the database for the Tan family. He then made provisions so that the kids and young adults they'd rescued, would be cared for once they became adults. In the meantime, they were in the hands of an organization that, with the very generous funding he gave them of $50 million dollars, promised to see to their education, health, and happiness.

After he had left Noi's office, James quickly toured the facility where he'd placed the kids, and met a few of the caretakers. After, he sat down with the director, and told her about the funding, and how it could be dispersed. She assured him she'd take care of everything, and that the money would go a long way. Her young assistant had been in the room with them, and not spoken, but gave James a slightly weird feeling.

Letting out a great yawn, James said, "I'm sure you and your group will do everything in your power to give these kids the life they deserve. No one else has, and chances are no one knows they are alive. They deserve a fresh start to be whatever they want. Please help them do that."

There were fifty-eight individuals in total, their ages ranging from just under three years old to over eighteen. The adult age children agreed to stay and help the younger ones with the transition for a few months. James didn't tell them they would have half-a-million dollars waiting for them when they left, but he did tell them that when they were ready to leave, money would be provided to help them get started.

The kids and young adults were still in a state of shock, but James was sure things would calm down soon. They would be happy once they realized they were free.

As James pulled away, he could see a lot of faces pressed to the windows. He waved, but only a few kids waved back. As he took the corner, someone came running out onto the sidewalk, but James didn't look in time to see who it was.

He felt proud for getting the children out, and establishing a life for them. He felt a sense of accomplishment for rising to the challenge and conquering it. This was what he loved to do, but he was happy to be alive, and even happier that he'd see Carissa soon.

The rest of the funds went, tax-free of course, to the guys involved. When James sat them down as a group, and told them what he was transferring to each of them, their mouths hit the floor. It was almost comical how they all responded the same way.

"Holy shit," said Rocker, breaking the silence.

James laughed and said, "Figured gabby here would be first to speak." Everyone laughed.

"James, we can't take this. We didn't do this for money," said Paul. The others nodded and murmured their agreement.

"The funds are coming from the Tan family," James said simply.

"The funds should be going to the kids," said Jason, "to make sure they're all right."

"The children each have an account set up with $500,000 dollars in it. They receive the funds when they move out into the world on their own. The funds awarded to each of you are for your services for allowing them to be free, while offering your lives in the attempt. I only wish I could honor all servicemen and women like this," James explained.

Ben stood up, and all eyes turned to him. "What about the others?"

"I've set aside money for the..." James began. He thought Ben meant the F-14 pilots.

"No, the other kids," Ben said, in a low voice.

Keegan spoke. "Dude, we got them all out. Remember? That's why you and James went back in."

James knew what Ben meant, and before Haiden could agree with his cousin, James spoke. "That's something I want to talk to you guys about. We have the records going back a good length of time. A high level of intel was gathered that the Tans kept as leverage. I'm not sure how long it'll be before others discover the Tan family is out of business, so we'll have to act quickly."

"How are we going to run all those operations? We can't be taking out a bunch of fortresses," said Paul doubtfully.

"I doubt they're all in fortresses, dip shit," said Kevin.

"Ooh ya, well for sure, I'm in, you betcha" Paul said, without a second thought.

Ben still had questions. "How are we going to fund this, and what about money for the other kids?"

James turned to the others, "What do you guys think?"

Jason cleared his throat. "Their masters have money, and that money goes to the kids. We can fund anything up front, and get reimbursed from each take-down. I'm in."

The discussion went on for over an hour. Everyone agreed this needed to be done tactfully. James struggled to persuade them to take their time bringing down these former clients of the Tans. If they acted too fast with too many, they would draw unwanted attention.

James was to keep the records, and whenever they had a mission somewhere, the major would contact James for names. James then could offer any additional assistance that he could.

Ben had just one remaining issue. "How are we going to get all of them? This sounds rather piecemeal. I want them all." There was a cold fire in his eyes.

"I'll make every effort to make sure each and every one of the people in those files suffers, and the kids reap the rewards. I know it's not ideal, and that some kids are suffering now," James admitted. "If I had a way to spring them all at the snap of my fingers, I'd do it, but we have to do what we can without jeopardizing our ability to help others."

Ben didn't look satisfied. James didn't blame him. But Ben still said, "I'm in."

James made eye contact with Ben and vowed, "Before my last day on this Earth, I'll make sure those bastards fall. You have my word."

Ben didn't know the things James had done before, or what skills he had. He only knew what he'd seen. He witnessed James's unflinching willingness to go back into hell and save a single child. That was enough to earn his buy-in.

The major promised to find a way to get the money to the guys who were involved in the F-14s, but since they thought it was just an exercise, he had to be tactful about it. James wanted Calvin and Raymond to get some of the money too, though, that wasn't what they were excited about.

They'd gotten some great information from the data they'd collected at the fortress. Both felt the money coming from that would make them richer than anyone could imagine, once they developed their ideas. They still took the cash, however, as it would help them independently fund their research, and get them out from underneath the thumb of Dr. Watterson.

Now that it was obvious Raymond would make a full recovery, minus some small scars, the twins were mostly back to their normal selves. James had talked with them about everything that had taken place. Though they were upset by the events, they promised to keep the mission to themselves.

They also acknowledged that they would have been happier not knowing, and they were smart enough to know they didn't want to know anymore. They wished it had been some secret plan the team had gone after, as thinking about child trafficking was horrifying.

"I'm sorry mate. I should have listened, and not had a go at getting that hard drive. I appreciate you coming for me. Saved me life, you did, and I will never forget that. You're a good man," Raymond had said, hugging James.

James couldn't help thinking of Daen at this moment, and his own mistake of not listening.

Calvin had been very quiet. James knew Raymond's near abandonment weighed heavily on him.

As they were saying farewells, Calvin said, privately to James, "I understand why you would have walked away from me brother. I understand that you didn't go back specifically for him. The fact is, he's alive because of you, and that is what I choose to remember. I don't ever want him to know we almost left him."

James started to say, "Than..."

Calvin continued, "I feel sorry for you. You lack basic human emotions, but there's still a chance that you could learn that emotions can save you. Thank you for saving me brother, James. I will never forget what you've done for us."

This wasn't what James had expected, and he was dumbfounded as he watched the twins walk away. He tried to process it, but he had other things to attend to.

Besides, he wasn't that devoid of emotion. He had some plans for himself and Carissa. These plans would get him mostly out of this life. Helping bring down other abusers wouldn't be too much of a stretch, and if he was honest with himself, he wasn't sure he could ever stop doing this type of thing completely.

James kept very little of the funds for himself, just enough to cover expenses, and $10,000 dollars extra for his upcoming medical costs. He felt rather beat up, and decided it would be smart to get checked out. None of the money would be going to the group however, as this wasn't a group sponsored mission.

His CT scan came back clean, as did the X-rays. Despite this, James felt he had a slight concussion, but there wasn't much to be done for it. The lack of broken bones didn't mean much either. It certainly didn't stop the pain James felt, or the fascinating colors appearing all over his body, even in places that didn't hurt. His back wasn't exactly damaged, but he now had some minor alignment issues in his lumbar from the fall. *Such is life*, he thought.

Later that night, following the end of Operation Joshua, James called Carissa. He wanted to fall asleep to the sound of her voice. He also wanted to talk with her, but his body was starting to shut down, and he needed to recharge. Plus, the muscle relaxers he had taken were having a sedative effect.

She didn't object or take offense. She didn't even ask why he was so tired. She merely talked, and he listened, drifting off as she described an error she'd found in someone's account. The error kept happening each quarter.

*He was running down black tunnels, searching for something. There were pipes, pipes he could jump down, but mushrooms were covering them, and children were laughing...*

The dream changed. It was more blurred and somehow felt more real.

*He was in pain and dragging himself down the hall to an open door. He could see outside to a very well maintained courtyard behind a beautiful large wooden desk...*

At 10 a.m., the alarm went off. James felt terrible, but he needed to catch a plane back to the USA. Two weeks would give him ample time to heal, and let him get a few things situated, so that he could smoothly transition the Spara investigation to someone else, and retire from the group. Then he'd get to be with Carissa forever.

# •Chapter Forty-Five•

As the plane touched down on the runway at Aberdeen's airport in Dyce, James turned on his phone to text Carissa that he'd be home soon. She always liked to know when he landed, but especially when he was home. It was late, and James had caught the last flight from Amsterdam. It had been a long trip with some unexpected delays. He'd hoped to be home a good eight hours earlier, but he was glad to be home all the same.

*Funny, Aberdeen really does feel like home now*, he reflected.

As the plane came to a halt, James noticed the familiar drizzle he'd come to associate with Scotland nights. He smiled a bit, remembering his first visit, and meeting Carissa. In the moments before the door to the plane opened, James continued reflecting on how much his life had changed. Hopefully, it was about to change more in less than forty hours when, he and Carissa, would celebrate their one-year anniversary of their first date at Paradise Stadium.

This was going to be the biggest day of his life, and it would end with a cleared conscious, an unencumbered path forward, and most importantly, with Carissa being his forever. Admittedly, she might be upset with him when he came clean, but he was certain she'd forgive him.

Carissa's reply text of, *"See you soon :),"* accompanied by an emoticon with a smiling face made him smile. To him, it wasn't just a happy smile, but, in fact, a smile of love. This was the same way his mother had ended her notes when he was growing up, and it never failed to remind him of her. Carissa didn't know it, but it was very meaningful to him that the woman he loved, had this small trait in common with his mother.

The journey home took a mere twenty minutes because of the late hour. As James pulled into the parking space, he saw the light on in the apartment that had become his and Carissa's, only a few months earlier. She was certainly staying awake late to see him. Her day would have started very early, but they both knew that once she was asleep, there was little chance of waking her.

"Sleeping Beauty," James called her sometimes in a teasing way.

Whenever she heard him say this, she'd reply, "Well, now, where is me prince ta wake me then, as your kiss doesn't."

The sass made him smile.

"Hello, Love, how was your trip?" Carissa stifled a yawn, and rose from the sofa to greet him as James opened the door.

"Hi Risa." James set down his bags and closed the door, then turned and kissed her.

They stared at each other, holding the moment, before resuming their normal manner of just enjoying one another's company. Theirs was different from most relationships, and James truly valued how they expressed their love, but didn't go on and on about it in some overly dramatized manner.

"The trip was okay, aside from the layovers. I'm just glad to be home. How was your day?" he asked.

"Ah, had a bit of a toss with the system this morning that caused some issues, but nothing we couldn't solve with a spot of help from the new consultant," she started. "And then there were some odd lads hanging about outside a good portion of the afternoon. One came in about half past three ta exchange some tenners for coin. Sara had ta come get me ta get him ta remove his sunglasses, you know. Odd, but no worries. Oh, and Rian, you know Susan's boy, had a nasty turn, and is in a cast now. Broken wrist, poor thing. Talked ta Jamie Smitty for Judy's party today..."

She paused a moment, and gave him a look. "You have ta be tired. Did you manage any sleep on the flights? By the look of you, I would say no then. Are you hungry?" she said, in her natural rambling way, though she seemed to be restraining herself out of consideration for him.

"I'm fine, but yes, tired. I didn't sleep, but that isn't all that different. I ate just before I left Amsterdam. Just want to get a shower before bed. I'm shattered," said James, truly exhausted now that he was home. He smiled at her, knowing she was tired too.

"Why don't you get to bed, and I'll be in soon." He walked his bags to the bedroom as Carissa followed.

"Well, be quick as poss," she said, grabbing him, and kissing him good night. She knew she wouldn't last the few minutes it would take James to shower, and he knew it too.

"Good night, sassy lassie," he said, as his fingers gently slipped from her shoulders.

As he showered, he thought about her description of her day, but was distracted by a slight acid smell, almost like something decaying. For some reason, the same feeling he got when things were about to happen came over him. It was strange to have that feeling in the shower in his home.

Perhaps it was the thirty hours he'd been awake, or the anticipation of the jet lag he always got when traveling east by more than four hours. Or perhaps it was what would happen this weekend. Or just the relief of finally being home after all that had happened.

A few minutes later, James smiled to himself as he quietly got into bed, and lay listening to the gentle sounds of Carissa breathing. Within moments, the rhythmic pulsing of the fan blades, and her body next to him had lulled him to sleep too.

The vibrations from Carissa's side of the bed came all too soon. As she always had trouble waking, James had created a device that would shake her side of the bed when set to an alarm. She typically needed a solid five minutes of shaking, and then a very loud alarm clock to get her to stir properly.

James was in the middle of a long unpleasant dream when the vibrations woke him. This annoyed him, but not as much as the headache he now had from the jet lag. He lay there, dreading the alarm, but it didn't go off that morning. Luckily, Carissa rose quickly.

"Good morning, my love, I will be quick and quiet as poss, then. Go back ta sleep." She ran her hand over his head as she left the bed. Her touch was as soothing a feeling as any he had ever known.

Fifty minutes later, he heard her depart. She made every effort to be quiet, but that wasn't really her strong suit. Feeling he could finally get back to sleep, James decided to set the alarm for a few hours later. He wanted to get up, and get a workout in. The endorphins would help him work through the jet lag. Plus, he needed to check on the arrangements for tomorrow. Unfortunately, his bladder was in need of relief, so that needed addressing before going back to sleep.

Slumping off to the bathroom, James let out a loud yawn before making use of the toilet. After flushing and turning to rinse his hands, he got that faint odor again. He started to look for the source when his cell phone rang. It was Carissa's ring tone, so he answered.

"Hello, Risa," he said, a slight crack in his voice.

"Sorry ta wake you, Love, though I was sure you weren't back asleep yet."

James smiled. She knew him well.

"I forgot ta tell you something. Well, truth is, I didn't want ta bother wit' you last night then, you know. But the telly is on the blink. I missed me shows last night. Can you have a look then, please? It just stays black, the picture, and I would like ta see that documentary tonight." As was customary for her, she said this all quickly, as if getting off the phone would make it easier for him to get back to sleep.

"I'll give it a go. I'm going to try to get a session of weights in before taking a nap. See you tonight then."

"Bye, Love," came Carissa's voice as he hung up.

James turned off the alarm, having walked to the bedroom, feeling he might as well stay up, and fix the television, and start the day. It turned out she'd somehow managed to unplug the TV from the power strip. The TV turned on when plugged in, and a BBC newscaster said ". . . has been missing for two weeks now. She is the daughter of the long-time Congress . . ." James turned it off.

Normally, this would annoy him, but with Carissa, it just made him laugh. Details weren't her strong suit in most everyday things, but somehow when it came to math and bank ledgers, she was as keen as could be. She had risen quickly within the Royal Bank of Scotland, and was on a fast track. Her coworkers adored her, and she had great relationships with customers. Everyone seemed to love her, and James constantly felt lucky to have her. For the life of him, he didn't see what Carissa saw in him, but he didn't care either. He was happy and in love.

James went to make some food, but quickly found they were out of eggs and bacon. He didn't want cereal with milk before going to the gym. After finding his gym clothes, and making a protein shake, he was off.

At the front desk, he greeted Janie.

"Hi there, stranger. Had another long trip?" she asked, as James handed her his identification.

"How'd you know?" James asked.

"Well, you haven't been here in as many months, it's the middle of the morning, and to be honest, you look a bit worked over, lad," she said with a smile.

"Is that your way of saying I look like hell in a hand basket, then?" James said.

"Yep." Janie smiled, handed him a towel, and returned to her work.

"How goes finding a lad of your own?" James asked with a slight smirk, knowing full well that Janie was a lesbian.

"Har, har, har," she replied, looking up at him, and giving him a rather rude hand gesture that made James chuckle as he walked away.

For James, this was leg day. He reminded himself of the saying, "Friends don't let friends skip leg day." After recent events, he clearly needed to build more leg, and lower back strength. *Then again, if I'm walk-*

*ing away from all this, what does it matter?* He then thought of Andy, and laughed to himself and carried on.

Sixty-five minutes of squats, lunges, presses, step-ups, abductors, adductors, and calf raises zapped all of his energy. James didn't feel his best as he made his way back to the locker room. He hadn't even finished his last set of calves. He sat down on the bench that split the middle stall where his locker, was and in-stantly downed half of the protein shake. He sat for a minute and felt better.

After finishing the shake, stripping down, and grab-bing his towel, he noticed that a man wearing sunglasses had walked in, and was looking around. James headed to the showers, but once again, he had that strange feeling that something was off. Simultane-ously, he noticed that faint acid odor again. For the life of him, he couldn't figure out what it was. Upon re-turning to get dressed, the odd fellow was gone, and James felt much better.

Before taking his nap, he called Paradise Stadium to speak with Larry, who was helping him get everything in place for the next day.

"Hi, is Mr. Flent there, please?" he asked the young woman who answered the phone with a cheerful, "Thank you for calling the home of the Celtic, how may I assist you?"

"One mo' please, sir, I will check to see if he's in," she replied, and a few seconds later Larry was on the line.

"Oops," came a voice. James heard a banging sound, then "Damn!" followed by, "Sorry 'bout that, dropped the phone, right, 'ello this is Larry Flent." He spoke rapidly, with a strong Scottish accent.

"No worries, mate, this is John Boyd, how does the day find you?" asked James, silently laughing.

"John, mate! Cheers. Back home, then? O'course you are. All set for tomorrow then, eh?" exclaimed Larry.

"That's what I was ringing you about," replied James. "We have everything in place as we discussed?"

"Ah, yeah, no worries t'all mate, won't be a trouble in the world. I will have the chef on board, and have the wait staff know what we got brewing. Mr. Stewart will be there, and we can get the team to help after the match. You done your part, then? You picked out the ring and 'ave it and all?" said Larry.

"I'm all set here, thanks, mate. Just wanted to make sure you're all set," answered James.

"Could I get a current picture of you two, so we know we have the right bloke and lass then?" Larry asked.

"Yes, sure enough. I will send it in a fax if that is all right?" asked James.

"Yer, no worries. Thanks again for paying up front in cash and all. This should go down well with the boss after some messes I had a few weeks' past. But this one, I have planned out, and it will go smooth, promise mate," Larry said.

James felt a little less reassured, but he didn't let Larry know that. "Right, thanks, Larry. Tomorrow is going to be a great day, and I seriously appreciate all the efforts, mate. I'll chat with you later, then."

"Yeah, alright then, cheers," said Larry.

James lay down to take a much deserved nap, deciding the fax could wait for 90 minutes. Just then, the phone rang. James listened to the ring tone deciding if he wanted to pick it up.

"Hey, Risa," he said.

"How was your workout?" she asked.

"Good, thanks, did legs. How's your day going?" James inquired.

"Not bad, just getting things going for the property's office. So for dinner tonight, would you like ta go ta a new pizza place? Sara was telling me all about it then. And it's a make your own pizza with a lot of add-ons. I'm really craving pizza, oh and blue cheese, oooh, and capers. The chair in me office broke today as well. It won't go back properly. And this cute old couple walked into today while Sara was training the new lad ta make deposits for their grandchildren, which is just so sweet."

Carissa said all of this in her normal way, to which James replied, "That's fine. Odd topping choices, especially for you, but pizza does sound great. Ask Jim to give the chair a look, and yes, that's sweet. Risa, I was going to have a quick lay down and..."

"Oh, you should do that, sorry, Love, but good then on dinner. Talk when I get home. Love you," she said quickly.

"Love you, too. See you tonight." James hung up the phone and collapsed, just as the phone rang again. It was Carissa.

*Ugh*, he thought, "Hello?"

"Sorry, Love, forgot ta tell you why I called ta start. I will be a bit late tonight. Have ta stop and check on something, but really shouldn't be more than an hour or so," she said.

"Right," said James, through a pillow.

"Sweet dreams," Carissa said, and hung up. This time, James shut his phone off.

The pizza parlor was very nice indeed. The center was the cook's area, and visible to the customers. A double-sided brick oven with multiple layers cooked the pizza. Carissa's friend had been right about the topping selection. You really could get just about anything you wanted.

"So can I get the small pizza, with the variety cheeses, plus blue cheese, and sliced prime rib with onions, and capers too, please? Oh, but I also want this bacon pizza. Look, John, it has two different kinds of cheeses, and four kinds of bacon, but I really want the other too, but..."

The waitress looked a bit dumbfounded as to what Carissa was trying to order, so James offered, "Risa, how about I get the bacon pizza, and you get the other, and we can share?"

"Oh yes, then, good idea," and she leaned in to kiss him.

James leaned in to meet her halfway, and noticed in a reflection in his water glass, what seemed to be a very short man in sunglasses staring at them. Thinking it would be rude not to finish the kiss, he did, so but quickly looked behind him when they broke apart. No one was there except a kid dancing in his seat, and drawing with crayons. James dismissed what he'd seen in the water glass. It must have been the kid, but that didn't explain that little feeling he had in his stomach. The evening passed uneventfully, unless you counted Carissa eating her entire pizza, of which James got one bite, and a third of his.

Climbing into bed later, after making up for lost time with Carissa on the couch, reminiscent of the night before he'd left for Operation Joshua, James felt excited for the next day. It would be a day he'd never forget. It was to be the first day of the rest of his life with the person he loved.

# •Chapter Forty-Six•

The next day started just like the one before. This was a little odd, as Carissa was never first up. When James awakened and came out of the bedroom, she greeted him with a big smile and a kiss. She immediately pushed him away, saying, "Ewww, go brush your teeth, eck," before patting him on the backside as he walked away.

"And don't be coming back out with that morning problem not sorted. We have ta be going soon, and don't have time for that, but you know, later we can have some fun with it," she said. James couldn't help but laugh.

After he had showered, he looked in the mirror, jubilant that today would be the last time he'd have to place these fake cosmetics on his face. Today would be the last day she called him John. Today, he'd finally let someone completely into his life and his heart.

While at home in the States, he saw his family and friends, and had been to work. He had made the needed arrangements to have everything, and he meant everything, settled for the group. He was done with any new operations; done living a crazy life. He was going out on top. He'd advise on operations for the kids with the major and his team, but that was the end of it. All he had left to do now was transfer the files, and that would be at the top of the list of things he'd take care of tomorrow.

Today was all about focusing on Carissa, and his marriage proposal. He felt confident that she'd say yes, but it wouldn't hurt to wait until after she knew everything to release that old life. He planned to get down on his knees, and with the ring in his hand, explain who he was, why he hadn't said something sooner, and ask for her hand.

Carissa finished getting ready while James double checked that he had the ticket confirmation and ring. He felt slightly nervous, just like he had at the start of Operation Joshua. No doubt, it was all of the change that was coming. It was a lot, even for him, and that feeling that something was coming that had started the previous night was legitimate. Something was coming, and it was going to be wonderful.

James smiled and called out, "Nearly ready then?"

"Just a mo'," called Carissa from the bathroom.

They were off five minutes later, heading toward the Celtic match. As they drove, they had a lively debate about their anniversary date.

"You're mad. How can you claim that today is an anniversary? You said yourself that tomorrow's date is the date we went to the match," Carissa said, her hands bouncing up and down.

"Aye, I do, but that doesn't stop today being an anniversary for us," said James. He knew what she was getting at, and he was really just having a bit of fun with her.

"What? You admit you're wrong, then?" she said, looking at him funny. "Need ta write that down as a real event, we do."

She dug in her bag as James laughed. She got out her organizer and wrote down, "John finally admits he is wrong about something." She said the words out loud as she wrote, then looked up and smiled. "We will have to celebrate this day, now."

"We have to celebrate it for a different reason, it's our anniversary," James said slyly.

Carissa tapped him on the head with the organizer. "You've gone around the twist."

"Risa, today is the day we met. Just like this morning, you hit my backside a year ago today. Tomorrow is just the anniversary of our first date, my love," James said softly.

Carissa melted. She even began to cry a bit, which was rather unusual for her, as she wasn't typically overly emotional. Then she hit him again, a bit harder this time, with the organizer.

"Ow, what was that for, then?" James said, taken by surprise. "Shouldn't be hitting a driver, you know."

"It's for being a prat. You could have said all that, and saved the whole argument. Oh, and I suppose I have ta erase the mark I put. Turns out you're right, sort of. Prat. Go figure, and I wrote it in ink, too," she grumbled.

James just laughed as she scratched it out. She looked stern, but James caught her eye and she smiled, and gave him a wink that made a tingle go through him. James thought the wink was odd, as it was just the two of them in the car, but he didn't dwell on it.

They parked, walked into the ticket office, and approached the counter like the first time. James thought it might even be the same chap who had given them their tickets last year.

"May I help you?" said the man.

"Hi, yes, two tickets under Boyd," said James.

"Seems like yesterday I was getting those tickets." Carissa smiled at James, and he smiled back.

"Right, Mr. Boyd, just a moment please, sir," and the man walked away.

James hoped Larry hadn't let out that anything special was happening with all the staff. That was supposed to be a surprise.

A moment later, the smiling young man appeared again, and handed him two tickets, saying, "Please, enjoy the match. You will find the stairs and the lift to your left."

They took the stairs as before. Each step gave James a greater and greater sense of excitement. His eyes did the normal scan of the facility, but only out of habit. Something wasn't right, but it didn't fully register, and he didn't care anyway.

They walked through the double door, and Carissa held out her hand. Thinking she wanted to hold hands, James took it.

"Oh, you actually took my hand! Well, this is somethin' then, as you hate public displays." Carissa grasped his hand tightly, as he pulled away at her words. She held out her other hand.

"Well, as you have a death grip on my hand now, I'm certainly not giving you the other to crush," James said, squeezing back a little.

"No, John, don't be silly. If we are repeating our date from last year, this is the part where you give me twenty quid." She smiled a huge, tooth-filled grin.

"Oh, same as last year, is it?" James smiled, knowing what was to come.

"Aye, you even got the same seats."

She stuck her tongue out as James gave her a look of surprise. "And just how the bloody hell do you know that?" James asked.

"I can read, you prat. It was on the tickets the bloke handed you," she said, and clicked her fingers at him.

The only comeback he could muster was "Oh, right," before handing her the money.

She placed the bet, and as they walked away, she said, "Oh, look!"

James looked up. He thought she was pointing at the security camera, but she was pointing at a couple in the distance. She dragged him over to the couple, as James now registered what he'd seen on the steps. He paused for a moment, unsure of why, and was pulled back to reality by Carissa's words.

"This is too funny. Mary and Joseph, fancy seeing you here!" she exclaimed.

It took the older couple a moment to remember them, but soon the ladies were off talking like the oldest of friends. Scottish people often spoke to one another like this. It was a part of their culture that James truly enjoyed. They talked to the couple for about fifteen minutes before venturing off to find some food. James almost thanked Joseph for his insight on castles and exits, but thought it would just lead to odd questions.

"Can you believe they were here, then? Did you arrange that? If you also found that wee Glassie lad and his dad and uncle, I'm not sure what I will do. Well, I will be saying something ta the lad and all if he still has that foul mouth. But oh, this is turning out ta be so brilliant. I'm loving today, and it has just begun. You didn't arrange that, did you?" she asked James.

James chuckled. "No, Risa, I didn't. They come to all the home games, remember?"

"Oh, right," she said, a faraway look in her eyes.

He smiled. "And if the lad is here, that is also by chance." He saw Larry waving at him from behind Carissa. "Going to visit the toilet. Back in a second."

"Oh, good idea," and she got up with him. She headed to the ladies room, and James turned to Larry, who spoke quickly and nervously.

"Everything is set for after the end of the match. Just have to get her to the dining room as everyone leaves," Larry said.

"Right. I'm planning on saying I dropped my wallet as we exit, so we have to go back for it," said the hopeful groom-to-be.

Larry returned a very brief smile, and wiped his forehead before saying, "Okay, great, have to dash," and he was gone.

*Weird guy*, James thought.

James made his way to the bathroom, as he actually did have to go, and then returned to his seat.

The match was soon underway. The lad wasn't there, but it was still a great contest. Carissa, smiling nonstop, kept stealing glances at James and biting her lip. James kept looking at her sideways and smiling. At one point, she took a deep breath, grabbed his hand, and looked into his eyes. James didn't pull away. She opened her mouth to speak, and then kissed him. He enjoyed the moment before breaking away. He really wasn't a fan of public displays of affection, but today was somehow different.

The Celtic had a 3 to 1 lead with one minute to go, and a lot of people had started to leave. James planted his wallet so that when they came back, he could easily find it. They left their seats a few minutes later, and made their way through the dining area before James stopped. He pretended to check his pockets, and then announced he'd lost his wallet. Carissa clucked her tongue at him, and they returned the way they'd come. By the time James retrieved his wallet their section was empty. James kept his hands in his pockets as they climbed the steps. In his right pocket, he was playing with the ring. They were at the end of the line of people filing out of the dining area, and about to push open the doors and leave, when James stopped again. He took two steps back, away from the doors.

"Forget something else, Love?" Carissa smiled at him.

James hesitated. He had worked out the words, and now that it was time, he froze for a moment. It was so unlike him that he became slightly annoyed.

"Well, whilst you go find it, I'm heading to the loo. Back in a jiffy," and she headed back the way they had just come toward the nearest bathroom.

The butterflies in his stomach were in full swing, and James felt very alert. It was just like when he saw a dream coming true, but now, instead of a feeling of dread, he felt happy and excited.

He dug the ring out of his pocket, and ran over the words two more times. He was about halfway through his third run, at the part where he'd get down on one knee, and extend the ring to her when he dropped it. It rolled under a table, and he bent to retrieve it, getting down on his knees, before sticking his head under the tablecloth, and extending his arm to retrieve the ring. He heard Carissa's footsteps approaching. She was coming, and he was already on his knees. He decided to present the ring, and simply ask, "Will you marry me?"

He smiled. This was the happiest he'd ever been, and he knew in his heart she would say yes. They would get their happily ever after.

# •ABOUT THE AUTHOR•

George is the third of six children and grew up in western Pennsylvania. He earned his BS in Biology from the University of Pittsburgh, his MSc in Biology and his MBA in Marketing and Management from Duquesne University. He is also a Master 5th degree black belt in the art of Taekwondo with Young Brothers in Pittsburgh. He currently working as a global marketing and strategy professional in science industries. He also has one son, Matthew.

www.ingramcontent.com/pod-product-compliance
Lightning Source LLC
Chambersburg PA
CBHW051933240626
47153CB00005B/1477